CRITICAL ACCLAIM FOR LEIGH GREENWOOD'S *VIOLET!*

"Readers will love this beautiful story!"

—*Affaire de Coeur*

"Take a bow, Leigh Greenwood . . . *Violet* was a delight to read!"

—Arnette Lamb, Bestselling Author

"Leigh Greenwood writes Americana at its best! Hold these books close to your heart. You care about these people. You absolutely love them!"

—*Romantic Times*

"This novel is the study of a man's struggle to learn to trust in the power of love."

—*Rendezvous*

SWEET NOTHINGS

"I don't know what you mean by the attention you've shown me," Violet said, "if indeed you mean anything at all. But if you should one day be interested in pursuing a woman with the purpose of establishing a serious relationship, let me tell you you're going about it in entirely the wrong way.

"You'll need to begin by trying to make yourself agreeable to the young woman. You might pretend you have an interest in someone other than yourself, even if you don't. You might say something nice. I realize that will be difficult for you. So I suggest you write down some things to say and memorize them.

"Once you get about a hundred memorized, you can start practicing them. Just sprinkle them in with the rest of your conversation. If you memorize enough phrases, you might fool some gullible female into thinking you mean what you say."

"But it wouldn't fool you," Jeff said.

"Not for as much as a second."

"Good. I find it impossible to admire stupid women."

Violet hoped she wasn't standing there with her mouth open. No matter how much she was around Jeff, he continued to have the power to stagger her with the things he said. But that was nothing compared to the shock she experienced when he kissed her.

SEVEN BRIDES

LEIGH GREENWOOD

VIOLET

LEISURE BOOKS   NEW YORK CITY

A LEISURE BOOK®

March 1999

Published by

Dorchester Publishing Co., Inc.
276 Fifth Avenue
New York, NY 10001

Cover art by John Ennis

ISBN 0-8439-4494-3

Printed in the United States of America.

WILLIAM HENRY RANDOLPH (1816-1865)—AURELIA PINCKNEY COLEMAN (1823-1863)
m. 1841

George Washington
b. July 14, 1842
m.
Elizabeth Rose Thornton
|
William Henry '67
|
Aurelia '71
Juliette, twins
|
stillborn son '74
|
Elizabeth Rose '77

James Madison
b. Feb. 14, 1845
m.
Fern Sproull
|
James Madison II '72
|
Robert Tazewell '74
|
John Tucker '76
|
Alexander Stuart '78
|
Carter Harrison '80

James Monroe "Monty"
b. Sept. 16, 1849
m.
Iris Richmond
|
Susan Irene '81

John Tyler
b. June 17, 1853
m.
Daisy Singleton
|
Lillian Diana '81

Zachary Taylor
b. Aug. 2, 1859

Thomas Jefferson
b. Nov. 12, 1843
m.
Violet Goodwin
|
Thomas Jefferson II '81

Juliette Coleman
b. May 21, 1847
died in infancy

William Henry "Hen" Harrison
b. Sept. 16, 1849
m.
Laurel Simpson Blackthorne
|
Adam Blackthorne (6-adopted '77)
Jordy McGinnis (9-adopted '77)
|
William Henry Harrison II '79
|
Peter Nathaniel '81

Chapter One

Denver, 1880

"I don't care about your appointments or what the commodities market is doing," Fern said to Jeff. "Someone has to go to that school to see about the twins, and I can't do it."

Fern leaned back against the several pillows behind her. Jeff was being impossible, but she shouldn't have expected anything else. In the nine years she'd been married to his brother, Jeff had never once tried to be cooperative.

"I don't know anything about schools or girls," Jeff said.

"You should have thought about that before you insisted that Madison go to Leadville," she said. "You know I can't get out of this bed for more than a few minutes at a time."

"Rose should have kept those girls in Texas," Jeff said. "They're wilder than antelope."

11

Leigh Greenwood

"She sent them here hoping the Wolfe School would give them a little polish. George says they're growing up to look like your mother and act like your father."

"Hell! If that's true, you might as well shoot them now and save everybody a lot of trouble."

"Jeff, they're only little girls!"

"That's even worse. Nobody will believe they can be as evil as my father was."

"It's been years since you've seen them. They're not evil, just high-spirited. Now stop being difficult and go see Miss Goodwin."

"You sure you can't get up for a short trip?"

"Do I look as if I'm enjoying staying here?" Fern asked. It annoyed her that Jeff made no attempt to hide his skepticism at her illness. He never got sick, and he had no sympathy for anybody who did.

"You shouldn't let Madison keep you pregnant all the time."

"That's none of your business," Fern snapped. "But even if it were, it's too late to do anything about it now. Since you saw fit to send my husband to Leadville, you can see about your nieces."

"I'm no lawyer. I can't—"

"You could have hired one. You have enough money. What are you saving it for? Did you know the twins call you Rusty Money?"

"Money doesn't rust."

Fern sighed. "I'm tired of talking to you. Amy has the card with Miss Goodwin's address and the time to call. Ask her for it on your way out."

"I'll call when I have time," Jeff said, his harsh expression robbing his face of some of its natural attractiveness. "Miss Goodson—"

"Goodwin."

"—will just have to make accommodations."

Fern sighed again. "Try not to get in a fight with her. You're supposed to help the girls, not add Miss Good-

12

win to the list of people who pray they'll never see you again.''

"I don't get into fights."

"Piss and vinegar! Half of Denver groans when they see you coming. If you weren't president of the largest bank west of San Francisco, nobody would speak to you."

"You shouldn't curse."

Jeff looked so affronted that Fern almost laughed. "Why not? As you so often remind me, I'm not one of your precious Southern belles. Now go away and talk to Miss Goodwin."

"Rose ought to come do it herself."

"You make a mess of this visit, and she probably will." Jeff would never admit it, but Fern knew he was a little afraid of Rose. His bitterness upset George, and nobody distressed George with impunity. Rose was small, but she was a veritable tigress when it came to protecting her husband.

Fern settled back against her pillows as the door closed behind Jeff, his bad temper and the twins forgotten. Her hand moved slowly over her swollen stomach. After four easy pregnancies, this one had gone wrong from the beginning. She had only a month to go, but she couldn't forget that her mother had died in childbirth. She was frightened the same thing was going to happen to her. She whispered her husband's name into the pillow. He would have stayed if she had asked him. She wished she had.

Ten days later, Jeff paused on the flagstone walk before the Wolfe School for Girls. Five years before, the wealthy mothers of Denver had decided they needed a way to educate their daughters without sending them back east. Taking up subscriptions among themselves, they'd built the school. Composed of several stone buildings, it occupied extensive grounds on the edge of

Denver's most exclusive residential district. The daughters of local millionaires were day students. For the rest, including the daughters of gold and silver barons and a few cattle kings who didn't live in Denver, the board had provided a dormitory.

Acres of brown grass and hundreds of young trees struggled to transform the piece of prairie at the foot of the Rocky Mountains into a setting reminiscent of some eastern city. Already the stone of the buildings was becoming a weathered gray. In a few years, the Wolfe School would look like the venerable institution the Denver matrons hoped it would become.

"You'll find Miss Goodwin in the dormitory," a matronly female in the main building told Jeff. "It'll be the second building on your right when you go back outside, just past the chapel. Dear me," she said, gazing at Jeff's empty left sleeve, "did you lose that in a mining accident?"

"An obliging Yankee shattered my elbow at Gettysburg," Jeff said, a brittle edge to his voice. "The Yankee doctors decided it was easier to cut it off than try to fix it."

"But there's no point going about with an empty sleeve. They make such good artificial arms."

"No, they don't! They're damnable."

Jeff turned and stalked out of the building. He wished people would keep their comments, and their curiosity, to themselves. He supposed they were trying to be kind, but in their ignorance, they did more harm than good.

He pulled a gold watch from his pocket and frowned. He started down the path at a rapid pace. He was already five minutes behind schedule. If he didn't hurry, he'd be late for his meeting. The bank directors were going to decide whether to purchase more mining property in Leadville. He intended to see they did.

He glanced at the chapel as he passed. It was a small

square building. He hadn't been inside a church since he'd lost his arm.

The dormitory was large, square, and ugly. Jeff had his hand on the door before he decided it might be best to ring the bell first. The thought of bursting in on young girls in dishabille terrified him. A uniformed maid answered the door.

"Could I help you?" the young woman asked in a clipped British accent.

"I'm here to see Miss Violet Goodwin."

The maid looked flustered. "She doesn't have any appointments for this afternoon."

"Good. Then she won't have any difficulty meeting with me."

"I mean, since she has no appointments, she's otherwise engaged."

"I'm sure she can put whatever she's doing off to another time," Jeff said, pushing his way inside. "Please tell her I'm here."

"But who are you?"

"Mr. Randolph."

When the maid looked at him blankly, he said, "The banker."

The woman's expression remained unchanged, so Jeff said, "The twins' uncle."

The maid smiled broadly. "You're Mr. Jefferson Randolph."

"That's what I said."

"But you could have been any Randolph, couldn't you? Have a seat. Let me take your hat and coat. I'll see if Miss Goodwin is free to see you."

"Miss Goodwin will see me."

"I'll ask." The maid made her escape.

Jeff remained standing. He let his gaze wander over the large room. Someone had furnished it with a dismal collection of dark, heavy Victorian pieces. He felt as if he was in a mausoleum and considered what would happen if the twins were locked up in there. After an hour, they'd be too depressed to get in trouble for at least a week.

Fifteen minutes later Jeff had completed a detailed study of every picture, piece of furniture, plaster decoration, and rug in the room. He had sat in each chair, stared out each window, and even picked out a tune on the square parlor piano. Still Miss Goodwin had not come. His patience had fled, taking with it tolerance and good humor.

He considered leaving, but coming back would entail an even greater loss of time. He looked at his watch again. It would be difficult to have any sort of conversation with Miss Goodwin and still be on time for his meeting. He closed the watch with a snap. His meeting was more important than whatever nonsense his nieces had been up to.

But at that moment, an apparition came into the room, stopping him in his tracks. The woman, of slim figure and medium height, was past the first blush of youth. She was attractive; her features were pretty without being unusual. Deep blue eyes stared at Jeff from under long lashes. An incredible mass of curly copper-red hair piled atop her head struggled to escape the bondage of an army of pins.

But it was her dress that riveted Jeff's attention. The garment was made of yards and yards of rose-colored satin trimmed with cream lace at the throat and wrists. It looked like a gown he would have seen at a ball before his father had been run out of Virginia, not something the housemother in a girls' school would wear. Against the setting of the dark, somber room, she looked like a bird of paradise.

She smiled. "Mr. Randolph? I'm Violet Goodwin. I apologize for keeping you waiting. Do sit down." She took a seat on a high-backed sofa, arranging her rustling skirts around her.

Jeff stood immobile. She was a Yankee. He could place her accent down to the exact county in Massachusetts. His jailer for the last two years of the war had spoken like her. Jeff would remember the sound of that man's voice until his dying day.

"I had expected to see the twins' mother," Miss Goodwin said. "I confess this is the first time I've had a visit from a father."

She spoke in a soft voice, rather slowly, completely unlike the man who had made Jeff's years in prison a living hell. She was very pretty when she smiled; she seemed friendly. But she was a Yankee. Jeff wanted to turn and leave without saying a word.

"I'm their uncle."

"Oh, it's wonderful of you to take so much interest in your nieces."

Recovering slightly, Jeff said, "My sister-in-law is in bed and her husband's away. I'm the only relative left." He took out his watch and glanced at it. "I'm going to be late for my meeting."

Miss Goodwin seemed surprised at his outburst. "I'm sure you consider your nieces' welfare more important than a meeting."

"No, I don't."

She looked rather startled. "They are your family."

"That's not my doing."

Her eyes opened a little wider. Their deep blue formed a startling contrast to her white skin and copper-red hair. She would have been arresting even if she hadn't been pretty. "Perhaps we should discuss your nieces' situation."

"What's to discuss? My brother is paying you to turn them into ladies instead of headstrong females more at home on horses than in a parlor. I can only suppose I've been called here because you have failed."

Her expression registered shock. "You seem to be

17

under a misapprehension as to the reason I requested this visit."

"I make it a point never to be under a misapprehension. It costs time and money."

"I'm sure it does, but in this case—"

"This case is no different from any other. You've been paid to do a job, and you haven't done it." She had no business sitting in judgment of his nieces. She couldn't understand Southern women. No female brought up in Massachusetts could. "I'm sure they haven't done anything any other spirited nine-year-old twins wouldn't do."

Miss Goodwin appeared to be stunned by his unexpected retort, but not intimidated. Her reaction aroused his interest. People usually became agitated and flustered when subjected to one of his verbal attacks.

"As to that," she said, "I can't say. I've never been around twins before, spirited or otherwise."

"Then why are you criticizing them?"

"If you would listen for just a moment, I think I could clear up this misunderstanding."

She was criticizing him. But he should have expected that. Yankees seemed to think they had all the answers.

"I wouldn't interrupt if you'd get to the point. Why do women always talk around things?"

"Are you finished?"

The woman spoke quietly, politely, but her meaning was much different. Her eyes gave her away. Jeff guessed he'd never set out of there if he didn't let her get whatever was bothering her off her chest.

And she had a well-formed chest. He hadn't noticed at first—her gown had grabbed his attention—but she had a very fine figure. She was slender without being thin. Maturity had given her curves a lushness most young women lacked.

"Say your piece," he said.

"I'd prefer you sit down while I did."

"I'll remain standing."

Miss Goodwin looked irritated, but she clearly had herself well under control. "I don't make the rules at the Wolfe School. Nor do I decide what to do when they've been broken. That's the responsibility of Miss Eleanor Settle, the headmistress. It's my responsibility to report any infractions and to oversee any disciplinary action."

"So why am I wasting time talking to you?"

Jeff could see the woman struggle to keep her temper under control. He didn't know why that should please him. He'd always disliked temperamental women.

"In the case of the boarders, I'm expected to confer with the parents when there has been a problem."

"Well, what is the problem?"

"The twins have been consistently breaking the rules."

"Then send them to bed without dinner and be done with it."

"We don't starve our students, Mr. Randolph."

"They won't starve by missing one meal. We went without food for days at a time during the War of Northern Aggression, but we never stopped fighting."

Miss Goodwin's gaze went directly to Jeff's empty left sleeve. "I'm well aware of the suffering caused by that war, but it has no bearing here."

"Well you have to do something besides talk at those girls. I'm not going to run over here every time they break a rule."

Miss Goodwin took a moment to answer. She probably couldn't think of anything to say at first. Finally, she said, "I don't know what you do for a living, but you apparently have little experience with girls."

"None."

"Then let me explain."

"I'm tired of all this explaining. Get to the nub of things."

Once again Miss Goodwin took her time answering, but Jeff had the feeling she wasn't searching for words so much as eliminating most of the ones that came to mind. That pleased him, too, though again he couldn't say why. He had no interest in what the woman thought of him.

"Perhaps that's best," she said, then paused, studying him.

Her perusal irritated Jeff. He didn't like bold females. She ought to be a little more deferential. Men would like her better, and she might not end up an old maid. Still, she was remarkably attractive to be unmarried.

"The headmistress wishes me to inform you that unless your nieces' behavior improves, disciplinary action will be taken."

Jeff felt cold anger seize him. "You mean you dragged me over here, made me miss an important meeting, and put me through a half hour of pointless prattle, just to tell me that!"

"Miss Settle wanted you to know—"

"I don't give a damn what Miss Settle wants!" Jeff snatched up his coat. "I have too much work to do to waste time listening to you complain because my nieces have been late with their assignments or have gone to bed without brushing their hair."

"It's a good deal more than that."

"Then for God's sake, say what it is!"

Miss Goodwin fixed him with an incendiary gaze. "As of this morning, your nieces have been placed on probation. Unless there is an immediate improvement in their behavior, they will be dismissed from the school."

Jeff paused, hat in hand. If the twins were kicked out while Fern was sick and Madison was away, he'd be responsible for them. He'd either have to take care of them until George came or take them to Texas himself. He'd almost rather go back to being a prisoner of war.

"I want to see them," Jeff said.

"They're studying."

"I don't care if they're sound asleep."

Miss Goodwin rose to her feet. "I'll see if they can be disturbed."

"They sure as hell can. I've been more than disturbed."

"Mr. Randolph, it's not the custom of the Wolfe School to put up with profanity."

"And it's not my custom to put up with people trying to put me off."

Violet closed the door behind her. She let her breath go in a long, slow sigh. She was so angry she was almost shaking. She had never met such an insufferable man in her whole life. Her sympathy had gone out to him when she noticed he was missing an arm. She had grown even more sympathetic when she had discovered that he had lost the limb in the Civil War. He had fought on the opposite side from her brother, but she knew pain made no allowances for the justice or injustice of a cause.

"Is Mr. Randolph gone?" the maid asked.

"No, he wants to see his nieces."

"Poor dears. He's liable to frighten them to death."

Violet laughed softly as she regained some of her composure. "If there are any females on this earth capable of giving Mr. Randolph back his own, they're Aurelia and Juliette."

The maid giggled. "They are a handful, aren't they?"

"They're more than that. I was anxious to meet their parents, but after meeting their uncle, I'm not so sure I want to. Go tell them to come here immediately. And, Beth, tell them not to take time to change or tidy up. That man might explode if he has to wait a minute longer."

Violet wondered whether it was wise to let the girls see their uncle. Still, doing so was the normal procedure. The school encouraged parents to become involved in the disciplining of their children. With wealthy clients, such a course of action was always the politic thing to do.

Violet smoothed a wrinkle out of her dress. She wondered if Mr. Randolph was rich. He certainly had all the arrogance of a man who had inherited money and thought himself all the better because he hadn't had to earn it.

And he was an unrepentant Southerner. If she'd had any doubts, his reaction to her would have put them to rest. He hadn't forgotten the war and didn't intend to. Well, that was okay. Neither had she.

But even as remembering the agony of her brother's lingering death stoked her anger, remembering Mr. Randolph's missing left arm cooled it. No one knew better than she what such a loss could do to a man. It was obvious that Mr. Randolph hadn't learned to accept his loss. Neither had Jonas, and she had loved and cared for him for ten years. The least she could do was try to be nice to Mr. Randolph for the next few minutes.

Civility wouldn't be hard if the man would just smile. He was extremely handsome. His physical similarity to the twins was remarkable. Anyone would have thought he was their father. Violet had never been attracted to blond men, but it was impossible not to think Mr. Randolph attractive. He was tall with the broadest, most powerful shoulders she could remember seeing. His coat fitted well, but she could see the strain his muscles put on the cut of the garment. And his eyes! They were as blue as the sky over Cape Cod on a summer afternoon.

The door opened, and Aurelia and Juliette Randolph exploded into the hall. Actually they walked in more calmly than Violet could ever remember seeing them move, but that was the effect the twins had on everyone. Violet shuddered to think what they would be like as adults.

At that moment, they looked like angels: blond, beautiful, and seemingly as sweet as any children God ever created. It was hard to believe so much devilry could hide behind two such angelic faces.

"Beth says Uncle Jeff is here," Aurelia said. At least Violet thought Aurelia spoke. She still had trouble telling the twins apart.

Juliette made a face. "Do we have to see him?"

"You can punish us," Aurelia said. "We won't say anything."

"You haven't earned any punishment yet."

"We will," Juliette said.

"You can't expect me to make a bargain like that," Violet said, smiling in spite of herself. "Now stop being silly, and go talk to your uncle."

"Will you come with us?" Juliette asked.

"I don't think he would like that."

"He won't like it no matter what you do. Uncle Jeff never likes anything," Juliette said.

"Mama says he's soured on life," Aurelia said.

"Maybe, but he can't be soured on his two beautiful nieces."

"Uncle Jeff can," Aurelia said.

"Then I suggest you march in there, apologize for causing him to miss his meeting, and promise you won't misbehave again."

"We can't do that," Aurelia said.

"Mama said we were never to tell a lie," Juliette said.

"Then promise to try to behave. Can you do that?"

The two children looked at each other. "I suppose so," Juliette said.

"Now give me your biggest smile," Violet said, and the twins grinned from ear to ear. "Good. That ought to dazzle your uncle right and proper. Now go on with you."

"You might as well be sending those children into a bear's den," Beth said when the door had closed behind the twins.

"I'm not moving one step," Violet said. "Let him so much as raise his voice, and he'll have me to deal with."

"You going to listen at the keyhole?" Beth asked.

"It's mortifying, but how else am I going to hear what he says?"

Chapter Two

Like puppies expecting to be whipped, Aurelia and Juliette entered the parlor with hanging heads. Jeff knew they were only acting. They had never been whipped in their lives. They should have been, but he doubted starting then would do any good. Nor had they ever been head-hanging contrite. They were headstrong, willful, and full of the devil.

"Hello, Uncle Jeff," Aurelia said.

"Hello, Uncle Jeff," Juliette said. "Where's Aunt Fern?"

"Home in bed."

"What's wrong?" Juliette asked.

"She's sick."

"Is she going to die?" Juliette said.

"No, she's just having a baby."

"Is it going to be another boy?" Aurelia asked, disgust heavy in her voice.

"I don't know, but considering the trouble you two keep getting into, I hope so." When the girls looked mulish, Jeff said, "I have a good mind to send for your mother."

"No!" the twins said in unison.

"Give me a good reason why I shouldn't. I can't take time from work to worry over whether you're not doing your assignments or brushing your teeth before going to bed."

"We wouldn't do anything that stupid," Aurelia said, clearly insulted by his limited imagination.

"It wouldn't be worth the trouble," Juliette said.

"Just what did you do?"

"Put ink in Betty Sue's hair," Aurelia said

"Hide the choir books in the chapel," Juliette said.

"What else? No, don't tell me. I don't want to know. You can tell your mother when she gets here."

"Please, don't tell Mama," Aurelia said.

"We'll try to do better," Juliette said, clearly uncomfortable at making such a promise.

"You'd better. That Yankee dragon says you've been so bad the headmistress has put you on probation. If you get kicked out, you'll have to come stay with me until your mother can come get you." When the girls directed shocked looks toward each other, Jeff said, "Either that, or I'll have to take you back to Texas myself."

Seeing their alarm increased, Jeff said, "That will keep me out of the office at least a week. Do you know how much work I won't get done? Maybe I'll send your father a bill. A thousand dollars a day ought to do it."

"We promise to try to be better," Juliette said more earnestly than before.

"This trouble is making your Aunt Fern worse," Jeff said.

Juliette sniffed. One eloquent tear welled up in her eye and rolled down her cheek. Jeff wasn't fooled. According to their mother, one of the twins' greatest accomplishments was the ability to shed tears any time they wanted.

"Your father will be shocked," Jeff said, angry that the little imps showed no sign of remorse. "Even William Henry hasn't gotten into this much trouble."

Aurelia's lower lip quivered. "I hate him."

"I don't want to think what your mother will say," Jeff said, even while losing hope that the twins would ever feel truly contrite. "She wanted you to learn to act like young ladies, not hoydens on horseback. How is she going to feel when she learns you've been so bad the school has put you on probation?"

"We'll be better," Juliette said. "We will."

Both girls were crying openly, but their false tears only served to make Jeff madder.

"That's what you told your Aunt Fern. But you lied to her, didn't you? Are you lying to me? Are you going to keep raising hell until the headmistress kicks you out? It would serve you right if I took my belt to you right now."

A woman's hard clipped voice caught Jeff's attention. "I think it's time the girls returned to their studies."

Jeff looked up, startled to see that Miss Goodwin had reentered the room. He hadn't heard her. He could see an angry glint in her eyes as she placed herself between him and the girls. She acted as if she thought he was going to beat the twins right there in front of her. Her assumption angered him.

Miss Goodwin handed each girl a handkerchief. "Here, dry your eyes. We don't want the other girls thinking your uncle has been unkind."

"I was trying to make them understand the consequences of their behavior," Jeff said, aware of how weak his explanation sounded.

"Now that you have, I'm certain they'll keep the consequences in mind. Thank your uncle for coming, girls," Miss Goodwin said as she shepherded them toward the door.

"Thank you," Aurelia said.

"Thank you," Juliette said. "Tell Aunt Fern I hope she feels better."

"I don't mind if she has another boy," Aurelia said.

Miss Goodwin closed the door behind the girls and turned around, her blazing gaze boring into Jeff. "I see no excuse for treating children as you just did. Considering they're your own flesh and blood, I find your behavior incomprehensible."

Jeff was furious at being caught by the twins' trick. He hadn't wanted to come, but he had. Then to be treated with such contempt—and by a Yankee female at that! Telling Miss Goodwin that the twins had only been pretending to cry would do no good. She wouldn't believe him. After seeing the girls' tearstained, angelic faces, he doubted anybody would.

"I wasn't really going to beat them," he said, righteous anger throbbing in his voice.

"Maybe not, but a threat is just as unacceptable."

"What did you expect me to do? Pat them on the head, tell them I understand, and go away again? If so, you can get somebody else. I won't waste my time."

"What makes your time so valuable?"

An alarm went off in Jeff's brain. Every time females found out he was president of the biggest bank in Denver, they started to fawn over him. He'd been hunted by enough women to populate a small city. And not all of them had been unmarried. Some had even pretended not to notice that he was missing an arm. He especially hated such falseness. Nobody could love a cripple.

"That's none of your business," Jeff said, aware he was being rude. If he could make the woman angry, maybe she wouldn't bother him again. But she didn't appear shocked by his present behavior.

"I didn't mean to seem nosy, but you've mentioned the value of your time so often you piqued my curiosity."

"Confine your curiosity to finding a way to teach my

nieces to behave. That's the least my brother can expect in exchange for the enormous tuition he's paying.''

"This school is paid to educate young ladies, not—"

"An equally important part of its purpose is to help form their character. It's in the school charter. That's why my brother sent the twins here."

Miss Goodwin faced Jeff squarely, her gaze sliding neither to the right nor to the left. "Mr. Randolph, that's the second time you've accused me of incompetence. Is that how you normally deal with people when they don't come up to your expectations?"

Jeff was boiling mad, but he couldn't, in all honesty, call the woman incompetent. Nobody could control those girls. Damn the woman! She looked as if he had hurt her feelings. He didn't care if he made her mad, but he didn't want to hurt her. He didn't act much like a gentleman anymore, but he knew it was wrong to take his anger out on a female, even if she was a Yankee.

"I know it's not easy dealing with the twins, but that's what my brother wanted when he sent them here. It still is. Now if you'll excuse me, I have to go." He hadn't exactly offered an apology, but he could manage no better reply.

"But I haven't finished."

Jeff paused in the act of turning away. "What more can there be?"

"The girls will be on probation for two weeks. If there are no further infractions during that time, the probation will end."

"And if they get into trouble again?"

"It will depend on the nature of the trouble. If it's something minor, I can ignore it or recommend their probation be extended."

"And if it's something major?" Jeff asked.

"I will be forced to recommend they be dismissed. It will be necessary for you to return in two weeks to review the situation."

"Come back again just to be told the brats are behaving? I won't do anything so stupid." He noticed Miss Goodwin's look of surprise at his reaction.

"You may speak to Miss Settle if you like."

"What for? All they did was put some ink in a girl's hair and hide a few hymn books."

"They poured ink over the head of the daughter of a board member. Black India ink—permanent ink. The child was very proud of her blond hair. We've had to cut at least a foot of it off. She wouldn't come out of her room for a day. She still cries whenever anyone mentions the incident. As for the hymn books, the girls hid those just before the bishop came to dedicate the chapel. Everyone was forced to stand silent while the organist played the hymns."

Jeff decided he wasn't ready to deal with two children willing to attack society from its foundations up. "Their aunt will be well by then. I'll let her decide what to do. Do you have any more orders for me?"

"I don't think anything more need be said at the moment. I'll inform you if anything happens during the next two weeks."

"Fine. I bid you good day."

Jeff turned and walked out the door without acknowledging the woman's parting nod. He was infuriated that the female could—and would, it seemed, if the girls didn't behave—recommend his nieces be dismissed from school. That she was a Yankee only made the bile more bitter.

What did Miss Settle mean by hiring such a person? The Wolfe School shouldn't have a woman like her teaching young girls. What could she know about turning them into ladies? Not much when she dressed in a style guaranteed to turn every head in the room. A lady was quiet, decorous, submissive. She didn't draw attention to her person or her opinions.

Miss Goodwin fitted none of those criteria. The sooner she went back to Massachusetts, the better.

"That has got to be the rudest man I've met in my entire life," Violet said.

"What he needs is a wife," Beth said as she set about tidying the parlor after Jeff had rearranged half its contents. "A good woman would straighten him out in no time."

"He'd probably put her in restraints if she tried. How do you know he's not married?"

"No wedding ring. Besides, he acts like a man who's used to having everything his way. You know that's no husband."

Both women laughed. Violet moved to the window. She watched Mr. Randolph as he walked down the flagstone path toward the street. Once again she was aware of his empty left sleeve. She watched him tuck the sleeve into his pocket to keep it from flapping about in the brisk autumn wind, and she felt some of her anger fade.

After watching her brother refuse to live after the war had so savagely mangled his beautiful young body, Violet could imagine some of what Mr. Randolph had suffered over the years. His pain didn't excuse his behavior, but it made his actions more understandable, more forgivable.

"He doesn't understand children," Violet said. "He has no more business being responsible for the twins than I have being the mayor."

"He says he's a banker," Beth said.

Violet doubted that. Mr. Jefferson Randolph didn't act like a banker. More likely his family owned stock in the bank where he worked. They might even own the bank outright, but surely they wouldn't let anybody that rude near customers. Most likely he worked in an office somewhere in the attic. His family might even have created a job to give him something to do. That could account for some of his ill temper. No one liked having to take charity, not even from one's own family.

As Violet watched, Mr. Randolph reached the street and started walking toward town. She was certain that, if he'd been as important as he acted, he would have had a carriage waiting.

Violet gave herself a mental shake and turned away from the window. "I'd better see how the twins are. They were pretty upset when they left."

"Those two," Beth said with a dismissive wave of her hand. "I wouldn't be surprised if their uncle made them so mad they're fixing to do something terrible."

"I hadn't thought about that," Violet said, hurrying from the parlor.

She was relieved a few minutes later to find the girls in their room, sitting on Aurelia's bed, their arms around each other. Violet noticed no sign of the tears that had flowed so copiously moments earlier. She began to wonder just how genuine they had been.

"He's going to send for Mama," Juliette said when Violet asked the reason for their subdued mood.

"Daddy will come, too," Aurelia said. "He never lets Mama go anywhere by herself."

"Mama doesn't understand why we can't be more like Elizabeth and William Henry."

"If Jordy and Adam were our brothers, nobody would ever pay us any attention," Aurelia said.

"Jordy is awful," Juliette said. "Uncle Hen said he's going to shoot him like a coyote."

"You're joking," Violet said.

"Aunt Laurel told Mama she was going to nail his hide up to dry."

Violet began to wonder just what kind of people the Randolphs were. Her family had been gentle and loving. Her father had never recovered from the shock of his wife's death. The spark of life within her brother had not been strong enough to survive coming home from the war an invalid. Even her mother, the linchpin of the family while she lived, had weakened and died under the strain of nursing wounded prisoners.

"I wish Uncle Monty were our father," Aurelia said. "He wouldn't care what we did."

"How many uncles do you have?" Violet asked, losing count.

"Six. And seven cousins," Aurelia said.

"All boys," Juliette said.

Violet began to understand a little better. With so many men around, it was no wonder the girls didn't know how to behave. And with that many brothers, all apparently active and healthy, no wonder Jeff Randolph brooded over his handicap. Her own brother had been sweet and appreciative to the end, but then he hadn't had Jeff's strength of character, his apparent willingness to attack anything that stood in his path. She could have endured anger, even verbal abuse, if Jonas had only been a fighter. Jeff was as surly as a Vermont farmer with nothing but daughters, but he wouldn't give up. Violet had to respect him for that, even admire him. But she didn't have to like him.

"Your nieces are terrorizing the entire school," Jeff said. "Nobody's safe, not even the bishop."

"They're your nieces, too," Fern said.

"No, they're not. I've disowned them. I'm not going back to that school or dealing with that Yankee female."

"Her name is Miss Goodwin."

"I don't care what she calls herself. She's a Yankee with an exaggerated opinion of her own importance."

"I still can't get up."

"You might not have to bother. I've sent for Rose."

Fern realized the situation was indeed serious. Despite the passage of 14 years, Jeff had never forgiven Rose for being the daughter of a Union officer. Not that his grudge bothered Rose. She was always ready to let Jeff know exactly what she thought of his behavior and attitude.

"When are they coming?" Fern asked.

"Probably not until after George finishes selling this year's steers. He always insists upon holding them back until he can get top dollar. With our four ranches, that's never easy."

Fern decided she would have to visit the school. It wouldn't do to have things in a muddle when Rose arrived.

"Go on back to your bank and forget about the twins," Fern said.

"That's exactly what I intend to do."

And he would, Fern told herself as Jeff left. He didn't seem to care about anything except making money.

"That's the best workout you've ever had," Jeff's trainer said as he massaged Jeff's sore muscles. "You had me worried there for a while. That stump can't take but so much strain."

"I have the same muscles in both shoulders," Jeff said. "I mean to see my left side is just as strong as my right."

"It is. There can't be a man in Denver with a better developed torso than you. You going to see Louise tonight?"

"Of course, it's Tuesday. Why do you ask?"

"You worked yourself pretty hard today. Maybe you ought to take it easy."

"You think I'm too weak to work out and visit a woman all in the same evening?" Jeff said.

"Of course not, but you wear her down too much when you're like this. Maybe you ought to take it easy this time."

Jeff sat up and grabbed a towel. "Mind your own business. Just be sure to tell Louise to expect me in the same mood as always."

"Trying to prove you're a bloody bull," his trainer muttered under his breath after Jeff had left. "You'd think being strong enough for two men would be enough for him. But, no, he has to exhaust that poor woman or he thinks he's not much of a man. What the hell is he trying to prove?"

"You have no progress at all to report, Mr. McKee?"

Violet faced her lawyer across a desk piled high with neatly stacked papers. He was a tall, spare, attractive man, probably in his forties. His hair was graying around the edges, but it was full and bushy. His office was large and well-appointed, his staff courteous and efficient. Violet didn't know how her uncle could have afforded such a successful lawyer. It had been very fortunate for her that he had. Mr. McKee was also a member of the board of the Wolfe School. It had been his recommendation that had gotten her a job.

"I'm afraid not, Miss Goodwin. The Leadville courts are full of disputed claims and counterclaims. It could be years before we're able to achieve any concrete results."

"But I don't have years, or enough money to pay you if I did."

"It's not necessary to pay me any more just yet." McKee smiled at her in a way that made her heart beat a little faster. "You can wait until I have something definite to report."

Violet tried not to let her desperation show, but she needed her inheritance. She wanted to go back to Massachusetts. Immediately.

Her father's brother had left Massachusetts to avoid the war. He had wandered over the West from one mining town to another. Occasionally he sent news of a small strike. Most often he told of empty holes and picked-over claims.

A short time after her father's death, her uncle wrote

that he had struck it rich and invited her to come live with him. Having no other family, Violet had sold everything she had and left Massachusetts. It had been a terrible shock to reach Denver and be told by Harvey McKee that her uncle had been killed in a mining accident. It had been even more of a shock to be told his claim was disputed and considered worthless.

Mr. McKee was certain the courts would recognize her ownership, but he had warned her not to expect quick results. To support herself while she waited, she had taken a job as housemother to the boarders at the Wolfe School for Girls. She didn't realize until later that Harvey McKee had become fond of her.

"There must be something you can do to hurry things along," Violet said. "Maybe if you went to Leadville—"

"There's no point in my leaving this office, Miss Goodwin. I have colleagues in Leadville. I can do as much here as they can there. Maybe even more."

"But you're not doing anything."

"Not achieving anything. Well, maybe a little. I have succeeded in getting your case on the docket."

"How long before it can be heard?"

"Maybe within a year."

Violet wanted to scream. Somebody had stolen her claim, and the court might let a year pass before getting around to even looking at her complaint. Her uncle had said prospectors were taking silver out of the earth as fast as possible. There might not be any left in a year.

"It's not an unreasonable delay," Harvey McKee said. "Many cases take much longer."

"I don't have longer."

"You have your position at the Wolfe School. You live and take your meals there."

"I know, but—"

"Besides, it's possible your situation may change."

"How do you mean?"

"You might decide to marry. You're a very attractive woman, always beautifully dressed," he said, eyeing Violet, who wore a dress of rich emerald green. "There must be many men who would be proud to have you for a wife."

"I don't expect to marry." Violet was shocked when thoughts of Jeff Randolph sprang into her mind. "I mean to return to Massachusetts as soon as I get my money. I have something I very much want to do."

"I had hoped you might allow me to advise you on investments."

"There's hardly any point if I'm as poor as a New England Quaker." Violet stood. "I'd best be going."

"I had hoped you would dine with me. It would give me time to explain what I plan to do."

Violet liked Harvey McKee and found his company enjoyable. After being locked up all week with little girls who never thought of anyone but themselves, she felt wonderful that someone was trying to please her for a change.

"Thank you, but I need to be back early. One of the girls is showing signs of coming down sick."

"I'm sure she'll recover soon."

Violet imagined the girl would get better a lot faster than she herself would recover from learning years might pass before she got any money. Such a fate upset her in more than one way. She didn't want to make any decisions about her future with the fear of poverty, or perpetual enslavement at the Wolfe School, staring her in the face.

Much to Violet's surprise, the image of Jeff Randolph flashed into her mind again. Honesty forced her to admit he was more attractive than Harvey. Also, Harvey was sometimes too restrained and polite. After years of having to depend on, and take care of, weak males, she wanted someone who could take care of her, a bear of a man who was willing to stand up and fight. But not one so full of growls and bared fangs as Jeff.

Jeff made his way toward the dormitory, his temper badly frayed. He didn't want to be there, but Fern was still not well. Miss Goodwin had stated he was to return on this day. He had heard nothing from her during the intervening two weeks; so he assumed the girls had managed to behave. He didn't know why Miss Goodwin couldn't have sent a note. He had had to cancel another meeting since Fern still wasn't well enough to leave the house and Madison hadn't returned from Leadville. Jeff pulled his coat closer about him. The gusts off the plains could practically lift a man into the air.

Jeff wasn't looking forward to meeting with the woman again. She was a bossy Yankee, and she dressed much too boldly. Most upsetting of all, he'd found himself thinking of her all week long. At first he had done little more than catalogue her shortcomings. When he had found her image breaking in on his thoughts, he became uneasy.

Not that he was worried he was overly attracted to her. He just hated knowing he found any Yankee woman appealing. Such an abomination hadn't happened before. He couldn't imagine why one should be happening at that time.

If those wretched twins could just have behaved themselves; if Fern hadn't been sick; if Madison hadn't been in Leadville; if Rose had sent the girls to St. Louis instead of Denver—but he'd get nowhere torturing himself with ifs. He was a fool to think Yankee women couldn't be beautiful. And as much as he hated to admit the fact, he was a fool to think he wouldn't be attracted to one sooner or later. He was a man, after all, with the Randolph appreciation for women. His lapse in judgment was nothing more than a momentary aberration. He would never see Miss Goodwin again after their appointment. He would forget her existence in less than a month.

Reaching the dormitory, Jeff knocked on the door. When no one answered, he knocked again with the same result. He thought of asking at the main building, but changed his mind. Miss Goodwin had told him to be back in two weeks.

Well, it was exactly two weeks, to the minute. He knocked a third time. Still no one came. Angered, he opened the door and went in.

The parlor looked just as he remembered it, except a fine layer of dust covered everything. The maid had been neglecting her duties. Apparently Miss Goodwin was unable to keep her staff up to their work. Clearly she was unsuited for her job. He knocked on the door Miss Goodwin had used to enter the parlor when he had been there before. The door remained closed.

The building might as well be empty for all the attention its inhabitants were paying him. But Jeff knew the dormitory wasn't empty. He'd seen one of the girls at an upper window.

He knocked harder and was pleased a moment later to hear a door open and footsteps scurrying along the hall. Beth opened the door just enough to see who was knocking.

"You're not supposed to be here!" she said. "Go away."

"I've come to see Miss Goodwin," Jeff said, miffed by her behavior. "I have an appointment."

"She won't see you."

Hot rage surged through Jeff. "Do you mean to say that, after letting me come all this way, she won't see me?"

"She's busy," Beth said.

"Busy be damned," Jeff said, pushing against the door. Since Beth didn't have a tenth of his strength, he pushed past her easily. "I mean to see her now. Where the hell is she hiding?"

"She's not hiding," Beth said when Jeff opened the nearest door. "And you can't go opening every door in the building."

"The hell I can't. If Miss Goodwin couldn't see me she should have sent a message."

"I'm sure she meant to. She probably just forgot."

"Responsible women don't forget," Jeff said, opening and closing another door. "She demanded I be here exactly on time. I am. I expect to be seen."

"Don't go in there!" Beth shrieked when Jeff reached the third door.

With a satisfied smile on his face, Jeff jerked the door open. "I've found you, Miss Goodwin," he said. "Now you'll have to come out and talk to me."

He pulled up short when Miss Goodwin, wearing a stunning dress of orange satin, blocked his path.

"No, I'm afraid you'll have to come in," she said. "We're under quarantine."

Chapter Three

Mr. Randolph's expression was one of such shock, horror, and disbelief, Violet's good humor was restored. She almost felt sorry for him. Then he opened his mouth.

"You're crazy if you think I'm going to stay locked up with a gaggle of giggling girls for I don't know how long."

"Five days," Violet said.

"That's nearly a week! I could be ruined by then."

There he went again, acting as if he owned a bank. Well, she wasn't going to argue with him. She didn't really care what kind of fantasies he indulged in.

"You should have thought of that before you came bursting in here."

"There's no sign on the door."

"We didn't put one up because a thing like this is liable to panic the community. After all, scarlet fever isn't terribly serious."

"Why didn't you send me a message?"

"Why should I have?"

"Because you ordered me to be here on this day at this time."

"I didn't do any such thing. I'd never—Oh, my God! I completely forgot!"

"Well it doesn't matter. I'm not staying here," Jeff said.

"You might carry the infection into the community."

"Don't be ridiculous. I never get sick."

"Maybe not, but you'll have to stay anyway. Oh, dear, what on earth am I going to do with you? This building wasn't designed to have a man in residence." When Jeff turned to go, Violet grabbed him by his right sleeve. "You can't leave."

He removed her hand from his coat. "Watch me."

"It's illegal to break a quarantine."

"I don't care." He started toward the door Beth had closed behind him.

"If you leave, I'll have you arrested," Violet said.

Jeff turned and gaped at her. "You'll do what?"

"I'll have you arrested. No one is allowed to break a quarantine. If you go out that door, everybody you meet, your family, business partners, the clerks and tellers at the bank, even the arresting policemen will have to be quarantined. I imagine you'd be the most unpopular man in Denver by nightfall."

Jeff looked from Violet to a tongue-tied Beth and back to Violet again. He obviously couldn't believe what had happened to him. He probably expected someone to tell him the quarantine was a joke. He should have left when no one had answered the door. Nevertheless, the woman had insisted someone return to the school. She should have remembered to tell him not to come. The whole situation was her fault.

For her part, Violet wondered what she was going to do with Jeff. He didn't look like a man who could entertain himself, especially under the circumstances.

"I'm afraid you'll have to stay on the third floor,"

Violet said. "There are no bedrooms down here, and the girls occupy all the rooms upstairs."

"That's impossible," Jeff said.

"Why?"

"The place is full of girls."

Violet had to smile at his remark. "That's not unusual in a girls' school."

"I probably know their fathers and mothers. I wouldn't be able to look them in the face after this."

Good Lord, Violet hadn't thought about that. Some of the parents would create a fuss if they knew of Jefferson Randolph's presence. Even if his bank did try to hide him in the attic, quite a few people probably knew him, at least socially. She'd let Miss Settle know immediately, but she'd have to keep his presence a secret until the quarantine was over.

"We won't advertise your presence," Violet said.

Jeff wasn't listening. He was staring into space. He looked furious. She dreaded what he would decide to do. Quite abruptly, his brow cleared and he said, "Show me my room."

She was immediately worried. Polite and gentlemanly acceptance of what couldn't be changed was the last thing she expected from him.

"My bedroom is on the third floor as well," she said.

He stopped in his tracks. "That's completely unacceptable."

"It would be if I were alone, but Beth sleeps up there, too. She will preserve my reputation."

"I was thinking of mine."

Violet looked at him with wry amusement. "When did a man ever wish to preserve his reputation, except to prove it's as bad as can be?"

"I have a position to uphold," Jeff said quite seriously. "It doesn't include squirreling myself away in the attic of a girls' dormitory. And there's no point trying to keep my presence a secret. It will be found out. Might as well make sure everyone knows. Then there'll be nothing to explain later.''

Violet wasn't sure Miss Settle would agree, but she had to respect Mr. Randolph's decision. He wasn't the most pleasant person in the world, but he didn't hesitate to face up to a difficult situation. Or was his decision merely obstinacy? She couldn't tell.

As they climbed the stairs, Violet was surprised to find herself very much aware of his physical presence. She supposed it was his size. Her father and brother had both been of medium size. Mr. Randolph was at least half a foot taller, much bigger, than either her father or brother. He'd have made Jonas look like a child.

Violet tried not to think of her brother as he was after he came home. But she could remember little else. She had been nine when he had left.

She was winded when she reached the top floor. Mr. Randolph didn't draw a deep breath.

"I'm afraid the rooms aren't well-appointed,'' she said.

"This room doesn't look bad. I'll take it,'' Mr. Randolph said, indicating the first room on the right.

"That's my room,'' Violet said. "Beth sleeps directly across the hall. You can have any of the others.''

Mr. Randolph stuck his head in each room. "They're full of trunks and old furniture.''

Violet looked into the room on her side of the hall. "There aren't many trunks here. It won't take you but a few minutes to drag them across the hall.''

"Don't you have someone to do that for you?''

"Not while we're in quarantine. Our food is delivered to the door. Other than that, we're on our own.''

Mr. Randolph proceeded to let her know, in colorful and concise terms, what he thought of the situation. So much for polite and gentlemanly acceptance. She wasn't too familiar with the workings of a bank, but she was certain Mr. Randolph had acquired neither his vocabulary nor his manners in one.

Using a maneuver she imagined he must have practiced a long time, since he seemed to do it so easily, he shrugged out of his coat. He handed the coat to her. She took it, her gaze glued to his body. Huge shoulders heavy with muscle tapered down to a trim waist. His heavily starched shirt did little to hide the muscles that rippled across his chest.

Without a word, he strode into the room. A moment later a large trunk sailed through the door, across the hall, and through the opposite doorway without stopping. A second and third followed almost immediately. For a man with only one arm, he was amazingly strong.

"Wait a minute," Violet said. "You can't jumble those trunks together like that."

"You straighten them out."

"Not while you're flinging them about like an angry gorilla."

He stuck his head through the doorway. "A what?"

"A gorilla—a large animal of great strength and uncertain temper."

Jeff didn't seem the least upset by her description. He crossed the hall to survey the jumble of trunks.

"They ought to be stacked," she said.

"I can't lift them by myself." He waved his stump at her. He was using it as a weapon to make her feel guilty, to get what he wanted. And he was succeeding.

"I can help." Violet didn't tell him she'd never been required to lift anything much heavier than a newborn baby. She didn't know how she would handle anything as large as a trunk. And soon they both could tell she wasn't cut out for such work.

"You're weak as a cat," Jeff said. "Maybe you'd better get that other girl up here."

"That other girl is busy. I'll manage."

"I doubt it."

His scorn provided Violet with the impetus she needed. She was certain every muscle in her back and shoulders would ache abominably the next morning, but she had the satisfaction of showing Mr. Jeff Randolph she wasn't quite useless. "I'll get some sheets and a blanket for the bed," she said when they had stacked the last trunk.

"Don't forget a pillow."

Violet was relieved to have a moment to herself. She felt uncomfortably hot. She knew her discomfort wasn't just from physical exertion. She couldn't understand why being around Jeff Randolph should unsettle her so. Her work had brought her into contact with so many men she had become virtually immune to their physical attractiveness.

Not so with Jeff Randolph. Violet had never seen anyone with such a sculptured physique. He was reminding her quite vividly that, even though 29 was considered well beyond the marriageable age, it was not beyond the age of being susceptible to a virile male. She blushed to think she was behaving in such a shocking manner. Miss Settle would grow faint if she had any notion of the ideas flashing through Violet's head.

Violet was feeling a little light-headed herself. She forced herself to concentrate on gathering the things she would need to make his bed. By the time she had climbed the stairs once again, she had herself reasonably under control.

"I need to send a message to my clerk," Jeff said when Violet reached his room. He had found a desk and chair in working condition. The bed, buried under the pile of trunks, was already there. She supposed he would need a chest of some kind, but there were several he could choose from.

"Beth will bring you pen and paper and see your message is sent out. I'll make up your bed while you're gone."

He left without thanking her, but then she hadn't expected thanks. She doubted he had ever felt thankful in his life or would have admitted it if he had. She'd have hated to have been part of his family and to have had to deal with his roughness all the time.

She spread a sheet over the mattress and began to tuck it in. Maybe she was being unfair. Just because he barked at her didn't mean he always acted that way. He was clearly out of his depth with his routine destroyed. Maybe he was better when he was in his bank.

As Violet began with the second sheet, she wondered if his family knew he went about pretending he ran the bank. Of course they must. Even in a city of 35,000 people, such an outrageous claim couldn't be kept quiet for long. It was a shame he felt the need to aggrandize himself. He was quite impressive as he was.

Violet smoothed the sheet as a tremor shot through her. Mr. Randolph's body would soon lie exactly where she placed her hand. A vision of him naked in bed flashed through her mind. She drew back. She flushed with embarrassment at her own reaction. She had to stop her imagination from running wild. No matter how handsome Jefferson Randolph was, he didn't like her and she wasn't very fond of him.

Telling herself that she had to stop being silly and that she was too old to let a fantasy affect her so strongly, Violet fluffed up a pillow and slipped it into a case. She placed a folded blanket at the foot of the bed and headed downstairs. Somehow she felt safer there.

Jeff sat alone in his spartan room. He had sent a note to Caspar Lawrence. The clerk would be there soon. Jeff rose and paced the hall. He had never been so inactive for such a long time. His lack of work was getting on his nerves.

President of the biggest bank in Denver, Jeff Randolph had a private office paneled in mahogany and furnished with leather-covered chairs, a fireplace, a desk the size of a bed, and a dozen men at his beck and call. But because of the blasted quarantine, he was forced to work in an attic room littered with trunks, suitcases, and discarded furniture and to sit in a ladder-back chair at a table consigned to the attic because of wobbly legs. Instead of his comfortable house with its expensive furniture, soft mattresses, and perfectly prepared food, he was to sleep on a metal bed with a thin mattress and make do with no heat and a small lamp. God only knew what kind of swill would come from the kitchen. And his horrible fate had come about because that woman had forgotten to cancel his appointment. He would have loved to choke her, even if he did have only one hand.

Worse yet, he was going to be locked up with her for five days. Not close, by God. He would keep to his room. She could keep to hers. He shook his head in disbelief. This ought to have been happening to George. They were his kids.

For a moment Jeff wondered if the whole situation was all a plan to trap him. Then he told himself not to be foolish. No woman wanted a man without an arm. How many more times did he have to learn that lesson? Women wanted his money, but they didn't want him. They didn't need him either.

That fact was important to Jeff. His family had needed him once. He drove himself to prove they still did.

Jeff didn't know why he was even thinking about those things. They had nothing to do with Violet Goodwin or being locked up in a girls' dormitory. Nevertheless, he would keep to himself. No telling what kind of trouble Violet would get him into if he didn't.

But the idea of days stretching ahead with no human contact didn't appeal to him. He always complained about having to meet people, but he didn't like isolation.

On the other hand, solitary confinement had to be better than being forced to fraternize with a Yankee female who insisted on wearing bold-as-brass colors. Her white skin and that mountain of coppery hair were no excuse to flaunt herself. Nor were her deep blue eyes, eyes as blue as the depths of a mountain lake.

Jeff cursed. He was annoyed that she should be pretty, that he should be attracted to her. He had disliked Yankees on principle for years, but disliking Violet Goodwin was hard when he kept wanting to look into her eyes.

Violet stopped midsentence. She was right. There was a man shouting somewhere outside the building. She walked to one of the windows at the back of the large room that served as a study hall for the girls. The man must be on the other side of the building. She left the room, crossed the hall, and entered an equally large room the girls were using for recreation and meals during the quarantine. Three of the girls had their noses to the window. Two of them were the Randolph twins.

"What is that man doing?" Violet asked.

"He's shouting up to Uncle Jeff," Aurelia said.

"He's from the bank," Juliette said.

The girls moved aside to allow Violet an unobstructed view of a man with his hands cupped to his mouth shouting to the upper floors.

"This must stop," Violet said.

She climbed the two flights of stairs as quickly as she could. She reached Jeff's room to find him leaning out the window. By the time she had recovered her breath sufficiently to speak, she had heard enough to understand he was instructing his clerk to set up an office in the parlor.

"Mr. Randolph, stop shouting out the window this minute. You'll have everybody in town wondering what's going on."

Jeff finished what he was saying, closed the window, then turned to face her. "I was just telling Caspar what

49

I wanted him to bring first thing in the morning. Got any wood? He says the parlor's cold."

"He can't use the parlor. We're under quarantine."

"He'll push everything through the door and your maid can bring it to me."

"Beth has a full load of duties already. She can't become your courier as well."

"Then you can bring everything to me."

"In case it has escaped your notice, there are sixteen girls in this building who are my responsibility. I don't intend to slight my duties to drag myself up and down those steps a dozen times a day."

"Let the twins do it. Maybe then they'll keep out of trouble." Jeff's gaze narrowed. "It wouldn't hurt you though. One trip has winded you. You're out of shape. You need some exercise."

Violet had never been more nonplussed. No one had ever told her she was out of shape. The few people who had dared make such personal comments had been flattering.

"My physical shape is none of your concern. I—"

Jeff eyed her quite brazenly. "Your shape is fine. It's your condition I'm talking about."

When he flashed a smile, Violet's knees nearly gave way. She had never seen him smile before. She was quite unprepared for how devastatingly handsome he was. Not even her acquaintance with the twins had warned her sufficiently. It was as though God had made a perfect man, then taken away one arm to make him mortal.

Only Jeff Randolph wasn't perfect. He had a lousy temper, and he was always taunting her to see how she would respond. She didn't like being manipulated for anyone's amusement.

"You can't imagine the pure joy your approval gives me," she said.

"Yes, I can," he said with brazen candor. "You're

ready to cut my throat. I can't spend five days locked up in this place with nothing to do. I'd murder the lot of you before Sunday morning.''

"What an appropriate day."

"If you don't want anybody running up and down those stairs, move the girls up here and give me the downstairs.''

"I can't move the girls just because you didn't go away as you were told.''

"I'm not going over that ground again," Jeff said. "My clerk has already put a box of papers in the parlor. Have somebody bring it to me, or I'll get it myself. Can I take off my coat? It's hot in here.''

"I'd rather you didn't," Violet said. "Open the window if you must, but keep your door closed. Beth and I are not hot.''

"Indeed, you seem damned cold to me.''

Violet's palms itched to slap that arrogant frown off Jeff's face. "It's undoubtedly the effect of your charm.'' Flashing a grim smile she hoped was as cold as his frown, she turned and headed toward the stairs. She stopped halfway there and turned back. "I have to inform Miss Settle of your presence. I'm sure you understand it would be impossible for me to do anything else.''

"Sure.''

"I'm certain she'll have your office removed from the parlor.''

"You let me worry about that.''

"I shall." Turning and heading down the steps, Violet met Juliette coming up, carrying a box of papers. Aurelia followed close behind with another. "Have you girls completed your assignments for the day?''

"Yes, Miss Goodwin.''

"Then you can help your uncle this afternoon. I imagine all this will be over by dinner.''

"Yes, Miss Goodwin.''

* * *

Fern laughed so hard she hurt. "Swear you're not making this up. He really is locked up with a bunch of little girls and a spinster housemother for five days?"

"Yes, Mrs. Randolph," Caspar Lawrence said." He's got everybody turning the bank inside out getting things ready to take over to him."

Fern turned to Daisy. "You know how he hates Yankees. The housemother is from Massachusetts. I'll bet he's mad enough to start the war all over again. I shouldn't laugh," she said, then went off into another peal of laughter, "but it serves him right."

"I thought you'd like to know where he was," the nervous clerk said. "Miss Aurelia and Miss Juliette are fine. They never did get the fever."

"I didn't expect they would. I suppose Jeff'll be all right until they let him out, but keep me informed. Though what I can do confined to this bed, I can't guess."

"Do you want me to go to the school?" Daisy asked after the clerk left.

"Not with you pregnant as well. No telling what you might pick up there. Though you do look healthy as a horse. Sorry. You can tell I was reared on a farm. Nine years in Chicago and Denver haven't turned me into a lady."

"Don't say that. I grew up in the New Mexico desert. There won't be any hope for me."

"There never was for either of us, according to Jeff. We weren't born in Virginia," Fern said, and both women laughed.

"Do you think he'll ever change?"

"Never! But that's enough about Jeff. Tell me about your hotel. Did you finally get everything finished? It must be even more luxurious than you and Tyler planned. I hear you have people practically climbing through the windows to get in."

* * *

The dinner hour came and went without word from Miss Settle. Violet had sent word to Mr. Randolph that dinner would be served in the social hall. He had sent back word he had too much work to dine. Violet decided he needed a break even if he didn't need food. Besides, guilt at forgetting to notify him of the quarantine had overcome her anger. She fixed him a tray and started up the stairs. She met the twins tearing down the steps, their arms loaded as usual.

"Is your uncle still working?" she asked.

"He's always working," Juliette said.

Violet started up again, but sudden curiosity made her stop and turn back. "What does your uncle do àt the bank?" she asked.

"He runs it," Juliette said, stopping on the landing and turning to face Violet.

"You mean he's the manager?"

"No, he owns it."

"Do you mean he's on the board of directors?" Violet felt a cold chill flood all through her body. When the twins didn't know, Violet asked, "What about the rest of your family? Do you have any more uncles?"

"Yes. Five."

"Don't they help him?"

"No, Uncle Jeff does it all by himself."

Violet experienced a sinking feeling in the pit of her stomach. "What's the name of his bank?"

"I don't know, but Mama says it's the biggest bank in town."

The First National Bank of Denver! Jefferson Randolph couldn't own that bank. She couldn't have the most powerful financial wizard that side of San Francisco shouting out of her upstairs window.

Good God! No wonder she hadn't heard anything from Miss Settle. The poor woman had probably fainted dead away when she had received the note. She was probably petrified every important member of the Denver financial community would soon be at the front door demanding her head. No, not Miss Settle's head. Violet's head.

Violet admitted to a moment of cowardice. She could go back downstairs and send Jeff's food up with the twins. She could lock herself in her room for the next five days and not see anybody at all. She wasn't cut out to be the housemother, nurse, and teacher for 16 girls between eight and 14. She hadn't had as much as five hours to herself since she had taken the job. And she wouldn't get them after making such an embarrassing mistake.

Violet started up the stairs. She stopped outside Jeff Randolph's door, surprised when she heard a child's voice coming from his room. She had passed the twins on the stairs. No one else was supposed to be up there.

"Do you have to do things with all those papers?" the child asked.

Essie Brown. She was the only eight-year-old boarder. A small, fragile child. Lonely, too. Violet had found her crying in her sleep several times in the last three months.

"Every one of them," Jeff said.

"But you've got so many."

"Hundreds."

"My daddy has lots of papers, too. He keeps them in a big black bag. He takes it with him everywhere."

"What does your daddy do?"

"I don't know."

"What's his name?" Jeff asked.

"Daddy."

"Yes, I suppose it would be."

Violet could hardly believe she was listening to Jeff Randolph. He sounded human, even kind. None of the girls had much time for Essie. She was too shy. Violet had to admit even she sometimes lost patience with the child. If the little girl would just try to have a little gumption, she would be happier. It was hard to believe Jeff Randolph was able to push back the curtain of fear that seemed to surround her.

"What's that?" Essie asked.

"Nothing but a long column of numbers," Jeff said.

"Do they mean anything?"

"They stand for quite a bit of money."

"My daddy has a lot of money." Essie was silent a moment. "He says money's the most important thing in the world."

Violet didn't like to spy on people, but she couldn't help herself. She stood just close enough to the door to be able to see into the room. Jeff had set his work aside, and he was looking at Essie.

"What do you think is the most important thing in the world?" Jeff asked.

"I don't know."

"What do you want most in the world?"

"To see my daddy."

"He can't come now because of the quarantine."

"You came."

"Yes, but I wasn't supposed to."

"My daddy never comes."

Essie started to cry. Violet decided it was time to intervene. Jeff wouldn't know what to do with a crying child. But much to her surprise, he simply reached over, put his arm around Essie, and drew her to him.

"Your father will come."

"No, he won't," Essie said.

"He will now."

The child looked up at Jeff, her cheeks wet with tears. "How do you know?"

"I just do."

Jeff glanced up and saw Violet outside the door. Then he withdrew into himself just as clearly as if he had closed a door.

Chapter Four

"You'd better run along now. Miss Goodwin is here to see I eat my dinner."

Essie grinned through her tears. "Can I watch?"

"No, she might spank me if I don't eat everything on my plate."

"Ladies don't spank men."

"Miss Goodwin might."

"Run along, Essie," Violet said. "You've got plenty to do before bedtime."

"Can I come back and say good night?" Essie asked.

"Sure," Jeff said, giving her a little push toward the door. "Come any time. I hardly ever go to sleep. And don't worry about your father. He'll come."

Violet watched Essie trudge along the hall and disappear down the staircase, but her thoughts remained on Jeff Randolph. She didn't understand him at all. She would have sworn he wasn't capable of gentleness or understanding anybody but himself, but he had been wonderfully gentle with Essie. She had seen his kindness with her own eyes and heard it with her own ears. She wondered just what kind of man hid behind that callous facade.

"I hope you can make good on your promise," Violet said when Essie was out of hearing range. She entered the room and stood waiting for Jeff to clear a space on his desk so she could put the tray down. "She'll be brokenhearted if her father doesn't come. He never has, despite several letters from Miss Settle."

"Is her father Harold Brown?" Jeff asked.

"How did you guess?"

"She looks exactly like him. He's a real bastard, but a father ought to see his daughter. Hell, I'd visit Essie if she were my kid."

Violet decided it would be pointless to get upset every time Jeff cursed. Just as long as he didn't swear in front of the girls. Besides, she was fascinated by the previously unseen side of Jeff Randolph.

"I'm surprised you got Essie to open up. She's terribly shy with everyone else," Violet said.

"She's just lonely," Jeff said. "All she wants is a little attention."

Violet knew Essie needed more than that. She hadn't been able to reach Essie in three months of trying. Yet Jeff had her chattering away like a normal eight-year-old in one afternoon.

"How do you propose to make her father come when no one else has?" she asked.

"Call in his loan. It's overdue."

Violet should have guessed. Wasn't that what all bankers did?

"It must be nice to have such power."

"I'm not interested in power, just money. Making loans is one of the ways I do it."

"Well, you need to take some time off, or you'll get a brain fever and do something crazy."

"I never do anything crazy, and I frequently work around the clock."

Violet should have known it was pointless to try to be helpful or considerate, but she tried anyway. "You can't work all night while you're here. The girls must get their sleep, and you make a great deal of noise. Besides, your staff should go home to their own dinners. Their families must be waiting for them."

"I mean to let them go at nine o'clock."

"Seven," Violet said.

"Nine."

"I have already given Beth orders that nothing is to be brought up after seven o'clock."

Mr. Randolph clearly wasn't used to being thwarted. But after only a small pause, he said, "I guess I'd better make sure I have everything I need before then. Now if you'll put that tray down, you'll be free to attend your girls."

"I'm waiting for you to clear a place on your desk."

"I don't intend to clear a space because I don't intend to eat. However, if you insist upon leaving the food, you can put it on the floor, the bed, or anywhere you like."

Violet opened her mouth, reconsidered her words, then said, "I don't approve of wasting food."

"Neither do I; so I suggest you take it back downstairs. Good night, Miss Goodwin. I have work to do."

Violet was not accustomed to being dismissed, but she had been, quite unmistakably. It was a severe strain on her temper. But since she prided herself on her control—it was an essential part of her job—she made the effort. She had to remain calm. She had to spend five days with this man.

"Good night, Mr. Randolph. I'm sorry your accommodations aren't better. If you need anything, don't hesitate to let me know. Breakfast will be at a quarter after eight."

Jeff merely nodded. Violet left, trying not to dislike

him for preferring columns of numbers to herself. After all, she didn't like him either.

Jeff paused in his work to stretch. He looked at his watch. 3:27 a.m. He took a few turns around the room to get the stiffness out of his muscles. He yawned, but he wasn't sleepy. He had to go to the toilet. He would have to use the one downstairs. Jeff had never gotten used to the noisy contraptions, but Tyler had insisted every room in his new hotel have one. Jeff wondered what Miss Goodwin thought about them.

He picked up his lamp and started downstairs. He stopped when he realized her door was open. Frowning, he wondered why she didn't lock it. She ought not to trust him. Men very often weren't what they pretended to be.

Not that she was in any danger. He wasn't immune to her allure, but he wouldn't have entered her room if she had invited him. If a Southern woman couldn't accept him, how could a Yankee?

He had tried to put the failure of his last trip to Virginia out of his mind, but the wound was still raw. He'd met Julia his first day there. She was lovely, exactly the kind of woman he'd hoped to find. Her beauty and serenity had reminded him of so much he had lost. Nothing had been said, but hope had been born and nourished. If it hadn't been for that terrible accident, he might have made an irrevocable mistake.

A wheel had come off during a carriage race. He could still hear the splintering of wood, the horrible screams as a man's body was torn by wood and metal. He was the only one who knew what to do. He remembered from the war. Shouting orders, he'd torn off his coat, ripped his shirt into pieces with his teeth to help stanch the blood.

Jeff had seen Julia recoil. He had hoped she was reacting to the carnage, even the unexpected sight of his bare chest. But that night he knew she had been horrified by his arm. The change had been subtle, but it was unmistakable.

That had been nearly ten years ago. Jeff hadn't been back to Virginia since, even though he knew in the end he must return. He had no intention of trying to discover if Violet Goodwin was more broad-minded. Being used to her brother's wounds, she probably wouldn't flinch. But he didn't want to be accepted because she had seen worse. He wanted to be thought of as being whole, complete. He wanted to be thought of just like anybody else. It would be a cruel irony if the first woman to do that was a busybody from Massachusetts.

Jeff reached the lower floor and entered the first bathroom. He set his lamp down and raised the toilet seat. He'd better lock the door. If one of the girls wandered in before he finished, she'd probably start screaming. That foolish Yankee woman would be bound to think he'd done something unspeakable.

Jeff wondered why she was in Colorado. She didn't dress like a housemother. Who was she trying to impress with those extravagant gowns? He had to admit the strong colors formed a wonderful contrast with her hair and eyes, but that was out of place in a girls' school dormitory. It was a good thing the Wolfe School wasn't for boys. He didn't like to think of the erotic dreams her presence would evoke.

Jeff flushed the contraption. He cringed at the resulting commotion. If toilets were going to catch on, somebody would have to figure out how to make them sound less like a flash flood roaring down a mountain canyon. He expected half the girls to stick their heads out of their rooms. But when he entered the hall, all the doors were closed and the hall was wrapped in silence.

As Jeff started up the stairs, he wondered what Violet did when she went out. She must leave the school occasionally. Any sane adult would go crazy locked up with 16 little girls all day, every day, week after week. But she had been in quarantine for more than a week. That almost made him feel sorry for her.

He paused outside her door. He didn't know why. If she were to suddenly wake up, he'd have a hard time explaining what he was doing.

Jeff went back to his room, his steps a little more rapid than necessary. He decided he had better get his mind off Violet Goodwin and back on his work. Specifically, he needed to study the Chicago futures market. Prices were behaving erratically. If he was lucky, he would make a great deal of money.

Violet jerked awake. She could swear she had heard the sound of a rachet outside her window. But no sound disturbed the morning quiet. She looked at her timepiece. 6:17 a.m. She lay back and burrowed under the covers. Winter had come early to Denver. It was bitterly cold in the attic.

She wondered what Mr. Randolph was doing. He had been up when she had gone to bed. The door to his room had been open, with light pouring out into the hall. Even after Violet had gone to bed, she had heard him moving around. He had probably worked far into the night. She hoped he would sleep late that morning. She would appreciate some time without having to deal with him. She was still trying to figure him out.

She had jumped to the conclusion that he was a mere flunky in a bank. It turned out that he not only ran the bank, but he owned it. She had decided he was cruel and without any human kindness, but he had shown both gentleness and understanding to Essie. She had been wrong about him twice. Could she be wrong in every other way?

No. He *was* an arrogant Southerner, bitter about the war and the loss of his arm, bent on taking it out on the rest of the world, especially Yankee women. But the way he acted with Essie proved he hadn't always been that way.

What had caused him to change? It wasn't just losing his arm or losing the war. Too many men had gone through both without having their characters altered so drastically. Something more had happened. Violet doubted she would ever know. Jeff Randolph didn't strike her as the kind of man to share his secrets, especially with a Yankee.

You're just trying to make excuses for him. You've been completely bowled over by his looks, and you're looking for a way to make him into someone you can admire. Don't. He seems to enjoy being an irascible recluse.

She had been mesmerized by his looks. She had lain in the bed for a good half hour the night before, aware that he was only a few feet away, aware that only a thin wall separated them, aware that she should be shocked for feeling that way.

She wasn't a young, impressionable girl. She was old enough to know there was a great deal more to a man than looks. She was also well aware Jeff's personality was far from charming. Yet she'd even dreamed about him. Clearly she had been locked away in the school too long. She hoped Harvey would ask her to dinner again soon. He wasn't as attractive as Jeff Randolph, but he was certainly more charming. That ought to stop her from—

The rachet sound started again. There was no mistake. Violet threw back the covers. The cold bit into her flesh. She reached for her robe and wrapped it around her. She pushed her feet into slippers and hurried to her window. Her eyes grew wide with surprise.

She saw several men milling around below. They had rigged up a kind of hoist outside Mr. Randolph's window. She couldn't tell what they were bringing up, but it looked like large circles of metal. She couldn't un--

derstand what he could want with something like that.

Violet's first thought was that the solution was wonderful. Jeff could get anything he needed without disturbing her or the girls. Then she became aware of a feeling of discontent. She told herself she hated losing control of the situation, of not being able to monitor what he did. But she knew it was more than that. She was disappointed she would have no reason for further contact with him.

How could that be? Maybe she was just jealous he had outthought her. Any man clever enough to do business with the smartest men in America could certainly outmaneuver a nurse from Massachusetts who couldn't even get her own silver mine back.

Violet thought of asking Jeff to help her, but discarded the idea immediately. She had no intention of being involved with him one minute longer than necessary.

The noise was terrible. She was certain none of the girls could sleep through it. She left her room. When she reached Jeff's doorway, she stopped, startled. He hadn't changed clothes. He hadn't slept. Neat bundles of paper covered most of the bed. Three of those iron disks lay on the floor. He reached out to take a fourth from the lift.

"What on earth are you doing?" she asked.

Jeff turned toward her, a bewildered expression on his face. "What happened to you?"

Violet's hand went instinctively to her hair. It cascaded over her shoulders like a lion's mane. She wore a faded blue housecoat. She probably appeared frumpy.

"If you mean I look unsightly enough to explain why I'm an old maid, I'll thank you to keep your opinions to yourself." He continued to stare at her. "I was waked out of a sound sleep by your infernal machine. I haven't had time to repair the damages of sleep."

"No damage," Jeff said, staring at her without apology. "You look pretty."

Violet wanted to believe him, but she didn't dare. If she did, there was no telling what foolishness she might start to believe.

Then he smiled, and she was nearly undone. How could he stay up all night and still look so deliciously attractive? He didn't even have bags under his eyes.

"I prefer a woman to wear her hair down."

"And go around in faded robes and threadbare slippers?"

"It makes them look more like the women I knew before the war."

The lift arrived, and Jeff pulled another cast iron disk into the room.

"What are those?" Violet asked.

"Weights. Since I can't go to my trainer, I've had him send the equipment to me."

Violet watched as Jeff held an iron disk between his knees and anchored one end of a bar through the hole in the middle. He did the same with the other end.

"What do you do with the others?"

"I add them as I go along. Now, unless you wish to watch me strip down to my waist, I suggest you go back to your room," he said, then seemed amused by her consternation.

"But you've only got one arm. How are you going to lift such a thing? It could fall on you."

Some of the ease went out of Jeff's expression. "Then I shall hope you and the twins rush up and lift it off me before I expire."

"I doubt all of us could lift that together."

"Then I guess I'd better not drop it on myself."

He was mocking her unfairly. She was only expressing concern. Locking Denver's most important financier in her attic was bad enough. Letting him kill himself would be unforgivable.

"You're not going to haul your clerk up on the lift, are you?" Violet asked.

"I was tempted, but you'd probably hold him hostage as well. Then there's the problem of where he would sleep. You're not willing to share your bed, are you?"

When Violet flushed crimson, Jeff said, "I didn't think so. So I plan to let him go home to his wife tonight."

"He probably hasn't seen the poor woman since yesterday. Undoubtedly he spent all night rounding up that infernal machine and putting it up. What time did your men arrive?"

"Shortly before five."

"Five!"

"It could have been earlier. I wasn't paying attention."

"Do you drive all your employees like this?"

"Ma'am, my employees are well paid. If they wish to leave, my recommendation will secure them a position in any bank in Denver."

"And how many have you worn out so far?"

"I haven't worn out anybody."

Violet's look was skeptical. "Don't you want to keep good people around you?"

"The world is full of capable employees. If one can't keep up, I can find one who can."

He wasn't human. Couldn't he see he had turned his mind into a machine? He was using those weights to do the same thing to his body. He would destroy himself just as surely as Jonas had.

"The girls won't have their breakfast until more than an hour from now," Violet said.

"Don't worry. My clerk will send my breakfast up the lift. He'll take the dirty dishes away the same way."

Somehow Violet was annoyed that Jeff had taken even his meals out of her hands as well. He was cutting off all contact between them, which bothered her.

The door at the end of the hall opened, and Essie

Brown peeped in. She broke into a smile when she saw Violet.

"What are you doing up so early?" Violet asked.

"I came to see the man."

"I think it would be better if you went back downstairs. He's not ready for company. And try not to wake the other girls."

"They're all up."

"Well, go back anyway. You can come up later."

Essie was disappointed, but she disappeared down the stairs.

Violet turned to Jeff. "Your infernal lift has waked everyone."

"You have only yourself to blame. You wouldn't let your maid bring anything up from the parlor, and you cut my men off at seven last night. I had to do something."

Violet decided it would be best if she didn't say what was on her mind. When she realized he had the audacity to look disappointed, she was determined to make no reply.

"I figured this would free your maid to go about her duties," Jeff said, "and the twins to start getting into trouble again."

"It's quite possible Miss Settle will have something to say about that," Violet said, unable to think of any way to stop the man from taking over her building. "I expect to hear from her this morning."

"Let me know what she says."

He began to undo the buttons on his shirt. Violet decided that, if she didn't leave, he'd probably take his shirt off in front of her just to see what she would do. She returned to her room. She seated herself before her mirror and began to brush her hair.

She tried hard to subdue her irritation at Mr. Randolph, but she was tempted to give in to her anger and throw something at him. He certainly wasn't trying to curb his temper.

She put down her brush and began to pin her heavy hair in place.

Jonas had been unfailingly pleasant, even cheerful, from the day he had come home from the hospital until he died ten years later. He always thanked her for everything she did for him. But he had decided to die, and she had been unable to stop him.

Violet wondered if Mr. Randolph had ever felt that way. His injuries weren't as severe as Jonas's, but she'd learned the most severe wounds were to the spirit, not the body. They were also the most difficult to heal. Mr. Randolph's temper might be the result of some hurt he couldn't heal. There was no way to know what he felt or what he might be hiding. Violet decided she should suspend judgment until she knew more about him. She certainly had to give him credit for what he had accomplished. And she had proof his achievements were the result of hard work.

Violet pushed the last pin in her hair and turned to the task of choosing her dress. She opened the doors of the large wardrobe, the only piece of furniture in her room besides her bed and her dressing table. The dresses inside were striking and lovely, but there were so few of them. She found herself mentally planning so she wouldn't wear the same dress twice while Mr. Randolph was here. She wanted to slap herself for being so foolish. She shouldn't have thrown away her nursing uniforms.

Violet didn't want Mr. Jefferson Randolph to think she liked him. Some women might have been able to overlook his character because of his money and position. She was not one of them.

Violet was shocked at the path her thoughts were taking. The strain of confinement was getting to her. It was absurd to think of the man in that way. She might think more kindly of him than he thought of her, but since he thought of her as something akin to a biblical plague, she could actively dislike him and still come out ahead.

Besides, she wasn't interested in marriage. She wanted to get her money, go back to Massachusetts, and find a way to help women who had sacrificed their lives as she herself had.

"Mr. Jefferson's clerks have taken over the parlor," Beth said as soon as she came downstairs. "They've even built a fire."

"The poor things have to keep warm," Violet said. "He has them outside working in the bitter cold."

"There must be six or seven of them in there now, each with his own desk. They're working just as if they were in a bank."

"How do you know that?" Violet asked.

"I can't help seeing when they open the door, can I?"

"You aren't supposed to be in the hall." When Beth blushed, Violet said, "You've been peeping."

"Well, just a little," Beth said. "There's ever so many handsome young men in there. I feel faint just thinking about it."

"Don't. I can't handle all this by myself."

"Yes, you can. Nothing ever gets you upset."

"This has. I wish Miss Settle would answer me. I feel uncomfortable not knowing what she expects me to do about Mr. Randolph."

"He's a nice-looking gentleman, isn't he?"

"Yes, but he's also a very demanding one. Now we'd better see about serving breakfast. The girls were up and about when I came down. I have to write Miss Settle about the lift. I shudder to think what might cross her mind if she sees it without having received some sort of warning."

Violet hadn't completed more than half her letter

when a series of girlish squeals from the second floor caught her attention.

"Beth, see what's going on. If it's the twins, send them to me immediately."

Violet turned her attention back to her letter. But she had hardly collected her thoughts and decided on the next sentence when Beth rushed breathless into the room.

"It's him, ma'am. He's in the bathroom, and he's practically naked."

Chapter Five

Everything was in turmoil when Violet reached the second floor. The girls were jumping about, squealing, holding on to each other. A few seemed to be on the verge of fainting. Some were dressed, but most were still in their nightgowns, their feet bare, their hair falling about their shoulders in untidy tangles. On the whole, they were having a delightful time.

"What's this I hear about—"

"He's in there!" Betty Sue shrieked, pointing to the bathroom as she bounced up and down like a rubber ball. "I saw him. He doesn't have any clothes on."

"He does, too, you stupid girl," Aurelia said, advancing on Betty Sue with an angry look.

Betty Sue retreated behind one of the bigger girls. "I saw him. He was naked."

When Juliette closed in from the other side, Betty Sue shrieked again. Her bobbed blond hair flew from side to side as she tried to watch both girls.

"What in hell is wrong with you?" a deep masculine voice demanded.

The girls froze, their screams cut off in midcry. Violet whirled around to find herself standing barely six inches from Jeff Randolph. He was naked from the waist up. She felt as though she'd been hit in the solar plexus. She could hardly breathe. She couldn't move. Jeff's rippling muscles were so close she could smell the muskiness that resulted from hard male exercise and see the sheen of perspiration that made his skin glisten in the light. His pulse throbbed in the veins of his neck. Violet could almost feel the heat radiating from his body. She could almost count the number of blond hairs nestled in the center of his chest. She felt sure she was going to faint.

Betty Sue's shrieks—a result of the twins finally getting their hands on her—plus the chorus of squeals erupting from every part of the hall pulled Violet back from the brink. The girls were her responsibility. She had to take charge of the situation.

"Please step back in the bathroom," she said to Jeff as calmly as she could. "I'll speak with you as soon as I can get everyone downstairs. Aurelia and Juliette, get your hands off Betty Sue this minute. Don't touch her again, or I'll have no choice but to recommend your dismissal."

"But she lied. She said Uncle Jeff was naked," Aurelia said.

"I realize that, and I will speak to her. Right now, however, I want everyone except the twins downstairs this instant. Don't stand there staring at me. Move!"

The girls broke into suppressed giggles and hurried off downstairs, where they could talk and exclaim without restraint.

"You, too, Essie."

"I told him he could come down here," Essie said, unwilling to leave. "I told him we had two bathrooms."

71

"What were you doing upstairs so early?"

"I wanted to ask him when Daddy was coming. He didn't smell good. You always tell us to take a bath when we smell bad."

Violet couldn't resist a glance in Jeff's direction. One glimpse of his stunned expression made her struggle to keep a straight face. "Okay, Essie. You can go downstairs with the other girls."

"Why do Aurelia and Juliette get to stay?" Essie asked.

"They're his nieces. Besides, I don't trust them with Betty Sue just now."

"I don't like Betty Sue," Essie said. "She's not nice."

"Take Essie and go to your room," Violet said to the twins. She didn't turn around until they had closed the door behind themselves. "Now—"

Once again Jeff's closeness struck her like a physical force. She had no choice but to retreat if she was to have any coherent thoughts. She hoped she managed it without looking as if she was running away.

Violet hadn't noticed Jeff's arm before. It had been taken off just above the elbow. In the intervening 14 years, the redness had faded from the scar. Only the stump showed the smooth shininess of scar tissue.

"What on earth possessed you to come down here?" she asked, redirecting her gaze from Jeff's arm to his face. She didn't want to pretend she hadn't noticed, but she didn't want him to think she showed more than ordinary interest.

Jeff's gaze met hers in the space between them, and the two of them stood like duelists, swords ready, each waiting for the other to advance. His gaze was defiant, hers hesitant.

"I thought Essie explained it rather well," he said. "I needed a bath."

"But to come down half naked—"

"I meant to be back upstairs before the girls appeared. This is the only shirt I have until my clerk brings me some fresh clothes."

"You could have stayed upstairs until he returned. You could have sent for me. You could have done several things instead of sending half my girls into hysterics."

"Nothing's wrong with them. They're enjoying themselves."

"I realize that. However, you have gotten some of them overly excited, especially Betty Sue."

"The exaggerating little heifer?"

"I must insist that you moderate your language," Violet said.

"Would you prefer lying little bitch?"

Violet took a deep breath and started to count to ten. She only made it to four. "No, I would not! I would prefer you go back to your room and not leave it until the quarantine is over."

"I can't do that. While I take my bath, you can think about your second favorite wish."

"After the disturbance you've caused, you can't still mean to take a bath."

"I still smell bad."

Violet couldn't deny the man the right to be clean any more than she could deny him the use of the bathroom for other purposes. Good Lord, she hadn't thought about that!

"But those are the girls' bathtubs." Her words sounded stupid, but they were all she could think to say.

"Do you have any other bathtubs?" Jeff asked.

"No."

"Do you use them?"

"Of course. I live here."

"So do I. I don't think I'll leave any nasty male germs, but I promise to wash the tub very carefully."

Seeing that he was again teasing her and enjoying her

agitation, she said, "Don't be ridiculous."

"My feeling exactly," Jeff said, more seriously. "Do you have towels? Or am I expected to run up and down the halls until I'm dry?"

Violet wondered why she'd thought he could be reasonable about anything. She marched over to a cabinet, extracted two towels, and thrust them at him.

"Do you think this will be enough?"

"I'll call you if I need more."

"I won't hear you. I'll be downstairs."

"You'd better stay. I might really come out naked next time."

Violet made herself pause before she spoke. He was just baiting her. "I'm sure you didn't mean to upset the girls. But as you can see, they're extremely impressionable."

"I would have said foolish. No man would act that way if he met a woman coming out of the bath."

"No woman would come out of the bath half naked."

Devilment danced in his eyes again. "Some I know would come out without a stitch."

Violet was sure she turned the color of her name. "Perhaps I should have said lady."

Jeff grinned at her. "I think I'll take my bath before I scandalize anyone else. Can you hold the girls at bay? Or should I lock myself in?"

"I would appreciate if you'd return to the upper floor as soon as possible. Should you need anything—" she didn't finish her sentence. Just thinking of possible requests caused heat to rise in her face again.

"Would you come rushing to my aid? No? Maybe if you closed your eyes first?"

Violet made herself turn away. She couldn't trust herself to be with Jeff for even one more minute. She didn't understand what his teasing was doing to her control, but she knew she was on the verge of losing it completely.

* * *

"Betty Sue said that to be mean," Aurelia said the moment Violet stepped into the room.

"She's always doing something like that," Juliette said.

"She said my daddy would never come," Essie said. "She said he was nothing but a grubby old trapper with the good luck to stumble over some gold when he was setting a beaver trap. He's not, Miss Goodwin. My daddy goes to an office every day just like that man."

"Mr. Randolph," Violet said.

"And he said my father was going to come see me. Betty Sue was wrong, the mean old goat."

"Listen, girls. Mr. Randolph is going to be here for several more days. We can't have this happening every time he wants to use the bathroom. You have to help me."

"How?"

Violet wished she knew. She didn't think Jeff would cooperate with the girls any more than with her. "I would like one of you to keep an eye on him. Let me know when he means to come downstairs. Above all, don't pay any attention to anything Betty Sue or the other girls might say. Right now they're too excited to think before they speak."

"Miss Goodwin." The plaintive call drew Violet into the hall. One of the older girls waited at the top of the stairs, her inquisitive gaze sweeping the hall for the whereabouts of Mr. Randolph.

"I thought I made it clear I didn't want any of you girls back up here until I told you," Violet said.

"It's a note from Miss Settle. Beth said you would want to see it right away."

"Thank you, Corrine. Now go straight back downstairs. Tell Beth to bring any additional message herself."

"Yes, Miss Goodwin."

Violet watched until the girl headed down the steps. Then, rather than go back into the twins' room, she opened the letter in the hall, where she was alone. The note was brief and to the point.

Pardon the tardiness of my answer, but your message literally took my breath away. I cannot imagine how such an extraordinary circumstance as Mr. Jefferson Randolph being quarantined in our school could have come about.

How could you have allowed such a thing to happen?

Do everything in your power to see he's comfortable. Allow him unlimited use of the building and the staff. Do not exclude yourself.

Encourage the girls to remark upon this as little as possible.

Eleanor Settle

Violet felt herself bristle at the note. Not only did Miss Settle hold her personally responsible for the situation, but she clearly expected Violet to handle it so that there would be no repercussions—to Miss Settle and the school, of course.

Allow him unlimited use of the building and the staff. There wasn't much likelihood Violet could deny him the use of the building even if she had wanted. He was a man who was used to having things his own way. As for the girls not remarking on his presence, his parading about half naked had taken care of that. They would talk of little else for months.

Do not exclude yourself.

Violet wouldn't allow her mind to carry that thought to its logical conclusion. Besides, if Mr. Randolph continued the way he had begun, he'd be lucky if she didn't murder him in his room.

She looked at the closed bathroom door. She doubted

Miss Settle had this in mind either, but she decided against telling the headmistress just how fully Mr. Randolph had availed himself of their hospitality.

The bathroom door opened, and Jeff Randolph stepped out half dressed. When he didn't pause to see if there were any girls about, Violet decided that he had been alone so long he was out of the habit of thinking about other people, which was sad. He was a prickly man, but surely some female could see past his arm and bad temper to the good that must be there if she would only take the trouble to look. Essie had in less than a day.

Jeff looked delicious, all flushed and warm from the heat of the bath, his wet hair slicked into place. The thin sheen of moisture simply accentuated the muscular definition of his body. Violet barely noticed his arm. How could she when the rest of him was so perfect? She was appalled she was so affected by the sheer physical presence of the man. She had always assumed a man's mind and heart would be the only part of him that was of any real importance. After all, the body was merely a vessel. Only Mr. Randolph's vessel was so splendid that she found it nearly impossible to remember the contents were badly spoiled.

"You can tell the girls to come out of hiding," Jeff said. He paused, then went toward Violet, some of the mockery fading from his eyes. "I expected you to hide your head under a pillow. Aren't all women from Massachusetts horrified by the sight of a man's body?"

"What do you know about Massachusetts or its women?"

All signs of amusement faded from his eyes to be replaced by a hardness that was chilling. "I was a Confederate prisoner there for two years. The women in the nearby town refused to nurse our wounded."

"I can't believe that! Nobody could be that cruel."

Violet saw savage emotion unleashed in Jeff's eyes.

"War is a cruel thing. It does strange things to people, even women." He turned and went up the stairs.

Another reason he hated Yankee women. Violet wondered if he'd ever forgive those women or stop assuming she was like them. She wanted to prove she wasn't, but she didn't know how.

Jeff balled up the note and tossed it out the window. His brothers could never mind their own business, and Tyler was no exception. Instead of the simple dinner Jeff had requested, Tyler had sent a banquet and suggested that Jeff invite the schoolmistress to share it with him.

Maybe it will improve the family image in her eyes.

Tyler had never cared about the family's image. He was just trying to annoy Jeff, and he had succeeded.

Fern says you've been a bastard. Nothing unusual there, but for the sake of the twins—and the rest of us, if Rose goes on the warpath—at least pretend to be a gentleman.

Tyler couldn't understand what it was like to have the very sound of Miss Goodwin's voice resurrect those two agonizing years in prison as if they had been yesterday. He tried not to take his anger out on her. If he looked into her eyes, if she smiled, he could control his temper. But when she spoke, the accent reminded him of the women who'd turned their backs on him. It was all he could do to keep the anger from exploding.

Fifteen years had not dulled the memory of the cold and the wet, the moans and screams of those dying around him, the smell of putrefied flesh, the sight of bodies being carried out stiff and cold to shallow, communal graves. Nor had he forgotten the pain in the arm that was no longer there. He, too, had wanted to die. But he had wanted to live even more, to prove that he was stronger, to show that they couldn't kill his spirit as they had tried to kill his body.

Hatred had kept Jeff alive through two bitterly cold

winters. He no longer needed his hatred, but sometimes it came back anyway. It irritated him that Tyler would try to force him to be civil to Violet. He tried not to blame her; she was merely the spark that ignited the gunpowder of his stored anger.

Jeff found a reasonably steady table made of solid oak in one of the storerooms. It was amazingly heavy. He was glad Violet wasn't around to see him struggle to pull it out of the storeroom, set it upright, and open the leaves. Even spreading a tablecloth or lighting candles was awkward for him.

He pulled up a chair and began transferring the food from the lift to the table. It was absurd to send so much food even for two people. Knowing Tyler, Jeff assumed he had sent at least five courses.

With everything served on crystal, silver, and fine china, the table looked like something out of the hotel dining room. Probably Miss Goodwin hadn't sat down to such a meal since she had left Massachusetts. She certainly wouldn't while she was housemother to 16 little girls. She was more likely to get soggy vegetables, overcooked meat, and indigestion.

Jeff looked at the table covered with food. He could never eat it all himself. And he had been rather hard on Violet. She had failed to tell him about the quarantine, but she had been left alone to take care of 16 girls. It was a wonder she hadn't lost her mind.

She'd never once lost her temper with him, even though he had done all he could to provoke her. It wouldn't hurt him to be nice to her just once. It was time he showed her he could control his temper.

Still he balked at the idea of inviting her to share his dinner. They were going to be thrown together a lot over the next few days. He didn't want to encourage any degree of familiarity. That sort of thing invariably led to expectations. And women's expectations always centered around marriage.

But to be fair, Violet hadn't shown any signs of being willing to accept his advances, had he been interested in making any. He looked at the table once again. He felt foolish for sitting down alone and selfish for keeping such a meal to himself. Maybe she wouldn't be so bad to talk to for an hour or so.

Jeff didn't want to hear about her girls or her family. But surely she could talk about something else. Oh, well, it didn't much matter. If she proved to be a bore, he'd never invite her again, no matter how much food Tyler sent.

Okay, he'd invite her up. He'd be doing her a favor to give her an hour away from the girls. She didn't like him any more than he liked her, but he doubted she would turn him down.

Or would she? That woman had enough brass to do anything, especially if it would irritate him. And it would irritate him to have his invitation refused. He knew why his pride was so fragile, but knowing didn't erase its fragility. He didn't accept refusal from a woman any more easily than failure in business.

He knew how to handle that. There wasn't a woman made who could get around Jeff Randolph, and that included Violet Goodwin.

"They're all correct," Violet said, handing the paper back to Essie. "How did you do it? You've always had so much trouble with math."

"The man helped me."

Violet had not gone upstairs all day. Jeff Randolph hadn't come down, but she was constantly being reminded of his presence. His helping Essie was just one instance.

"Mr. Randolph, Essie. If you are going to keep visiting him, you have to learn his name."

"He said he didn't care."

"Maybe not, but you should always learn a person's

name. It's a sign of courtesy. Do you understand all of that?'' Violet said, indicating the perfect math assignment.

"Uh-huh. Mr. Randolph made me do all the problems myself. He said I should never depend on other people to do things for me. He said sooner or later they wouldn't come through for me. Then I'd be in a pickle.''

Violet wished Mr. Randolph would keep his philosophy to himself. Essie had enough trouble dealing with being separated from her father.

"Explain it to me.''

It took Violet only a few minutes to realize Essie really did understand the lesson. She wondered what it was about Essie that caused Jeff to be so kind. He didn't treat his own nieces half as well.

"I'm proud of you,'' Violet said when the child had finished explaining the assignment. "I hope you will do this well in the future.''

"Mr. Randolph said, if I didn't understand anything, I was to ask him and he'd explain it to me.''

Violet wondered if Mr. Randolph had given any thought to what would happen to Essie when he left. He didn't seem to understand that he couldn't take up a child one day and disappear a few days later without hurting that child very deeply. It was possible that, being alone, he needed Essie as much as she needed him. But he would have to understand he was better able to cope with the loss of a friend than she was.

But Violet wondered if that was true. He might be just as desperate for someone to reach out to him as Essie was to believe her father loved her.

"That's Beth calling everybody to dinner,'' Violet said, getting up from her chair. "You'd better hurry, or the other girls will eat everything up before you arrive.''

"Not anymore,'' Essie said, grinning. "Aurelia and Juliette said they'd save me a place between them.''

If Mr. Randolph had gotten his nieces to take Essie

under their wings, he had done the child a good turn after all. No one but Betty Sue wanted to take on the Randolph twins. Even without an uncle like Mr. Randolph, they could hold their own.

Violet stood, unable to decide whether to eat with the girls or take her dinner to her room. She didn't want to do either. She was unusually restless. She would have given a month's wages to be able to leave the building for a few minutes.

She sighed. She was just as much a prisoner as Mr. Randolph, only she'd been there for ten days while he'd been there for just one. She wondered how he'd bear it for four more days.

Don't be a fool. Four days is nothing compared to being a prisoner for two years.

The tales she had heard about the suffering in prison camps were enough to turn her stomach. She couldn't imagine how anyone with a serious wound had survived nor how any woman could have refused to nurse a wounded man, Confederate or Yankee. No wonder Jeff Randolph was angry at the world, and at Yankees in particular. Violet had less reason, and she was just as angry at the South.

Juliette came tumbling down the stairs. She skidded to a halt at the sight of Violet.

"Uncle Jeff says you're to have your dinner with him," she said. "He said eating dinner with the enemy can't be worse than with sixteen chattering females."

"And he promises to keep his shirt on," Aurelia said with a mischievous grin.

"Juliette, tell him I appreciate his invitation, but I will eat with the sixteen chattering females."

"He won't like it," Aurelia said as Juliette took the stairs two at a time.

"I didn't expect he would. Now you'd better get to the table. Essie is depending on you."

"If that miserable Betty Sue so much as says a word—"

"I'm sure she won't. But try not to antagonize her. She isn't any better than you in knowing when to sit down and be quiet."

"Randolphs never sit down and be quiet," Aurelia said. "We always stand up to be counted."

"That might be fine for little boys, but little girls ought to—"

"Papa says girls ought to have just as much guts as boys."

"What does your mother say?" Violet asked, certain George Randolph must have phrased his advice a little differently.

"Mama says, if there weren't any women around, men would be animals. She says Randolph men would be the worst of all."

"I'd like to meet your mama. She sounds like quite a woman."

"Uncle Madison says Mama's a Tartar. I don't know what that means, but it makes Aunt Fern laugh."

Juliette came tumbling down the steps. Despite her best efforts, Violet had not been able to teach the Randolph twins how to walk. Their world moved at a gallop.

"Uncle Jeff says, if you don't come up, he's going to come down. He says I'm to tell you he can't remember what he did with his shirt."

"That's blackmail," Violet said before she realized she had spoken aloud.

"He said I was to tell you that, too."

Each step Violet took caused her breath to come a little faster. She couldn't decide if that came from being out of shape—Jeff's words still rang in her mind—from fear, or from excitement. She told herself she had no business going anywhere near him. She told herself she was merely going to get a few things straight. She told herself he really wouldn't come downstairs without his shirt. But she knew he would.

It was about time somebody taught him he couldn't force other people to fall in with his wishes whether they wanted or not. It was time he learned the loss of his arm didn't entitle him to permanent indulgence.

When she reached the top of the stairs and stepped into the hall, she stopped dead in her tracks. He had set up a table in the middle of the hall and covered it with things she hadn't seen in years—two silver candelabra with blazing candles, crystal wineglasses, a bottle of wine, a silver chafing dish, and much more. He came from his room bearing another dish.

"My brother sent all this over from his hotel," Jeff said by way of explanation. "He's an outstanding cook. It would be a shame to waste it."

He seemed a little nervous, as if he still expected Violet to refuse. She had intended to do just that, but she felt her resolve melt faster than butter on a hot corn cake. She was touched he had gone to so much trouble. It had to be for her. He would never have done it for himself alone.

"All that came up your lift?" she asked as she slowly approached the table, her eyes still wide in wonder.

"Every bit."

"I'm surprised you haven't escaped down it."

"Fear of being arrested," Jeff said, a hint of a smile in his eyes. "Very embarrassing to a man in my position. Besides, now that I have things set up, it's not bad. With no interruptions, I got twice as much work done."

Violet allowed him to hold her chair, every word of her intended reproof utterly forgotten. The harsh, uncompromising lines of the bare walls retreated beyond the aura of candlelight, leaving Violet at the center of an isle of enchantment. The Wolfe School, Miss Settle, the girls—everything else seemed to fade into insignificance as Jeff Randolph loomed even larger.

Always incredibly handsome, he could do full justice to any woman's image of Prince Charming. He had put on a fresh shirt and changed his coat. He had also combed his hair. She cautioned herself not to read anything into his invitation other than loneliness or impersonal courtesy, but she was helpless to halt the flutter that invaded her stomach, taking up what threatened to be long-term residence.

It had been many years since she had been alone with a man who aroused a more tender emotion in her than wondering how long before she could bring the evening to an end. Being alone with Jeff gave rise to thoughts her ruthless common sense told her were as dangerous as they were foolish.

But she didn't feel like herself. Such thoughts might not be silly for the woman she felt like that night.

Jeff opened a bottle of wine. Violet put her hand over her glass. She noticed the Waterford crystal goblet next to his place contained milk.

"Why aren't you having any?" she asked.

"Drink ruined Pa. Madison drinks brandy occasionally, but the rest of us won't touch anything."

"I'll have milk, too." Violet didn't know why she had said that. She hadn't had milk with a meal since she was a child.

"Are you sure? It's an excellent wine. Tyler sent it especially for you."

"My father drank himself to death. I could never touch wine after that."

For a brief moment, she felt a kinship with him. Then it was gone, as ephemeral as his smile.

Violet accepted something from every dish, but she was more concerned with Jeff than with food. She didn't understand him. He smiled as he served her, but his conversation was limited to describing the contents of the dish and asking how much she wanted. She couldn't figure out whether he was too unused to company to be able to carry on an ordinary conversation or whether he simply had nothing to say to her.

She soon decided it was the latter. He served himself and began to eat. As she sat there, watching him in silence, the magical mood began to fade. She felt that they were two people occupying the same room, but separated by an invisible barrier.

The milk was cold, the food hot and excellent. "I've never tasted such wonderful food," she said, hoping praise for his brother's cooking might encourage him to talk.

"Umm."

She was used to conversation at dinner. Jeff seemed to be determined to avoid it. She felt the chill of disappointment settle around her. The last spark of excitement cooled; the last flutter trembled and fell still. Jeff was still handsome, but the magic was gone. She had been invited to dinner, and if she didn't start eating, the food would be cold.

She noticed the monogram on the napkins. The Windsor Hotel. The finest and most luxurious hotel in Denver. It had opened during the summer and been full ever since.

"So your brother is one of the cooks at the Windsor Hotel."

"Yes."

"I've heard it's the most expensive hotel in Denver."

"It is. My brother owns it."

"Your brother owns the Windsor Hotel?"

"Half of it. His wife owns the other half."

Violet wasn't hungry anymore. She was clearly out of her depth. She didn't know what the twins' father did, nor their Uncle Madison, but she knew they were very rich. Apparently all the Randolphs were.

She wondered what it would feel like to be able to buy whatever she wanted without thinking of the cost. Even when her father had been well and working, she had always had to budget carefully. It was hard not to be a little jealous of so much wealth.

"Eat up," Jeff said.

"I'm full."

"You can't be. There's dessert."

"Maybe we could send it down to the girls. They never get anything like this."

"There's not enough for sixteen. Besides, kids that age don't appreciate the taste of food. They just want lots of it."

Naturally, since it was too late, he wanted to talk. Then again, maybe her idea about the dinner was all a misperception. Jeff had never pretended his invitation was anything more than courtesy. Thinking it might be had been her mistake. It was time she put aside fantasy. She was too old for it anyway.

"You obviously haven't been around girls very much. They may not be as concerned with taste as adults, but I constantly have to encourage them to eat more."

"Why?"

"Fear of being fat. They're already worried about finding husbands."

"Good God! They're just children."

"Every woman, regardless of age or fortune, learns very early that catching a husband is her primary task."

"Did you learn that lesson?"

Violet felt heat flame in her face. "Yes, but I chose to do other things."

"What?"

"Take care of my brother and father," Violet said.

"Do you have anyone to take care of now?" Jeff asked.

"No."

"Then why aren't you married? You're pretty enough."

Chapter Six

Was Violet desperate enough for Jeff's attention to answer a question that a gentleman wouldn't put to a lady? But then he didn't think a Yankee could be a lady. She imagined it would be useless to try to convince him otherwise.

"Don't tell me no one has asked you," Jeff said. "I won't believe you."

Violet had always avoided answering questions about herself. Most people were polite enough not to ask. Her life was really no one's business but her own. Obviously Jeff Randolph didn't subscribe to that belief.

"Why not?" she asked.

"I just said. You're pretty."

"Is that all you expect of a wife? To be pretty?"

"I don't have a wife."

"If you did, if you were going to choose one tomorrow."

"No."

"What else would you look for?"

Jeff put down his fork. He didn't appear to want to answer her. But if he was going to ask her personal questions, she had the right to do the same thing. Besides, the longer she kept him talking, the longer she could put off answering.

Jeff refilled his glass with milk and said, "She'd have to be kind and gentle, soft-spoken, caring. She'd be able to manage the household. Above all, she would be a lady."

Jeff didn't want much, she thought with sarcasm. If women made similar demands of men, there wouldn't be a dozen marriages a year in the whole country.

"Have you found such a woman in Denver?" Violet asked.

"I haven't looked."

"Why?"

"When I choose a wife, she will be a true daughter of the South."

"Aren't there any Southern daughters out here?" She hoped she didn't sound too sarcastic, but he was being absurd.

"I would never choose a woman who had come to Colorado. I'll wait until I return to Virginia."

Jeff was serious! He really believed leaving the South could change a woman's nature. Violet wondered if he had considered what 15 years away from Virginia might have done to him. Of course he hadn't. Men never did. They assumed they were exactly what they wanted to be.

"Are you saying a good Southern woman doesn't transplant?"

"If you want to put it that way. My mother went to Texas. She couldn't endure it. She died within two years."

"Texas is part of the South."

"The true South is Virginia and Carolina and maybe parts of Georgia."

Thinking that Jeff sounded as. if he could do with a geography lesson, and a history lesson as well, Violet said, "Where were you born?"

"Virginia."

"Why did you leave?"

"You're full of questions. And you still haven't answered mine."

"I don't really know you. I don't feel I can discuss my reasons for not marrying with a virtual stranger."

Jeff regarded the woman for a moment over his glass. Violet could never remember being studied over milk. It somehow made the entire situation ludicrous.

"You won't get around me by clever answers. But I will tell you my father was a cruel, drunken bastard. After he killed his best friend, our neighbors decided they didn't want him around anymore. They agreed to pay his debts if he'd move to Texas."

Violet didn't know what to say to that. It must have been hard for Jeff to have been exiled from the home he loved.

"How did you end up in Denver?" she asked.

"By degrees. When our ranch made a little money, we had to invest it. First it was Chicago. Now it's Denver. We could end up in San Francisco."

"Where do you want to go?"

"I don't care as long as I make money."

"But you must have a lot by now. I don't mean to be nosy, but the twins said you owned the bank."

"The family owns the bank."

Along with cattle ranches and the Windsor Hotel, Violet thought. Then, she asked, "Are you going to start another bank in San Francisco?"

"I doubt it. I don't care much about banking."

"But—"

"It's the way I make money," Jeff said.

"Why do you need so much?"

"So we can go back to Virginia."

"You mean the whole family?" Violet asked.

"Yes."

So that was his reason for working around the clock. "But why do you want to go back?" When Jeff looked at her as if she was simpleminded, Violet said, "You're president of a bank. One of your brothers is an important businessman, one owns the most successful hotel in Denver, and others have ranches. Each has carved out a life for himself. Why would they want to uproot their families to go back to Virginia?"

Jeff leaned forward, his eyes glowing ardently. "Do you plan to stay in Denver?"

"No."

"Where do you want to go when you leave here?"

"Back home. I have something I want to do," Violet said.

"Couldn't you do it somewhere else?"

"I expect so."

"But you're going back home."

"Yes."

"Because it's home," Jeff said.

"Well, yes."

He leaned back, obviously satisfied that he had made his point.

But it wasn't the same with Violet. "I don't have any reason to stay in Colorado. I have no family, no financial empire. Your family hasn't been in Virginia for twenty years. Everything must have changed." She didn't ask him about his home. She had a feeling it had been destroyed.

"Now tell me why you aren't married," Jeff said, ignoring Violet's remarks. Clearly he'd said all he was going to say. She should have known he wouldn't be sidetracked for long.

Violet wasn't sure why she wanted to tell Jeff, except that, every time she got close to him or looked into his eyes, it was the same as being put under a spell. She ought to be ashamed, but as long as his undivided attention made her feel as if she was the only person in the world, she didn't care.

She wasn't sure what to tell him. She could say that she didn't want to or that no one had asked, but those responses would be lies. She was certain he would know.

"I guess you could say the time never seemed right," she said. "Then when it was, it was too late."

"Don't be ridiculous. You're an attractive woman and still relatively young. How old are you anyway?"

Didn't the man have any sensitivity? Didn't he realize a woman of her years had no desire to discuss her age? "I told you earlier."

"I forgot."

People usually did when it came to old maids. "I'm twenty-nine. Well past prime marrying age."

"I'm thirty-seven, and I consider myself to be of prime marrying age."

"I doubt a woman of sixteen or seventeen would think so," she responded with some asperity.

He looked genuinely startled. "Good God, I don't plan to marry a child."

"That's the prime marrying age for women." She didn't know what he'd been thinking, but clearly she had surprised him. Good. She was glad she wasn't the only one being unnerved by their interminable meal. "If you don't want a wife still in her teens, just what are you looking for?"

Jeff looked at her the way she imagined he'd look at a novice clerk who'd just bungled his first task. "You're not to ask me any more questions until you've answered mine."

"It's a long, sad story," she said, reluctant to begin. "You'll think I'm looking for pity."

"I never pity people. It only encourages them to wallow in their own helplessness."

She hoped no woman would ever truly love him. Her life would be a misery of unfulfilled hopes. She wondered why he cared that she wasn't married. He wasn't the kind of man to indulge in idle curiosity. He certainly wasn't interested in her.

"My brother joined the Union Army when I was nine. My father was a doctor. He was drafted to tend the wounded. He was a brilliant doctor, but he didn't have a strong mind. He always depended on Mother. She helped nurse prisoners, but she caught dysentery from one of the men and died. The army let Daddy come home then, but he wasn't the same. He used to talk about the piles of arms and legs that collected outside the medical tents after a battle, of the men who died in the fields because no one could get to them, of the men who were beyond helping, who screamed in agony until death finally brought peace. He could forget only by drinking."

"What about you?" Jeff asked.

"I was thirteen. What can a girl of thirteen do for a man suffering as he was?" Violet realized that not even her mother could have helped her father. His gentle soul had seen too much. "He might have recovered if my brother hadn't come home an invalid. Jonas lost his legs, but there was something wrong inside him. No matter what my father or the other doctors did, he wouldn't heal. He grew weaker each year until he died.

"After that my father had no desire to live. He quit going to the hospital or seeing patients. He was drunk most of the time. One night he fell down some stairs and broke his neck."

"Don't you have any other family?"

"I came out here to be near my uncle." She had no intention of telling Jeff about her uncle's death or the loss of the mine. She just didn't want to go into it.

She was relieved he didn't start saying how sorry he was, how her loss would grow less painful with time. It would never go away. She would simply get used to it.

"What are you looking for in a wife that makes it impossible for you to find her outside of Virginia?" Violet asked.

"I already told you."

"You can find gentle, soft-spoken women able to manage a household just about anywhere. What makes one born in Virginia so special?"

Violet thought at first that Jeff wasn't going to answer her. Then she realized he was slipping off into a world all his own. She wasn't certain he still knew she was there.

"It's a question of quality," he finally said. "Diamonds and pearls come in all grades, from flawless to useless, but you always search for ones of the finest quality. A true Southern woman is like a flawless gem. She's as gracious as she is beautiful. She instinctively knows how to act, what to do for every occasion. She orders her household for the comfort of her husband. His word is law, and she will never question or contradict him. Her love is as unfailing as it is limitless. She knows when to speak up and when to remain silent.

"She will see that the servants and children are trained to show her husband the respect and deference she herself gives him. Her home will be a haven for his rest, a welcoming spot for his friends. She will do her best to give him many strong, healthy sons, and she will never withhold the comfort of her body. She will find no higher joy than his happiness."

Jeff might as well have been talking about a slave or a concubine! Violet couldn't believe intelligent men still thought like that.

"Are there many women like that in Virginia?" she asked in apparent innocence. "I daresay you could find just as many foolish—or should I say spineless—females in the North. In fact, I doubt you would have to look very hard."

Jeff looked surprised, shocked, and absolutely furious.

"I should have known a Yankee wouldn't be able to understand what I was talking about.

"I understand perfectly," Violet said as she folded her napkin and pushed back her chair. "I can only assume the deteriorating quality of the Southern woman was the reason you lost the war. Southern men must be truly remarkable to have compensated for their deficiencies for so long. Are you sure men like George Washington and Thomas Jefferson weren't smuggled in from the North as babies?"

Violet thought Jeff really would explode as she got to her feet. "Thank you for dinner. Give your brother my compliments. I can't wish you well in your search for a wife. I'd hate to think such a woman exists. However, if she does, and you should find her, I hope you will take good care of her. She obviously won't be capable of taking care of herself."

"Miss Goodwin, you have a very peculiar notion of Southern women." His voice was cold, the tone cutting.

"If I do, you have given it to me. I never dreamed an intelligent woman would turn herself into such a caricature, or that such a caricature would interest a man of your intelligence. Maybe you have a blind spot when it comes to women. I guess that's why you're not married. You're certainly handsome enough." She executed what she thought would be a Southern lady's curtsy. "Good night, Mr. Randolph."

Jeff would be damned if he ever invited that female to eat with him again. He practically threw the dishes onto the lift. If Tyler sent a five-course banquet again tomorrow, he'd invite Miss Settle.

What did Violet know about Southern women? No Yankee could understand what it meant to be born in the South. They lived an entirely different kind of life. They were always in a hurry, always trying to get the upper hand over their neighbors, always trying to get something they didn't have, to become something they weren't. Nothing was ever enough. They always wanted more; they had to have the most.

They didn't understand that Southerners didn't care if everybody else was richer. They helped each other. They shared. They would rather die or endure poverty than be dishonored.

Jeff shouldn't be getting so angry. He had never expected Violet to understand anything so foreign to her nature. Maybe she could learn, but he doubted it. It was something one needed to be born to. It was like learning to stand the heat.

He told himself it didn't matter what Violet thought, but it did. She irritated him. Maybe it came from being locked up together. Maybe he couldn't stand to see a woman that attractive go around with a head full of such wrong ideas.

And he hadn't helped matters. He'd choked up when she had appeared at the top of the stairs looking like a vision in a deep blue gown that made her eyes glisten like sapphires. He couldn't think of anything to do except put more food on her plate.

When he finally did recover the use of his tongue, he'd started badgering her about her past. And he'd been worried she couldn't carry on an interesting conversation! A child could have done better than he had.

But it had taken him a while to recover from the shock of discovering he was thinking things that were contrary to everything he'd said and believed for the last 20 years. He had admitted that he thought Violet was pretty, that he was attracted to her. Suddenly he realized that he liked her, that he found her interesting.

He had to remind himself that, even if she had been a Southerner, she would be an impossible female. She might appear soft-spoken and agreeable, but she was the kind of female who kept her real opinions carefully hidden. He wanted nothing to do with a woman like that.

He couldn't imagine Violet Goodwin's husband being happy unless he agreed with her.

It undoubtedly came from being allowed to order the lives of two grown men since she was fourteen. She couldn't know what it was like to be protected by a man strong and capable enough to shield her from the uncertainties of life.

You're nothing but a miserable little coward. You ought to be ashamed to call yourself a man. I'm ashamed to call you my son.

Jeff could feel beads of perspiration pop out on his forehead. It had been years since his father's words had broken through the barriers he had constructed in his mind. Only during sleep was he vulnerable.

Don't call yourself a man unless you're willing to act like a man. But you can't. You're weak as a woman.

Jeff shook his head. He wouldn't allow himself to remember those cruel taunts. He didn't know what could have happened that night to cause his guard to collapse. It hadn't happened in years.

Gradually he lifted the barriers back into place. He didn't want to think of his father or Violet. He had work to do. Work had always kept his demons at bay.

Violet woke to a loud clanking noise that seemed to shake the building down to its foundations. She didn't know what it was, but she did know it came from Jeff Randolph's room.

She didn't have to look at her watch to know it was early. The sun was just coming over the horizon. 6:47 a.m. She could have killed him! The man had only been in the building two nights, and he'd waked her at a disgraceful hour both mornings. She was sure the girls were awake, too.

Violet got out of bed, put on her robe, and stepped into her slippers. Even though she knew he'd make some comment about her hair, she didn't bother to cover it.

She nearly fainted when she reached his open doorway. He was in the process of lifting that bar with all four iron disks over his head, but he was using only one hand. He used the stump to steady it. His only clothing was some kind of short, tight pants. He might as well have been naked.

Violet had been around men all her life. As a nurse, she had become accustomed to seeing them in nearly every possible condition, but everything felt different at that moment. She clamped her hand over her eyes. "Mr. Randolph! Have you no shame?"

The bar dropped to the floor with a terrifying crash. The entire building shook. Violet expected the girls to come running up the stairs any minute, wanting to know if they were having an earthquake.

"Don't ever shout at me when I have weights over my head," Jeff said, anger throbbing in his voice. "If anybody had been in the room with me, he could have gotten hurt."

"I should fervently hope that, in your present state of undress, no one would venture to enter your room." She thought she heard him chuckle, but she didn't dare move her hand to check.

"Take your hands down. I'm sure you've seen men in less."

"Yes, but he was my brother."

"Well, I'm not your brother, but I'm not any different."

"It's not the same."

"I should hope not. We Randolphs are known for our—how should I put it—attributes."

"Mr. Randolph! I know you're doing this intentionally to mortify me. I think it's terribly unfair. I can't possibly go away for fear one of the girls might come up to discover the cause of the noise. I refuse to take my hands down and stare at you. You'd have every right to think me the brazen Yankee female you want me to be.''

''Then turn around and take your hand down. I'll tell you when you can turn back.''

''What are you doing?''

''I'm lifting the weights three more times. I haven't finished my exercise.''

''Mr. Randolph—''

''Don't talk. You'll break my concentration.''

Violet needed to talk. She needed to do something to block out the picture of his body from her mind. But she was afraid it would be there for as long as she lived.

If she'd been overwhelmed by the sight of his bare chest, she'd nearly fainted at the sight of his bare legs. He had almost no hair on his chest. The little on his arms and legs seemed to disappear in the morning light, leaving the straining muscles of his powerful calves and thighs exposed to her shocked gaze. Even his feet looked strong and muscular.

But it was the almost nonexistent pants that had nearly caused her to feel faint. Jeff Randolph was very well endowed. And being a nurse, rather than some weak-minded Southern belle, she wasn't plagued by a shadowy notion of the male anatomy. She knew exactly what that endowment was meant to do.

Violet was certain she was beet red, a horrible combination with her copper-red hair. Worse still, as she listened to his grunts and visualized his straining body, his muscles standing out in clearly defined lines, her own body began to react as it never had before. Her breasts tingled and arcs of white-hot sensation exploded through her. Some landed in her belly and set off a throbbing reaction that left her weak. She trembled from head to toe. She felt too hot and too cold. She longed to sit down before she fell. She jumped a foot when the metal weights hit the floor.

99

"I'm putting on a robe," Jeff said. "You can turn around now."

Violet turned slowly. She didn't trust him not to lie to her just to see her reaction. But when she completed her turn, he was wearing a long white robe that covered him from head to toe.

"Why didn't you wear that yesterday?"

"I didn't have it yesterday. Nor did I have my own towels and soap."

He was going downstairs to take another bath! And there was no chance she could talk him out of it.

"Wait! Let me make certain the girls are in their rooms."

"They should still be asleep."

"Not with you throwing hundreds of pounds of iron about. Don't come down the stairs until I call." Violet hoped that Beth would stay in her room. She didn't need another woman squealing or fainting.

As Violet had feared, the girls were up, whispering, wondering. "As you probably suspected, it was Mr. Randolph. He's coming down to take his bath. So I want all of you to stay in your rooms until I tell you it's okay to come out."

"Which bathroom is he going to use?" Betty Sue asked.

"I don't know," Violet said, wondering what mischief Betty Sue was up to.

"I can't use the same bathtub as a man."

Trying to ignore her feeling of foreboding, Violet said, "Anyone caught out of her room before I give her permission will have to stay in one day past the end of quarantine."

Every head disappeared. Apparently the girls were feeling the confinement as much as she was. Violet waited a minute, but no one stuck her head out. All seemed quiet.

"Are all your ducklings safely tucked in?" Jeff asked suddenly.

Chapter Seven

Violet nearly jumped a foot. "I told you to stay upstairs until I could make sure the girls were in their rooms." She was as angry at Jeff for refusing to cooperate as she was at herself for being so jittery. Wondering if he was naked under that robe didn't improve things at all. She didn't think she could stand much more.

"Go ahead and take your bath," Violet said. "No matter what you do, don't come into the hall until I tell you it's okay."

She breathed a sigh of relief when the bathroom door closed behind Jeff. She moved away when she heard the water running into the tub. She walked slowly along the hall, checking each of the eight doors as she walked by. They were all closed, but she felt certain that behind each the topic of conversation was the same.

Jeff Randolph. His presence completely dominated their little group. To the girls he was a curious—possibly even scandalous—diversion, but they would forget about him in a few days. By Christmas they probably wouldn't remember what he looked like. Violet would never forget him. She didn't see how any woman could forget that body. Just thinking about it started the sensations and feelings stirring again.

Violet forced her mind to focus on the view from the window at the end of the hall. A dusting of early morning frost had turned the brown grass silvery in the cold, early morning light. The blustery winds had robbed the young trees of their fluttering leaves, leaving bare limbs traced in thin lines against the sky. Denver clustered all around the trees—the tall gray buildings of the business community, the massive homes of the silver barons, the muddy streets that teemed with traffic, the noisy streetcars bringing people in from the new suburbs.

Violet could see the snow-covered peaks of the Rocky Mountains in the distance. In a few months the mountains would be completely covered in a thick mantle of snow, their passes closed until spring. Leadville was out there somewhere—Leadville and the silver mine that should have been her hedge against the future. She had come to suspect that Harvey McKee wanted to be her hedge.

She forced her thoughts away from Leadville, the mine, and Harvey. While she was locked up, she had more than enough to do worrying what Jeff Randolph would do next.

You'd better give some thought to what he's doing to you. You've never acted like this over a man. You can't be falling in love with him, can you?

The thought was so absurd that Violet didn't give it any further consideration. But it was beyond question that Jeff had had a very strong, and unexpected, effect on her. Her childhood sweetheart Nathan Wainwright had certainly never affected her that way, and he had wanted to marry her. It couldn't be Jeff Randolph the person; it had to be his body. All she had to do was take one look and she practically started shaking.

My God, she was lusting after Jeff Randolph! That had to be the answer. It was the only explanation that fit. She, Violet Ankum Goodwin, was lusting after a man she didn't even like. Her first reaction was horror that she could have succumbed to such a base emotion.

Next she felt like laughing at the irony of it. She had spent her entire life concerned only with the mind, the spirit, the true essence of life—she had actually been heard to say that she scorned the body as a reason for two human beings to be attracted to each other—only to have her body betray her at the first opportunity.

Her nipples were so sensitive that she could feel the stiffness of her corset through her chemise. A simple movement of her shoulders caused them to ache as they rubbed against the fabric.

An even greater surprise was the feeling in her belly. Violet had never experienced that before. She didn't even understand what it meant at first, it was so unlike anything she'd expected. But then she felt heat, moisture in the most private recesses of her body. She knew exactly what that was all about. Her body was responding directly to the presence of Jeff Randolph.

Violet turned away from the window, but that brought her gaze into direct line with the bathroom door. Knowing Jeff was behind that door, naked in his bath, intensified all the feelings which tormented her.

"Miss Goodwin." The sound of a student's voice jerked Violet out of reverie.

"What is it, Corrine?"

"I have to go to the bathroom."

"Can't it wait?" All she needed was for Jeff to step out into the hall stark naked. She wouldn't put it past him to do it just to mortify her.

"No," Corrine said.

Violet squared her shoulders and hurried down the hall. "Okay. Follow me. Use that one," she said, pointing to the second bathroom. "And don't come out until I tell you."

"Yes, ma'am." Corrine disappeared into the bathroom.

Violet placed herself in front of Jeff's door despite the fact that, every second she stood there, a voice inside her mind shouted more and more loudly that Jeff was naked just through that wall. She tried to push the image out of her mind, but it became more vivid. All she had to do was. . . . Violet wouldn't allow herself to finish that thought.

It was Saturday. The girls would spend only half the day on their studies. Violet would have her hands full keeping them occupied. Sunday would be even worse. She ought to run through her list of activities to make sure she had enough things for the students to do.

Violet hadn't worked very far down her list when Corrine knocked. Violet listened, but couldn't hear anything from Jeff. She hoped he was still in the tub. "You can come out now."

Corrine emerged from the bathroom and hurried down the hall. The door had barely closed behind her when the bathroom door behind Violet opened. She turned and came face-to-face with Jeff.

She was immediately aware of a fresh spicy scent tinged with the smell of soap. She'd never known a man could smell so good. She fought to regain the control that threatened to vanish as though it had never been. She backed up. "I asked you to knock before you came out. Why do you refuse to do even the little things I ask of you?"

"Sorry, I forgot."

"Please go to your room. The girls are beginning to stir. You just missed one returning from the bathroom. Thank God, she didn't see you."

"I never knew Yankee women were such prudes." He had a strange look in his eyes and appeared to be wondering what he could do to her next.

Violet didn't know if she believed what he said, but she did know he was trying to provoke her. "If it were just myself, I wouldn't care what you did," she said, lying as brazenly as she could. "But I can't allow you to embarrass these girls. If it ever became known that you wandered the halls in front of the girls, it would injure the reputation of the school."

Jeff cocked an eyebrow. "Or bring in more applications."

"Mr. Randolph, you've completely destroyed any chance these girls had of getting a full night's rest. Please allow me to get on with my day."

"I thought everybody got Saturday off."

"The girl's have no classes, but my responsibilities are unchanged." Violet could hear the sound of the lift outside the building. "Apparently yours as well. I believe your first load of work just went up."

Jeff seemed reluctant to leave, which surprised her. She had thought he lived for his work. There didn't seem to be anything else in his life.

"I expect your staff is already at work in the parlor," she said.

"They must be if the lift is working, mustn't they?"

"Why don't you give them the weekend off?"

"They get Sunday."

"That's only one day."

"It's more than I get."

"It's okay if you want to kill yourself staying up all night and working seven days a week, but I imagine some of them would like to see their families."

"Which they go home to every night."

"They don't leave here until too late to see their children. Their supper must be cold."

"Miss Goodwin, I'm not a ladies' aid society. I pay my people well. If they don't like the work or the hours, they're free to go elsewhere."

"I'm not surprised you're forced to turn to your work for company. You're not human. And you don't have any compassion for those who are."

"I prefer to think I don't confuse compassion with sentimentality. People don't need all this useless emotion. It doesn't make their lives any better, and it encourages them to be weak."

"Not everyone is as strong as you, Mr. Randolph."

"Perhaps not, but you can't expect me to change my requirements because of it."

"But you can't—"

"This is a fruitless conversation. We'll never agree. Good morning. I hope your day goes well."

"Miss Goodwin! Miss Goodwin!" Essie cried. She raced toward Violet waving a piece of paper in her hand. "Papa wrote me a letter. Mr. Randolph said he would."

The child's face was absolutely beatific with happiness as she gave Violet a tremendous hug. "They wouldn't let him come in to see me, but he made them give me this letter. He said he's going to come back the day the quarantine is over. When is it over, Miss Goodwin? I want to write and tell him right away."

"If no one comes down with anything else, it'll be over Monday at noon. Do you want me to help you with your letter?"

"I've got to show Aurelia and Juliette," Essie said, breaking away and heading for the twins, who were in the corner with their heads together.

They had been that way all morning. Violet was worried they were cooking up some new trouble.

"I'm going to show it to that mean, nasty Betty Sue, too. I want to show her she was wrong. Then I'm going to show it to Mr. Randolph. He promised to help me write Daddy."

Violet felt a little hurt that Essie should prefer Jeff to her. Though she told herself the child desperately needed the approval of a man, she still experienced a twinge of jealousy.

Be fair. He was able to get Essie's father to write and promise to visit. No one else has managed to do so much.

Essie came streaking by Violet and hit the stairs at a gallop. "I'm taking my letter to Mr. Randolph," she said over her shoulder as she took the stairs two at a time. Essie was beginning to take after the twins in many ways.

Violet realized that she was feeling terribly curious about what Jeff Randolph was going to say when Essie showed him the letter. She even thought of a couple of reasons why she needed to go upstairs, but she resolutely put them aside. The less she saw of him, the better. Just remembering the experiences of the morning caused her pulse to race.

Violet made a conscious effort to get herself under control. In addition to not wanting to be attracted to Jeff, she didn't want her emotions to be at the mercy of her physical nature. That morning's experience had proved to her she couldn't control her body. And if she couldn't control that, she couldn't control her emotions. And if she couldn't control her emotions, she had no control over herself. And if she wasn't controlling herself, then Randolph would be. Violet couldn't accept that. No matter what she had to do, she would shake his hold on her.

"But I don't know what to say," Essie said to Jeff. "I never wrote a letter before."

"Why?"

"I'm only eight. Little girls like me don't write letters."

"I'm sure Miss Goodwin will be happy to help you."

"I want you."

Jeff realized there was no way around helping Essie write her letter. He didn't really mind, but she had interrupted him in the middle of figuring up some pressing orders. If he took time out to help her, he'd have to start over again. Oh, well, his concentration was already broken. He put the papers aside.

"You think about what you want to say. Then tell me. I'll write it down, and you can copy it over."

"Why do I have to copy it over?"

"Your father will like it more if he knows you wrote it. Just as that letter is special to you because your father wrote it himself."

"It's my first letter."

"I know," Jeff said, smiling. "You've told me that five times already. Now tell me what to write."

. Essie positioned herself at Jeff's elbow so she could watch as he wrote down her words.

Hi, Daddy!
I got your letter. It was real nice. I showed it to the twins. Their names are Aurelia and Juliette. They're my best friends. They promised to cut off the rest of Betty Sue's hair if she said anything else mean about you.

"I think maybe we'd better leave that last part out," Jeff said.

Essie looked disappointed, but she didn't argue.

Mr. Randolph is helping me write this letter. He writes real pretty, but he says you'll like it better if I write it. I don't write real good. Miss Goodwin says I need to practice more.

"Tell him when the quarantine's over," Jeff said. "You've got to tell him when he can come back and see you."

*Miss Goodwin says the sickness will be all gone
on Monday after we eat lunch. You can come back
then. Miss Goodwin says I can go away with you
all afternoon. Can I, Daddy?*

Essie watched as Jeff finished writing the last sentence. "That's a lot," she said.

"It's not enough. You've got to tell your daddy you love him and miss him."

"But he knows that."

"I know, but you have to tell him. Sometimes daddies forget."

"How can they do that?"

"I don't know," Jeff said, thinking of his own father rather than of Harold Brown. His father had been surrounded by people yearning to give him love. He never seemed to see that, or that he hurt them deeply by his indifference. Harold Brown might be a cold, heartless man, but he worked to give his child a good life. His father had done nothing but destroy what little they had. "But they do forget. Sometimes they need to be reminded."

"I love you, Daddy. I miss you. Please don't forget to come. That's all."

"That's a very good letter," Jeff said. "Miss Goodwin will be proud of you. Now take it downstairs and copy it exactly as I wrote it. Then you bring it back to me. I'll see that your father gets it."

"Can I stay here?"

Jeff kind of liked having Essie there. Besides, it would hurt her feelings if he sent her away. "Sure."

He slid some of his papers over to give her room. He handed her a fresh piece of paper and a pen. "Get a chair. You can sit right next to me."

* * *

Violet found it difficult to concentrate. Essie had been upstairs with Jeff for more than an hour. She couldn't imagine why Jeff Randolph had allowed her to stay so long. He had banished his nieces the minute the lift was installed. Not that the twins minded. They had been as good as gold. Violet shuddered to think what they'd do once Jeff was gone and their period of self-imposed good behavior came to an end.

But at the moment it seemed nothing the terrible twins might do had the power to keep her thoughts from their uncle. That was something else she had to change. The twins were her responsibility, not their uncle. But it was Jeff's relationship with Essie that caused her to wonder if there might not be a different Jeff Randolph from the one she had been allowed to see. The other girls were frightened of him. But shy, gentle, childlike Essie adored him, and he seemed perfectly content to let her stay with him as long as she wanted. Why?

Could it be that he saw something of himself in Essie? Violet almost rejected the notion. It was impossible to imagine that a man like Jeff Randolph had ever been gentle or shy. But even as Violet searched for other explanations, that idea would not go away.

Maybe he had been very different as a child. Maybe something had forced him to change in order to survive. She needed to find out what it was. She could sense something was changing between them besides the physical response, something that made it necessary for her to try to understand him.

Don't be foolish. He's not going to give you a chance to get that close to him. Besides, there's no point. You'll never see him again once the quarantine ends.

Nevertheless, Violet made up her mind to find out what had turned Jeff Randolph into a miserable old crank.

* * *

Jeff took one look at the dinner that had just arrived on the lift and started cursing so violently that the men outside looked afraid to send anything else up. Tyler had sent just as much food as the night before. And along with the food came the silver, china, and linen to serve it on. More wine. More crystal. More candles. Jeff didn't know what Tyler was trying to do, but he was going to break his brother's neck as soon after noon on Monday as he could manage.

Jeff had sworn he would have nothing more to do with that sharp-tongued Yankee woman. He didn't relish having his ideas about womanhood mocked. He hadn't expected her to understand, but he hadn't expected her to be sarcastic.

He had thought a lot about her having to watch her brother die. That changed his opinion of her, at least a little. No woman could have endured that without gaining some understanding of what Jeff had suffered. At least, more than his own family had. She had lost her parents as well. She had almost as much reason to be bitter as he did.

Yet she wasn't. She didn't like to talk about it or brood over it, as his brothers accused him of doing.

Jeff glanced down at what remained of his left arm. He knew why he had never considered using an artificial limb. Everybody else wanted to forget the war, to put the bitterness behind them, to act as though it had never happened. He wanted to keep that arm just the way it was as a visible reminder to himself and everyone else of what the war had cost.

Violet must have felt the same way even though she didn't let it show. She always seemed cheerful and happy, at least when she wasn't dealing with him. He could hear her with the girls, helping them with their studies, sharing their confidences, laughing with them. He didn't eavesdrop, but he couldn't help overhearing them whenever he went to the bathroom. The twins stood guard for him. Violet was never far away, but she kept her distance.

He laughed when he remembered her reaction when she saw him exercising that morning. She couldn't have been more embarrassed if she'd been a Virginia belle. He had to admit he had come out of the bathroom without knocking just to disconcert her. She was such a managing female, it was fun to upset her just enough to give him a chuckle. She might pretend she thought he was an old crust, but he could turn her into a fluttering, blushing woman.

Violet was a mature woman, but her embarrassment made her seem younger. Not exactly girlish, but innocent. He supposed innocent wasn't the right word either. There was something about her that softened the effect of the years, that made her very appealing, even when she was acting most like a school mistress. She pretended she was hard and self-sufficient, but something about her whispered different words.

Jeff didn't know what he was doing thinking so much about Violet Goodwin. He supposed it was only natural when a man found himself around an attractive women, even a Yankee woman—especially if she was the only woman in sight. But Violet had shown no interest in him. He couldn't imagine why he should be thinking about her so much.

Neither did Jeff know why he should suddenly want her to share his dinner. He must have been exhausted from spending the afternoon with Essie. She was a sweet child, but as much as he liked her, children were a mystery to him, one he wasn't certain he would ever solve.

He picked up a serving dish and began transferring everything to the table. Several minutes later he had the table set. He figured he might as well summon Miss Goodwin if he was going to, but the question remained of how to do it. He didn't want to go downstairs and issue a public invitation. He wanted to get her upstairs. But how?

Suddenly an idea came to him that caused him to break into a broad smile.

Beth and some of the older girls had finished laying out supper. Violet climbed the stairs to summon the younger girls to the table. She had barely opened her mouth when a shriek caused her to close it again. The twins came tumbling out of their room.

"There's something outside our window!" Aurelia cried, pointing back into their room.

"What is it?" Violet asked, hurrying forward.

"It looks like a bat," Juliette said.

Violet didn't know why a bat should have flown into a closed window—she couldn't remember one having done that before—but it was nothing to worry about.

"Go downstairs," she said to the other girls, who had started to gather around the twins' doorway. "Beth has supper on the table."

"Can't we see?" Corrine asked.

"I bet it's nothing," Betty Sue said.

"Downstairs, all of you. You two as well," Violet said to the twins. "Whatever it is, I'll see to it."

"But it's our room," Aurelia said. "Can't we stay?"

"No, I'm sure it's some trash blown against the window by the wind. Maybe it blew off your uncle's lift."

"I told you it was nothing," Betty Sue said. "I wouldn't be afraid of a piece of trash blowing against my window."

"Don't either of you say a word to her," Violet said when she saw the twins' stormy looks. "Now scoot."

The girls departed with lagging footsteps. She knew the twins would find a way to retaliate against Betty Sue. She couldn't really blame them, but she hoped it would be something she could overlook. She liked the twins. They had spunk. And their protection had turned Essie from a nervous, withdrawn child into a happy, energetic one. For that alone, Violet could forgive them a lot.

Violet entered the twins' bedroom expecting to see a piece of paper flapping against the window. She was aghast when she realized that the strange-looking object gently swaying in the breeze outside the window was the very brief pair of pants that Jeff Randolph had been wearing the morning she had found him exercising. She would remember that particular piece of clothing as long as she lived.

Good Lord! He'd be mortified if he knew. She'd have to go up and tell him at once. It wouldn't do for anyone to discover what they were.

She hurried downstairs to tell the twins it was just a piece of their uncle's clothing that must have blown out the window and caught on one of the lift cables. She allowed that it did look a lot like a bat beating against the window. She stayed a moment to make certain Betty Sue wasn't going to say anything that would start trouble. Once the girls were occupied with their food, she left the room.

She made herself climb the stairs slowly. She refused to arrive on the top floor out of breath again. She came to an abrupt halt when she reached the upper landing. Jeff was standing behind a set table with one chair pulled out, just as if he were waiting to help her sit down.

"Would you like to have dinner with me?" he asked.

Chapter Eight

Violet was too stunned to speak. The table, Jeff's near smiling welcome—everything was outside her expectations. The dangling pants went completely out of her mind. So did her resolve to have nothing more to do with Jeff Randolph. All she felt was pleasure that he wanted her to dine with him again.

She walked forward and allowed him to help her with her chair. Once she was seated, a little of her presence of mind returned. "I didn't think you'd invite me back after last night."

"My brother sent too much food again."

That was what she'd expected him to say. She certainly never thought he'd have asked for extra food.

"I could always send the twins up."

"Essie was up here all afternoon. I wanted company a bit more mature this time."

The table was set for two, and he had been standing there, just as if he was waiting for her. He had been waiting for her. Those pants weren't dangling in front

115

of the twins' window by accident. He'd done it because he knew it would send her running up the stairs. He had wanted to invite her to dinner. He just hadn't wanted to ask her in the usual way, though he would undoubtedly deny he had wanted her company enough to spend time thinking up that silly way to get her upstairs.

Violet was shocked. She would never have expected it of Jeff. But she was even more shocked at herself. She was feeling slightly giddy. She stopped herself just as she was raising her hand to see if her hair was still in place.

She was acting like a self-conscious young woman with her first gentleman caller. She hadn't done that ten years ago. It was foolish to be doing it that night. She was building nothing into something. Jeff might be crabby, but he was human enough to want company. And he was lonely enough to settle for a Yankee woman because she was all that was available.

Still the feeling of excitement continued to simmer and bubble. It was impossible to sit down to a candle-light dinner with a handsome man and not feel some thrill of anticipation. Besides, he had changed clothes. Apparently he didn't consider her a complete heathen. She was coming up in his estimation. Maybe one day he would actually want to have dinner with her.

Heaven help her! This went farther than mere lust. She realized that she liked him and wanted him to like her as he poured milk for both of them without asking.

"What did your brother cook tonight?" Violet needed to talk. It helped her gather her wits. "I have to admit I wasn't looking forward to eating shepherd's pie with the girls."

Jeff started lifting covers. "Beef in a pastry casing, whole potatoes in butter and herbs, peas in a white cream sauce, and asparagus in aspic. There's something chocolate filled with cream for dessert."

"It's a good thing I don't eat like this every evening.

No wonder you exercise so hard.''

The mention of exercise brought back the picture of his virtually naked body. Violet hoped she didn't blush, but was certain she did.

"Tyler's just sending all this food as a bribe to keep you from kicking the twins out of school," Jeff said.

Violet became aware of Jeff's closeness as he held a dish for her to serve herself. He was tall. Even when he bent over, he seemed to tower over her. She wondered if he was equally aware of her proximity. She glanced up. His eyes were empty of expression.

Violet felt a twinge of disappointment. She told herself she was being foolish to want more, but she couldn't help it. Considering how strongly he affected her, she thought that it was only fair that she have some effect on him.

"You should know a bribe won't work."

"I'm not the one trying to bribe you."

Violet decided not to point out he was the one who had invited her to dinner. She was still too surprised at her own feelings to start probing his.

"I'm very fond of the twins," Violet said. "They do get into trouble, but I like spirited girls."

"They have plenty of that."

His leg brushed hers when he sat down. He glanced up at her, a questioning look in his eye.

"Sorry," she said. "It's a small table."

She hoped her voice didn't betray the jolt of excitement she felt. She couldn't help wondering if he had done it on purpose, maybe even to tease her.

They talked of the twins, of Violet's life at the Wolfe School, of the little headaches and triumphs that were part of her job. It was soon clear that his touching her had been an accident. If Jeff Randolph felt anything, could feel anything, it was the best-kept secret in Colorado.

"Being a housemother must get boring sometimes," Jeff said.

"I don't mean to stay here. I expect to be coming into some money soon."

Violet reached for her glass, and Jeff reached for it at the same time. For a moment his hand covered hers. He jerked his hand back.

"I was going to refill it." His gaze was steady. Only his voice betrayed his reaction.

"No, thank you." He had felt it. It was nothing like his effect on her, but he had felt something. Just knowing that helped to steady her nerves. She didn't feel nearly so clumsy, so out of control.

"Will you have enough money to live on?" he asked.

"More than that. At least, I hope so."

"You'll need to invest it. Money will disappear if you just let it sit around."

The eternal banker. Mention money and everything else went out of his head.

"I have something I want to do with it," Violet said.

"What?"

Violet hesitated, but realized she'd been wanting to tell him about her project for some time. Maybe he could help her, even give her some ideas about how to bring it about.

"It was very difficult for me to take care of my father and brother and still work. There must be many women in the same position since the war. Many must have much less money than I did. I want to do something to help them. Only I can't figure out what."

"You must be expecting a large fortune."

"I don't know that it's a fortune at all," Violet said, still unwilling to tell him about the mine. "I'm just hoping I'll have enough to do something worthwhile. Now we've talked about me long enough. Tell me something about yourself."

She realized that he'd spent the whole evening listening to her talk about herself. He had also been watching her closely. She had been too nervous to notice at first, too aware of his closeness.

"There's nothing to tell," Jeff said.

"Of course, there is. I don't mean about your arm or the war. I don't imagine you want to talk about that. Jonas never did. That's why he wouldn't see people. That was all they wanted to talk about."

She saw the cloud pass over Jeff's face. She wondered if he would ever be able to think of the war or his arm without bitterness. He'd never learn to be happy until he did. But she wasn't about to tell him that. She was certain others had already tried.

"You're one of the wealthiest men in Denver, yet you do nothing but work. Why?"

Violet wondered about the women in Jeff's life. He couldn't be that rich and prominent and not draw interest. Besides, he was so attractive, women would have chased him even without the money. There must have been at least one who had broken through that cold reserve.

"I explained that last night," Jeff said.

"You must have had enough money to go back to Virginia years ago. Why haven't you gone?"

"It wasn't time."

"Why?"

There Jeff went again, looking as if the sun was about to set on his world. Violet wondered what it was about his home that still drew him 20 years later. Massachusetts would always be her home, but she could easily imagine never going back. She didn't think Jeff could.

"We were driven out of Virginia," Jeff said, subjecting his coffee to a minute inspection. "True, it was our pa they were getting rid of, but we felt as if they were getting rid of us just as much. I don't think any one of my brothers would consider going back unless he felt he had been successful enough to wipe clean that disgrace.''

Violet wondered what kind of man their father must have been, what he could have done to saddle his sons with such a deep-seated need for redemption. "Is that why you work so hard at the bank?"

"It's my job," Jeff said. "It's what I do."

But Jeff's guard had slipped for a moment, allowing Violet to see his need to feel necessary to somebody, his need to belong. His work at the bank was just his way of feeling successful. She didn't know which was more important: his need to be successful because of his father or his need to be successful because of his arm. She wasn't sure it mattered. Both were unfair burdens. Both drove him hard.

"Then you need to find something else, something to do for fun," Violet said.

"I like my work."

"Maybe, but you're too intense. It makes you short-tempered. It'll probably kill you before you're fifty. Now before I say anything else, I think it's time I left. Thank you for dinner. I hope I get to meet your brother one day to tell him how much I've enjoyed his cooking."

"He's always at the Windsor."

"I'm sure I'd feel very out of place there. By the way, chapel service tomorrow is at ten o'clock. They're going to close the balcony off so we can use it. You're welcome to join us."

"I haven't been to church in twenty years."

"Then it's about time you went. I imagine your voice is quite rusty."

"I don't sing."

"That's unfortunate. The girls love it. You'll be surrounded by an awful din."

"No, I won't. I'll be working."

"Surely you can spare an hour from your work."

"I can't keep my clerks sitting around while I sing

hymns. The competition would soon get ahead of me if I were forever taking mornings off.''

Violet stared hard at him. ''You said they got Sunday off.''

''Something unusual has come up. I have to take advantage of it before it disappears.''

''That's your choice.''

''If my employees don't like—''

Violet slid her chair back so abruptly it scraped the floor. ''Don't you dare tell me if they don't like it they can go somewhere else. It's not that easy to get a good job, especially one that pays enough to support a family. They may want to throw your columns of figures in your face, but they have families to feed. I insist that you give them the day off.''

''Why do you care about them? You don't even know them.''

''I care about anyone who's being tyrannized, and holding a job over a man's head is tyranny.''

Jeff's attitude was one of irritated puzzlement. He was probably looking for a hidden motive. That was just the thing a cynical banker would do.

''Besides, Sunday is a special day for the girls. If we weren't under quarantine, they'd be having visitors. I plan to use the parlor. We'll build a fire and tell stories. I can't have it full of your minions and the lift creaking and screeching all day.''

''Let them stick their fingers in their ears.''

''I will not have their day ruined any more than it already is. Besides, you owe it to your clerks in compensation for being here at such ridiculous hours.''

''It's none of your business what my clerks do.''

''It is as long as they do it in my building.''

''They can move to the lawn.''

''There won't be any point in that if I dismantle your lift.''

''How would you manage that?''

"I don't know," Violet said. "But I'll find some way to keep it from working. Not one paper will travel up that lift to your window tomorrow."

Jeff's face was a study in emotions. Violet watched in fascination. She could almost see the thoughts as they tumbled about in his mind.

"Okay," he said, "I'll give them tomorrow off."

He caught her completely off guard. She hadn't expected him to give in, certainly not so quickly.

"Thank you," Violet said, unable to think of anything else to say. "I'd better be going. I imagine the girls are through with their dinner by now."

Violet descended the stairs in deep thought. Nothing much during the evening had gone as she expected, least of all their last exchange. Jeff couldn't have given his men the day off because she asked him to, could he?

No. Still, something was different. She could feel it.

Jeff practically flung the dishes off the table, he was so angry at himself. It had been his intention to give his men the day off all along. Only occasionally did he ask them to work on Sunday and then only on a voluntary basis. He enjoyed the quiet and solitude of having the bank to himself. So why had he virtually told Violet he expected them to work?

He'd never been obstructive just for the sake of being hard to get along with. So why was he doing so now? Probably for the same reason he'd invited her to eat with him. She had gotten under his skin, and he couldn't get her out. Though why she was there at all was a mystery to him.

He dropped a stack of dishes on the lift so hard one of them broke. He felt like throwing the crystal after it, but he was old enough to control his temper and try to solve his problems in a quiet, adult fashion. Only he felt anything but.

He couldn't believe he was attracted to that woman.

He might as well admit it. There was no other explanation for his behavior. Why else would he go out of his way to dine with a woman who represented nearly everything he wished to avoid? Why else would he do it a second time when his every doubt had been confirmed? And why else would he say he was going to do something he hadn't planned to do just to annoy her?

Jeff loaded the serving dishes on the lift. Fortunately they were made of silver, or he'd probably have broken at least one of them, too.

All during dinner, he had kept noticing how the candlelight sparkled in Violet's eyes. They were such a deep blue that they seemed almost like bottomless pools. Against the white of her skin they were almost black.

Her hair fascinated him. He couldn't decide what color it was. In the sunlight it almost looked red. In the normal light it was a deep copper color. In candlelight it turned almost as dark as her jet brows and lashes.

Everything about her was a study in contrasts between strong, bold colors, even her dress of emerald green.

Why hadn't she said anything about the dangling pants? She had to have known what she was looking at and that he'd put them outside on purpose. He'd expected her to get into a temper over it, yet she hadn't mentioned it. She wasn't acting as he had expected.

Nor was she like the women who had visited the prison in Massachusetts. She was more gentle, softspoken—he had to say it—more ladylike. And though she had very strong opinions that she held to despite anything he might say, he knew she would never have refused to help a prisoner, even a Confederate.

That still didn't excuse his liking her. All he could figure was that he had been away from Louise too long. He had always had a strong physical appetite. Being around a beautiful woman without being able to satisfy his needs was apparently causing him to do, say, and feel all kinds of unusual things.

He had less than two days to go. He could keep to himself until Monday afternoon. There was no point in asking for trouble. Women were unaccountable creatures. They could ensnare a man even when he thought he was safe. He had proved too vulnerable when and where he hadn't expected. He would have to watch himself more closely. He intended to return to Virginia a bachelor.

Violet woke to the sound of Jeff's weights again. At least that morning the clanking noises had started later and weren't so loud. He was obviously making some attempt not to wake the girls. Violet doubted he would be successful. He clearly didn't know how to live with other people.

She refused to get out of bed. She didn't want to have to come face-to-face with him when he was wearing nothing but those shorts. She assumed he'd hauled them up after she'd left last night. The twins hadn't complained of bats when they had gone to bed. She'd forgotten to tax him with the matter. Now that she'd forgotten it once, she couldn't very well bring it up later. She'd have enough trouble with his using the bathroom.

"Is that man in there again?" Betty Sue asked.

"He has to take a bath," Violet said.

"I don't see why he has to use our bathrooms."

"There aren't any others. What are you doing up so early? You usually don't get out of bed until I've called you at least twice."

"I couldn't sleep with all that noise," Betty Sue said.

"Are you ready to take your bath?"

"No, I just wanted to know if that man was in there again. My father's going to be very angry when he finds out."

Violet had been expecting that remark to be made eventually. It was unreasonable to think that the girls wouldn't mention Jeff's presence, but she wished it could have been anyone other than Betty Sue who had brought the subject up.

"Nobody's happy about it, but Mr. Randolph can't leave any more than you or I can."

"He shouldn't be here."

"Well, he is. So we might as well do the best we can until tomorrow afternoon. Then the quarantine will be over, he can go home, and we can all get back to normal."

"I'm still going to tell my father."

"I imagine Miss Settle has already done that, but you can tell him if you like."

"I'll tell him about the twins, too."

"What about the twins?" Violet asked, wondering what they had done.

"I'm going to tell him about that ugly little weasel, Essie Brown, too."

So that was it. The twins' protection had brought Betty Sue's harassment of Essie to an end, and she was angry.

"Betty Sue, you have lots of friends in this school. Your father is a rich and powerful man. Your mother is a prominent member of Denver society. Why can't you ignore those girls?"

"I hate them."

"If you don't like them, just ignore them."

"They think they're so pretty they can do anything they like. They said their uncle was as rich and important as my father. They even say their aunt's prettier than my mother."

Jealousy. The canker in the bosom of so many girls when brought face-to-face with a prettier girl. Only there were two of them in the present case. Violet guessed, if she'd been at the school longer, she'd have seen the jealousy more quickly.

Until the twins had arrived, Betty Sue had been the

prettiest girl with the richest and most socially prominent parents. Even though her friends had remained faithful, she didn't like having her position threatened.

"I should have thought you were too old to care about anything they said one way or the other," Violet said. "After all, they're only little girls. You're thirteen."

Violet was pleased her words had caused Betty Sue to stop and think.

"They're just so annoying," Betty Sue finally said.

"Little girls often are, but they grow out of it. Now I suggest you go back to your room. I don't hear any more splashing. I expect Mr. Randolph will come out soon."

"Why doesn't he have somebody make him an arm?" Betty Sue asked. "Mother says people find it upsetting to constantly have to be aware of his stump."

Violet felt her entire body flame with anger, not just for Jeff, but for any man who had fought for a cause he believed in, then was forced to see people turn away because he had to shoulder a burden they had been spared. There were times when she thought people like Betty Sue's mother would have preferred their friends, relatives, and lovers to come back dead rather than maimed.

"I can't answer that question," Violet said, trying to keep her voice as calm as possible. "If it bothers your mother, I suggest she avoid him."

"Mother says he's too important to ignore."

Violet tried to remind herself that Betty Sue probably didn't mean anything by what she said. She was merely repeating what she'd heard her mother say.

"I really don't know what you can do about that. Maybe if you try to remember he lost his arm in a war, it won't seem so terrible."

"Mother says he fought on the wrong side. She said he deserved to lose his arm."

Violet realized she was so furious she was shaking. If

this was an example of what Jeff Randolph had had to endure over the last 15 years, it was no wonder he worked all the time. It was probably the only way he could forget the cruelty of people who ought to be grateful that he, rather than they, had been the one to pay the price of the long and bitterly fought war.

"I wouldn't repeat that if I were you. It's not a very charitable thing to say, particularly on Sunday."

"But mother said—"

"In this instance your mother is wrong," Violet said flatly. "Mr. Randolph was willing to fight for what he believed. For that alone he deserves your admiration and respect. Many of our gallant men never came home. We should welcome the ones who did, even if their bodies are no longer whole. In Mr. Randolph's case, the fact that he has made such a great success in spite of his handicap is even more remarkable. Your mother should be proud to know such a man."

Seeing that Betty Sue had the grace to look abashed, Violet said, "The same thing could have happened to your father or one of your uncles. I'm sure you wouldn't want people to turn their backs on someone you loved."

"I guess not."

"I didn't think you would. Now you'd better go back to your room. I'll let you know when Mr. Randolph has gone upstairs."

Even after Betty Sue had returned to her room, anger continued to burn in the pit of Violet's stomach. She had never seen that kind of cruelty before. No one had ever said anything like that about Jonas. Maybe Colorado was different from Massachusetts. Everyone at home was so partisan and had believed so strongly in the justice of the war that they honored their veterans. All of them.

"Do you always make a practice of defending the enemy?"

Violet jumped at the sound of Jeff Randolph's voice.

Chapter Nine

Jeff grinned as Violet stared at him, her mouth slightly open to accommodate the quick intake of breath. Her gaze traveled from his face to the triangle of skin showing through his open robe.

"Will you never learn to give me some warning before you step out into the hall?" she asked in a faint voice.

"Blame it on your eloquence. It made me forget."

"I'm sure it did no such thing. I didn't say much."

She looked embarrassed that he had overheard what she said. But her agitation couldn't be any greater than his own surprise. Not that he had expected her to feel as Clara Rabin did. Clara was a selfish bitch who drove her husband to make more and more money to fuel her social ambitions. Jeff didn't give a damn what Clara thought of him, and Clara knew it. After one heated encounter several years earlier, Clara had given Jeff a wide berth.

But he was surprised Violet would defend him. He

didn't know for sure, but he had the feeling she harbored a deep resentment against the South.

"I've never heard anyone say as much," Jeff said. "Most of the time, people prefer to ignore my arm or pretend there's nothing wrong. Even my family would like to forget."

"It's hard to remember and forget at the same time."

He hated riddles. "What the hell is that supposed to mean?"

Violet smiled. It was remarkable how her eyes seemed to change color with her moods. Not change color exactly, but go from a deep blue, almost black, to a lighter shade more akin to a deep mountain lake drenched in summer sunlight. It would be easy for a man to forget she was a Yankee and remember only that she was a beautiful woman.

"I don't pretend to know as much about Southern belles as you," Violet said, "but I imagine you're going to have to acquire some manners before you'll be able to convince your paragon to marry you. You're abrupt, rude, and given to cursing when anything annoys you."

"It doesn't seem to bother you."

"Would it make any difference if I objected?"

"No," Jeff said.

"Then it's a good thing I don't."

He wasn't about to get into another verbal exchange with her. She'd already proved she was more than a match for him. "You still haven't explained your remark."

"You won't like what I have to say."

"I rarely do."

She leveled a dubious look at him and took a deep breath. "Your disability has put your family in a very difficult position. I know because I was there myself. It's impossible to forget a wound such as yours. It would be unfair and unkind. Truly forgetting would mean forgetting your sacrifice, not giving you the credit and respect you deserve for what you did. It would also mean ignoring the added effort you must make to do things others do more easily, to ignore the extra effort that went into your success, to ignore the hurts and slights you endure from people like Betty Sue Rabin's mother. It would also mean they would ignore the added depth of character you have developed to deal with all of this.''

''Don't make me sound like some kind of saint.''

When Violet smiled again, Jeff wished she would stop that. It played havoc with his control. All he could think of was that her mouth looked wonderfully inviting.

''I'd never confuse you with a saint,'' Violet said. ''They're too fragile to survive long in this world. Sour-tempered bears like you endure.''

Jeff felt like smiling back at her, and he didn't understand why. She disagreed with him. She called him a sour-tempered bear, and he still wanted to smile. The woman was a witch. They used to burn women like her at the stake a few hundred years earlier. He wasn't sure it was wise to have given up the practice.

''Finish explaining what you meant,'' he said. ''Why should people forget?''

''You're not going to like this part.''

''I haven't liked any of what you've said,'' Jeff said.

''You can't go around making people feel guilty for the rest of your life. They'll grow to resent it. Finally they'll hate you. The loss of your arm is one of the risks that comes with being alive. It could just as easily have happened to someone else. It could have been worse. People have to be allowed to forget so that they can begin to treat you like a normal human being.''

''But I'm not normal,'' Jeff said, waving his empty sleeve. ''I can't forget it.''

''But you must, or you'll become crippled emotionally. My brother did. He looked at himself and saw only the ruin. He didn't see the wonderful person that was left, the person who hadn't changed just because he had lost part of his body. You didn't let misfortune destroy you. You channeled your energies into your work. You made something of your life."

Jeff didn't feel like smiling. He felt a bit angry that Violet would dismiss his handicap so easily. She couldn't know how it made him feel less of a man. She didn't know what it meant to have to continually fight people like Clara Rabin to keep from being considered a social leper. He didn't like society, but he'd be damned if he'd let anybody push him out of it. Arm or no arm, he was as good as anybody else.

At the same time, he felt a little ashamed of himself. Violet had given him more credit than he deserved. He had never let anyone forget what happened to him—not his family, not his business associates, not even his customers. He fanned the flames of memory at every opportunity. He'd never let anyone forget he hated every Yankee who had ever drawn breath.

Yet he didn't hate Violet, even though she irritated him, even though she reminded him of two bitter years of imprisonment.

He smiled. He could feel the muscles tighten in his face. He could feel the gentle rise of the corners of his mouth. He could feel a change in his mood. He didn't know why he smiled. It had just happened.

"You've got a rosy view of the world, Miss Goodwin."

Violet smiled back. He was going to have to ask her to stop doing that. He didn't think as well as he ought when she smiled. It encouraged that awful pink color to invade his own view of life, and he had more than enough evidence to prove life was at best a dark gray.

"Don't you think it's time we stopped calling each other Miss and Mister? I realize you'll be leaving in a few days, but I'd rather you called me Violet."

"My name is Jeff. Thomas Jefferson Randolph. You can guess my namesake."

"Thomas Jefferson! How wonderful to be named for one of the greatest minds in the history of our country."

"Actually he was a distant cousin."

He didn't know why he told her that. He and his brothers had always made it a point never to let anybody know their father had named them for presidents. They'd also avoided claiming connection with their famous relatives. Half the people didn't believe them. The other half liked them only because of it.

Violet stared at him in disbelief; then a look of amazement bloomed in her eyes. "You're telling the truth, aren't you?"

"I don't know why I told you that. I shouldn't have. But now that I have, you might as well know I'm related to Gen. Robert E. Lee as well."

He saw the warmth and pleasure fade from her eyes to be replaced by a steely quality he had only seen hinted at before.

"Usually my brothers and I don't tell people much about our family. It seems to do more harm than good."

Violet tried to smile, but it wasn't much of a success. "Don't worry. I won't hold you responsible for the misdeeds of your relatives. Now before the girls start waking up, I suggest you go upstairs."

Jeff hesitated. He couldn't imagine why learning he was related to Robert E. Lee should have caused such a reaction, but there was something there, something buried deep, something she didn't want to tell him. It obviously made her very angry.

She had started to walk away, but she turned back. "You're welcome to go to chapel with us."

"No."

"If it's because of your arm, it's time you made your peace with your Maker."

"And if it's not?" Jeff said.

"You still ought to go. There is a great deal of unresolved anger inside you. You'll never be happy until you get rid of it.''

"And you think going to chapel will help?"

"Maybe. I keep hoping it will help me."

With that, she turned away and began knocking on each of the doors. "Time to get up, girls. We're due in chapel in an hour."

Jeff wanted to ask what she meant, but she was clearly through talking for the time being. He started up the stairs. Maybe he would ask her later that night. She might want him to believe she was more at peace with her life than he was, but something clearly bothered her.

He didn't like to see the kind of brooding anger he'd lived with so long in her eyes. He knew what it had done to him. He didn't want it to do the same thing to Violet.

Essie poked her head through the doorway. "Miss Goodwin wants to know if you're going to chapel with us."

Frowning, Jeff looked up from his notes. "I have too much work to do." He pointed to several stacks of paper in front of him.

"My daddy's coming. He sent me a letter." She showed it to him. "He's here already."

"Then you certainly don't need me," Jeff said, preparing to go back to work.

"He'll be far away. They're going to put us in the balcony. It's way high. I'm afraid of the balcony."

"Then you hold on to Miss Goodwin's hand." When Essie didn't move, Jeff said, "You'd better get dressed, or you'll be late."

"I'm already dressed," Essie said. She stepped into the room and pirouetted so that he could see her dress.

Jeff told himself he was going to have to pay more attention to what he was saying. If he'd made that comment to a woman who'd just spent considerable time getting ready to be seen, she'd probably be mad enough to rip his papers to shreds.

"You look very nice. I'm sure your father will be very proud of you."

"He's coming tomorrow, too."

"You already told me. Now you'd better get back downstairs. It'll soon be time to go."

"Are you sure you're not going?" another girl's voice asked. It was Aurelia. Her angelic face was matched by Juliette's.

"What are you two doing up here?"

"We came to find out if you're going to chapel."

"I already told Miss Goodwin I wasn't going."

Both twins looked delighted. "Good," they said.

Jeff instantly felt uneasy. He had a gut feeling danger loomed ahead. "Why is it good?"

"We don't want to go to chapel either. Miss Goodwin says if you're not going, we can stay with you."

Blackmail. She had turned his own game on him. He wouldn't have a moment's peace with those two hellions downstairs.

"Betty Sue doesn't want to go either."

Great! If those three were left by themselves for an hour, the consequences were liable to start a war that would involve every female in Denver before it was done. Jeff slammed down his pen. "Tell Miss Goodwin I'll be down in ten minutes, dressed and ready to go to chapel. You may also tell her the last time I was in a church, blackmail was still not considered Christian, not to say illegal."

"Miss Goodwin didn't say anything about blackmail," Juliette said.

"No, I don't expect she did."

"What's blackmail?" Essie asked.

"Making people do what they don't want to do," Jeff said.

"That happens to kids all the time," Aurelia said,

obviously disappointed in the mysterious word.

"Can I stay while you get dressed?" Essie asked.

"Of course you can't, silly," Aurelia said. "Girls don't ever watch men get dressed."

"Why?"

"Because you'll get a baby."

"How?"

"I don't know, but Corrine says that's what happened to some lady her mother knew. She said everybody got so mad the lady had to go to another town."

Jeff decided there were pitfalls to being around young girls. This was a particularly deep one. He hated to think what Denver society could do with their conversation!

"All three of you are going downstairs this very minute."

"Don't you want to read my letter?" Essie asked.

"Not now. If I don't hurry, I'm going to be late."

Besides, he needed his mind free to think of what he was going to do to Violet. He couldn't let this blatant blackmail go unanswered.

Violet wished she could stop thinking how handsome Jeff was. She also wished she could keep her gaze from turning in his direction at least once a minute. If she didn't get better control over herself, everybody in the chapel was going to be whispering about her.

She looked down at the people on the ground floor. Miss Settle had looked up once, visibly paled to see Jeff in the balcony; she had practically stumbled to her pew. She had been in constant prayer ever since.

Harold Brown was also present. He, too, had paled when he saw his daughter walk in holding Jeff's hand. Violet wondered how much money he'd borrowed from Jeff. She wondered if he would be able to pay it back. She was certain he would visit Essie regularly from then on.

Violet sent a silent prayer heavenward that no other

parents would choose to attend the service. If she didn't have to make an explanation, it couldn't be misunderstood. Besides, Betty Sue had enough mischief in mind for everybody. Her mother visited twice a week, Tuesday and Friday, and Violet was certain Betty Sue would tell her everything that had happened, as well as a few things that existed only in Betty Sue's imagination.

Violet knew she ought to be paying attention to the sermon, but her gaze involuntarily turned back to Jeff. He had scowled at her when he had come down the stairs. She'd smiled in spite of herself, and instantly his expression had softened. She knew he wasn't mad. She expected he would try to retaliate—she would have to be on the alert—but that didn't bother her as much as the fact that she liked the man.

And she wasn't talking about lust at the moment. That was still as strong as ever, but she actually liked him, sour temper and all. She didn't want to like a Southern man. There were too many unresolved issues in her own mind.

It made no sense. She did admire Jeff for his success, but he was an irascible man, hardheaded, prejudiced, and determined that any woman born above the Mason-Dixon Line might as well be a spawn of the Devil. Not that she had any desire to be the kind of woman he wanted to marry. She couldn't imagine a more miserable example of the female sex than Jeff's ideal Southern belle. Every self-respecting woman in the world should weep with fury just thinking about it.

But neither of those things bothered her as much as the awareness that she had no control over her feelings. She liked Jeff in spite of the fact it was a stupid thing to do.

She studied his classic profile. But a woman didn't fall for a man because he had a classic profile, did she? The image of Jeff exercising in those skimpy pants flashed into her mind. Even men tried to pretend they loved a woman as much for her inner qualities as for her body.

Not that she believed them. To hear Jeff tell it, he wanted a beautiful shell. Any inner qualities beyond complete obedience were unacceptable.

She ought to be listening to the minister. His sermon was practically written for her. Forgive your enemies. Be kind to them who persecute you, who despise you. The timing wasn't very good for her. She couldn't forgive the people who were trying to steal her mine any more than she could forgive the men who had destroyed her family.

She wondered what Jeff was feeling. He held to his anger even more tenaciously than she did. Maybe she shouldn't have forced him to come.

The organ broke into the final hymn. Violet tried to regather her thoughts and focus them on the text of the hymn. She might as well have stayed in the dormitory for all the good chapel had done her.

The noise from downstairs finally broke Jeff's concentration. It hadn't been very good anyway, not since he'd gone to chapel services. He was still irritated he'd lost time from his work. He was irritated he'd let Violet trick him into going and furious about the sermon. The minister had practically glared at him the entire time. He didn't know the sanctimonious little bastard's name, but he had a good mind to have him sacked.

Another series of squeals, thuds of running feet, and a barrage of shrill, preadolescent voices shattered any remaining shred of calm. The last figures flew out of Jeff's head and refused to be recaptured. Uttering a particularly colorful oath he'd picked up from Monty, he pushed the table aside and got up.

Jeff looked out the window. It was a little overcast, but the temperature was above normal, the wind calm. It was a fine afternoon to be out and about. He hoped his clerks were taking advantage of the day. He meant to keep their noses to the grindstone all the next week.

Jeff turned away from the window, but there was nothing except his work to engage his interest. He was tired of that. He had slept nearly four hours last night, and he didn't feel tired. Just impatient, frustrated, and irritable, as though he was being held back from something he wanted to do. Only he didn't know what.

Jeff left his room. He walked to the end of the hall and looked out the window. From this height he could see his house on Fourteenth Street. Some of the homes in the newly fashionable area of Capital Hill were visible, particularly the monstrous house of Philip and Clara Rabin. He could also see the spot Horace Tabor was preparing for the house he meant to build.

Madison's home was out on the plain a mile beyond the end of Broadway. Fern had insisted that he build outside Denver, where she would have enough space to ride her horses. Not that he'd given her time to do so. She'd been pregnant or nursing ever since they had moved from Chicago. As a result, Madison found himself sitting on a huge piece of real estate that would one day be worth a fortune. Jeff never ceased to marvel how everything Madison touched seemed to turn to gold.

Jeff noticed a family walking down the sidewalk in front of the school. Two small boys held on to their father's hands, pulling him this way and that, shouting and laughing. A woman walked sedately at his side pushing a carriage. Jeff was surprised to find he knew the man, had done business with him. He would never have suspected that the man took such an interest in his family. He was a hard man to do business with. Yet there he was, looking as if he'd be unable to deny his family anything they wanted.

The scene had the unaccountable effect of reminding Jeff of his own loneliness. He wondered if Violet missed having a family. She was surrounded by more than enough children, but surely that wasn't the same as having her own. She'd said that she didn't want to get married, that she wanted to help women like herself. He wondered if that would compensate her for the family most women seemed to want so badly.

Something drew his attention to the fact the building had fallen silent. Listening intently, he couldn't catch even the slightest sound. He turned back to his room, but he wasn't in the mood to go back to work. He was curious as to why the building was quiet after sounding like a battlefield all afternoon.

When he reached the landing below, he found the second floor empty. All the doors stood open with light pouring into the hall, but not a sound was to be heard.

The hall of the main floor was just as quiet. For a moment Jeff wondered if the quarantine had been ended early. No, in that case, he would be the one to leave, not the girls.

Jeff opened the door to the room on the right side of the hall. Beth was setting the table for the evening meal. She appeared startled when she looked up and saw him.

"I'm looking for Violet . . . Miss Goodwin," he said, unable to think of any other reason for being downstairs at this time.

"She's across the hall supervising study period," Beth said. "Since the quarantine's over tomorrow, the girls will have to go back to class."

He closed the door, crossed the hall, and opened the only door he saw. Instead of being filled with tables, the room was filled with desks. A girl sat at each, with a book open in front of her. Violet was standing at the front of the room next to a blackboard with about a dozen names written on it.

"It's Mr. Randolph," Essie said. "Can you help me with my arithmetic?"

"I need help, too," Aurelia said, "and he's my uncle."

"Come on in, Mr. Randolph," Violet said. "You're just in time to help us with our lesson on the Civil War."

Chapter Ten

Jeff's survival instincts were nearly as good as George's, and they were in full cry. The message was unmistakable: He should retreat, run for his life. He was entering a mine field; he'd never come out alive. The enemy had heavy artillery aimed at his heart, and he was standing there in nothing but his shirttail.

But Jeff also had the instinctive response of an old war horse. Once the smell of battle was in his nostrils, he could no more avoid the conflict than he could refuse to draw breath. He felt his body grow tense, the sweat pop out on his forehead. Just thinking about it brought back all the horror of those awful years. He could smell the blood, hear the scream of cannonballs, see the carnage all around him, taste the grit that filled the air, and feel the scorching heat of the big guns.

He could also see the faces of the dead and maimed, faces of friends, of men who had sacrificed their lives, the flower of Southern manhood reduced to bloody meat. The cruel injustice of it all rose in his throat like bile.

"I've done my history," Essie said.

"Maybe Mr. Randolph will help you when he's finished talking to the class. It's not often we get to learn about a war from a man who actually took part in it. He's a relative of Gen. Robert E. Lee. Maybe he can tell us why the general did everything he could to prolong the war."

Jeff's shocked gaze riveted itself on Violet.

"Our father fought in the war," Juliette said, "but he never talks about it. He has a sword he keeps in his office. He won't tell us about that either."

"That was his officer's sword," Jeff said, his mystified gaze still on Violet.

"Why don't you begin by telling us the causes of the war?" Violet said.

She didn't seem like the same woman he'd been talking to the past few days. It wasn't a matter of being angry or unfriendly. She seemed to have changed into somebody cold and remote.

"It was a question of states' rights," Jeff said. "The Southern states believed they had the right to decide their own destiny. When they no longer wanted to be part of the United States, they felt they had the right to secede."

"What's secede?" Essie asked.

"To break off and start their own country," Violet said.

"Do you mean Texas would be in a different country from Colorado?" Juliette asked.

"It would have been if the South had won the war," Violet said.

"Wyoming, too?" Aurelia asked.

"Yes."

The twins looked at each other. "I wouldn't like it if Uncle Monty lived in a different country," Juliette said.

"You would have been able to go back and forth," Jeff said, "the same way we do with Mexico."

"Papa won't let us go to Mexico," Juliette said. "He said it's not safe for daughters of rich American ranchers."

Jeff had the feeling control of the situation was slipping away from him before he even started. He looked at Violet, but her expression hadn't changed.

"That has nothing to do with why the war started," Jeff said.

"What about the slaves?" Violet asked.

The tone of her voice was warning enough. It told him of her anger, buried and carefully controlled, but as deep and abiding as his own.

"Isn't it true that the South started the war because landowners wanted to keep their slaves and their huge plantations? Isn't it true that all the talk about states' rights was just to cover the real reason they were willing to fight such a long, bloody war?"

There it was, the attack he had been expecting, the one he'd seen in her eyes from the moment he entered the room. He knew she wasn't his friend at that moment.

"That may have been true of some people, but most Southerners didn't own slaves. My family didn't. We didn't have a plantation either. We lived on a dirt ranch in Texas with barely enough to eat and hardly enough money to buy bullets to fight off the rustlers, bandits, and Indians."

Violet looked surprised. She hadn't expected that. She was just like everybody else from Massachusetts. They thought every Southerner had hundreds of slaves, did nothing but drink mint juleps all day and gamble or go to parties every night. Violet should have seen his mother the way he remembered her that day he left for the war, her dress stained, her hair dry and lifeless, her skin burned and cracked.

"Girls, go on with your reading," Violet said. "We'll discuss it when you finish. Mr. Randolph and I will continue our discussion outside. I'll be in the hall if you need me."

She was still coldly angry. Jeff wondered what she wanted to say that couldn't be said in front of the students.

"You know the South fought the war because of slaves," Violet said the minute she closed the door behind her. "There was no other reason."

"I wouldn't have risked my life so other men could keep their slaves," Jeff said, his voice as angry as hers.

"What about your plantation in Virginia?" She confronted him in the empty hall, their voices echoing from one end to the other.

"Our land was rented out. Anybody who worked for us received a wage."

"Then why did you fight?" She sounded genuinely confused. "Surely you didn't think the South would be better off as a separate country."

Jeff had thought so, but he had thought they could achieve their aims without fighting a war. He had said so to his father, whose angry reply still had the power to thunder in his ears.

You only think that because you're a coward. You're afraid to fight because you know you won't measure up. You've always been a weakling. The twins have more guts than you.

He had tried to forget that day, to block it completely from his memory, but 19 years later it still remained as vivid as the moment it happened. He could remember the anger and the hatred he'd felt for his father. The bastard didn't care about his son, only that the family name shouldn't be disgraced. Jeff had never understood why being a wastrel, a liar, a drunk, a seducer, a man so vile his neighbors had paid to have him leave the state could possibly be less disgraceful than not wanting to fight.

You're afraid some Yankee will shoot you. If you

don't fight, I'll shoot you myself.

Jeff never doubted his father would have done exactly that. His father had killed his own best friend, and he only had one of those. He had seven sons.

"I did think we'd be better off as a separate country," Jeff said finally.

"Do you feel that way now?"

Jeff found it difficult to say what he felt then. One part of him wanted to shout that the South would have been better off dead than yoked with the North, that the war had killed everything good and worthwhile. But the banker in Jeff was prepared to argue loudly that the South would have been at a grave economic disadvantage if it had had to survive on its own.

"In my heart, I wish we were free. The North may be stronger and richer, but they didn't share either their strength or wealth with us. You only had to live through the Reconstruction to know how much they hated us."

"You sound like a man who holds tight to his prejudices."

"It's just like a Yankee to equate beliefs they can't share with prejudice. I won't be talked out of what I believe by anyone, but I wouldn't start a war to settle the differences."

Violet moved a few steps closer to him. "You don't sound like a man who believes in war."

"I don't." He never had. "It's a stupid way to try to settle an argument. The outcome has nothing to do with what's right or wrong, only who's stronger. The problems still exist." He couldn't help looking at his empty sleeve. "And it's a stupid waste of men. It ruins so many lives."

He'd volunteered only because his father had shamed him into it. But what he couldn't come to grips with was the knowledge he was such a lousy soldier. George had come through four years without a scratch. He had even reached the rank of captain without having been to military school.

Jeff had been wounded and captured, his squadron wiped out at Gettysburg. He had been struggling to make up for his feeling of failure ever since.

"You know slavery was the real reason for the war," Violet said, the anger in her voice dispersing his own thoughts. "Your family might not have had slaves—maybe most Southerners didn't—but the people who made the decisions did." She moved closer to him, an angry glint in her eyes.

"There were lots of other reasons we wanted to secede," Jeff said, angry she couldn't see past that one issue. "For one, your merchants were strangling us."

"You would have strangled anyway," she said, using her hands in big circling gestures that showed her anger more than her voice or expression. "Your economy depended on unlimited virgin land that you could exploit and an unlimited market for cotton, which you glutted in your desire for more and more money."

"We had no monopoly on exploitation. Hundreds of Yankee fortunes were made on the slave trade. When that was outlawed, you exploited the poor and their children under murderous factory conditions. You raped the land for its mineral wealth. If you want to see how it's done, go see what they've done to the mountains outside of Leadville."

"You're talking around the issue," Violet said. "The South was wrong, and they knew it. They were fighting to hold on to a morally indefensible position. They tried to cover it up by running away—seceding if that's what you want to call it—but they only succeeded in starting a war that killed hundreds of thousands of fine, beautiful men. And I hold Robert E. Lee responsible as much as anyone."

Jeff had started to turn away, to go back upstairs. But at that, he turned back, so surprised he almost forgot his anger. "How on earth can you hate the most respected man besides Lincoln to emerge from that bloody mess?"

"Because he was too good a soldier, too admirable a man. He should have fought for the Union. He was in the Union Army."

"No, he was in the United States Army. He resigned before it became the Union Army."

"He resigned so he could fight for a cause he didn't even believe in."

They were standing nose to nose, shouting at each other like irate dock hands.

"He believed in Virginia and its right to secede," Jeff said.

"If he had led the Union Army instead, the war would have been over in one battle. You would still have your arm. My brother would still be alive."

That was what came from letting women think that they knew something about wars and history. They couldn't see past their emotions.

"Not even Robert E. Lee could have ended that war in a single battle," Jeff said. "Feelings ran too deep. It could only have been fought as it was—a bloody slugfest in which one side knocked the other down time after time until one was too weak to stand up again. The Union Army was twice as strong. It had unlimited resources and it blockaded the whole South. Still it took four years. Lee couldn't have changed that by himself."

"People would have listened to him. If he had remained loyal to his oath, others would have."

"You don't know what you're talking about."

Jeff hated it when people tried to tell him what the South should have done, how it should have behaved, how it should be ashamed of what it had done. He especially hated it when the person telling him was a Yankee.

"You didn't live in the South. You don't have any notion of how we think, how we feel, how we can feel honor bound to give our lives for something we believe in.''

''Honor!'' She made the word sound like a curse.

Beth opened the door to the hall. ''Are you all right, Miss Goodwin?''

''You don't understand what that word means,'' Violet said, ignoring Beth. ''There's nothing honorable about fighting a war for a dishonorable reason.''

''You're so narrow-minded you can't see anything except what you want to see. You may think I'm wrong, but a million Southern men believed enough to risk their lives and everything they had. Thousands lost their lives. Thousands more were left maimed and cut up like me, and all because Lincoln thought we ought to stay one country. Maybe we should, but was it worth so many lives?''

''I think I'll look in on the girls,'' Beth said. She tiptoed across the hall, giving the combatants a wide berth.

''You're so bigoted you couldn't see the truth if it hit you in the face,'' Violet said. ''You're so busy feeling sorry for yourself, thinking the world owes you a life-long apology, you can't see that losing your arm is just one of the things that happens to some people in life. You could have been dead.''

''I would have preferred it.''

For the first several months after he'd been wounded, the doctors had kept him restrained. He had threatened to take his life. What they didn't understand—what even he didn't understand until years later—was that his will to live was too strong. His father might not have given his brothers or him much, but every one of them had an indomitable will, an absolute certainty he was right. He might have to die, but he wouldn't give up. His father had been wrong. He wasn't a coward, and he would never take a coward's way out.

''Look at you,'' Violet said. ''You think you've suffered, but you've been brilliantly successful even without that arm."

"I would trade every bit of it for my arm."

"There's no use dwelling on the loss of that arm. It's time to put it out of your mind."

That was what everybody who had never lost so much as a fingernail tried to tell him. They didn't know what it was to be stared at, pointed out, pitied, cross-examined. People wouldn't allow him to forget if he tried.

"I have, as much as common sense will allow."

"Is that how you justify hiding in your office and working around the clock? All it's gotten you is plenty of money and even more self-pity."

"I—"

"You've retreated into yourself. You've turned making money into a way of compensating for your arm."

Violet was wrong there. He'd turned it into a way of compensating for his sense of failure as a soldier, his feeling of being only part of a man. Only it never seemed to work. No matter how successful he became, how much money he earned, the failing was still there.

"I make money because it's what I do for a living. I also make money so the family can return to Virginia."

"So you can go back rich."

"You can't expect us to want to go back poor."

They couldn't. It would be the same as admitting that the people who had driven his father out had been right.

"That's not a worthy goal," Violet said. "Your family has so much money now having more is pointless. What have you done to help any of those poor maimed men you're so concerned about? Have you offered them medical care or artificial arms? Have you helped their families get back on their feet while they struggle to care for their disabled loved ones?"

"Have you?"

He had to turn the question back on her. He didn't

dare face it himself. He had never considered doing anything like that. To do so, he would have had to come to terms with his own loss, and he hadn't been able to do that.

He'd been back to Virginia only twice. He'd seen the destruction of land and property, even human life, but he'd been unable to face the destruction of the human spirit. He'd repurchased Ashburn. He'd bought up several of the farms that surrounded it, always paying more than the property was actually worth. He told himself he was helping by giving some people the means to start over again. But he was still avoiding the real issues, and he knew it.

"No, I haven't," Violet said. "Until I came to Denver, I was too busy taking care of my brother, then my father. But my uncle left me a mine, which is supposed to be worth a fortune. There's some trouble over it—I have a lawyer working on it for me—but when I get my money, I intend to do everything I can. Massachusetts men died and were maimed, too, you know."

"If those men had minded their own affairs, if they hadn't tried to force their ideas down our throats—"

"There's no point in continuing this conversation, Mr. Randolph. We are not likely to agree on even the smallest point. I suggest you return to your pile of papers. There must be several thousand dollars that have escaped your grasp while you've been wasting your time talking to me."

Violet turned and disappeared into the room with the girls before he could respond, which was just as well. He couldn't think of anything to say that he wouldn't have had to apologize for afterward. And feeling as he did then, he would have choked before he apologized to that woman.

She had attacked him where he was most vulnerable. He had always been uneasy about some of the reasons for the war. Trying to ignore them didn't work. Violet's bringing them up and throwing them in his face merely made the situation worse.

It revived all his anger at men like his father who didn't understand that honor was something more than pigheadedly keeping to one side of an issue just because they'd declared that was where they were going to stay. Honor required that they be right. Too many lives hung in the balance.

Violet had reminded him of the futility, the cruelty, the brutality of war, of the men who had lost their lives, who had suffered more than he, all because some men were not willing to compromise, were not willing to look for other ways to solve their problems.

She had brought back into the center of his consciousness a battle he had fought with himself and never won: the conflict between his love for Virginia and all it represented to him, and his dislike of the war that had destroyed it.

Damn the woman! She had thrown him back into the hell he'd been trying to escape for 15 years.

Violet wished she had somewhere to retreat until she stopped shaking, but she couldn't think of anyplace where Jeff couldn't follow her. Beth and the girls eyed her curiously when she walked into the room. She had to smile, pretend everything was normal, but she was sure hers was a strained smile. Her control was stretched dangerously tight.

"Is Mr. Randolph going to come back?" Essie asked.

"Maybe after dinner," Violet said. "He's busy right now."

Busy wanting to wring her neck. She shouldn't have attacked him, but she couldn't remain quiet when he spouted such rubbish. Maybe he believed everything he said—she couldn't answer to that—but not everyone in the South had the same sense of moral justice. He probably did fight purely for the right to secede. He was the

151

kind of idealist who could do something like that. When it failed, he would have had a difficult time adjusting to the failure of his ideal.

"Are we going to talk about our reading?" Juliette asked.

"Has everyone finished?" Violet asked. Only the twins and Corrine raised their hands. "I think we need a little more time."

She shouldn't have attacked Jeff personally. She could tell he hadn't been able to put the war behind him. Her brother had felt that way, too. His life had stopped the minute that twisted piece of metal had entered his body and tried to tear up everything inside him.

But Jeff hadn't given up. He simply refused to forget. Violet wouldn't have cared about that. It would be unreasonable to ask anyone to forget something as momentous as a war, being disabled, being a prisoner. However, it hadn't ended his life. She couldn't understand why he still let it weigh him down.

"I'm bored," Juliette said.

"Me, too," Aurelia said.

Violet glanced at Corrine, but the girl didn't say anything. "Can either of you help Essie with her math?"

"I can," Juliette said.

"Me, too," Aurelia said.

"Will you help them, Corrine?" Violet asked. Corrine was older. She was good at arithmetic and could be relied on to keep the twins from doing anything outrageous.

"Yes, Miss Goodwin."

"Then the four of you can go into the dining room. You can use one of Beth's tables, but you must set it properly when you're through working."

"Yes, Miss Goodwin," they said together.

"And I want you to return to your seats as soon as you're done. Study period is not over until six."

"Yes, Miss Goodwin."

The room settled into quiet, and Violet's thoughts soon returned to Jeff, where they always seemed to be those days.

She had guessed some time ago that he used his work as an escape, a way to hide, but she was beginning to suspect there was more to it than that. He hated war as much as she did. He had said it was a stupid, ineffectual way to settle a dispute, yet he had fought in one. She didn't understand that. Robert and her father had believed in the war. They had supported Lincoln's position from the first. She had argued with both of them, but they had discounted everything she said because she was a woman who, they had claimed, didn't know what she was talking about. Exactly the same phrase Jeff had used.

Yet there was something behind his words, something he probably wouldn't admit to himself, much less to her, that robbed them of some of their sting. She couldn't help wondering what it was.

"Miss Goodwin!"

"Yes, Betty Sue."

"I'm bored, too."

Violet discovered that she had no taste for beef stew. It was a good thing Jeff hadn't asked her to share his dinner. She wasn't the least bit hungry.

She hadn't expected him to invite her that night, not after the argument they'd had. In fact, she had memorized what she meant to say to decline his invitation. She ought to be relieved. It would have been awkward at best. Nevertheless, she was disappointed. There was a great deal of difference between being able to refuse an invitation and not having it extended in the first place.

Her life was a shambles, she thought as she stared at the cooling stew. She didn't have any money. She had no prospects for a job outside the walls of the Wolfe School, and she had just alienated the one man who was powerful enough to help her get both. All because she couldn't forgive the South for destroying her family.

She was just as bad as Jeff was. She accused him of holding on to the past. So did she. She had no visible wound, no empty sleeve to wave in people's faces, but she had her memories to keep her anger warm and alive. And when the South seemed much too insubstantial to hate, she could focus on Robert E. Lee.

Wouldn't you know he would end up being one of Jeff's relatives? She didn't know why she was surprised. Lee had to be related to somebody. Lots of people, if she could judge from the size of most Southern families. She could have run across his relatives just about anywhere. But she had run across one of them there, and he'd been the first man to attract her interest since Nathan Wainwright had asked her to marry him.

That was stupid, too. Jeff had made it abundantly clear he would never marry any woman who'd set foot out of the South. Fortunately she wasn't in love with him, at least not yet, but she liked him a lot. And it was the kind of like that leaned in the direction of marriage. Just her luck to fall for a man who hated everything about her, past and present.

"Miss Goodwin, can I go see Mr. Randolph now?" Essie asked, breaking into Violet's thoughts.

Chapter Eleven

Jeff watched as Essie started her last problem. He couldn't understand why the child had so much trouble with arithmetic. She ought to be good at it. Harold Brown certainly had no trouble understanding the principles of addition and multiplication. At the rate he was applying them, he would soon be one of Denver's richest men. And Essie, his only child, would be one of Denver's greatest heiresses.

Jeff's work lay in front of him, scattered and largely ignored. He hadn't been able to think of anything but Violet since their argument. At first he was so angry he had never wanted to speak to her again. He didn't even want to think about her. But of course he couldn't think of anything else.

The intensity of her anger had surprised him. She had constantly needled him with her gentle criticism. At times he was certain she was laughing at him, but she had always seemed in control of herself. Then she had taken the gloves off and landed him a facer right in front of a room full of gaping girls.

"Is that right?" Essie asked as she held her paper up for him to see.

"Exactly. Now why can't you do that all the time?"

"I don't know."

"Yes, you do. Tell me."

"I don't like my teacher," Essie finally said. "She scares me."

"What does she do?"

"She glares at me. I can't think when I'm scared."

"Are you afraid of Miss Goodwin?"

"No, I like her. I like Juliette and Aurelia, too. They're my friends."

"Do you think you could do your arithmetic for Miss Goodwin?" Seeing that Essie was weighing her answer, Jeff said, "It would make her happy."

"Would it make her stop making those funny sounds?"

"What funny sounds?" When Essie seemed reluctant to explain, he asked; "You have to tell me, Essie. It might be important. If you don't, I'll have to ask Miss Goodwin."

"No!"

The child looked so miserable that he felt sorry for her. "Did you do something you weren't supposed to do?" She nodded, and he asked, "What?"

"It's all Betty Sue's fault. She's a mean old cat. I hate her."

"What did you do?"

"Betty Sue said mean things about my daddy, and I was crying. Priscilla—she's the girl who sleeps in my room—told me, if I was going to cry, I could sleep in the hall. But it was dark in the hall. I was scared. Miss Goodwin told us she always sleeps with her door open so she can hear us if we need her. So I went upstairs."

"To sleep in Miss Goodwin's room?"

Essie shook her head. "Outside her door. But the floor

was hard, and I couldn't sleep. I'd stopped crying by then. So I went back downstairs to my bed.''

"What about the strange noises?" Jeff prodded.

"She talked funny. Not like she does all the time. Like she was upset about something. She wasn't crying, but she kept making funny noises like she wanted to cry.''

"Did she call out a name?"

"I forget."

"Was it Jonas?"

"I don't know," Essie said.

"Did you ever hear her make those funny noises again?"

"No."

Jeff glanced at his watch, which he kept on the table. "You'd better gather up your books and run downstairs. It's almost bedtime.''

"Will you help me tomorrow?"

"Your father will be here tomorrow. I bet he'd like it if you asked him.''

"Daddy never likes to help me."

"Ask him again. People change their minds sometimes.''

"Daddy doesn't."

"Even your father. Now run along. I don't want Miss Goodwin coming after you. She's liable to take a switch to me for keeping you up so late.''

Essie giggled. But she gathered up her things, pulled Jeff down so she could give him a kiss, and ran off downstairs.

Jeff touched his hand to his cheek. He wondered what it was about Essie that made her so unafraid of him. Even his own nieces wouldn't have thought to kiss him good night.

Kids wouldn't be so bad if they were all like Essie. Of course they weren't. No point in thinking about it. What kid would want a father without an arm?

The dormitory was getting to him. First he started inviting a Yankee female to dinner. Next he was thinking about kids. Soon he'd be thinking about marriage.

Jeff wasn't aware of the noise until it stopped. He listened intently, but heard nothing. He glanced at his watch. 2:37 a.m. The building had been quiet for hours. Violet and Beth had gone to bed before ten. The girls earlier. Monday would be a school day. Monday would be the day the quarantine ended.

Maybe he hadn't heard anything. Maybe Essie's talk about strange noises had planted the idea in his mind. Violet or Beth could have turned over in their beds or mumbled in a dream. It certainly wasn't anything he should concern himself with.

2:51 a.m. He was certain he had heard a whimper, a faint moan. Less than 15 minutes had passed. He paused. The figures in his head gradually lost their grip on his concentration and slid from his thoughts. What could he do if something was wrong? Even if Violet did cry in her sleep, it was probably best to leave her alone. Besides, the noise might have come from Beth's room.

Jeff tried to go back to his work, but part of his mind kept listening for the sound again. He wondered if he was imagining things. He'd heard nothing the previous nights.

When the whimpering sound came a third time, he was almost relieved. He started to get up, but settled back in his chair. What could he do? In all his 37 years, he'd never had to comfort an upset woman. In fact, he'd never had to do anything for a woman. He'd always been too far away.

The sound came again. That time it did sound as if Violet was crying. He got to his feet, undecided. She must have done that before. He doubted she would appreciate his knowing about it.

He left his room, but stopped just outside her door.

Violet's room was hardly more than eight by ten feet with a window in the center of the far wall. An oak frame bed stood to the right of the window. A table and wardrobe stood against the left wall.

Moonlight fell on the bed, making Violet's face visible. She was having some kind of dream. She moved restlessly, her lips forming silent words, her head moving from side to side, her fists clenched tightly at her sides.

Suddenly she spoke with absolutely clarity. "Jonas, you can't do this!"

Her brother.

"You're all I've got. You can't die!"

She was becoming more agitated. Jeff teetered on the brink of indecision. He entered her room. What was he doing there? He didn't know what to do, and he felt terribly out of place. He had no experience with that kind of intimacy. He couldn't change anything. Considering what had passed between them earlier in the day, he doubted she'd want any comfort he could offer. But the sound of her distress drew him deeper into the room, closer to her bedside.

Even though her skin seemed unnaturally white, her loveliness was not diminished by the moonlight. Her magnificent halo of hair gleamed nearly black, her brows and lashes ebony. Only her lips retained their warm, lustrous color. Inviting lips. Lips that begged to be kissed.

"Jonas!"

It was almost a shout. Violet rolled over so far Jeff feared she would fall out of the bed.

He dropped to his knees and reached out with an arm to keep her from falling. It was awkward. He had to support her with his stump. With his right arm, he tried to lift her and move her back onto the bed. Instead she threw her arms around him and held him tight.

"Jonas!" It was a sigh of relief, of near contentment.

He didn't dare move. He couldn't, but not just from fear of waking her. No woman had ever clung to him for comfort. He just knelt there, as still as a statue, wondering what to do next.

His brothers would have laughed at him. Well, maybe not George, but the rest would have enjoyed the scene. Rose would have told him it served him right for being such a cross-grained cuss.

Even as Jeff slipped his right arm around Violet's shoulders to support her, he was acutely aware of his stump, of a desire to move it away from her, of a need to hide it. But his instinctive reaction was to fold her in both arms.

He ought to get out of there as soon as possible. He shouldn't even be touching her. What if Beth woke up? But Violet's distress affected him as no other woman's ever had. He was upset because she was upset. He felt the need to comfort her even though he knew it was a mistake. Violet was a Yankee. He shouldn't be feeling that way about her. He couldn't let himself.

He must be crazy! He was only trying to comfort a woman who had cried out in her sleep. He was making far too much out of the whole thing.

But he knew better than that. From the moment she had stepped into the parlor two weeks earlier, Violet Goodwin had inflamed his emotions, muddled his thoughts, and stirred up feelings he had hoped were dead and buried.

Jeff brushed aside the hair that had fallen across her face. Despite the years he had spent going to see Louise, he'd never touched a woman. Not really touched her. It felt different, as if he was experiencing it for the first time. He'd never known skin could be so soft, like warm velvet. He wanted to caress every part of her face until he memorized the contours of her cheeks, the stiffness of her lashes, the softness of her lips.

Jeff didn't know what caused him to do it—he would

have said it was the last thing he'd ever do—but he kissed her. It was more a brushing of the lips than a real kiss, but its effect on him was the same as if it had been a passionate embrace. He wanted to kiss her again, really kiss her. He also wanted to drop her, scramble down the lift, and tramp about in the bitter cold until this hot madness left him.

Then Violet stirred awake. She raised her head from his chest and a look of panic spread over her face. ''What are you doing here?'' she asked pushing him away.

Jeff hardly knew how to respond. Did she know he had kissed her? She seemed truly shocked to find herself in his arms. Almost frightened. Surely she didn't think—no, not even a Yankee could think he would attack a woman in her sleep.

''You were having a bad dream. You nearly fell off the bed. When I tried to lift you back—''

She pulled the covers up around her shoulders. Only then did he realize her nightgown was cut low and made of some silky looking material.

''Thank you.''

''Can I do anything to help?'' He wanted to do something, though he had no idea what. She was alone. She needed comfort.

''I'm all right now. You can go back to your room.''

He felt a spasm of relief. She didn't know. ''Are you sure you're all right?''

''Yes.''

''You cried out for Jonas. Why?''

''I told you. He died.''

''But that wouldn't make you dream about him. You didn't the other nights.''

''Talking about the war brought it all back. I knew it would. I shouldn't have brought it up.''

''What happened to him?''

''I told you. He died,'' Violet said.

"But there was something else."

Violet pulled the cover closer around her and slipped back down into the bed. "He didn't have to die. The doctors said he could get well if he wanted to. But he wanted to die. He wouldn't take his medicine. He wouldn't eat. He wouldn't see anyone or do anything. He just lay there waiting."

Jeff understood. He had felt the same way at first. But it wasn't long before he had gotten over it, started wanting to live again. Life hadn't held much promise for him either, but he hadn't been ready to trade it for angel wings—or, according to Monty, devil's horns.

"There was a sweet young girl who loved him. She would have married him as he was. She was rich. He could have had the best medical care available. But he wouldn't see her. He wouldn't read her letters. He told her that his life was ruined and she should not ruin hers as well."

"What did she do?"

"She finally went away. She wanted a husband and a family. She found somebody else. She's happy now. But I could never see her husband without thinking that he could have been Jonas if he had just had the courage to live. I loved my brother dearly. I would have done anything for him, but I think I almost came to hate him for being such a coward."

Coward! His father's voice echoed down the deeply eroded canyons of Jeff's memory. Coward! Coward!

Jeff felt himself pull away. Violet seemed to sense it.

"You'd better go," she said. "Thank you for coming."

Jeff stood. He felt awkward. "Are you sure you'll be all right?" That was a damned stupid question. Nobody ever got hurt by a bad dream.

"I'm fine. I'd better get back to sleep. Tomorrow will be a busy day."

He didn't know why he didn't feel right leaving her.

He didn't know what he could do if he stayed.

"Haven't you been to bed yet?" she asked.

"I still have work to do."

"Jonas missed his life because he died. You're going to miss yours because you never stop working. I don't know which is worse."

That remark stung. There she was, only half awake, scared out of her mind because of some damned nightmare, and she couldn't stop criticizing him.

"I've got to catch up with all that money I let slip past me this afternoon," Jeff said.

Violet looked puzzled. She didn't remember. He felt foolish for being so caustic. Then she did remember and looked embarrassed. He felt like a scoundrel for bringing it up.

"I know better than to let myself start talking about the war," she said. "I always say something I shouldn't. And then I always dream of Jonas."

Damn her! She made him feel as if he ought to apologize. And he'd never apologized to anybody. He was too old to start doing it now.

"I guess all of us say things when we're angry that we later wish we hadn't."

Hell, that was practically an apology. What was wrong with his tongue? It seemed to be rattling on without any regard for what his brain was telling it. He backed toward the door before he could say anything else.

"Call me if you need anything," he said. "I'll be up a while yet."

"Go to sleep. I'm sure you'll catch up with that money sooner or later. People like you always do."

Jeff took one last look. She had pulled the covers up to her chin and was lying on her side, her face toward him, her eyes closed.

"Should I close the door?" he asked.

"No."

He knew that. Essie had told him. He was casting about for an excuse to linger. He was trying to explain to himself the reason for that kiss. He was hoping to understand why the woman was so different from all the rest. The answer was almost there, just out of reach. If he left, he might never find it.

But there was no reason to stay, no reason to know. He never meant to kiss her again. The sooner he forgot about it, the sooner he could put these five days behind him.

Jeff turned and headed toward his room. Inside, he dropped into his chair like a runner at the end of a race. He was going to have to face it. His feeling for Violet was more than physical. He didn't understand how it could have happened, but it obviously had.

His brothers would give half of everything they owned to know. After what he'd said about their wives, the way he'd acted over the years, they'd never let him forget it. It didn't matter that his feelings were little more than liking. By the time they got through with it, Romeo and Juliet's love would sound like a passing fancy.

He picked up his papers and forced his mind back on his work. He didn't have long to endure. By tomorrow afternoon he'd be gone and forgotten.

Violet appeared in his doorway while he was still exercising. He wore a pair of pants and a cotton shirt. He lowered the bar when he saw her.

"I want to thank you for last night," she said. "I'm sorry I pushed you away. I was upset."

She seemed unsure of herself, almost shy. He wondered if she felt the change between them. He couldn't define it, but he knew it was there. They had shared something, and it had formed a link, however tenuous, between them.

"I had no business staying so long," Jeff said. "Somebody could have come up."

She definitely looked nervous. "I know you don't like women much, especially Yankee women. It meant a lot."

Denial rose to his lips, but it was too late. He was leaving soon. It wouldn't make any difference.

"I don't usually have nightmares like that unless I'm tired," she said. "I didn't get my last two days off." She brightened. "But it won't be so bad once the quarantine's over. The girls will be outside or in class most of the day."

"And I'll be gone."

Violet looked agitated again, as if she needed to say something, but didn't want to.

"I'm sure you'll be relieved," Jeff said. "These last few days must have been a strain on you, not to mention your staff."

He'd done everything but pray for the end of the quarantine, but with it there, he felt something important was about to end. Violet was a bossy, opinionated woman, but he'd be a little sorry not to see her again. It was hard to believe it could have happened so fast, but he'd gotten used to having her around. She could make him mad as fire, but she had touched places inside him that had been gathering dust. She was a fresh wind that made him feel more alive, feel less numb.

"It hasn't been as bad as I expected. I hope Essie gets better with her arithmetic," Jeff said.

Violet seemed to gather herself, take a deep breath, and go back to her usual, businesslike self. "I'm sure she will. Now you'd better hurry up and finish with the bathroom. This is a school day. The girls will be up early."

He watched as she walked down the hall, her rich coral satin dress swaying as she moved. In a moment, she disappeared down the stairs. In a few hours, he would go down those steps for the last time, but he would leave the building a different man. He didn't know yet whether that was good or bad.

Iris eased open the door and looked in. Fern was sitting up in the bed, staring out the window, her breakfast tray across her lap.

"I told Monty you'd be up," Iris said, practically bouncing into the room. "He was sure you'd sleep until noon."

"Iris! What are you doing here?" Suspicious moisture glistened in Fern's eyes. "When did you get in? I thought you were fixed at the ranch at least until Christmas."

Fern gave her sister-in-law a warm hug, then dropped down on the bed. The breakfast tray tilted to one side, and the remains of Fern's coffee slopped into the saucer.

"Let me take that before I make an unholy mess." Iris put the tray on a table by the bed. "Now tell me how you're doing?"

"Not until you tell me why you're here," Fern said.

Iris grinned and dropped back on the bed. "I didn't want to be, but my hardheaded husband insisted."

"Where is he?"

"Playing with the boys."

"I can't imagine why he does, but I'm grateful. They adore him. Now stop trying to change the subject, and tell me why you're here."

"The miracle finally happened."

"What miracle? It can't be that Monty has finally grown up."

"Maybe I should have let your coffee splash all over you."

"I take it back. Besides, I like Monty just the way he is."

"So do I, most of the time," Iris said, her good humor restored.

"Out with it."

"I'm pregnant. I'm finally pregnant." Iris hugged her sister-in-law once more. "As soon as he found out, Monty decided I was too weak and fragile to spend one moment of the next seven months not under a doctor's eye. If I hadn't come on my own, he would have picked me up and carried me."

"Daisy's expecting, too."

"I know. We got into the hotel last night. I couldn't believe that place. It's a good thing Tyler found an entire gold mine. It must have cost a fortune."

"And it's making one. Daisy says they have people fighting over the rooms."

Iris laughed. "Tyler looked disgusted when I told him I was pregnant. He said the family was going to have to build a maternity hospital." Iris sobered. "How are you doing? Daisy says you've been having a rough time."

"Nobody seems to know what's wrong. I never slowed down for a minute the other times. This time I knew something was different right from the start."

"Probably means it's going to be a girl," Iris said, trying to sound cheerful. "Even before she gets here, she's letting you know she's not going to put up with anything from her four older brothers."

"I hope you're right. It would be nice to have a girl. I love the boys dearly, but I'd like one child who was a little less noisy than a herd of elk."

"Where is your handsome husband?"

"Jeff sent him to Leadville. There's some trouble about the mines."

"Why didn't Jeff go himself?"

"You know Jeff. He won't leave that bank unless he's made to." Suddenly Fern started laughing. "You won't believe what happened."

By the time Fern had finished the story, both women were laughing so hard they were crying.

"Wait until Monty hears this," Iris said between bursts of laughter. "He likes Jeff even less than Madison

167

does. Do you think he'll come here when he gets out?''

"Probably. Why?''

"I expect he's about to go crazy. I know it's not nice of me, but I'd love to see Jeff fall apart. Just once, I'd like to see him shaken out of his I-know-everything stance.''

"If anything could do it, being shut up with sixteen little girls and a Yankee housemother would.''

Iris didn't like the lines of fatigue she saw etched in Fern's face. It was only morning.

"Have you been sleeping well?''

"Not really. I never sleep well when Madison's away.''

"You poor woman! He's away half the year. You have four years of sleep to catch up on.''

Fern smiled. "It's not that bad, but I do wish he'd finish this business soon. The boys need at least one parent who can stand up. They tend not to take me very seriously when I'm lying down.''

"I can take care of that,'' Iris said. "Now I have to find Monty before he teaches them to ignore every rule you've ever taught them.''

Fern smiled. "That's not many. Considering they have Madison and me for parents, I'm surprised they've learned to live indoors.''

"No, my child is the one who's going to be labeled wolfman. It'll serve Monty right if it's a girl. Can you imagine him trying to deal with a wolfgirl?''

They both went into peals of laughter.

"I said I was going, and here I still am,'' Iris said. She pulled the bedclothes up around Fern. "You lie back. I have a few things to do, but I'll come back and sit with you this afternoon.''

The moment she closed the door, Iris went in search of Monty. When she found him, she said, "You get on that telegraph—or whatever it takes to reach Leadville— and tell Madison to come home this instant. Something is dreadfully wrong with Fern.''

Chapter Twelve

Violet paced the parlor. Jeff's clerks had spent most of the morning removing their files and desks and putting the furniture back the way they had found it. Even at that moment, they were waiting to dismantle the lift that had creaked and groaned for several days, carrying the steady flow of papers, food, and clothes to Jeff's room. The parlor seemed strangely quiet. Only the smell of fresh ashes in the fireplace hinted at the frenzied activity that had centered around this room.

Inside, the girls were eating their lunch. Violet ought to have been eating hers as well, but she wasn't hungry. Any minute, Beth would announce the end of the quarantine. Violet's two weeks of incarceration would be over. But she wasn't thinking about herself. She was thinking of Jeff Randolph.

After their argument of the previous day, she was sure she never wanted to speak to him again. But after the past night, she wondered. He wasn't an easy man to understand. He wasn't easy on himself or others. He didn't know very much about women. He did the wrong thing more often than not, but there was something about him that wouldn't let her forget him.

She had seen too many instances of his temper and lack of consideration; she had heard far more than she ever wanted about the war. If she never heard the word Yankee again, she'd be thankful. The man had more blind spots than a one-eyed mule, and he was just about as stubborn.

But there was something very different buried deep inside him. Essie had seen it right away. Violet had caught only a glimpse. Until the previous night she thought she was fooling herself. It was so easy to make excuses for a man who looked like Jeff Randolph.

Something quivered deep in her belly every time she remembered what he looked like in those short pants. It was shocking to think she was so susceptible to a physical attraction, but she had to face the truth. Where Jeff Randolph was concerned, she was nonsensical. And she was beginning to imagine things. She must be. She was convinced he'd kissed her while she'd slept.

The strain of being in quarantine must have been getting to her. She couldn't think of anything more unlikely. She had been surprised he'd forgotten his work long enough to know she was having a bad dream. She was stunned to find herself in his arms, even after he explained she'd been about to fall out of the bed. She was surprised he hadn't let her tumble onto the floor.

No, that was unfair. He might have disliked her, but there was a certain gallantry about him that would make him behave the same way to her as he did all women, even if she was a Yankee. But it wouldn't make him kiss her. She wished it had.

The thought appalled her. Surely she hadn't become so captivated by his looks that she wanted him to kiss her. She'd dreamed of him, but that was a natural reaction to being around an attractive man. Wanting him to kiss her meant something else entirely. The door to the dormitory opened, cutting off the thread of her thoughts.

"It's twelve o'clock," Beth said. "The quarantine is ended."

Violet didn't have a chance to feel relief or disappointment before the girls came streaming past her like puppies released from a pen. She had said they could spend an hour enjoying themselves outside. They seemed determined not to miss a minute. When the twins reached the door, Violet put a hand on their shoulders and pulled them aside.

"Aren't you going to say good-bye to your uncle?" she asked.

"We can wave to him," Aurelia said.

"I don't think that's enough," Violet said. "You're the reason he's here. And you haven't spent much time with him."

"He's too crabby," Juliette said.

"He likes Essie better than us," Aurelia said.

"Nevertheless, you must tell him good-bye and thank him for coming by to talk to me about you," Violet said.

"Can we wait outside?" Aurelia asked.

"He might be forever coming down," Juliette said.

"Okay, but don't go so far you can't hear me when I call you."

"We won't," the girls chanted in chorus. Then they scampered through the door before Violet could change her mind.

"You think the girls will be ready to come inside after an hour?" Beth asked. They both watched as the girls chased each other across the wide lawn, whooping and laughing as they went.

"After two weeks of inactivity, they'll be so exhausted they won't be able to stand."

Beth looked over her shoulder at the door leading into the dormitory. "When is he leaving?"

"Soon. I don't imagine he'll want to stay a minute longer than he must."

It was as though her words drew him forth. The door opened and Jeff and Essie entered the parlor. Violet hadn't set eyes on him since early that morning—she had forced herself to stay away from him—but she couldn't get enough of him at that moment. He was so handsome, dressed in a dark blue wool suit with a crisp white shirt and a black bow tie. His blond hair had been combed into place while still wet, but enough strands had escaped to relieve the severity of his appearance. His eyes were as blue as she remembered, his shoulders as broad. Violet had to remind herself to breathe.

Jeff was leaving. She wouldn't have to worry about avoiding him anymore. She wouldn't have to worry about his using the bathtub, waking her up with his exercising, or asking her to dinner. She wouldn't have to worry about her body's unexpected reaction to his presence. Her life could return to normal. Never had normalcy held so little appeal.

Essie threw herself at Violet. "Please make him stay."

"I'm sure he's anxious to get back to his office," Violet said, startled by Essie's request. "You can't expect him to want to stay in a building full of little girls."

"You're not a little girl."

Violet's gaze flew to Jeff's face before she could stop herself. He looked as uncomfortable as she felt. "Mr. Randolph has a job and a family and lots of things to do."

"The twins said, if they were bad, you'd make him come back."

"I don't think that's a good idea," Violet said.

"But I want him to meet my daddy."

"I've already met your father," Jeff said.

"But I want to show you to him."

"Maybe some other time," Violet said.

Essie turned from Violet to Jeff. She tugged on his arm. "You will come back, won't you? Please."

Violet thought Jeff looked close to losing his temper. Essie had probably been plaguing him all morning. Violet should have been paying attention to her job instead of wallowing in her own confusion.

"I have a better idea," Jeff said. "Suppose I have your father bring you to the bank sometime?"

Essie practically bounced up and down. "Promise?"

"I promise."

"I see your papa down by the road," Beth said.

"Why don't you run out to meet him?" Violet said.

"You can see Daddy now," Essie cried. "You won't go away before I get back, will you?"

"I promise to wait right here," Jeff said.

Relieved of that worry, Essie shot through the door Beth held open and dashed across the lawn to meet her father.

"I'm sorry. I never thought she'd plague you so," Violet said.

"She'll forget about me soon enough," Jeff said, but his expression was tight about the eyes.

Violet doubted any of the residents of the dormitory would forget him that easily. They stood there in awkward silence.

"Do you have a carriage coming for you?" Violet asked after a while.

"I never ride," Jeff said. "Walking is some of the best exercise. You ought to try it."

"I do," Violet said, stung. "But I can't get away from my duties for very long."

"You ought to make it part of the girls' regime. Maybe I'll speak to Miss Settle."

"You'll get your chance right now," Beth said. "She's coming down the walk."

They moved outside. Miss Settle, her assistant, and two members of the school board must have been waiting. They started forward as soon as they saw Jeff.

Violet held back. She watched them fawn over him, showering him with the kind of attention they would only bestow on a rich and powerful man. Once he glanced in her direction, and she thought he looked as if he wished she would rescue him. But that was ridiculous. He was used to that kind of attention. He must know how to handle it.

She tried to focus her thoughts on the girls, on Essie, on anything but Jeff and the fact he was leaving. He had already gone—Miss Settle and the others had closed around him—he just wasn't out of sight.

Violet had started down the walk to meet Essie and her father when Jeff broke away from the group. He came over, took Violet by the hand, and drew her over to Miss Settle.

"Miss Goodwin handled everything very well," he said. With his hand in the small of her back, he placed her directly in front of him. "It can't be easy to be shut up with so many girls for two weeks. I think you ought to give her a week off to recover."

Violet was stunned, but hardly less so than Miss Settle.

"We have no one to replace her!" the headmistress exclaimed.

"What about yourself?" Jeff asked.

The board members looked shocked. Miss Settle looked ready to faint.

Violet turned to scan Jeff's face, searching for a reason why he would make such a suggestion. Was he trying to provoke Miss Settle the way he had provoked her? He looked at her out of blue eyes that gave no hint of what he might be thinking.

"That won't be necessary," Violet said to Miss Settle. Her words sounded overly loud as they tumbled into the shocked silence. "I'll be quite recovered in no time."

"Nonsense," Jeff said. "You're exhausted. You're going to spend a couple of days at Tyler's hotel. I insist."

A couple of days! He remembered.

"The Windsor!" Miss Settle gasped. "But they never have any rooms."

"Tyler keeps two suites for the family," Jeff said. "She can stay in one of those."

"But—" Violet said.

"There's nothing more to discuss," Jeff said. "Tyler will send a carriage for you at four o'clock. That'll give you time to get settled before dinner. You can find somebody to stay with the girls by then, can't you, Eleanor?" Jeff said to Miss Settle, who gaped at him. "You'd better if you don't want the girls running loose. Imagine the twins left on their own for two days."

Miss Settle looked as nonplussed as Violet felt, but Jeff just said, "Now where are the little monsters? I guess I ought to take a last look to make sure they haven't broken anything since I saw them."

Violet pulled herself together sufficiently to motion to the twins. Essie dragged her father up first.

"This is my daddy," the little girl said proudly.

Despite not having recovered from the shock of Jeff's invitation, Violet felt her eyes water. She'd never seen Essie so happy. She looked up at her father as though he were the only person in the whole world. Even her adored Jeff was almost invisible in her father's presence. Harold Brown was tall and thin, an austere man with a thick black mustache and muttonchop whiskers. He looked miserably uncomfortable. Violet wanted to pull his mustache out hair by hair for ignoring Essie for so long. She hoped Jeff would hold that loan over Harold's head for as long as possible.

"Glad to see you're so prompt," Jeff said, a cold warning in his voice. "Essie's been missing you."

"I've been busy," Mr. Brown said. "What with work and this quarantine, I—"

"It's been hard on all of us," Miss Settle said, recovering sufficiently to speak to another wealthy patron. "I'm sure you're glad to have your precious daughter restored to you happy and healthy."

"For which you have Miss Goodwin to thank," Jeff said.

"No one else was allowed to enter the building," one board member said. He was a self-important little man, fat and bald, too old to have any but a granddaughter in the school. "The law forbids it."

"It's been good to see you, Brown. I don't want to take up your time with your daughter," Jeff said, then turned to Miss Settle. "Don't forget that Miss Goodwin is to be ready to leave at four. Oh, God, here come my nieces."

As Aurelia and Juliette approached cautiously, Violet said, "Come on. He won't bite you."

"Maybe not," Jeff said, "but if you get into any more trouble, I'm liable to murder you and hide your bodies."

The adults laughed easily. The twins weren't so confident.

"You proved you could behave this week, so I expect you to keep doing it."

"Yes, Uncle Jeff," the twins said in unison.

"Good. Now get lost."

Taking him at his word, the twins disappeared as fast as they could run.

"Such beautiful little girls," Miss Settle said. "You must be extremely proud of them."

"I'd be a lot prouder if they weren't so damned much trouble," Jeff said before turning to Violet. "We dress for dinner," he said. With that, he turned on his heel and headed toward the road. Violet and the others stared after him in silence.

"I guess you'd better start your packing, Miss Goodwin," the first board member said to her. "You don't want to keep him waiting."

"Where am I going to find someone to take her place on such short notice?" Miss Settle asked. "The twins are such troublesome girls."

"Try to find someone they'll like," the second board member said. He was also fat and bald, but he was young and clean shaven. Violet had met his daughter. "Our boys' school will be finished next year. We can't afford to have all those male Randolphs go somewhere else."

"I'll expect you back no later than noon on Wednesday, Miss Goodwin," Miss Settle said. "I really don't know what that man expects me to do without you."

Violet didn't have any thoughts to spare for Miss Settle. She was trying to calm the upheaval of emotion inside her. Hope, fear, fantasy, cynicism, speculation, common sense, and a dozen other feelings fought for primacy. She was also trying to figure out what had prompted Jeff's invitation. He had remembered what she had said last night. He had arranged time off for her. What more might he want to do?

He had invited her to stay in the family hotel. The possible interpretations were endless. Violet told herself it would be a waste of time to try to sort them out. She would find out what he meant soon enough.

Jeff surveyed Fern's drawing room with open revulsion. Just his luck to find that every member of his family within a hundred miles was gathered here. He was even more disgusted that Iris and Daisy were pregnant and Monty and Tyler acted as if they'd done something to be proud of. No one had reacted well to his observation that even gophers managed to have babies.

He probably should have gone to see Louise instead. He was sure physical release would help him banish the image of Violet Goodwin from his mind. But he wasn't in the mood for Louise's company. He had no appetite for her boisterous gaiety. Frustrated and confused by his feelings, he had decided to make his report to Fern.

"The little monsters behaved themselves while I was there," he said, "but I wouldn't put it past them to do something disgraceful any minute now. I don't know how anybody as dull as George could have fathered those two hellcats."

"It's just high spirits," Iris said. "I remember being sent away to boarding school. I hated every minute of it until I was old enough to go to parties."

"Then you can go stay with them."

"I might, to get away from Monty. I'd probably have more freedom."

Jeff felt slightly nauseated by the way Monty grinned at his wife. Monty wasn't his favorite brother, but until Monty had met Iris, he'd never turned foolish over women. Tyler seemed to be holding up better. At least he had the good sense to keep working. They'd all go crazy if they had Monty around all winter with nothing to do.

"I wish you hadn't telegraphed Rose," Fern said. "After all, I did promise to take care of those girls."

"You can't be expected to do that when you can't get out of bed," Daisy said.

"No one can control those girls," Monty said. "I dread to think of what they'll be like in ten years."

"Well I'm not having anything to do with them," Jeff said, "not ten minutes from now or ten years. I got more than enough being locked up with them for four days."

Devilment stirred in Monty's eyes. "Fern tells me the housemother is a beautiful Yankee temptress."

"She had red hair. I expect you'd know more about that than I would," Jeff said.

"Just what do you mean by that?" Monty asked, firing up.

"What's she like?" Iris asked, trying to prevent an

argument. "Fern says she's quite nice."

That wasn't a word he'd have used to describe Violet. Spirited, intelligent, pretty, and dangerous all came closer to the elusive qualities that made her impossible to forget.

"She's from Massachusetts," Jeff said as five pairs of eyes watched him. "What else do you want to know?"

He wasn't going to tell them about her skin, her hair, or the way she looked when she covered her eyes to keep from seeing his body.

"Good God, Jeff," Fern said, "millions of people come from Massachusetts. I imagine quite a few of them have red hair. They can't all be the same."

"I wouldn't know." He was certain none of them were like Violet.

"You did speak to her, didn't you?" Tyler asked. "You did invite her to share all that food I sent you?"

"Yes, I did," Jeff said, turning on his taciturn brother. "And I'll thank you not to do anything like that again. She was just as miserable as I was."

No, he was the one who had been miserable. She had tried to act as if she had enjoyed being with him, but no woman could like spending an evening with a man who was alternately silent and argumentative.

"Nobody could be miserable eating Tyler's food," Iris said.

"They would if they had to eat it with Jeff," Monty said.

"What did she think of the Beef Randolph?" Iris asked. "We had some for dinner when we arrived. I swear I could have eaten another meal."

"She didn't come to dinner that night," Jeff told them. He had wondered if she would. He hadn't invited her, but he couldn't help but wonder.

"Why?" Fern asked.

"Do you need to ask?" Monty said. "Two meals with

him, and she's probably given up eating.''

"Why not?" Fern said, ignoring Monty. "You did invite her, didn't you?"

"No," Jeff said. Angry as he had been, he had been tempted. He'd spent the whole meal wondering what she was doing.

"You ought to have invited her just for putting up with you," Iris said.

"She wouldn't have come."

"Why?" Fern asked.

Jeff shouldn't have come. His relatives were going to squeeze every bit of information out of him, and they weren't going to like any of it. He didn't like it either.

"We had a disagreement," he said.

"You didn't mention the war, did you?" Fern asked, her brow furrowed.

"She asked me to explain the causes to the girls," Jeff said, and everyone in the room groaned.

"I thought you said she was an intelligent woman," Monty said. "She can't be if she couldn't tell within ten seconds that Jeff is a fool when it comes to that war."

"Fortunately for me, she didn't feel that way," Jeff said angrily. "Her brother was wounded during the last campaign. She doesn't ignore it like the rest of you."

After another round of groans, Monty asked, "If she's so understanding, why isn't she home looking after him?"

"Because he died," Jeff said.

"We weren't so fortunate."

"Monty!" Fern said.

"Hell, I get tired of hearing about something that happened fourteen years ago. If you're going to discuss it, I'll leave." Monty got up and opened the door, but the sound of pounding feet stopped him. He turned to Fern, a quizzical look on his face. "You keep cows in the house? It sounds like a damned stampede."

Fern smiled happily. "It's the boys. Their classes are

over. It's time to visit me before they go outside.''

Jeff started toward the door. ''This seems like a good time to make my escape. By the way, since you're all so interested in Miss Goodwin, you'll be happy to know you'll be able to make her acquaintance. After her harrowing experience with the twins, I invited her to spend two days at the hotel.''

''What?'' Fern said, stunned.

''I don't believe it!'' Iris said.

''Where are we going to put her?'' Daisy said. ''We're full up.''

''In George and Rose's suite,'' Jeff said.

''You can't just invite someone to stay in the hotel without telling us,'' Tyler said.

''Well, I have. And before I forget it, she'll be expecting you to send a carriage for her at four o'clock.''

''I simply can't believe it,'' Iris said, more to herself than anyone else.

''How will you get your work done at the hotel?'' Daisy asked. ''You know you always complain of the noise.''

''I'll be in my office as usual,'' Jeff said.

''But who's going to entertain Miss Goodwin?'' Daisy asked.

''You. I did it for four days.'' Jeff smiled at their looks of outrage. ''Just consider it your contribution to the twins' education.''

He almost got through the door before three raven-headed boys looking like stair-step versions of each other raced into the room. A nurse followed with a fourth child of about two. The two oldest boys threw themselves at Monty.

''Can you play now?'' the older one asked.

''I want to ride in your lap this time,'' the younger one said.

''James, you and Tazewell come here,'' Fern said. ''And don't run over Tucker and Stuart to do it.''

"I don't know why you let Madison saddle those boys with such ridiculous names," Monty said. "They'll have to fight their way all through school."

"They're good Randolph names," Jeff said, finding himself in the unusual position of defending one of his brothers.

"They're no worse than Aurelia and Juliette," Fern said.

"From what Jeff says, they're fighting their way through the entire city of Denver," Iris said.

As the others continued their conversation, Jeff made his escape. For a good 20 minutes, all talk was dominated by Fern's young sons. But after they had gone off with Monty and their nurse, Fern turned to Iris.

"Why on earth do you think Jeff invited Miss Goodwin to spend two days at the hotel?"

"I don't know, but you could have knocked me over when he said it," Iris said.

"Do you think he likes her?" Daisy asked.

Iris laughed. "You haven't been in the family very long, but one thing you'll soon learn is that Jeff doesn't like anybody who ever had any connection with the North. Poor man, he doesn't like me at all, but I'm the only sister-in-law his conscience will allow him to approve of."

"He deserves to fall in love with her," Daisy said. "Not only that, but it would serve him right if she turned him down flat."

"God Almighty!" Tyler said, sitting up faster than anyone could ever remember seeing him move. "Don't wish that on the family. We're not the nicest people in the world, but we don't deserve that."

One man let down the steps and held the door of the carriage for Violet to step out on the street in front of the Windsor Hotel. Another removed her luggage from the carriage and carried it inside. A third held the door for her to enter. A fourth guided her toward the lobby.

If she had been astonished before, she was suddenly overwhelmed. The hotel exceeded anything she had imagined. The lobby was huge. It seemed to stretch for the entire block. Floors and columns of white marble made it bright. Furniture and hangings in crimson and gold made it breathtaking. But Violet was truly overcome when a woman who stood at least six feet tall and was obviously pregnant approached her.

"You must be Miss Goodwin. I'm Daisy Randolph, Jeff's sister-in-law."

"Is he here?" Violet said, desperate to see at least one familiar face in the terrifyingly palatial establishment.

"Unfortunately, the pressure of business will keep him at the bank. I'm afraid you'll have to do with just family tonight. Unless, of course, you'd prefer your own company. Jeff says you're to be rewarded with two days of peace and quiet for being locked up with the terrible twins."

"I'd be delighted to join you, if you don't mind," Violet said, more terrified of being alone in the awe-inspiring place than meeting strangers. "I'll be glad for a chance to talk with Mrs. Madison Randolph."

"You do seem out of luck," a stunning woman with red hair said. Violet had always been teased about her red hair. But at that moment, she knew what red really looked like. "I'm Iris Randolph, another sister-in-law. Fern's doctor won't allow her to leave the house, but she insists you come to dinner tomorrow."

Feeling overawed by the two women, Violet nodded her agreement and allowed herself to be escorted toward an elevator. No wonder Jeff hadn't felt inclined to leave his work to be with her. Compared to the Randolph wives, Violet was hardly memorable. If they hadn't been shut up together because of the quarantine, Jeff certainly would never have noticed her.

"We're eating in the private dining room," Daisy said with a smile. "So don't feel you have to dress up. I'm sure you've guessed I'm expecting a child. Iris is, too. So we take every chance we can to be comfortable."

"My husband will be joining us if he can tear himself away from Fern's boys," Iris said.

"Mine, too," Daisy said, "if I can get him out of the kitchen. I never thought when we agreed to build this hotel together that I'd practically have to beg him to help me make a decision."

"You mean you run this place by yourself?" Violet said, wondering what Jeff thought about that. She couldn't imagine he approved of giving a woman so much power. But then he didn't have any control over his sisters-in-law. Maybe that was why he was staying away.

No, don't try to fool yourself. He's staying away because you're not reason enough for him to leave his work.

"I like running the hotel," Daisy said. She smiled as if she was sharing a secret among friends. "It's great fun telling men what to do. I do a good job, too, but everybody knows it's the food that keeps people clamoring for reservations."

Violet could believe that. She hadn't forgotten a single mouthful, or minute, of those two meals she had shared with Jeff. The elevator arrived on the second floor, and they stepped out.

"I'm putting you in the suite we keep for Rose and George. That's only fair since you've had to put up with their twins."

Daisy opened a door and ushered Violet into a fairy-tale room. Violet didn't think putting up with a houseful of genuine monsters could earn her the privilege of spending two nights in such luxury.

The sitting room was nearly the size of the school

parlor. After the spare simplicity of New England styles, the Louis XV furniture upholstered in royal-blue silk trimmed in silver seemed unbelievably sumptuous. The wall panels were white trimmed in gold. The carpet was blue and white with a crest in gold. The window hangings were blue velvet with silver tassels and chords.

The bedroom, dominated by a huge four-poster bed, was a vision of blue and white. A maid was already unpacking Violet's clothes and putting them away. When Violet realized she would have her own private bath, her heaven was complete.

"Dinner's at seven-thirty," Daisy said, then showed Violet a buzzer. "Ring if you want anything."

"We'll leave you alone to enjoy the peace and quiet," Iris said, "but I'll be next door in case you have any questions. I'll come for you when it's time for dinner."

Violet could only mumble her thanks, then stand in dumb amazement as she realized she was to spend two days as a pampered guest in the biggest suite in the fanciest, most-sought-after hotel in Denver.

She let out a whoop and collapsed on the bed. Certain some guests would think they were being attacked by Indians, she clamped her hand over her mouth, then broke out laughing. The walls were so thick, no one could have heard her. She would have to go back to being a housemother in two days, but until then she was going to enjoy every minute of the unbelievable luxury.

She couldn't imagine why Jeff had invited her and then had decided not to show up. But that really shouldn't have surprised her. It was just like him to feel he had to offer her some kind of compensation for putting up with him, but not feel he had to be part of it.

She was disappointed. She admitted that. She liked the stiff-necked cuss despite himself. She told herself she was being foolish to rate the will to survive so highly.

But after having lost her entire family because they lacked it, she couldn't help it. She didn't mind that he was a fighter, even if it meant she collected a few scratches along the way.

Chapter Thirteen

"You don't seem your usual self this evening, Jeff," Louise said. She opened her wrapper to give him a better view of her black-lace-covered corset. "It's not like you to want to eat first."

"Just tired," Jeff said. "I've been working harder than usual."

She eyed him over a glass of wine. "I wondered what kept you away so long. That's not like you." She threw her shoulders back. It made her ample bust seem even more impressive.

They sat at a table burdened with the remains of supper. Not nearly as good a supper as he would have enjoyed had he gone to the hotel rather than come here. Nor was the company as satisfying. Not that Louise seemed to be any different this evening from hundreds of other nights they'd spent together. Yet the whole evening had felt dull, pointless. He hadn't done what he'd come to do.

"Business not going well?" Louise asked. She leaned

forward so he could get a clearer view of the deep cleft between her breasts.

"Fine, and except for some trouble with a mine in Leadville, better than usual."

They often discussed business. Afterward. Louise was a clever woman who managed to make use of the tips Jeff gave her from time to time in appreciation of what she had done for him. He was able to relieve his sexual need with her without feeling inadequate because of his arm.

"You look preoccupied." She pursed her lips in an inviting pucker.

"Mmm."

They had met nine years earlier. Jeff had saved Louise from a beating by an irate customer. She had offered to repay him the only way she could. He had found her a place of her own where she didn't have to accept just anybody off the street. She had responded by keeping two nights a week for him. Their relationship had matured over the years into friendship. Jeff had not slept with another woman since.

Louise got up and came around in front of Jeff. Straddling his legs, she put her arms around his neck and pushed her breasts forward until his face was practically buried in them. When he didn't respond, she fondled him between his legs. Jeff felt the familiar stirring in his loins, but the usual desire to bury himself in her body was absent, which stunned him.

They had established a friendly, easygoing relationship over the years, but suddenly he wanted more. He wasn't certain exactly what that more would be, but he did know Violet was responsible for creating the desire within him.

Louise leaned back far enough to look at him. "You sure something's not wrong? You've never ignored me once you got your hands on me."

Jeff thought that she showed more pique at his lack

of interest than concern for him. He guessed it was normal. If a woman in her profession started to lose her appeal, she was in serious trouble.

"There's nothing wrong with you," Jeff said, dropping a kiss on one creamy bosom. "I'm just not feeling up to par tonight."

Louise was also an ambitious woman. Using the connections she had made through Jeff, she had educated her tastes, kept herself informed on business and political affairs, and improved her choice and style of clothes. She could look and act more like a lady than some of Denver's society matrons.

"What have you been doing with yourself?" Louise asked. "I haven't known you to act like this in nine years."

He couldn't tell her she'd been replaced in his fantasies by a copper-haired housemother. She'd never forgive him. "I guess it comes from being locked up in quarantine."

"What!" Louise jumped away from him as though he was contaminated by a deadly disease. "You came in here infected and didn't tell me?"

"I'm not infected," Jeff said. "I went to see about some trouble my nieces got into, and I got caught in the last few days of a quarantine. The sickness was already gone. Besides, they kept me away from the girls."

"You got caught in a girls' school? Not that real fancy school up on Seventeenth Street?"

"That's the one."

Louise went off into peals of laughter. "You poor man. You must have gone crazy locked up with a bunch of squealing virgins. But you had no right to come here. You can never tell about sickness. You might be carrying some of it now. You could infect me, and I could infect my girls. It could ruin us."

"I'm not infected."

"Maybe not, but you're sure acting peculiar. I could

tell right off.'' She backed away a little farther. She grabbed up a handkerchief and waved it in the air as though to keep all the disease on his side of the room. ''Maybe you ought to go home.''

Jeff was surprised at his feeling of relief. It didn't make sense. Louise and he had always been so comfortable together.

''Maybe I should,'' he said, rising. ''I'm clearly not good company.''

''It's not your company that worries me.''

''I know. It's the sickness that might be hiding somewhere on me.''

''It could,'' Louise said. ''You shouldn't have come. It wasn't fair not to tell me.''

''Don't worry. I won't come back until I'm sure every bit of sickness is gone.''

Jeff was irritated. Louise was being ridiculous. He wasn't sick, and he wasn't carrying any disease. But he wouldn't stay. He needed some time to himself. He needed to figure out why every time he looked at Louise he saw Violet instead.

Violet let herself sink into the feather mattress. It would be hard to go back to Wolfe School after two days of such luxury. She stared at the molded plaster decorations on the ceiling, the Tiffany lamps, the marble-topped table, and the enormous mirror. The bedroom furnishings alone must have cost more than her father's house.

She had been terribly nervous about meeting Jeff's family, but the evening had turned out to be fun. The food was wonderful, and she liked his relatives, especially Iris and Monty. She liked their energy, their fierce enjoyment of life, their willingness to rip, scratch, and tear. She couldn't wait to see what kind of child they had. She wondered whether they would send it to the Wolfe School if it was a girl. Violet was certain she would still be there if Harvey McKee didn't do something about her mine.

She found Daisy and Tyler more of a puzzle. Of course that might be due to the fact that Tyler hardly stayed long enough to take a dozen bites of his food, and Daisy had to leave twice to deal with hotel business. The feeling of constantly living in demand would have driven Violet crazy, but they seemed to thrive on it. They were as bad as Jeff.

Violet had tried to banish Jeff from her thoughts, but dozens of things during the evening had brought him to mind. She remembered the china and crystal from their dinners together. Even the candelabra looked familiar.

She thought of how much she longed to see Jeff again and was angry at herself. She had to get over feeling hurt that he hadn't shown up at dinner. He had made no promises. She had known better than to think he would.

The feeling at the table had been festive, lighthearted. She figured it always would be when Monty and Iris were present. They had so much energy and felt things so intensely that they made her feel like an old woman. Jeff had the same intensity, but it was quiet, almost hidden. It ran deep rather than bubbling to the surface.

Violet couldn't help wondering how the girls were doing. She smiled to herself at the thought of Miss Settle having to cope with the twins and Betty Sue. She hoped Essie had had a good visit with her father. She wished he had come on his own without Jeff having had to force him.

Those thoughts brought her back to Jeff. Everything did. She guessed it was to be expected. She wouldn't be there if it weren't for him. Maybe that was the problem. Since he wasn't interested enough to come see if she was enjoying herself, she couldn't figure out why he had issued the invitation at all.

Violet decided she'd probably get a migraine if she insisted upon trying to understand Jeff. Either that or brain fever, and she didn't want either. She made up her mind to enjoy her stay and not worry why it had happened. It had. It wouldn't have any consequences; so it didn't matter.

But the clearest impression of the evening was the happiness the two couples shared. She'd long ago given up hoping for such joy for herself, but she found herself wanting it more than ever—wanting it with Jeff.

Violet didn't need to tell herself again how foolish that was. She snuggled under the covers, but found that she didn't need any but the lightest blanket. The heat from the radiator kept the room toasty warm. After sleeping in an ice-cold attic, it was a wonderful luxury.

Violet found herself hoping Harry McKee could get the business with her mine settled soon. She still intended to do what she could for women like herself, but she had a longing to indulge herself in a little luxury. Not all of that silver money would find its way back to Massachusetts.

"Violet! What are you doing here?" Harvey McKee hurried across the lobby in her direction. "When was the quarantine over? I thought you'd be playing mother hen while your charges worked off their cabin fever."

Violet laughed. "I would be, but Jeff invited me to spend two days recuperating here. Then he bullied Miss Settle into hiring someone to take my place."

Harvey's smiling greeting began to fade. "Jeff? Jeff who?"

"Jeff Randolph."

The smile seemed forced. "Jeff Randolph invited you to spend two days here? Where? They never have any rooms."

"I'm staying in a family suite."

His smile disappeared altogether. "I can't imagine why he did this. You know he hates Yankees, don't you?"

Violet didn't understand why Harvey should suddenly become so serious. "Of course. He never misses an opportunity to tell me."

"Then why did you come?"

"Because I was tired, and I'd missed my two days off. What else should I have done?" She was irritated. She was also tired of everyone trying to disparage Jeff.

"Nothing." Harvey forced a smile. "Since you're here, why don't you have dinner with me?"

"I can't. I'm invited to Fern Randolph's house this evening."

"Is Jeff taking you?"

She stiffened. "No."

"Is he going to be there?"

Violet was getting angry again. "I expect he'll spend the evening working."

"Tell them you can't go," Harvey said. "They're a hard family."

"I couldn't do that, not after accepting their hospitality."

"Don't let their good looks fool you. They're the most ruthless family I've ever met."

Violet didn't understand Harvey. He'd never acted in that manner before. "I like them. I think they're charming."

Harvey paused. "I had hoped you would think me charming."

"I do. You're also one of the nicest men I know."

"Then you'll—"

"I'll see you next week at the usual time. I'll go to dinner with you then if you like."

"And you'll remember what I've said?"

"Harvey, you know I wouldn't let anybody say a word to me against you. Surely you would expect me to do the same for Jeff."

Harvey accepted defeat with grace. "I'll try to remember that the next time jealousy makes me say something I shouldn't.''

"Jealousy? Because of me?" Violet asked, surprised.

"Surely you know I'm very fond of you."

"Of course, but jealousy? I never thought—"

"We'll talk when we have dinner," Harvey said. "In the meantime, beware of the Randolph charm."

Philip Rabin entered Jeff's office. Jeff allowed his irritation at the interruption to show.

"I won't take a minute," Rabin said.

Jeff didn't understand why such a successful man always looked as if he was angry at the rest of the world. Probably living with Clara and being cursed with a daughter like Betty Sue had made him want to take his anger out on the rest of the human race.

Jeff didn't offer him a seat, but Rabin seemed more interested in warming his hands by the fire.

"As the chairman of the school board, I've come to extend our apologies for your getting caught by the quarantine. I don't know what Miss Goodwin was thinking about letting you in like that."

Jeff wondered what Miss Settle had been telling the board members. Obviously she didn't want any of the blame to settle on her shoulders.

"Miss Goodwin had nothing to do with it," Jeff said. "I got caught by my own mistake. She did all she could to make the best of a bad situation."

Rabin didn't look convinced. Jeff wondered if his wife or daughter had been telling tales. Clara Rabin hated Jeff, but she'd have no reason to want to blame Violet for what happened, which wasn't necessarily true of Betty Sue.

Rabin cleared his throat. "I heard she slept in the room next to you."

It had to be Betty Sue, the spiteful little witch. She was angry because Violet had defended the twins, and she was trying to get back at her. Jeff couldn't imagine why a grown man should believe everything a 13-year-old girl told him, but then he didn't understand why Philip allowed himself to be dominated by his wife either.

"She slept in the room next to me because there were no beds anywhere else," Jeff said in sharp, curt words. "Did Betty Sue tell you that the maid also slept upstairs and that Miss Goodwin kept her door open at all times so she could hear the girls if they called out to her?"

"What makes you think—"

"Miss Goodwin wasn't the least bit pleased to have a man in her dormitory. She constantly placed herself between me and the girls. She never let me go downstairs without her being present, not even to use the bathroom."

"Is it true she dined alone with you on at least two occasions?"

"Yes." Jeff decided maybe he'd have a word with the twins. If they were determined to get themselves kicked out, they might as well take care of Betty Sue at the same time. He eyed Philip distrustfully. The man looked too pleased with himself.

"Then I'm afraid the board will have to reconsider her employment. We can't afford to keep staff who exercise such poor judgment. If the parents ever found out—"

"They won't, unless you tell them," Jeff said. His voice was quiet, but Philip's expression showed he had heard the menace in it.

"But we can't hide the fact that—"

"Miss Goodwin dined with me at a table set up in the hall, in full view of anyone who came upstairs. I invited her to give her a few minutes' rest from the constant supervision of sixteen girls. Have you ever tried to take care of sixteen girls for as much as five minutes?"

Philip looked blank, and Jeff said, "It would drive

any man crazy. That's why I insisted Miss Settle let her spend a couple of days in the hotel.''

''As to that—''

''In case you're still inclined to let gossip and rumor lead you about by the nose, you can easily prove to yourself I haven't gone within five blocks of the hotel since. I don't intend to until after she has returned to her duties.''

Philip looked momentarily stymied. Jeff wasn't sure the man believed everything he'd told him, but he couldn't very well say so. However much he might adore his daughter, he had to know it would be easy to prove if she were lying.

''I'm glad to hear that,'' Philip said, stepping away from the fire. ''It was an awkward situation. Naturally Miss Settle and the board were concerned.''

''Not enough to come see for yourselves what was going on,'' Jeff said. ''Now I know you have business awaiting you.''

Philip Rabin clearly didn't relish being dismissed, not even by a bank president, but there wasn't anything he could do about it. ''I'm glad to know Miss Goodwin managed things so well. Clara will be relieved to hear it.''

''Clara would only be happy if I disgraced myself so completely that no one in Denver would speak to me.''

Philip Rabin looked more agitated than usual. ''You and Clara never did see eye to eye.''

''But we do,'' Jeff said. ''Neither one of us can stand the other. Now I have work I must get done.''

But the moment the door closed behind Philip Rabin, Jeff laid down his pen. He was furious over Philip's attempt to slander Violet. He was also surprised at the strength of his anger. He had come close to attacking the man.

It infuriated him anyone should suspect Violet of questionable behavior. She might have been a Yankee, but she took her responsibilities seriously. She had done everything in her power to shield the girls from the consequences of sharing their living space with a man.

He smiled at the memory of Violet standing guard outside the bathroom, of the shock on her face when he had appeared at the door naked to the waist, the way she had looked standing in his doorway with her hand clamped over her eyes. It was a good thing Clara Rabin didn't know about that.

Jeff wondered if Violet was enjoying her stay at the Windsor. He still didn't know what had caused him to make the offer. The words had popped out before he had known what he was saying. He guessed it was partly irritation at Miss Settle and the board for acting as if they had been put to some trouble. Violet had done all the work.

Iris had sent him a note saying that they'd had a lovely time the previous evening. She'd also told him they were all gathering at Fern's home for dinner. She'd invited him, but she'd ended by saying she expected he had work to do, which irked Jeff. He was tempted to go just to annoy Iris. Besides, he wanted to know if Violet had gotten any rest. He remembered how weary she'd looked when she left. Tense, as well. She needed more than two days.

He remembered the kiss. It still had the power to make him break out in a cold sweat. He remembered the softness of her lips. He'd never wanted to kiss Louise, not even under the sway of passion. It was different with Violet. It was tender and sweet. Almost youthfully shy. He had forgotten what innocence felt like. All of a sudden he could remember the kisses he stole from Amelia Bland the summer they were 16.

They had sat under the mulberry trees in the garden one hot June afternoon. He could still remember the heavy, sweet smell of honeysuckle on the garden wall, hear sounds that drifted down from the house, up from the orchard, along the farm road that ran beside the garden. He could still remember the magic that made the sounds seem far away and unimportant.

That had been 21 years ago, a lifetime, before his family had been forced to leave Virginia, before the war, before the loss of his arm, before he had learned to hate the world. He had ceased to be that boy so long ago that he had forgotten all about him. Yet Violet had brought him back with a single kiss.

Jeff wasn't sure he wanted that. It made him feel weak and vulnerable again. He had become strong. He knew what he had to do to be a successful banker. He knew himself, what he could do and what he had to avoid. His life and emotions were under careful control, each doing exactly what he expected of them.

That boy hadn't been in control of anything. He had been petrified of his father. He had had no idea what he wanted to do with his life. And even though he still had both of his arms, he hadn't felt strong enough to compete for Amelia against an older cousin. He had been weak and frightened. Jeff didn't ever want to feel that way again.

But Violet's kiss had reminded him of something he'd forgotten. That boy had had an enjoyment of life, an eagerness to rush headlong toward the future that Jeff had lost. He had trembled as his lips touched Amelia's, as his fingertips had brushed the soft skin of her inner arm. He had felt on the brink of something wonderful and exciting. He was in love with love, enchanted with enchantment. He was absolutely, unshakably certain that someday he would find a woman who would make him totally, deliriously, almost painfully happy.

At 37, all that boundless hope, and all that untrammeled enthusiasm, was gone. Jeff wasn't sure such a future existed for anyone. He was certain it didn't exist for him, and it was foolish even to remember it. Experience was a ruthless but very thorough teacher, and he wasn't one to forget its lessons.

But even as he picked up his pen, he remembered how Violet had looked across the table in candlelight—her eyes so dark and deep, her hair glistening thick and richly colored, her voice soft and comforting—and his resolve weakened. He wanted to see her once more, to kiss her again. There was more of that boy still in him than he would have imagined.

That was foolish, Jeff told himself as he drew a set of papers toward him. He refused to allow a Yankee female to upset him. Besides, just the thought of spending the evening in the bosom of his family made him decide his desire wasn't that strong.

Violet couldn't put her finger on why she was so uncomfortable about Fern's appearance, but her years as a nurse had helped her to develop certain instincts. Those instincts told her Fern Randolph was not well.

Madison and Fern had built a fine two-story stone house on a small hill three miles from the center of Denver. The family had gathered in a large Victorian parlor furnished with dark expensive furniture. The flickering flames of a feeble fire struggled to consume a pair of logs, but soft gaslights made the room bright, and steam radiators kept out the biting winter cold.

"Don't get up," Violet said, crossing the room quickly, her steps muffled by a thick carpet. "Are you sure you should be out of bed?"

Fern smiled, but the effort was apparent. "I have to get out of that room once in a while. Besides, I wanted to thank you for putting up with the twins and Jeff. That's more than should be asked of anyone."

"They were actually quite good while their uncle was there." She had almost said Jeff, but caught herself in time. "They spent the whole first day running up and down the stairs doing his errands. I think they were relieved when he finally had that lift erected outside his window."

"Tell us about that," Iris said. "I can just imagine what anyone passing along the street must have thought."

Violet faced Iris with an answering smile. "Fortunately, it wasn't visible from the street. But the half-dozen clerks racing about were. I'm surprised some parent didn't come demanding to know what was going on."

"Being locked up with Jeff must have been like being locked up with a tiger," Iris said. "Show us your scars."

"Miss Goodwin looks as if she's capable of taking care of herself," Monty said. "Tell us about Jeff's scars."

"You're going to give Miss Goodwin a terrible impression of us," Fern said.

"Please call me Violet."

"She already has one," Iris said. "After last night and a day of shopping at half the stores in Denver, she knows all the Randolph family secrets."

"How about yours?" Daisy asked.

"They're not Randolph secrets," Iris said. "I kept them to myself."

"I know them all," Monty said to Violet in a mock conspiratorial whisper. "Suppose you meet me for a ride early tomorrow morning."

Violet knew Iris and Monty were devoted to each other. Still she found herself flushing at being caught in the middle of their banter. She didn't quite know what to do. Her family had never done anything like that.

"Don't mind them," Fern said, "they always—"

The rest of Fern's sentence was forgotten. Jeff had just entered the parlor. In the resulting clamor of surprise and dismay, Violet hoped her sudden loss of color passed unnoticed.

She had told herself she would never see Jeff again. When she had arrived that night and he wasn't present, the last persistent shred of hope had vanished. She had accepted the fact that tomorrow her fairy tale would end, she would go back to the Wolfe School, and her life would take up where it had left off. Seeing Jeff had destroyed that calm and caused hope to dance wildly in her heart.

She was aware that his gaze immediately searched the room until he found her. He paused a moment, as though to drink in all he saw, before the family outcry claimed his attention.

"What the hell are you doing here?" Monty said.

"I figured I couldn't leave Miss Goodwin in your company for two nights running. She'd get a peculiar notion of what the family was like."

"This family is peculiar," Tyler said. "If she has any other notion, she ought to get rid of it."

"You're certainly strange enough," Jeff said.

"If you came here to get people upset, you can go home," Fern said, her expression severe, her voice firm. "I still haven't forgiven you for sending Madison away. I won't have you ruin the only evening I feel up to having company."

"Shall I toss him out?" Monty said.

The two men faced each other, bristling. Violet was shocked at the resemblance between them. Monty was slightly taller. But despite the fact that Jeff seemed to have smaller bones and a slimmer frame, their bodies were equally heavy with muscle, their hair equally blond, their faces equally handsome.

"Nobody's throwing anybody anywhere," Fern said. "Now sit down and stop acting as if you're about to have a brawl. They're always like this," she said, apologizing to Violet.

"Monty behaves just fine when Jeff doesn't antagonize him," Iris said, determined to defend her husband.

Violet felt a strong urge to defend Jeff, and she might

have spoken up if he hadn't caught her eye. He actually smiled at her and gave his head an almost imperceptible shake.

Monty laughed. "I've never been fit for company, and you know it. That's why the family's so happy to have me stay in Wyoming."

"I'd be perfectly happy to have you in Denver," Fern said. "The boys would be delighted, but I won't have you and Jeff fighting. I don't feel up to it just now."

"Maybe I should go find the boys," Monty said.

"Don't you dare. If you get them stirred up, they'll never go to bed."

"Invite the twins over," Jeff said. "The boys will be so worn out trying to keep up with those whirligigs, they'll be happy to fall into bed."

"Miss Goodwin was just telling us how well they behaved during the quarantine."

"They took one of the younger girls under their protection," Jeff said. "That way they could be ready to fight without actually having to do it."

"All the excitement without the danger," Iris said.

"They are really very kind to Essie Brown," Violet said, "but Jeff was the one who stole her heart."

"Jeff!" five voices exclaimed at once.

"She had trouble with her arithmetic," Jeff said.

"You helped a child with her homework?" Iris said, stunned. "I don't believe it."

"If you'd said he'd scared her half to death, I could have believed that," Monty said.

"Or gotten rid of her down the lift," Tyler said.

Violet could stand it no longer. "You obviously don't know your brother very well. Essie adores him. Her father never visited. Jeff not only saw that he was on the steps the minute the quarantine was over, but he also helped Essie write him a letter."

Violet realized everyone in the room was staring at Jeff. She also realized Jeff was embarrassed.

Chapter Fourteen

It had never occurred to Violet that Jeff wouldn't want his family to know what he'd done for Essie. But he was clearly more at ease with their thinking of him as a bitter loner, which shocked her. She couldn't imagine how anyone could be comfortable as an outcast.

"It was help her or have her camp outside my door," Jeff said, dropping into a chair across the room from Violet. "The twins decided she needed protecting from Clara Rabin's daughter."

"A grizzly bear would need protection from a child of Clara Rabin," Fern said. "That woman is vicious."

"I had Philip in my office today telling me how sorry he was I got caught by the quarantine."

"I'd watch him closely," Fern said. "Madison says that, ever since you took away his railroad business, he hates us. He'll make trouble for us any time he can."

"I'm not worried about him," Jeff said, dismissing Philip Rabin along with his wife and daughter. He glanced around the room. "I do wish you'd get someone to gut this place. It looks more like a funeral parlor than a place for people to enjoy themselves.''

Violet thought Fern's taste too heavily Victorian, but she liked the room. She was startled Jeff would condemn it so bluntly.

''You can do anything you want with it,'' Fern said, her eyes glittering dangerously as she smiled at Jeff. ''You can even choose the decorator as long as you pay the bill.''

''I'll be damned if I spend a cent on one of Madison's houses,'' Jeff said. ''He has more money than the rest of us put together.''

Violet was relieved when dinner was announced. She didn't know how much longer peaceful relations could have been maintained under the assault of Jeff's sharp tongue. She didn't understand why he was as anxious to provoke his brothers as they were to criticize him.

Dinner went off better than expected. Jeff sat at the end of the table between Daisy, who largely ignored him, and Madison's empty chair. He seemed to direct most of his attention to his food and to thoughts that troubled him. Every so often he would glance up at Violet, but since he usually seemed to be frowning when he did so, Violet was not moved to offer him a penny for his thoughts.

Besides, she was worried about Fern. Her concern grew more earnest as the meal progressed. Fern ate little of the first course. She waved away all dishes after that. Just before dessert, Fern's strength gave out.

Violet was out of her chair immediately. Fern didn't seem to have a fever, but she had lost her color, her skin was clammy and cold, and her heart was beating much too fast.

''You ought to be in bed,'' Violet said.

''I'll be all right in a minute,'' Fern said. ''It's just a spell.''

''It's no such thing,'' Iris said. She was only slightly

behind Violet in reaching Fern. "We're going to put you to bed whether you like it or not. Monty, carry her upstairs."

"This is ridiculous," Fern said. "I can walk."

"There's no point in Monty having all those muscles if he doesn't get to use them once in a while."

Violet couldn't help glancing at Jeff. He had the same muscles, the same strength, but no one had thought of him because he had only one arm. She wondered how many times that happened without anyone realizing. Jeff's expression of unconcern didn't change, but Violet knew it must hurt. She forced her attention back to Fern. Monty had picked the other woman up and was carrying her out of the room.

"You'd better stay here," Iris said to Daisy. "Three Randolph brothers can't be left alone without a referee, and I don't think we ought to sacrifice Violet just yet. Anyway, I need her help."

Daisy just smiled. Violet wondered how Daisy and her husband remained so calm in the midst of such a tempestuous family.

By the time they got Fern undressed and in bed, Violet was so worried she had the housekeeper send for the doctor. She motioned Iris to follow her into the hall. "I've helped with expectant mothers for ten years," Violet said after they closed the door. "I don't know what's wrong, but something is. Why isn't her husband here?"

"I wrote him to come home," Iris said.

"When?"

"Yesterday."

"Can he be reached by telegraph?"

"I suppose so."

"I'm going to ask Jeff to send him a telegram."

"Right now?" Iris asked.

"Yes."

"You think it's serious?"

"Yes, I do."

Violet's opinion didn't change later, even though the doctor decided Fern was merely overtired.

"He's a fool," Violet said angrily when the family had reassembled in the parlor after the doctor's departure. "Something is seriously wrong. If something isn't done, I'm afraid—"

"Fern's mother died in childbirth," Iris said. "Is that what you're afraid of?"

Violet nodded. "When her husband gets here, please ask him to consult another doctor. I know nothing about the reputation of the man who just left, but I have no confidence in him."

"He's the best in Denver," Tyler said.

"Then Denver needs a new doctor." Violet had allowed her feelings to make her forget she spoke to two women who were themselves pregnant. She didn't want to do anything to cause them concern. "I'm sure in a normal situation, Dr. Keener is quite capable, but Fern needs somebody who can give her special care."

"I don't think there is anybody else," Tyler said.

"I know a doctor in Boston who has taken care of many women in Fern's condition. Maybe he can recommend somebody."

"I wouldn't trust any doctor from Boston," Jeff said.

"But Madison graduated from Harvard," Monty said. "He might."

Violet stood. "If Madison would like the doctor's name, he can get in touch with me. Now I think I'd better be getting back to the hotel. No one has to go with me," Violet said when Tyler and Monty both got up. "I'm sure you'll want to stay and make certain Fern is okay."

"Jeff can take you back," Iris said. "He must have his carriage. He couldn't have walked this far."

"That's not necessary," Violet said. "It's not necessary—"

"You can't go alone," Jeff said, getting to his feet.

Violet wanted to be with Jeff. At the same time, she didn't want to be with him. She knew it would revive all the feelings she'd worked so hard to suppress. His being there that night hadn't changed anything.

Violet took her seat in the carriage, cautioning herself to expect nothing. But when Jeff chose to sit next to her rather than across from her, she found herself hoping his coolness had been due to a reluctance to divulge his feelings to his family.

"Do you really think Fern is in trouble?" he asked as the carriage bowled down the rough track toward town.

Violet knew she shouldn't be disappointed Jeff was more interested in his sister-in-law than herself, but she could not deny her disappointment. She didn't know what she had expected Jeff to say—they really had nothing else to talk about except the twins—but she had hoped for something.

"Yes, I do. That's the kind of nursing I used to do. I can recognize trouble without having to know what causes it."

"Will you go back to nursing if you don't get your money?"

Violet didn't want to talk about nursing. She wanted to know why Jeff had stayed away, why he'd come that night, why he'd offered to take her home. She wanted to know if she meant any more to him than someone to needle because she'd been born north of the Mason-Dixon Line. She wanted to know if he was going to continue popping up in her life only to disappear again.

"I don't know," she said. The thought of going back to Massachusetts to be a drudge for the rest of her life was too dismal to face. "It's either that or continue working as a housemother for the school."

Much to her surprise, she realized that choice hadn't

been such a horrible prospect just a few weeks earlier. Nor had going back to nursing. She had enjoyed her work. After her family had moved to Boston, she had worked with some of the finest doctors in the country.

With something of a shock, Violet realized the difference was that going back to Massachusetts meant never seeing Jeff again. She was horrified that she had let her feelings get so far out of control. If she thought one imagined kiss could become real just because she wanted it to, then she was stupid and deserved to be left to molder on the dusty shelf of spinsterhood.

"You could always get married," Jeff said.

"We've discussed that before, remember? I'm too old. Besides, I'm not as tolerant as I was years ago. I don't know that I could find anyone who would come up to my standards."

"What are they?"

Jeff didn't look amused or cynical. He looked as if he really wanted to know, which surprised her. Men didn't want to know what a woman looked for in marriage. They expected any woman they asked to accept gratefully. They figured that, if they could put a roof over her head, clothes on her back, food in her mouth, and babies in her belly, they'd done more than enough. Jeff had already told her exactly what he wanted. He must know it wasn't anything like what she wanted.

"You'll start calling me a foolish Yankee female," she said. Then she thought she could detect a trace of a smile on his face.

"Probably, but tell me anyway. I'm used to hearing things I don't want to hear."

Good Lord, what did she want? She wasn't sure she knew. "It's hard to say. I've never tried to put it in words before."

"You should always know exactly what you're after," Jeff said. "Otherwise, you'll take what's offered only to realize later it's not what you wanted."

"Don't you believe in some give and take," Violet asked, "in the power of love to help you tolerate faults or shortcomings?"

"No."

A flat, unequivocal answer. It was a jolt. A bad one. She knew he was harsh, demanding, critical, but she had always assumed he believed in love. She did, even though she had never found it.

"Emotion just clouds the issue," he said. "It doesn't change anything."

"Don't you believe in love at all? What about your brothers?"

"Love's not for everybody. It's a kind of emotional weakness that only the very strongest men can risk. Madison has managed it."

"Why, because he could leave his wife when she's pregnant?"

"Look at Monty. He jumps whenever Iris speaks."

Violet had the feeling that Monty did pretty much what he wanted, that Iris had to do most of the accommodating, but it was obvious Jeff didn't see it that way.

"If that's the way you feel, you certainly don't want to know what I look for in a man, because the first requirement would be that he be deeply in love with me. The second would be that he value my opinions as much as I value his. Daisy and Tyler do that."

"It just seems that way. Daisy runs the hotel because Tyler can't be bothered to come out of his kitchens. I knew from the beginning he wasn't cut out to be a hotel manger."

"Then why is it the most successful hotel in Denver?"

"Because it's the most luxurious and has the best food."

"Who designed it?"

"Tyler."

"Seems to me you've just disproved your point," Violet said.

"I don't agree, but I'm not interested in Tyler. What else will you require in a husband?"

"Why do you want to know?"

"I'm always curious about Yankees. They're such an odd breed," Jeff said.

"We're not a breed! We're people, just like you."

"You keep avoiding my question."

"I require that my husband not think of Yankees as a breed," Violet said. "He has to know we're people with the same feelings and needs as anyone born in Virginia. The same right to happiness."

"I'm sure you have additional requirements."

Violet didn't want to talk anymore. She wondered if Jeff had come just to dispel any hopes that she might have had about him. Well, he'd done it. So he should go home and leave her alone.

"You'll find as women grow older and see more of men, they become less willing to trust themselves to just any man," Violet said.

"Would you trust yourself to your husband?"

"I would have to, wouldn't I? The laws are such that—"

"I'm not talking about the laws. I'm talking about you."

There was nothing distant or disdainful about him at that moment. He appeared to be quite interested in her answer. She didn't know why he wanted to know. He expected a woman to abandon herself to her husband. That wasn't the same thing as trust, but she wasn't certain he knew the difference.

"I wouldn't marry him if I couldn't," Violet said.

"But doesn't that mean you could trust him to make all your decisions for you?"

"Don't willfully misunderstand me," Violet said. "I don't mean to abandon control of my own life. As long as I'm well and strong, I expect to be given full consideration. That's my right as a human being. I don't give that up just because I decide to marry. However, it does mean that, if I were unable for whatever reason to make a decision, I would trust my husband to make it for me, certain he would consider my desires equally with his own.''

''Wouldn't it be easier to hand over all such decisions to your husband and concern yourself with your home and family?''

Violet fixed Jeff with an angry gaze. ''I'm not stupid. Nor am I lazy. For ten years I looked after my father and brother, managed the household, and worked to support us. I have no intention of suddenly being told that I can no longer think or that there is no necessity for me to do so.''

''Do you really want to get married?''

''Has anybody ever told you you're the rudest man in Denver?''

''Frequently. Now answer my question,'' Jeff said.

Violet was weary, but she was also angry. ''I used to take it for granted that I did, but meeting men like you has made me question whether it would be a good idea.''

He laughed at her. He sat right there and laughed, as if she'd said something funny, as if he was indulging her whimsy. ''You'll lead some poor fool a merry chase some day, but I don't think he'll feel cheated.''

Violet was speechless. She didn't know why she liked the man. She didn't know how she could possibly consider a serious relationship with a man who had nothing to recommend him but a gorgeous body and the fact that he laughed about once a week. At her.

''Thank you, I guess,'' Violet said. ''I wouldn't even consider asking why you hold such an opinion. I would probably have to be restrained to keep from doing violence to you.''

Violet used to be shocked at the number of times

she'd considered violence since she had met Jeff, but that didn't surprise her anymore. She didn't see how anyone could know him and not be prey to wild thoughts at least once an hour. He was the most infuriating man alive. Fortunately the carriage pulled up in front of the hotel.

"Thank you for escorting me back to the hotel," she said, trying to be as formal as possible. "It was unnecessary, but it was kind."

"I'm coming inside." He got out and helped her down.

"It's not necessary."

"I know."

Violet tried to leave Jeff behind. She stalked into the hotel, leaving him to keep up. He did. Easily. She stopped in front of the elevator. He pushed the button.

"I don't know what you mean by the attention you've shown me, if indeed you mean anything at all. But if you should one day be interested in pursuing a woman with the purpose of establishing a serious relationship, let me tell you you're going about it in entirely the wrong way."

The elevator door opened. She didn't let the fact that a wide-eyed young man was operating the elevator stop her from saying what she had on her mind.

"You'll need to begin by trying to be likable, trying to make yourself agreeable to the young woman. It's hard for a woman to fall in love with a man when she's constantly getting mad at him. You might pretend you have an interest in someone other than yourself, even if you don't. You might say something nice. I realize that will be difficult for you. So I suggest you write down some things to say and memorize them."

The elevator door opened and Violet stepped out into the hall. "I don't expect you to actually come up with these phrases yourself. I realize anything in the way of flattery or kindness is foreign to your nature. Maybe you could get one of your clerks to do it for you.''

They had reached her door, but she wasn't through yet. ''Once you get about a hundred memorized, you can start practicing them. Don't try to make sense of them. You won't understand them. Just sprinkle them in with the rest of your conversation. If you do this enough times, memorize enough phrases, you might actually fool some poor, gullible female into thinking you mean what you say.''

''But it wouldn't fool you?'' Jeff said.

''Not for as much as a second.''

''Good. I find it impossible to admire stupid women.''

Violet hoped she wasn't standing there with her mouth open. No matter how much she was around Jeff, he continued to have the power to stagger her with the things he said. But that was nothing compared to the shock she experienced when he kissed her.

She was too stunned to respond, so stunned she wasn't even in touch with her physical response to him. She just stood there, as immobile as a statue, angry at herself, angry at him, letting him kiss her.

''Why did you do that?'' she asked, breathless and bewildered, when he released her.

''I've been wanting to do that all evening,'' Jeff said.

''But why?''

''I like you.''

''But I'm a Yankee. You hate everything I am. You disagree with everything I believe.''

''I'm trying to forget that. Do you have to go in just now?''

''It depends,'' she stammered, wondering what he was going to do next.

Jeff kissed her again. That time she kissed him back. She was mortified, but she couldn't stop herself. She had thought about kissing him for days, dreamed of it every night. The fact that he was a prejudiced, narrow-minded, insensitive, miserable human being didn't change a thing. It should have, but it didn't.

She didn't know how long they might have stood there, kissing like two youngsters, if they hadn't heard the elevator opening. She had to give Jeff credit. He hadn't flinched. She was the one who jumped back. She was glad she had. It was Iris and Monty.

"I thought you'd be back in your office up to your elbows in work by now," Iris said.

"Miss Goodwin and I were just discussing the traits she looks for in a husband."

"Why? The two of you couldn't have anything in common."

"Intellectual curiosity."

Iris eyed Jeff distrustfully. "When he gets like this, he's dangerous. I'd lock myself in my room if I were you."

"She's safe from Jeff," Monty said. "She's from Massachusetts, remember?"

Iris's gaze hadn't left Jeff. "I still wouldn't trust him. None of you Randolphs are really trustworthy."

"Not even me?" Monty asked.

"Especially you. Why do you think I never let you out of my sight?"

"Because you can't wait to jump my bones."

Iris blushed faintly. She opened the door to their suite and pushed Monty in ahead of her. "The Randolph men are so modest," she said.

"But we have so much to be immodest about," Monty said before Iris closed the door on the rest of their conversation.

Violet felt the need to be safely on the other side of her own door. She had some thinking to do, and she couldn't do it in the hall, especially not with Jeff staring at her.

"I want to thank you for giving me these two days," she said, extending her hand to Jeff in an effort to put some distance between them. "It isn't all that hard to put up with the twins, but it's nice to have my efforts appreciated.''

Jeff took her hand, but he didn't shake it or let it go.

"If I don't see you tomorrow, I want you to know I appreciate the way your family welcomed me." She smiled despite her nervousness. "I don't imagine they are any more comfortable with a Yankee than you are."

"Three of them married Yankees."

"Iris told me about that. But I was the only real Yankee in that room tonight."

"You were the prettiest."

"See. I told you it was easy to recite memorized phrases. You did that just as if you meant it. Keep it up, and you'll soon be ready for moonlight and magnolias. That is the favorite tree down South, isn't it?"

Jeff released her hand. "I'm rather partial to honeysuckle."

"See. It comes naturally, just like making all that money. Now I have to go. It must be close to midnight. I know I'm not Cinderella, but I don't trust this night not to end with mice and pumpkins."

The muffled sound of laughter and some thumping noises from Iris and Monty's suite distracted Jeff long enough for her to open her door.

"Thanks again." Violet slipped inside and closed the door behind her. She leaned against it, tears beginning to run down her cheeks. She felt like Cinderella all right. Maybe her gown hadn't turned to rags, but her evening had turned to ashes.

Violet had been telling herself all morning not to expect Jeff to escort her back to school. Just because he had kissed a Yankee to find out what it was like didn't mean he had any other experiments he was anxious to conduct. She kept telling herself she didn't want him to be downstairs, but she knew she was lying to herself.

She realized how much when she saw his empty carriage waiting for her.

"It's been wonderful having you," Iris had said.

"You'll have to come stay again," Daisy said.

Violet smiled, thanked them, and settled back against the cushions. She would never be back, and she knew it.

"I want those loan agreements on my desk in fifteen minutes," Jeff said to one of his clerks. The man stood before Jeff's huge desk, his body stiff, his eyes wider than normal. "The mine reports, too. And stop looking at me like you've come face-to-face with a wounded cougar, Caspar. Anybody would think you were afraid I was about to cut your throat."

"Yes, sir."

"And don't speak to me as if you're in the army. This is a bank. I pay you a damned good salary, and you still get to go home to your wife and family for dinner every night."

When Caspar's gaze didn't waver, Jeff said, "Well, almost every night."

It was Saturday morning, and Caspar had worked with Jeff through the night. Jeff had worked through every night since he'd left Violet at the hotel four days earlier. A different clerk had stayed each time. They hadn't complained. They expected it. It had been part of their job from the beginning. It accounted in part for the size of their salary.

Jeff kept reminding himself of that fact so that he wouldn't feel guilty about Caspar's bleary-eyed stare, his lagging footsteps, or his wife who had eaten her dinner alone and his children who had gone to bed without seeing their father.

It was all because of that Yankee woman. He'd never given a thought to keeping his men working around the clock or through the weekend until she had jumped all over him. Suddenly, one or another of her numerous criticisms was constantly popping into his head when it was least welcome.

"Is there anybody else in the office?" Jeff asked.

"Young Bledsoe came in a little while ago," Caspar said.

Jerry Bledsoe didn't know his head from the rest of him just yet, though he was coming around fast. He was so new that it would take Jeff more time to tell him what to do than do it himself.

"Go on home," Jeff said to Caspar. "I'll use young Bledsoe."

"But he doesn't know where anything is," Caspar said. "Besides, I don't think it's wise to trust him with some of the documents. His loyalty hasn't been proved yet."

"Don't worry. I'll handle anything sensitive myself." Conscience. When in hell had Jeff gotten one? Had the little bastard been hiding inside all along just waiting for some busybody like Violet Goodwin to come along and give it a swift kick in the pants? "You help him find the files I need and go on home."

He could tell Caspar wasn't sure he had heard correctly, but he could also see the man wasn't going to stand around and give Jeff a chance to change his mind. The speed with which he disappeared was a further prick to Jeff's newly awakened conscience.

Violet! Why in hell couldn't he forget that woman! Because he didn't want to! There he was, mesmerized by a woman for the first time in his life, and she was a Yankee from Massachusetts. Massachusetts, of all godforsaken places, the hellhole where he'd been forced to waste two years of his life, being treated little better than a penned animal.

Jeff forced the memory of those years out of his mind. It had nothing to do with Violet. And to be perfectly honest, it had little to do with him any longer. He would never forget, and he would never forgive, but he had put it behind him. He had seen enough of Violet to know that, if she had been a nurse there, she'd have given Capt. Sedgwick an earful.

Jeff smiled at the thought of Violet bullying the commander of the prison camp until he had let her do just about anything she wanted. She'd have seen that the men had gotten decent food, clean beds, and medical care.

Once more Jeff jerked his thoughts back from those terrible years. He didn't know why he kept trying to put Violet on some kind of pedestal. He didn't like managing women. They might be useful on occasion, but they were still to be avoided.

But Violet didn't exactly manage. True, she wasn't reluctant to say how she felt about something, but she didn't try to force Jeff to do anything. She just brought it to his attention and left it up to his conscience to do the dirty work.

He wondered why she had managed to stir up his conscience when no one in his family had. He'd met women more beautiful than Violet, but their beauty had never affected him the way Violet's did. It did something to him every time he thought about her mane of red hair. It wasn't the right color. It was too dark, too stark, but for some reason it stuck in his memory.

And her penchant for bright-colored dresses was a definite aberration in taste, yet he could still hear the rustle of her skirts as she moved about the dormitory. He could remember the feel of the stiff satin the night he had kissed her outside her room in the hotel. He could remember the smell of her perfume.

It was impossible to miss. He couldn't imagine her wearing any scent that merely hinted at its presence. He wondered when she had learned to be so assertive. He wondered why it had been necessary.

A knock sounded at the door, and Caspar entered. He dropped several folders on Jeff's desk.

"I thought I told you to go home," Jeff said.

"I just wanted to make sure you got the papers you wanted."

"No, you wanted to make sure I hadn't changed my mind," Jeff said, knowing that Caspar realized that what he was doing was completely out of character. The clerk wanted to make certain he could come back to a job on Monday morning. "Now get out of here. If Bledsoe can't handle the work, it's time I found out."

Caspar disappeared, closing the door silently behind him. Jeff settled down into his chair and opened the first folder. Several minutes later he realized he'd been staring at it without having any idea what was in front of him. His mind had been wandering over the first evening he and Violet had had dinner together. He had to admit that, no matter how much he might try, he could not forget Violet Goodwin.

He laughed at the irony of it. If it hadn't been for his stubbornness and his temper, he'd never have forced his way into the dormitory. And they were the very qualities Violet disliked the most.

His thoughts were interrupted by Bledsoe entering the office without knocking first. That was one thing the boy would have to learn right away, or he'd be looking for a new employer before the next week was out.

"Mr. Randolph, there's a wrought-up female out here to see you," Bledsoe said, looking completely unsure what to do in the situation. "She says it's urgent."

To Jeff's astonishment, Violet pushed her way into his office. "I'm sorry to bother you," she said, "but the twins have disappeared."

Chapter Fifteen

Jeff was out of his chair and around his desk in an instant. To his surprise, he wasn't thinking about the twins. He was more concerned that Violet should be so upset. He tried to offer her a chair, but she wouldn't take it. She was too agitated. Some of the color had drained from her face, and her hair showed signs of escaping from its pins again.

"I don't have time to sit. We must go after them," Violet said.

"When did you miss them?"

"Not until nearly ten o'clock. I should have known Essie wasn't telling the truth. The twins never sleep late. Sometimes I think they never sleep at all. They're as bad as you."

Jeff steered her toward a chair while telling Bledsoe to call his carriage, but she didn't sit. Her jade-green skirt rustled noisily as she moved about with short, jerky motions.

"We'll find them, and they'll be all right," Jeff said.

He offered her some of the coffee he kept hot on a small stove, but she refused. "They're more likely to have half of Denver at their beck and call before noon."

"It shouldn't have taken me so long to find that they were missing."

Jeff steered Violet back to the chair. She sat down, immediately got to her feet, and said, "We have to leave right away. We can't walk. I've exhausted myself coming this far."

"You should have asked Miss Settle to lend you her buggy."

"I didn't dare. She was so upset when I told her I was afraid she would fire me on the spot."

"Nobody's going to fire you over anything the twins do. If that were the case, the entire staff would have been gone by now."

Violet smiled, and Jeff felt a little less tense.

Bledsoe stuck his head in the door. "The carriage is coming around right now."

When Violet headed for the door immediately, Jeff had no choice but to follow. "Bledsoe, tell everyone to keep on as they are until I return. Where do you think we ought to look?" he asked as he helped Violet into the carriage.

"I was depending upon you to know that," Violet said.

"To the hotel," Jeff told his driver. "It's the closest place they know."

But the girls weren't there. Daisy hadn't seen them. Monty had gone out, but Iris was still in her room.

"You have to find them before Rose finds out," Iris said. "We can't let her know half-a-dozen adults can't keep track of two little girls."

"A half-dozen Pinkertons couldn't keep up with those infidels," Jeff said.

"What are you going to do now?" Iris asked. "And whatever it is, it had better not upset Fern."

"I think we ought to talk to Essie," Violet said. "I suspect she knows more than she's telling."

Violet didn't wait for Jeff once they reached the school. Without even thinking, Jeff attempted to follow her into the dormitory. Beth made him wait while Violet found Essie. The child looked scared when Violet marched her into the parlor.

"She still says she doesn't know where the twins went, but I don't believe her," Violet said.

Nor did Jeff. Guilt was written all over the little girl's face. He was certain that the twins had sworn her to secrecy. Since they had taken it upon themselves to become her champion, it wasn't likely she would rat on them.

"Come here, Essie," Jeff said, and the child approached reluctantly. "You know where the twins went, don't you?"

When she didn't move, Jeff asked, "They told you to tell Miss Goodwin they were sleeping so that nobody would catch them until they were far away, didn't they?"

Still Essie didn't answer, but Jeff could see in her eyes that he was right. "They could run away if they wanted, but it wasn't right to make you lie for them. That forced you to do something wrong, too. They took advantage of your loyalty."

Essie was watching him with big eyes as he said, "You can't let the twins use you. They'll be sorry when you get into trouble, but they'll do it again. I know. They're my nieces. My whole family is like that." He didn't look at Violet. He didn't want to know how she reacted to that statement. "We have to find them before something terrible happens to them."

Essie still didn't respond; so Jeff leaned back. "If you're not going to help me, I guess I'll just have to stop helping you."

Essie didn't say anything, but she looked apprehensive when Jeff said, "Do you want to know what I'm going to do? I don't want to take advantage of our friendship. I want you to know exactly what I'm going to do. I made your father come visit you, didn't I? I can also make him stop."

Jeff heard a sharp intake of breath. He knew Violet didn't approve of what he was doing, but he couldn't think of any other way.

Essie's lip started to tremble. Seeing her made Jeff feel rotten. He knew what it was like to feel deserted. He would have taken a beating rather than rat on one of his friends. He could only make Essie break her promise and risk losing the twins' friendship by threatening to take away something even more important.

"That's how important it is that you tell me where the twins have gone," Jeff said.

Tears ran down Essie's cheeks. Jeff had to stifle a desire to pull her to him, give her a big hug, and promise he would never do anything that terrible.

But Essie was made of stern stuff. She didn't show any signs of breaking down. Jeff admired her will, but he couldn't afford to let her win.

"Miss Goodwin, I want you to go to the window and watch for Essie's father. When he comes, please go outside and tell him what has happened. Explain why he can't see Essie today."

Jeff had never felt so much like a snake in his life. Essie looked at him with shattered faith in her eyes, and Violet looked at him as if he was a murderer. He wasn't certain she would do what he asked.

"Please," he said. "It's the only way."

Violet cast him an angry look, but she moved to the window. He settled back in the sofa. Harold Brown would be there in a few minutes. They had passed him several blocks from the school.

Jeff watched Essie and saw the hurt and distrust in her eyes. For the first time in his life, he felt the loss of someone's liking for him. He'd never felt that way before, not even with his family. He'd fought for them many times, but he never expected their thanks, never missed the feeling of warmth that didn't exist between them. He did what he did because they were family.

Only it wasn't so simple in the present situation. Violet had turned her back on him as well, but he didn't know what else he could have done.

He saw Violet's back stiffen, then she said, "Mr. Brown is here."

"Go talk to him."

She looked at him, her gaze begging him to find another way, not to make her part of this.

Essie started forward, but Jeff put his arm out to block her path. "Please go," he said rather sharply to Violet, who cast him an angry look and went outside to meet Essie's father.

Essie hurried to the window. She watched her father, her lower lip between her teeth, as he talked with Violet. She gasped when they started walking slowly down the walk back to the road. Jeff knew he ought to be talking to her, putting pressure on her, but he couldn't. He sat quietly, waiting.

Violet and Mr. Brown reached the road, stood talking for a moment, and then Mr. Brown started back toward town.

"They wanted to go riding," Essie said. "They told me they'd hand me over to Betty Sue if I told."

"Where did they go?" Jeff asked.

"Somewhere with lots of horses."

"But where?"

"I don't know."

"Who were they going to see?"

"I don't know," Essie said.

"Did they say it was their cousins?" When Essie shook her head, Jeff asked, "Did they mention any names? James or Tazewell?''

Essie shook her head again, and Jeff realized that he was getting desperate. Time was getting short. He couldn't dismiss the possibility that the twins had been kidnapped. Everybody knew the Randolph family was rich.

"Did they say anything you can remember?" Jeff asked. Essie was watching her father. "Please try to think."

Essie turned back to Jeff. "Aurelia said she wanted to ride Nightmare. But Juliette said not to be stupid. Uncle Monty wouldn't have brought his horse all the way from Wyoming."

Jeff felt as though a great weight had been lifted from his shoulders. The twins had gone to Madison's ranch. He only hoped to God that they had arrived there safely. He stood up, went to the door, and beckoned to Violet. She called to Mr. Brown, and he began retracing his steps.

"Your father will be here in a minute," Jeff said. "I'm sorry I had to do this, but it's very dangerous for little girls to be alone."

"Is Daddy going to be mad at me?"

Suddenly, Jeff wondered what Violet had told Mr. Brown. "No. He'll be angry at the twins. All of us are."

"But I gave my word."

"It doesn't count when somebody asks you to do something wrong."

Essie didn't look as if she was sure Jeff was right, but she wanted to believe him.

"Why don't you go meet your father?" Jeff said. "I'm sure Miss Goodwin won't mind."

Essie escaped like a bird released from its cage. Jeff followed slowly, thoughtfully. He didn't look forward to spending the next 20 minutes closed up in a carriage with Violet's angry disapproval.

* * *

"You might as well say it and get it out of your system," Jeff said after they'd ridden in uneasy silence for ten minutes. "Then maybe you'll stop looking as if you've just bitten into a sour pomegranate."

Violet didn't want to say what she was feeling. At first she had been simply angry. Then she had been furious that Jeff had made her part of something she disliked so much. But she had been reluctant to speak because, even though she didn't like his methods, Jeff had been successful where she hadn't.

The twins were his nieces. It was only natural he would be more concerned about their safety than protecting Essie's feelings. To a degree, Violet felt the same way. Essie was safe. It was the twins who were in possible danger. Violet prayed that they had made it to Madison's ranch unharmed.

"It won't do any good to tell you what I think," Violet said. "It's over and done with. Nothing I say can change it."

"So you're going to sit over there, glaring at me, not saying a word and enjoying your anger. How like a woman to use silence to make a man feel guilty when she can't do it with words."

"It has never been my purpose to make you feel guilty," Violet said with grim composure. She was determined to deny Jeff the pleasure of seeing her lose her temper. "Not even when your own stubbornness and ill temper caused you to force your way into the dormitory. I didn't try to make you feel guilty when you did your best to upset me and the girls by running around indecently clothed. I have no intention of doing so now, even though I wish you had managed to find another way. Under the circumstances, I think success may have been more important than Essie's feelings."

She had the pleasure of knowing she had caught him by surprise. "I expect you know Essie will never entirely trust you again."

When Jeff nodded, Violet thought he looked sorry for the loss. "Wasn't there some other way?"

"Probably, but I couldn't think of it. What did you tell her father? Essie was worried he would be angry with her."

"He won't. He understood the importance of finding little girls lost in a city of more than thirty thousand people, most of them men."

"You really don't blame me?"

Violet couldn't imagine that Jeff really cared what she thought. She was a Yankee, and Yankees by definition were a defective breed. That word still had the power to make her angry. But there was something new in Jeff's attitude, the tone of his voice, the way he looked at her, that was much more interesting and intriguing than her anger.

He actually did care what she thought of him. Really. Honestly. The great Jeff Randolph—the impregnable bastion of self-confidence, of indifference to the wants, feelings, and desires of the rest of the world—had cracked. And he had cracked because of a Yankee female.

Violet wanted to laugh. She wanted to dance about wildly until all her hairpins came loose. Instead she told her foolish heart to go back to beating in a steady, dependable fashion. Jeff might truly care, but his mind was set on his image of the perfect Southern belle. He was equally convinced Yankees had to have their horns and tails removed at birth. He might feel a physical attraction for her, but it would go no deeper than that.

"As I said, I can't blame you for succeeding where I failed," Violet said.

"I would have blamed you."

Jeff's reply shocked her. "Why?"

"I always blame people who don't behave as I want them to, even when they succeed."

"Why?"

"Because I have no tolerance."

Violet wondered why he was telling her that. Confession might be good for the soul, but she was certain that occasion was the first time Jeff had ever tried it. If his expression was any indication, his soul wasn't liking it too much.

"I always know the answers," he said. "I never cared about protecting people's feelings before. It seemed such a waste of time. It also got in the way of getting things done, of getting them done right."

"What made you change your mind?" She was vain enough to hope he would say she had. Women didn't have much power. To be able to influence a man such as Jeff Randolph would add greatly to her sense of worth.

"I don't know that I have. I'll probably always act like that—I have for so long I don't know how to behave any other way—but I don't want you to dislike me."

"I don't."

Violet couldn't. She never would. Her problem was just the reverse. She liked him too much. And though she was trying desperately to control her feelings, they were growing steadily out of control. Moments like that one didn't help.

He could make her so furious that she was certain she'd never again be susceptible to his charm. Then just a tiny show of vulnerability would cause her to melt like an icicle on a stove top. She was dangerously close to falling in love with this man.

The realization shocked Violet in so many ways, on so many levels, that her brain felt paralyzed. She had to put a stop to such foolishness. Jeff might have occasional moments when he wasn't as hard as granite. He might even be thoughtful at times. But he thought that he knew better than everyone about everything, that Yankees were only a slight step up from wharf rats, and that all a stupid, spineless female had to do to achieve

Madonna status was be born somewhere in Virginia. Their arrival at Madison's ranch saved her from having to continue the conversation, a task for which she felt unequal.

"Do we have to disturb Fern?" Violet asked, mindful of Iris's injunction not to upset her sister-in-law.

"If anybody knows if the girls are here, it'll be Fern," Jeff said.

But Fern didn't know. She hadn't left her bedroom all morning. And despite Iris's letter, Madison still hadn't returned from Leadville.

"If they came here, they could be anywhere," Fern said. "The boys are out riding with Monty."

"He's here?" Jeff asked, suddenly looking more hopeful.

"He's been coming every afternoon to ride with the boys. Today's Saturday and they're off from school. He was here before I woke."

Violet had caught the change in Jeff's expression. She decided it was a mixture of relief and anger. Unfortunately, she felt he had a right to be angry. Aside from the trouble and worry the twins had caused, they had exposed themselves to the possibility of serious danger. They had to be made to understand the gravity of what they had done.

"I'll go down to the barn to see if anybody has seen them," Jeff said. "You can stay here with Fern."

"I'm going with you," Violet said.

"It's not necessary."

"I'm still going with you."

Fern smiled, easing the worried look on her face. "You don't have to protect the twins from Jeff. They manage to get out of everything with very little damage to their spirits."

"Rose will be here soon," Jeff said. "We'll see how they like that."

"You didn't telegraph Rose that they had run away?"

"I'm not such a sap as that. I wrote her earlier. But I will telegraph her once I get the brats safely back at school. I haven't had a minute's peace this past month because of those two. This is worse than anything yet."

Violet didn't say so, but she agreed. It probably was time their parents came to deal with the situation in person.

"Sure, them girls are here," the groom said to Jeff a few minutes later. "Turned up practically with the sun. I don't know who they got to bring 'em out this far, but Mr. Monty and the boys wasn't even down yet before they was saddled up and off."

"Where are they now?"

"Can't say, but I imagine they'll be coming over that ridge right soon. Mr. Monty's not one to miss his lunch."

Violet glanced at her watch. She was surprised to discover it was already past noon. She had been so busy that she was hardly aware of the passing time.

They didn't have to wait long. Two horses topped the rise at a gallop. Violet wasn't the least bit surprised to discover it was the twins. Three boys followed. Monty brought up the rear.

"Those gals sure know how to ride," the groom said. "It's rare females can handle horses like they can."

"They were born in the middle of a kidnapping, then spent nine years on a ranch in Texas," Jeff said. "I guess that explains why they're as wild as longhorns."

Violet turned to gape at Jeff. "A kidnapping?"

"Ask Fern sometime." He stepped out of the shadow of the barn, making himself clearly visible to the group galloping toward the barn.

Violet noticed a visible check in the twins' forward motion. They glanced at each other. One glanced back at Monty. Violet had to give them credit. They had guts. They didn't wait for their cousins or their uncle to catch up. They rode right up to Jeff at a gallop. For one terrifying moment, Violet thought they were going to gallop their horses right over him. But he stood unmoving. They pulled up their rearing mounts only a few feet away.

"Well," Jeff said as the girls calmed their dancing mounts. "Do you want me to give you your beating now? Or would you prefer I wait until we get back to the school?"

Chapter Sixteen

The twins lost color. They looked at each other, at Jeff, and finally at Violet. She couldn't decide if they were asking for her protection or if they wanted her to tell them their uncle was serious. Violet could give them no answer. She didn't know herself. Jeff had a right to be angry, but to spank children not his own?

"Get down. Let the groom take your horses," Jeff said.

"We ought to unsaddle them," Aurelia said. "We rode them."

"You will. He's just going to walk them for a few minutes."

The girls dismounted and handed the reins over to the groom, who took them without a word. Violet looked up, expecting to see Monty and the boys. She was surprised to see they were still some distance away. Monty was in the front and they were walking their horses. He was giving Jeff a chance to have his say in private.

Jeff glared at the girls. Violet couldn't detect any of

the kindness or understanding that he had shown toward her and Essie. He looked more like a judge facing two convicted criminals before he sentenced them.

"Do you have any idea what you have done?" he asked.

"We only wanted to—" Juliette said.

"You have upset the entire school," Jeff said, brusquely cutting off his niece. "You have upset Miss Settle. You have also upset Miss Goodwin. Furthermore, she will undoubtedly receive a reprimand for failing to keep the two of you under control."

Violet hadn't considered that aspect of it, but she was certain Jeff was right. Miss Settle would be anxious to blame someone for the inexcusable lapse.

The twins glanced at Violet, then back at their uncle. "That's not fair," Aurelia said. "No one can keep us under control."

"Worse than that, you forced Essie Brown to tell a lie. All because you wanted to do something you weren't supposed to do in the first place. That's unworthy of a Randolph. If you're going to do something wrong, you should make certain you don't cause anybody else to end up taking the blame for it. But you were too selfish, too determined to get your own way to think of that."

As usual, when faced with the consequences of what they had done, the twins were sorry. Violet didn't doubt the sincerity of their repentance that time. But she knew they'd be ready to do something just as bad a week or ten days from then. Still, she couldn't help admiring their spirit. There was nothing weak or spineless about the girls. She was beginning to think an unconquerable spirit was a Randolph family trait.

"Are you really going to beat us?" Aurelia asked.

"Don't you think I should?" Jeff said.

"Beat us here," Juliette said. "If you beat us at school, we'll just have to run away again."

Violet could hardly believe what the girl had said, but

she realized immediately it was true. If the twins received any kind of unusual punishment at school, Betty Sue would make continued enrollment at the Wolfe School impossible.

Before Jeff could say anything more, Monty and the boys rode up. "You finished giving them a piece of your mind yet?" Monty asked Jeff. He dismounted, seemingly unperturbed by the morning's events.

"He's going to spank us," Juliette said.

"Go take care of your horses," Monty said. "Come back here the minute you're finished."

Violet didn't like the tension she sensed between the brothers. Neither spoke while the girls went to their horses, but she could feel the antagonism building between them. She wondered for a moment if she should leave with the girls.

"You'd better stay, Miss Goodwin," Monty said. "You'll have to deal with the girls and the school when we're done."

"I'm afraid any action the school may take is out of my hands," Violet said. "I doubt I'll even be asked to offer an opinion."

"I still want you to stay."

Violet stayed. In their present frames of mind, she wasn't certain either brother was capable of making a sound decision. They seemed to bring out the worst in each other.

"I should have known you'd be encouraging them," Jeff said.

"It's not encouraging them to run away to go for a ride with them," Monty said. "Besides, they were already in the saddle when I got here."

"You knew they weren't supposed to be here. You should have taken them back."

"I figured I might as well let them enjoy their ride. I knew you'd be along sooner or later to take them back."

"Fine. Let me be the ogre."

"It's a role you seem to enjoy."

"You shouldn't have let them go riding with you," Jeff said.

"Short of riding them down and taking them out of the saddle, there wasn't much I could do to prevent it. Besides, they broke out of that place for a reason. Maybe having a morning free will make them more willing to stay put for a while."

"It's more likely to make them think they can leave whenever they like." When Monty shrugged, Jeff said, "They simply don't obey rules. They think they're meant for everyone but them."

"They never have behaved," Monty said. "They've given Rose gray hair."

"And you've made sure she'll get some more."

"Stow it, Jeff. And you're not going to beat them."

"I never intended to. I ought to beat you instead."

The two men faced each other like a pair of angry bull elk. They didn't shake their heads or paw the earth, but they did glare at each other, their powerful shoulders bunched and tense, ready for action. Violet wondered if they would actually come to blows. She knew that Jeff wouldn't back down just because he was missing an arm.

"For grown men, you two talk a lot of nonsense," she said. "I don't know how you expect nine-year-old girls to behave when you can't do any better than this."

Jeff looked at Violet, then the twins before turning back to Monty. He made a gesture of disgust. "You can go to Monty next time the twins get in trouble," he said to Violet. "I wash my hands of them."

He stalked off, leaving Violet to face Monty and five wide-eyed Randolph grandchildren. There wasn't much she could do except put a brave face on things until they got back to the school. After that, it would be out of her hands.

"I suppose the best thing to do is get some lunch,"

she said. "Head for the house, and make sure to wash your hands."

The five children set off at a run. The twins, older than the three boys, were soon well in front.

Jeff was waiting for Violet when she reached the house. "You think I was wrong, don't you?" he said when the others had gone in.

"In various ways, you're both right," she said. She didn't approve of his being so harsh with the twins. Yet she knew that Monty's indulgent attitude would only encourage them to continue to flout authority.

"Monty and I have never agreed on anything."

"Never?"

"Not that I remember."

"Don't you even like each other?" She would have beaten her brother senseless if it would have given him the will to live, but she had loved him deeply.

"No, I guess not."

"But you're brothers."

"We can't help that."

Violet didn't know what to say. It was a concept she simply couldn't understand.

"I have to go back to the bank," he said. "I'll send the carriage to take you and the twins back to school when you've finished lunch."

"Aren't you going to come with me to find out what Miss Settle decides?"

"Nobody likes what I've done. As long as Monty's here, he'll interfere. Let Fern deal with them—or Iris if Fern's not up to it."

"I like most of what you've done," Violet said.

She really did. She didn't agree with him on everything, but she agreed with his stern attitude. Life wasn't easy. It wasn't accommodating. If people didn't exercise some kind of control, they were in for a lot of trouble. And it was her experience that, when someone got in trouble, the people who suffered the most were the people who loved them. She didn't think that was fair, but it seemed to be the way things worked.

"Most is not good enough," Jeff said. "Besides, Rose and George will soon be here."

"They really are coming?"

"When they hear about this latest escapade, they'll come right away."

"What are they like?" Violet had often wondered what kind of people could have produced the twins.

"They're nothing like those hellions, if that's what you're wondering. But I'll let you make up your own mind. Is there anything you'd like me to do before I leave?"

Violet was almost too startled to answer. Jeff had never said anything like that to her before. He usually just turned and left. Period. "I've taken up enough of your morning as it is."

Jeff gave a rare smile. "Don't worry. I still have all night to catch up with the money that got away this morning."

He was never going to let her forget that remark, but she wished she hadn't said it. It had obviously touched a sensitive nerve.

She watched him go, but for the first time she didn't feel he was walking out of her life. It seemed that she had always known him, that he had always been there. She marveled that it could have happened so quickly, so easily, when she was a damned Yankee and he a stiff-necked Southerner.

What a combination, yet despite their differences, he answered some need in her. Even then she felt herself trying to reach out to him, to will him to come back. She hadn't felt that way when Nathan Wainwright asked her to marry him. She had watched him leave, sad, but certain she had been right to refuse him. She was equally certain that she couldn't let Jeff go.

* * *

Violet was stunned to see Jeff waiting at the school when she arrived with the girls. She immediately ordered the twins inside to their room.

"I thought you had work to do," she said the minute the twins were out of sight.

"I do, but I'm determined Miss Settle is not going to blame you for what those brats did. Nobody can control them. I'll be happy to let her try if she thinks differently."

Violet was immensely pleased. "I'm not afraid of Miss Settle."

"I'm sure you're not, but she's not likely to take her displeasure out on you if I'm present."

Violet had no desire to have a peal rung over her head. She had done the best she could, but with 14 other girls to care for, she simply couldn't keep an eye on the twins every minute.

"I thought you never played the knight errant." She shouldn't have teased him. He wouldn't like it, and it wasn't kind after what he'd done for her.

"What are you talking about?"

"Helping the damsel in distress."

Jeff looked at a loss. Then as understanding dawned, Violet saw a series of emotions mold his expression. She was surprised when the one that won out was a smile. Her heart did a little flip-flop. She wished he would smile more often.

"That's a Randolph tradition, but it's not one I've bothered with before. It inevitably lands us in a lot of trouble."

"Aren't you afraid it'll do that to you?"

"It already has."

Since his statement was too provocative, too potentially interesting to leave alone, Violet asked, "What kind of trouble are you in?"

"Female trouble."

That wasn't exactly how she hoped he would phrase it. She decided to give him another chance. His damsel-rescuing skills were rusty. But then he'd just admitted he had kept them on the shelf most of his life.

"I think it a little unkind to say female in that manner when you're talking about your nieces. I admit they're a lot of trouble, but they are basically sweet girls."

They had reached the steps of the building that held Miss Settle's office. Jeff stopped. Violet paused and turned toward him.

"They are holy terrors, completely uncontrollable. But it's you I'm talking about, and you know it."

She gaped at him. It was the answer she'd been hoping for, but she was still unprepared when she got it.

"I like you, damn it, and I don't want to."

That she expected. In fact, it was so much what she expected that she couldn't help but smile. Things were back to normal. She understood this Jeff.

"Not all Yankees are wicked," she said. "Some of us have been known to be quite nice."

Good God! She could feel her eyelashes lower, then flutter provocatively. She just knew her smile was teasing. She was flirting right there within sight of half of Denver, and with Jeff Randolph, the most flirt-resistant man God had ever made. She tried to pull herself together. She wasn't certain she knew how she wanted to rearrange her feelings. Things didn't feel all that bad just then.

"Stop being intentionally dense," Jeff said. "And unless you have something in your eye, stop screwing up your face and look at me."

Definitely rusty. In fact, he had no skills at all. She wondered if he would ever develop any. From the depth of the frown he wore, she didn't figure it was high on his priority list.

"It was okay when I just thought you were pretty," Jeff said. "Even the most terrible females can be pretty.

My nieces spring immediately to mind. It wasn't even too bad when I wanted to kiss you. Has anybody ever told you you have a very kissable mouth? You don't paint your lips, but they're full and pink, not thin and white. It was okay that I find the rest of you attractive as well. But I started to like you. I started to admire you. Not much,'' he said hastily, ''but some.''

Jeff turned away, as though he wanted to leave, to escape the whole embarrassing business. ''Then I started to think about you all the time. I found your image getting in the way of my work. I'd be staring at a column of figures or reading a report, and I'd see your face. I'd have no idea what I'd just read. I'd remember something you said, something you did. You ruined my entire working schedule. Now I'm here!''

He seemed to find that the most unacceptable of all. ''I have a desk covered with work, an office full of clerks waiting for me. Am I at my desk, doing my work, keeping my clerks running until their tongues hang out? No! I'm here to make sure that dragon doesn't try to blame this whole thing on you.''

He looked stunned at his own folly. Violet hoped she wasn't screwing up her face, but she just knew she was smiling again and acting as if there was something caught in her eye. Never had a string of complaints sounded so much like music to her ears. She was delighted to know Jeff was caught and dangling on the same hook that had caught in her heart almost from the first.

She figured she had to be crazy to want to spend as much as five minutes in the company of this misogynist. Her father and brother had been two of the most mild-mannered men ever born. Her mother had been gentle and understanding. Violet could only assume that, as an antidote to all that sweetness, she needed a dose of vinegar with a little vitriol thrown in to give it bite. Jeff Randolph certainly qualified on both counts.

"You don't have to stay," Violet said. "I'm really quite capable of facing Miss Settle by myself."

"I'll stay." He took her elbow and started her toward the door.

"You don't want to be here."

"I'd be miserable anywhere else."

When they were finally ushered into Miss Settle's office, Violet had to admit that she was glad Jeff had come with her. Miss Settle appeared to be on the verge of having some sort of fit. The first words were almost out of her mouth when Jeff followed Violet through the doorway into her office. Miss Settle's startled reaction was almost comical.

"Mr. Randolph, what are you doing here? I hope your nieces are safely returned."

"They are. For the moment, Miss Goodwin has confined them to their room."

Miss Settle did seem relieved to hear that. "Good. I would hate for your family to think we couldn't take proper care of our students."

"Nobody can take proper care of those demons," Jeff said. "If you really want to control them, buy yourself a jail cell, lock them up, and throw away the key. Then post two guards just in case they figure some way out."

Miss Settle tittered nervously. "Mr. Randolph, the Wolfe School does not lock up its students."

"Then don't blame Miss Goodwin when they get out again."

Miss Settle's smile was tight. "I'm certain Miss Goodwin will see that they don't. Now you must have many important decisions awaiting your attention. I appreciate your coming, but I know you won't want to sit through a tedious discussion of rules and behavior policies."

"I came to make certain you didn't try to blame all this on Miss Goodwin," Jeff said, blunt as always.

For a moment Miss Settle was too stunned to speak. Finally she managed to say, "Of course not."

"Good," Jeff said. "It never does to shift the blame for problems onto those below you. They never have the power to change anything. Only you can do that. It's a principle I go by. Hire the best people you can find— like Miss Goodwin here—give them the best tools to work with, and then let them do their work. If you do that, when something goes wrong, it's your fault."

"I beg your pardon!" Miss Settle said weakly.

"You've obviously given her an impossible task. That's your blunder. So it's up to you to figure out what she needs in order to do the job the way you want it done and then give it to her at once."

Jeff sat back in his chair, apparently satisfied that he had explained his theory so that even Miss Settle could understand it.

"It works like a charm for me. Nearly every man in my bank has been with me more than ten years. Saves times, as well. You're not forever training new people, and you have the advantage of all that experience."

"I see," Miss Settle said, still nearly speechless. "I'm sure it's a most excellent system." She seemed to finally gather her wits. "I'm sure you will want to see your nieces before you leave. I'll let you know what I decide. Miss Goodwin, accompany Mr. Randolph."

"Kick them out," Jeff said. "George won't like it, but it'll save you a lot of headaches."

"Jeff Randolph, how could you say such a thing about your own nieces!" Violet said once they were outside. "They're only nine."

"It's the truth. I don't know what's gotten into them. They didn't used to be this bad."

"I'm afraid Miss Settle will expel them. There's not much else she can do."

"Serves them right."

"Is that all you're going to say?"

"What else can I say? Do you think I can make them stay here, follow the rules, and act all sweetness and light?"

"No, I doubt anybody will ever be able to do that."

"I say cut your losses and move on." Jeff glanced at his watch. "I'd better be getting back. If I drive everybody mercilessly, I can catch up before midnight."

"You're not going to keep all those poor men there that late on Saturday."

"Why not? With me running all over Denver, they haven't had a thing to do all day. Don't start in on me. I won't make them work on Sunday."

"How generous of you."

"Why don't you say what you really mean: that I'm a mean-spirited Scrooge who'd squeeze the last drop of blood out of a turnip?"

"There's no point in saying that when you seem to take pride in it."

"It's just the way I am. I stopped trying to fight that years ago."

"That's not true. You've been fighting everything and everybody so hard you've completely lost sight of the man you really are."

The easy feeling of companionship vanished instantly to be replaced by brittle tension.

"What do you mean by that?" Jeff asked, his mask of civility slipping away. "And don't think you're going to get by with some mealymouthed answer. I want to know exactly what you think you're talking about."

Violet wasn't sure it was wise for her to say anything further. She wasn't certain she had the right. She was venturing into an area that was none of her business, an area clearly marked with a no-trespassing sign.

She couldn't afford to say the wrong thing. If she was going to stick her nose into forbidden territory, she at least owed it to Jeff to know what she was talking about.

Chapter Seventeen

"I shouldn't have said that," Violet said. "I don't know you well enough to pass judgment."

"But you already have, and I'm not going to let you back out with a coward's answer like that," Jeff said.

"It's not a coward's answer. You've closed yourself up tighter than a New England clam."

"Stop stalling, and spit it out."

She shouldn't have said anything in the first place. But she had the consolation of knowing Jeff could only blame himself if he didn't like what he heard. She had tried to back down.

"I think you actually like having everybody disapprove of you. Maybe since nobody expects you to try to please them, they don't get upset when you do the opposite. They expect it of you."

"Why should I like that?"

"Because you can go around doing exactly as you please. Most of us have to make some attempt to get along. You don't. Nobody expects it."

"What else?"

Violet sighed. She doubted she'd ever learn to keep her mouth shut. Men didn't like the truth. Nobody did really. If she wanted to drive Jeff away, telling him exactly what she thought of him was a good way to start.

"I don't know how much the war still bothers you after all these years—I suspect it's a lot less than you want anybody to believe—but you intentionally keep the wound open. You wave your arm about to make people feel guilty. I think it was originally the way you worked off your anger at losing the war, the loss of your arm, and your imprisonment."

"You don't think that was important?"

"Of course, but you outgrew that long ago. You found something you could do, and you did it. You're too busy to have time to think about that arm or brood on the war."

Violet could tell Jeff wanted to interrupt, but she was determined not to let him. He'd say plenty when he got started, but she meant to get it all out of her system.

"I don't mean that you don't feel angry about what the war did to you, Virginia, or the thousands of men who lost their lives or their limbs. But the heat of the anger has cooled. You've grown past it. You've accepted it as a part of your life and moved on. But you've used the war and your arm as a battering ram for so long, it's become a habit. Everybody else has fallen into the habit of letting you."

Jeff looked at her in the same manner Violet imagined a mother wolf would look at any animal that threatened her pups.

"It amazes me that I actually thought I might need to protect you from Miss Settle," he said. "I forgot you're a Yankee. And a Yankee is equal to two or three lesser mortals. You didn't need my help. You could just have sunk your teeth into that poor woman and chewed and chewed until there was nothing left."

Violet had been prepared for anger, but his retort was more than she had expected. He wasn't just angry at her. He was angry at himself. He had let himself feel, and she had rewarded him by not needing him. He was wrong, but he wouldn't believe her if she told him. She'd been so busy trying to show him that she knew everything there was to know about him that she'd lost the moment.

She wasn't one of his simpering, helpless, clinging Southern belles, and she didn't want to be. She didn't need anybody to take up for her. If that was the way he was hoping to restore his image of himself, he'd have to look somewhere else. But just because she could stand on her own two feet didn't mean she didn't need someone to lean on occasionally.

Standing alone was a weary, lonely job. It denied her too much of what life had to offer, most of what made it worthwhile. Jeff wouldn't understand that. To him, life was a battle, a continual struggle against something, against somebody. He would never understand that just knowing that he was at her side, that she was in his thoughts, that he missed her, was the greatest gift he could give her. She didn't need his money, his social standing, or even his protection. She needed just a small corner of his heart.

"I do appreciate your going with me to see Miss Settle," she said. "I'll always cherish the look on her face when you told her the twins' escape was really her fault. But I did tell you that I could face her alone."

"I remember, but you'll forgive me for hoping my presence would help prevent at least one little scratch. I didn't realize I was protecting Miss Settle."

They stood in the middle of the walk. One direction led toward the girl's dormitory. The other led to the road and back to town. It was time they went in those two different directions. It was time they parted.

"I have to get back to the twins. They may be little

terrors, but they're still nine years old, and I imagine they could use some reassurance right about now. And you," she said, before he could speak, "need to get back to your waiting clerks."

Violet put out her hand. "I'm sorry for all the inconvenience. I appreciate your help and your kindnesses. I'll always remember my two days at the Windsor."

Rather than take her hand, Jeff abruptly slipped his arm around her and drew her to him. "You're a witch. You ought to be burned at the stake!"

Then he kissed her so roughly her senses were suspended. Violet abandoned reason, common sense, even basic caution, and kissed him back. She didn't understand why she should be so willing to put up with rough handling from the man, but she couldn't fight her feelings for him any longer.

She forgot that they could be seen by half the school. She forgot that she and Jeff couldn't agree on anything. She was only aware that he held her in his arms and that she'd never felt better in her life.

His strength amazed her. She felt crushed, imprisoned, incapable of moving. His kiss was rough and angry, but she didn't care. She felt rough and angry, too. She wanted to grab him and rip apart all the walls that he had built around himself, to explode the barricades of his mind.

She wanted to hold him and kiss him until he knew she loved him, knew she didn't care whether he had one arm or three, knew no matter how bad-tempered and cruel he might be she understood that he was just as vulnerable, just as desperate for love as everybody else.

So she held him. She kissed him. She clung to him long after he would have let her go. She pressed her body against him so that he would know she would withhold nothing from him. She promised all. She demanded nothing.

When he released her, Violet felt as if she had been

ravaged. Her lips burned, her body ached, her skin felt on fire, and her hair was coming down. Before either of them could collect their thoughts enough to speak, she saw Harvey McKee coming along the street.

Suddenly Violet felt less brazen. She couldn't possibly explain her conduct to Harvey. "I've got to go in," she said, trying to sound as composed as possible. "Even witches have to give their brooms a rest now and then. If I don't, I'm liable to get a very different name."

"Let anyone say a word against you and I'll—"

She smiled. Jeff might have been angry, but he was still ready to protect her. That was something to remember. "There you go again, trying to defend me. Didn't you decide I was more than capable of protecting myself?"

Harvey was crossing the street. He would reach the flagstone path to the school soon.

"Men like to feel that women need protection. Take that away, and what use are we?" Jeff said.

Violet couldn't help feeling sad that Jeff should think his appeal so limited. "Ask me again when I have time to answer that question. Now I must go."

"Not before I have the last word." He kissed her quickly, turned, and walked away.

Violet watched Jeff leave, completely bewildered at the unexpected turn of events. If he were about to fall in love with her—and she knew he wasn't—she would have expected some tenderness, not banter. If he were merely irritated with her, she didn't understand the kiss. More importantly, it proved beyond all doubt that she had fallen in love with Jeff. There was no reason for it. It defied logic, but she had fallen in love anyway. And she wasn't even sure she liked the man!

She admired him, lusted after him, and thought about him constantly. It wasn't enough for love, but it was too much to ignore. Far too much to forget.

But she must try. Jeff had no intention of falling in

love with a Yankee. She didn't think he was constitutionally capable, no matter how attractive he found her. And if he did love her, he would fight it for the rest of his life. Any way she looked at it, it would be a miserable existence for both of them. The only sensible thing to do was put him out of her mind.

She watched as Jeff and Harvey met on the walkway. Even at that distance she could see Jeff's frown and Harvey's raised eyebrow. They glanced in her direction, then back at each other. She smiled to herself. It was nice to be snarled over by two tomcats. It had never happened to her before. She found it quite bracing.

The two men separated. Violet almost broke out laughing when Jeff looked back twice. It would have served him right if he suffered a few pangs of jealousy over her. He had caused her enough already. She was certain he would cause her more before she finally got him out of her system.

The twins climbed out of the carriage and followed Violet up the walk, their heads hanging, their expressions solemn. Miss Settle had dismissed them from the Wolfe School, and Violet was taking them to stay with their Aunt Fern until their parents arrived. Her first thought had been to tell Jeff, but it was impossible for the girls to stay with him. Even if he had had the time, he wouldn't know what to do with them.

"Papa's going to be upset," Aurelia said.

"Mama's going to be mad," Juliette said.

"Probably," Violet said. "I'm sure she had hoped you'd do well in school."

"We told her we wouldn't," Aurelia said.

"No Randolph likes school except William Henry," Juliette said.

Violet rang the doorbell. "I know it must be hard being cooped up all the time, but the school can't afford to let you keep running away. Something might happen."

"Nothing ever happens to us," Aurelia said.

"Papa says we lead charmed lives," Juliette said.

"Maybe, but you weren't very charming to Miss Settle."

A maid opened the door and led them to a small parlor. "I'll tell Mr. Randolph you're here," she said and disappeared.

"I don't want to see Uncle Madison," Aurelia said.

"He doesn't like girls," Juliette said.

"He must like children," Violet said.

"He likes boys," Aurelia said.

"He says you don't have to worry about boys," Juliette said. "He says they bring themselves up."

"His boys could have been girls," Violet said.

Aurelia shook her head. "He said he'd have given them away."

Before Violet had time to wonder whether the twins had made part or all of their remarks up, a tall, dark, handsome man entered the parlor. She could see some similarities to Jeff. He glared at the twins. They cringed before him.

"So you finally kicked the little monsters out. That's the first sensible thing you've done. Shouldn't have accepted them in the first place. I told George he ought to break them to harness himself."

Violet stared at Madison Randolph in disbelief. He sounded exactly like Jeff. "These girls are not horses," she said, rather too severely she feared, "to be whipped and tethered."

"It would probably do them good," Madison said. He turned away from the girls and approached Violet. "I'm Madison Randolph. Fern will be down in a minute. You girls go find the boys. I'm sure Miss Goodwin has seen enough of you. I know I have. Don't worry," he said to Violet when she looked undecided. "I've warned everyone. They'll be treated like prisoners until George and Rose arrive.''

"When will that be?" Violet said, unsure of what to say to the man, who seemed even more uninterested in his nieces than Jeff.

"Tomorrow," Madison said. "I got a telegram this morning."

Violet had barely managed to get used to the idea that a person could travel from Texas to Colorado in two days. She couldn't get used to the concept of a telegraph. She had heard some people in Denver had bought the new craze, the telephone. She was anxious to see one. How could anybody talk into a little box and be heard miles away? She glanced at the gas lamps that lit the parlor. So many things had changed in the last few years, but her father hadn't had the money to take advantage of them. Obviously the Randolphs had.

"I'm sorry about their dismissal," Violet said. "They're really good girls. They just don't follow rules well."

Fern entered the room in time to hear that last remark. "They never have. I don't think Rose thought that they would last very long."

Violet was shocked. Fern seemed worse than when Violet had seen her only a week earlier. Violet had to repress an impulse to help her to a chair, but it was unnecessary. Madison was on his feet the moment his wife entered the room. He might not have been interested in little girls, but Violet could tell he adored his wife. She waited until Fern was seated and Madison was satisfied that she was as comfortable as he could make her.

"I'm sorry to put you to the trouble of delivering the twins, but you can see I couldn't go after them myself," Fern said. She looked up at her husband, her eyes brimming with love, and Violet wondered if she'd ever feel like that about any man. "And now that Madison is

Leigh Greenwood

back, I don't mean to let him leave my side until this child is born."

"Miss Settle agreed I should deliver the girls in person," Violet said.

"Then if we should lose them, it's no fault of yours," Madison said.

That was exactly what Miss Settle had said, but Violet had no intention of saying so. "I was just about to tell your husband the girls are fine students, bright and willing, but they could never accustom themselves to living within the rules. That doesn't make them bad, but you can see that it would be impossible for the school to keep them under the circumstances."

"I always did suspect Rose put them in school just to give herself a rest," Madison said.

"Shame on you," Fern said. "You know that, if anybody can control those girls, it's Rose."

"Well I don't believe anybody can. God help the men who marry them."

Violet thought that an unfair evaluation. The same behavior in a boy would have been characterized as high-spirited. If he were blessed with a similar amount of money and good looks, every female of marrying age would be after him. But Violet had learned the folly of struggling against prejudices that couldn't be changed.

"Miss Settle did say if the girls became more settled in a year or two, she would be willing to consider their re-enrollment."

"How much did Jeff pay her to say that?" Madison asked.

"He doesn't know they've been dismissed," Violet said. "I thought you might want to tell him yourself."

"I doubt he'll care," Madison said.

"He was very helpful while you were away," Fern said. She laughed suddenly. "I would have given a lot to see him while he was quarantined with you."

Violet smiled in response. "He wasn't happy about

it. But for a man of his nature, he handled it remarkably well.''

She was the one who hadn't been able to handle it. She had succumbed to an emotion that was as foolish as it was futile.

''For a man of his nature? I don't know why you didn't take a gun to him,'' Madison said.

Violet bit her tongue. She had met three of Jeff's brothers, all of them brutally unkind to him. She knew he was difficult at times—she could vouch for that from her own experience—but they were his brothers. If anybody should be able to understand him, they should.

''He had a lot to put up with,'' Violet said.

Fern eyed her closely, seeing more than Violet wanted anybody to see. ''I think Miss Goodwin believes Jeff's family is too rough on him.''

Violet had no desire to be the object of so much attention, nor could she listen to Jeff being maligned and not defend him. At the same time, his relatives must have known him better than she did. How could she presume to tell them how they should treat their own brother?

''I feel responsible since I failed to tell him about the quarantine,'' Violet said.

''If you are really from Massachusetts, and I can tell from your accent you are,'' Madison said, ''the fact that he's speaking to you is a marvel. I don't mean to be insulting, but none of us can figure out how you did it.''

''Jeff's not really that troublesome. He just likes to seem difficult. You spoil him. You let him do and say what he wants, no matter how ridiculous.''

Madison and Fern stared at Violet in amazement. She felt herself flush. She hadn't meant to say so much. She certainly hadn't meant to criticize anyone.

''You should ignore him when he starts in on one of his pet subjects or show him how absurd he's being.

He's really quite intelligent and doesn't like being made to look a fool.''

"You and Rose will get along famously," Madison said.

"No, they won't," Fern said.

"They've come to the same conclusion," Madison said.

"But from entirely different directions," Fern said.

Clearly Madison didn't understand his wife's statement. And just as clearly he intended to demand an explanation. Violet didn't think she could endure that, so she stood.

"I'd better be getting back to the school. They always tell you not to worry about things while you're gone, but if I have to fix something, I'd rather be there when it goes wrong."

"You're an intelligent woman," Madison said. "Why don't you ask Jeff about a job in his bank?"

"I don't think his opinion of my abilities is as great as yours." She wasn't about to tell them that she could never control her feelings enough to work that close to Jeff. "Thank you, but I'm perfectly suited with my present position. I—"

She broke off because Fern had tried to stand up but was unable to get out of the chair.

"I'm all right," Fern insisted when both Violet and Madison attempted to go to her aid. "Sometimes I just don't have any strength. I'll be all right."

"I don't think so," Violet said. "I've had some experience with women in your condition, and something is wrong. I don't care what your doctor says," Violet said when Fern started to protest. "Did you feel like this any of the other times?"

"No," Fern said, clearly relieved to be able to admit her own fears.

"I've had every doctor in Denver to see her," Madison said. "They all say there's nothing wrong."

Violet knew how useless it was for a nurse to put her opinion up against a doctor's—for a woman to contradict a man—but she felt certain Fern was in danger. "You both know something's wrong."

They didn't need to answer. Their looks told Violet they knew.

"There's a doctor in Boston who's absolutely wonderful in situations like this. You could go see him."

"She's too weak," Madison said.

"There are trains."

Fern and Madison looked at each other, then Madison asked, "What's his name?"

"Dr. Frederick Ulmstead. If you have a piece of paper, I can give you his address." Madison produced pen and paper from his coat pocket. Violet quickly wrote down the necessary information. "Tell him I asked you to contact him. He'll remember me. He was a colleague of my father." Violet realized having a doctor for a father gave her opinion added weight. "He's very busy, but I'm sure he will find time to see you."

She left the house worried about the twins, Fern, Jeff, and herself. She forgot to worry about her silver mine.

Rose entered Fern's bedroom like a small whirlwind. "Madison says you're not well," she said, giving her sister-in-law a brisk hug. "Tell me exactly how you're feeling."

"Weak," Fern said, "but otherwise I'm fine."

"You don't have any strange pains?"

"Only once in a while, and then not very bad," Fern said, but Rose didn't look relieved.

"Hello, George," Fern said, welcoming the tall handsome man, who stood quietly behind his wife. Seeing George always gave her a start. He looked so much like Madison.

"Madison says he's taking you to Boston to see a specialist," George said.

Rose whirled to face her husband and Madison. "She's not stirring one foot out of this house. You telegraph that doctor back and tell him to get on the first train to Denver. Where is he?"

"Boston."

"How soon can he be here if he leaves today?"

"He's not leaving, Rose. He expects us to meet him in Boston."

Rose turned back to Fern. The understanding between the two women was instantaneous and absolutely clear.

"She's too weak to travel to Boston, even in one of your special cars. What do the local doctors say?"

"That she's weak."

"Any fool can see that. Who told you about this Boston doctor?"

"Miss Goodwin. She's the housemother at the Wolfe School."

Rose's brow puckered. "I'll see her tomorrow. I'll let you know what I think. Now I need to see the twins before we return to the hotel."

She turned back to Fern, her brow puckered again. "I don't think I want to stay in a hotel. I'm too old for that kind of thing. Besides, Monty's there. I'll fall out with him before the day's over. Do you mind if George and I stay here? You have so much room, you'll hardly know we're here. I can look after the boys so Madison can devote all his time to you. I promise not to meddle."

Fern smiled, relieved. She knew Rose was asking for permission to take over running the household for her. She was grateful Rose could see and understand so much so quickly.

"It's probably best. The twins are here."

"That's something else," Rose said, looking less worried. "George, see about our luggage. I think it's time I talked to our daughters."

Chapter Eighteen

The twins hesitated for a moment when their mother entered their room. But seeing her welcoming smile, they threw themselves into her arms. Rose held them both close, covering the tops of their heads with kisses. They didn't see the tears that sprang into her eyes. If they had, they wouldn't have understood.

She was glad to see them. She had missed them terribly. She had had misgivings about sending them to Denver. They were so young. She had only done it because they were twins. Together they could have faced the world. And they had proved her right.

But it was the second reason for her tears that they wouldn't understand. They were the children of her body, dear to her heart, and she knew they were unhappy. They wouldn't have behaved so badly otherwise. But they had to learn to live in the world. They couldn't remake it to suit themselves. She cried for the heartache they would encounter in the future. She cried because she could. Later she would have to be strong.

"Let me look at you," she said, stepping back from them.

"Why are you crying?" Juliette asked.

"Because I haven't seen you in a long time and I missed you."

Juliette gave her mother another big hug. Rose hugged her back, then set her at a distance from her. "You're just as much alike as always. Do you still pass yourselves off as each other?"

"Nobody can tell us apart except Miss Goodwin," Juliette said.

"You're prettier than ever. Your father's going to be so proud of you he'll probably forget you're in disgrace." Rose dried her eyes with a lace handkerchief that she had tucked in her sleeve. She picked up the chair by the door, placed it between the beds, and sat down. "Now we're going to have to talk about your behavior."

The twins subsided, each on her bed, their smiles gone.

"You realize you've made your father very unhappy," Rose said, and the twins hung their heads. "He has such a strong sense of responsibility that he simply doesn't understand how you can behave as you have."

That wasn't quite true. The girls were exactly like his father, George had told her, a deep sadness in his voice. Even if they had wanted to behave, they couldn't have. There was something inside that drove them toward their own destruction. Rose wasn't about to argue with George about his father, but she had made up her mind that her daughters weren't going to destroy themselves, not as long as she was around to do something about it.

"I ought to take both of you back to that school, let Miss Settle give you a good whipping, then put you back in your room with a lock on the door if necessary."

The girls looked horrified. "That's what Uncle Jeff wanted to do," Aurelia said.

"It seems we finally agree on something," Rose said.

"I don't normally hold with spanking, but I won't tolerate this continued wild behavior."

"We tried to be good," Juliette said.

"We wanted to be lots worse," Aurelia said.

Rose couldn't repress a smile. "I'm sure you did. All you Randolphs have to struggle to behave like ordinary people."

"Lizzie and William Henry behave."

"I think they're Thorntons. Thorntons always do what they're told. That's why they make good soldiers."

"Why can't we be Thorntons?" Juliette asked.

"I don't know, but you're unmistakably Randolphs. You look like them, you act like them, and you think like them. But that's going to have to change."

"Why?"

"You can't grow up wild. It'll make you very unhappy. And you can't keep upsetting your father. We had to leave before he was through selling the herds. You've wasted a great deal of money by getting yourselves thrown out of school. It doesn't grow on trees. Your father has to work very hard to earn it. Now you have a choice: You can come home, or you can stay here."

"We want to go home," Aurelia said.

"No, we don't," Juliette said.

"If you come home," Rose said, keenly aware of the unusual circumstance of the twins not being in instant agreement, "you will be confined to the house. You will not be able to ride your ponies, attend parties, or go on the roundup. I'll hire a private teacher for you. You'll spend your days doing your lessons, your evenings studying. I will personally supervise you."

The girls looked dumbfounded. Then Aurelia asked, "What's the other choice?"

"If the Wolfe School will take you back—"

"Miss Settle said she didn't want to see us again."

"She might be persuaded to change her mind," Rose

said. "Anyway, if they will take you back, I'll take away your allowance and your prettiest dresses. If you last a week without a single complaint against you, you can have your dresses back. If you last a month, you can have your allowance. Do you think you can do that?"

"I don't know," Aurelia said dubiously.

"Well, you'll have this evening to think about it," Rose said. "I won't let you go back to the school unless you give me your word you'll behave."

"But then we'll have to do it," Juliette said.

"That's the good thing about being a Randolph," Rose said. "Once you give your word, even little Randolphs don't go back on it."

"Do we have any other choices?" Aurelia asked.

"No, and don't think you can wheedle your father into giving you one. He has agreed to let me handle this situation." Rose relaxed her severe expression. "Now tell me what has made you so unhappy. You're not normally this bad."

"It's the twins back again," Beth said to Violet. "And their mother's with them."

"Back?" Violet asked, startled. "I don't understand. Miss Settle dismissed them."

"Mrs. Randolph says Miss Settle has agreed to reconsider if you will."

Violet couldn't imagine her opinion would weigh with the headmistress. Ever since Jeff's most recent visit, Violet had been aware of a coolness in Miss Settle's attitude toward her, almost a distrust. She was certain that it had to do with that kiss in front of the school. Miss Settle hadn't said anything, but people had to have seen it. Someone was bound to have told the headmistress.

Violet put aside the book she had been reading. She checked her image in the mirror. She was wearing a ruby-red dress. She wondered what Mrs. Randolph would think of such a bold gown.

"They're in the parlor," Beth said. "She says they have something to say to you."

Violet entered the parlor, prey to rampant curiosity. In physical appearance, Rose Randolph didn't look a thing what Violet had expected. She was small of stature, slim, and attractive without being beautiful. She had dark brown hair beginning to show silver at the temples. The look in her eye, however, was everything she had expected of a woman who could control two such tempestuous children.

"Good afternoon, Miss Goodwin," Rose said, rising to her feet. "I'm so glad to meet you at last."

"I've been wanting to meet you, too," Violet said. She let her gaze slide to where the twins sat demurely. They didn't look downcast or even unhappy. Rather they looked determined, which made Violet uneasy. She never knew what to expect from them.

Both women took seats. Rose glanced at the twins before looking back at Violet. "I apologize for the trouble the girls have given you. We have had a long talk, and they have given me their word to behave for the rest of the term."

Violet glanced at the twins. They nodded their heads in agreement.

"I have also had a talk with Miss Settle," Rose said. "As long as you are in agreement, she will allow Aurelia and Juliette to return to school. If they get into any more trouble, they will be dismissed without any possibility of returning."

Violet liked the twins and was happy to welcome them back, but she had a feeling there was more to come.

"Things aren't that simple," Rose continued, "which is why everything depends upon your willingness to take personal charge of the twins once more. Girls," Rose said, turning to her daughters.

"We want to apologize for being so bad," Juliette said.

"We're not sorry about Betty Sue," Aurelia said, "but we didn't mean to get you in trouble."

"What else?" their mother asked.

"Miss Settle says we have to ask you if we can go visit Aunt Fern every weekend to ride our horses."

Violet looked back at Rose, who said, "Miss Settle refuses to take responsibility for them once they leave the campus. Would you be willing to do that for me?"

"What about the rest of the girls and my duties here?" Violet asked.

"I've taken care of that for you," Rose said.

Violet was a little bewildered by the power the Randolph family seemed to wield. "Of course, I won't mind." It would give her some time to herself, some relief from the constant demands of her duties.

"The girls would also like to try to explain why they've been so bad. I leave it to you to see if you feel you can come up with any solution to the problem."

"Nobody likes us," Aurelia said, almost before her mother had finished speaking.

"They call us buffalo babies," Juliette said.

"Betty Sue said we're nothing but calico cowgirls who couldn't be happy unless we were all dusty and dirty."

"She said we were—"

"I don't think Miss Goodwin needs to hear any more of that," Rose said. "If you could think of some way to help the older girls accept them, it would help a lot. I don't mean to excuse their behavior, but I remember what it was like being the daughter of a colonel in the Union Army, living in a Confederate town during the War. I'd have done just about anything to get back at the people for what they said, especially about my father."

Violet could understand that. She had listened to

whispers about her own father for years. Knowing some of them were true made it all the more difficult to defend herself against those that weren't.

"It seems we need a way to make the girls more respectful of what it takes to be a rancher," Violet said. "I don't think most of them have ever seen a cow or been on a horse more than once or twice."

"Betty Sue's afraid of horses," Aurelia said.

"I don't want you to mention Betty Sue again," Rose said. "We're trying to improve things, not dwell on what's done and can't be changed."

Violet realized that it must be very difficult to be nine and be required to act grown-up. A lot of adults couldn't manage acting mature. Jeff Randolph immediately sprang to mind, but she reminded herself his problem was prejudice, not immaturity. But then wasn't prejudice a kind of immaturity? Or in Jeff's case, was it just plain stubbornness? There seemed to be plenty of it in the family. The twins had a sizable portion.

"It's a shame we can't invite all the girls to Texas with us," Rose said, "and let them watch us work cows."

"There must be ranches close to Denver," Violet said.

"We could ride our ponies," Aurora said.

"And William Henry could shoot targets," Juliette said. "He's a real drip, but he's a dead shot."

"What you need is a kind of rodeo," Violet said. "I saw one advertised when I reached Denver.

"We could do it at Aunt Fern's," Juliette said, her eyes bright with excitement. "She's got lots of cows."

"And the space," Rose said, immediately thoughtful. Then she laughed at her daughters' enthusiasm. "You realize that you won't be able to keep Monty away, don't you?"

"Could you bring our ponies from Texas?" Aurelia asked.

"Uncle Monty will bring Nightmare. You know he will."

Rose turned to Violet. "Do you think the school would countenance such a thing?"

"I don't know," Violet said. "I know nothing about rodeos. I couldn't possibly organize one."

"We'll take care of that," Rose said. "All you need to do is get Miss Settle's approval for the girls to attend. We'll see to everything else."

"Do you think it will answer?" Violet asked.

"I don't know, but it'll go a long way toward making the twins more content. It'll give them a chance to take pride in being from Texas."

"We can practice when we go to Aunt Fern's," Aurelia said.

"Will Daddy help us?" Juliette asked.

"I'm sure he will. But I think you ought to invite James and Tazewell to participate."

"They're so little," Aurelia said.

"They're not much younger than you. And since their mother is undoubtedly the best horsewoman in the family, I imagine they can hold their own. Besides, if you plan to hold your rodeo on their ranch, I don't see how you can do anything else."

"If you'll choose a date, I'll talk to Miss Settle," Violet said. "I don't know about the day students, but all the boarders will come."

"We'll make it a real festive occasion, something all the girls will want to attend," Rose said.

"Would you like to go tell the girls you're back?" Violet said. "You can tell them about the rodeo, too. I'm certain Miss Settle will approve."

When the twins disappeared, anxious to spread the news, Rose said, "I appreciate your doing this for me."

"I'm not doing anything," Violet said. "You've cleared their return with Miss Settle, and you're going to take care of all arrangements for the rodeo. All I have to do is enjoy my afternoons off.''

"I expect it will be more than that," Rose said, "but thank you for feeling that way."

"Have you talked to Jeff? I mean, he's the one who spent the most time with the twins recently." Jeff couldn't tell Rose anything other people hadn't, but Violet wanted to know where he was, what he was doing. She hadn't heard from him since that morning.

Rose laughed softly. "The girls told me that he forced his way in here because he thought you were hiding from him. It sounds exactly like something Jeff would do. After putting up with him, I'm surprised you didn't flatly refuse to have anything else to do with our family.''

"He wasn't that bad," Violet said, wondering if there was anybody in his family who liked Jeff. No wonder he was about as cheerful as a Puritan. It must have been difficult knowing not even his own family wanted him around. "It was awkward at times, but we managed."

"Now I understand why you were so willing to take the twins back—even they won't seem so terrible after Jeff.''

Violet found it impossible to hold her tongue. She didn't know what had occurred between Rose and Jeff 14 years earlier, but she did feel it was time the family tried to treat him like a human being.

"The twins and Jeff are difficult people to deal with, but I've found it worth the effort," Violet said. She hoped Rose's raised eyebrows indicated surprise rather than anger, but she really didn't care.

"I'm glad you like him," Rose said. "Jeff needs that. Most of the time he won't believe anyone can, even his family."

Violet was relieved by Rose's quick understanding. She was also glad of her willingness to go straight to the heart of the matter without beating around the bush. It allowed her to do the same. "Then why does everyone say such cruel things to him?''

"The Randolphs are a strange family. I've been married to George for fourteen years, and I still don't understand why they're the way they are. You can't have two of them in the same room for five minutes without a fight—even Hen and Monty, and they're twins—but they'd travel around the world if any one of them was in trouble. Jeff has been more unforgiving than any of them, but he accepts their unkindness in return. Sometimes I think he feels it's all he deserves.''

"But he's not really like that. I thought he was, but you should have seen him with Essie Brown. She's only eight, and the shiest child, but Jeff had her chattering like a magpie. She absolutely adores him.''

"George says that Jeff was different before the war, that it destroyed something in him forever. I don't know. I've tried to like him, but he has never forgotten that my father was a colonel in the Union Army. As far as he's concerned, I might as well have enlisted myself.''

"But he's not like that now. Oh, he says a lot of stuff, but it's out of habit. He doesn't believe it.''

Rose's gaze narrowed. "What makes you say that?''

"I'm from Massachusetts, and my brother fought in the war. Jeff was a prisoner in a town near where I was born, but he gave me two days in the Windsor Hotel after the quarantine was over. And after the twins ran away, he came back with me to make sure the headmistress didn't blame it on me.''

"Maybe he has changed. I hadn't noticed, but I haven't seen much of him since he left Texas. George will be glad to hear it. He worries about Jeff.''

Violet wanted to meet George. She liked him already.

Rose stood. "I've taken too much of your time. The girls are to give up their six most favorite dresses for a week. Make sure they don't pick out the worst of their wardrobe. If you need me to talk to Miss Settle about the rodeo, just let me know. And thank you again.

You've been more than generous to all of us.''

"I'm happy to do it. I've always liked Aurelia and
Juliette.''

"And you didn't find Jeff to be a trial?''

Violet didn't trust the way Rose was looking at her.
She understood why everyone was a little uncomfortable
around her. No one could hide a thing from Rose Randolph.

"When a man looks that handsome and can be charming when he tries, it's not too hard to put up with him
for a few days. Besides, he was more scared of us than
we were of him.''

Rose smiled knowingly. "You're either a very courageous woman, or you have a liking for difficult people.''

Violet laughed. "I think I like difficult people, which
is quite perverse of me since my own family was so
kind and gentle.''

Violet remained in the parlor for several minutes after
Rose had left. She had to organize in her mind all she
would have to do over the next few weeks. It wasn't
going to mean a lot of work for her, but she would have
to keep a lot of people working together, not the least
of whom were the twins and Betty Sue. Everything depended on that.

Violet rose to her feet determined that the girls would
get along if she had to house them on separate floors for
the rest of the term. As long as she was involved with
the Randolph family, there was a chance she would see
Jeff again. She didn't mean to let three capricious little
girls rob her of that chance.

"I didn't think I'd live to see the day,'' Rose said to
George when they had retired to their room for the night,
"but after fourteen years, I think Jeff has found the
woman for him.''

"Who is she?'' George asked, his glance skeptical.

"Promise you won't laugh."

"Why should I?"

"She's a Yankee housemother from Massachusetts."

"Do you mean that woman you went to see this afternoon about the twins, the one who got him locked up in the quarantine?"

"The very one."

"What's she like?"

"She's got brassy red hair, wears boldly colored gowns, has a liking for difficult people, speaks her mind, and thinks Jeff is miserably rude out of habit."

The description seemed to clinch it in George's mind. "He'll never marry anybody like that. He still thinks women ought to act like Ma. He wouldn't marry a Yankee in any case. He'd have to take back half of what he's said over the last twenty years, and he's too proud to do that."

"I'll bet you."

George regarded his wife indulgently. A slow grin spread across his face. "I'd never bet against you when you look like a cat at a bowl of cream."

Violet hurried down the stairs. She couldn't imagine what Jeff was doing downstairs in the parlor, but Beth had sent up a note saying Mr. Randolph was waiting for her. She was wearing her emerald-green gown. It was her favorite because it struck such a contrast with her eyes and hair. She was brought up short when she entered the parlor to see Madison Randolph pacing rapidly around the room.

"He won't come," he said without preamble.

"I beg your pardon. Who won't come?" Violet asked, struggling hard to overcome her disappointment and to grasp hold of the conversation.

"Your doctor. He said he can't come all this way just for one appointment."

"I thought you were taking your wife to Boston."

"Her doctor says she's too weak even for a train trip."

Violet was disappointed. Dr. Ulmstead was the only man she felt sure would know what was wrong with Fern.

"I'm sorry, but I don't know how I can help you."

"I want you to try to persuade him for me."

"I'll be happy to write any number of letters, but I don't think we have enough time."

"I don't mean letters. I mean the telegraph."

"I don't understand."

"He's going to be in Chicago in a week for a conference. I want you to talk him into coming to Denver after it's over."

"Did you offer him more money?"

"More money and a private car from Chicago to Denver, but he still wouldn't come."

"Then I don't see how I—"

"But he knows you. You said he was a friend of your father. Surely he'll do more for you than for a stranger."

Violet didn't feel confident that old loyalties would move Dr. Ulmstead where money hadn't.

"He's agreed to be near a telegraph at eight o'clock tonight," Madison said. "I want you to go with me and talk to him."

"I don't know how to use a telegraph," Violet said.

"You don't have to know. I have my own operator."

"I can't leave the girls. Miss Settle—"

"One of the teachers is going to stay with the girls until you get back."

Violet felt swept away by the tide of Madison's urgency. "All right," she said. "If you think I can help."

"Good. I'll be back for you at seven-thirty."

"Where will we be going?"

"To Jeff's office. We'll use the bank's telegraph."

Chapter Nineteen

Jeff looked the same as Violet remembered. She hadn't forgotten a single detail. He seemed stiffer, more reserved than usual. There was another man present who looked so much like Madison it was uncanny.

"I'm George Randolph," the man said, introducing himself, "the father of the terrible twins."

Violet had never seen Jeff with George or Madison. She knew he stood in awe of his oldest brother. She had also gathered that Madison was a dynamic, somewhat abrasive character. Jeff pretended to be tough, but she knew he wasn't. She wondered if that could account for his withdrawal. Was that the only way he could cope with his brothers?

Despite the confusion and excitement of the moment, Violet couldn't help comparing Jeff's office with the attic he had occupied for five days. The difference made her cringe. She was surrounded by mahogany, leather, and polished brass. There was even a telephone on the wall. It was the office of a man who controlled millions from Chicago to San Francisco. She had been brought there by a man who casually spoke of private railway cars ready to travel a thousand miles at any moment. And the third man oversaw an empire made up of at least three cattle ranches in three different states. She felt more out of place than in the Windsor Hotel.

"Who's going to operate the telegraph?" Violet asked. There was no one in the room but the three brothers.

"I am," Jeff said, a faint smile easing the downward curve of his mouth. "Don't look so surprised. I don't like anybody knowing what I'm sending."

"Is the doctor at the telegraph?" Madison asked.

"Yes," Jeff said. "I just received confirmation."

"Then write your first message, Miss Goodwin."

Violet had dreaded that moment. She didn't know what to say. She didn't know how to go about convincing a man to do something he'd already decided not to do. She didn't know how to do it with Jeff and Madison looking over her shoulder. The aura of coiled intensity around them was so strong it interfered with her thinking. She found herself drawn to George because he seemed to be the only calming influence in the room.

"How does this work?" she asked.

"You write the message on a piece of paper, and I send it," Jeff said. "Then we wait for his answer. Once we have that, you write your reply, and we start all over again."

Violet racked her brain, her thoughts disturbed by the three men waiting in silence. She was certain Madison had already used every logical argument. That left Fern's medical condition. But Madison was going to follow the conversation, and she didn't want to worry him any more than necessary.

Dear Dr. Ulmstead,
 Please come, if only as a favor to me. None of

*the local doctors can help Mrs. Randolph, and I
fear for her health and the safety of the baby.*

"I've already told him that," Madison said, clearly
unhappy with her message. "Can't you think of
something else?"

"Let's see what he says," George said while Jeff
started a nerve-racking tapping at the telegraph key.
"She can't threaten him."

Violet felt sorry for Madison, who knew his wife was
dangerously ill and believed there was someone who
could bring her safely through the pregnancy, but was
unable to use his money or his forceful personality to
save her.

*Would love to help, but schedule full. Chicago next
week. Then back to Boston to raise money for
clinic. Couldn't possibly come for three to six
months. Do you still have Indians loose on the
plains?*

Violet felt a cold chill descend over her as she read
the reply. Dr. Ulmstead didn't seem the least bit interested in coming to Denver, and she couldn't think of
anything to make him change his mind.

"That crazy fool!" Madison said. "He's afraid he'll
be scalped. Doesn't he know Colorado's been a state for
four years? Maybe he thinks the Indians mine the gold
and silver, cut the timber, and grow the cattle we ship
back east to feed those fat, lazy Bostonians."

Violet's gaze flew to Madison. He sounded so much
like his brother she wondered if all the Randolphs
scorned Yankees.

"He's probably more curious than anything," George
said. "Most Easterners are. You should hear what Jeff
said the people in Virginia asked him the last time he
was there."

272

"I don't give a damn about Virginia. Just one lily-livered Boston doctor!" Madison said.

While Madison vented his rage at George, Violet handed Jeff a brief message. His gaze flew to hers when he read it. His eyebrows rose in a question. Violet nodded her head. Jeff tossed the message in the fire before beginning to send it.

> *You must come. She will die if you don't. Do it as a favor to me in memory of your friendship with my father.*

"What did she say?" Madison asked.

Shaking his head, Jeff kept sending, but Violet said, "I asked him to come as a favor to me."

"You did that already."

"I didn't think it would hurt to try again."

A message came in:

> *Are you sure?*

Violet nodded. Jeff sent the one-word reply.

"What did he say?" Violet asked.

"Nothing," Jeff said.

The line was quiet for a long time. Jeff sat behind his desk, waiting to transcribe the message when it came. George stood by the fire, his calm gaze on Madison, who paced the room with increasing impatience. Violet waited. She felt like an interloper in the drama that swirled around her, but which really didn't include her. She was helpless to avoid the tragedy that loomed ahead.

Maybe she shouldn't have said anything about Dr. Ulmstead. Maybe it was wrong to have given the family false hope. Maybe she should have encouraged them to take Fern to Boston despite the risks.

But it was too late for that. Their only hope was to convince Dr. Ulmstead to come to Denver.

The telegraph came alive. The tension in the room was awful. Jeff handed Madison the message.

Sorry. Clinic more important. Can save many women that way.

"Damn him to hell!" Madison said. "He'll come if I have to go to Boston and drag him all the way myself."

While Madison thundered out his anger and frustration to George, Violet quickly read the message, then wrote out a fresh response.

How much money do you need?

The answer came back almost immediately:

$30,000.

"We may be able to convince him to come after all," Violet said to Madison.

"How?"

"He's trying to raise money for a clinic. He needs thirty thousand dollars. If you could manage to raise that much money, or at least a good portion of it, I think—"

Madison turned to Jeff. "Tell him I'll give him ten thousand in cash the minute he sees my wife. I'll give him an extra thousand dollars for every day less than thirty it takes him to get here. I'll have a private car waiting in Chicago."

It took Jeff a while to send the message. The quiet in the room deepened. But it was better than the tension that filled the room when the telegraph key began its rhythmic dance. All four of them knew the response was the last chance. Afterward, there would be no appeal.

Jeff didn't write anything down. He just listened. Violet found herself afraid to breathe, afraid to move, afraid anything she did might prejudice the outcome.

Then the key fell silent. As they waited to see if there would be any more to the message, the tension in the room grew even more strained.

"Dr. Ulmstead says he will come," Jeff said. "He'll send us details after he reaches Chicago."

Madison gave a whoop, pulled Violet out of the chair, gave her a resounding kiss on the mouth, and headed for the door. "I've got to tell Fern!"

"I'd better go with him," George said to Jeff.

"I'll see Miss Goodwin back to the school," Jeff said.

George advanced toward Violet. He took her hands in his. "I don't know what it was you said that changed the doctor's mind. I suppose it's best it remain between you and Jeff, but the family owes you a great debt. I doubt we will be able to repay it, but we'll try."

"There's no need. I didn't—" Violet broke off, startled when George kissed her on the cheek.

"Rose said you were very generous. She was right. Have Jeff bring you around sometime. I would like to get to know you."

Violet watched openmouthed as George left the room.

"You didn't say you thought she'd die just to make the doctor come?" Jeff asked.

She shook her head. "I saw a woman suffering like that once before."

"What happened?"

"She insisted upon having her baby at home as she'd always done."

"Did she die?"

When Violet nodded her head, Jeff remained in his chair, staring into space. Violet didn't know whether to speak, remain silent, sit still, or leave the room. She felt her presence was an imposition.

Yet she didn't want to leave. She had looked forward to seeing Jeff again. She hadn't had a chance to do more than compose messages. She wanted to know how he was doing, if he had forgotten her.

He looked drained, as though the last half hour had taken all the energy out of him. He also looked worried. She wanted to say something comforting, to share the moment with him, but she didn't feel she had the right to intrude.

"I'm sorry. Do you need to get back to the school right away?" he asked.

"No, I could wait a few minutes if you need."

"Do you mind walking?"

Violet didn't look forward to that. It wasn't very far—six short blocks and two long ones—but it was cold outside. At least there was no snow or ice on the ground yet. "No, I don't mind."

"Of course, you do. It's freezing outside."

"I brought my coat and gloves."

Violet felt like kicking herself. There she was acting like one of those brainless women who would endanger her health to spend five minutes with a handsome man. And that handsome man was very likely to say something rude and hurtful before they left the building.

They were silent as they put on their coats, while she waited for Jeff to lock up, and as they went down the steps into the street. Fifteenth Street was quiet. City Hall across the street was dark, closed, everybody had gone home, but the streets shimmered in the light of gas lamps. The sound of their heels on the sidewalk echoed down the empty corridor.

Sounds of music and raised voices could be heard coming from saloons, around corners, even out of doors on the ground floor of the Palace Theater back toward Cherry Creek, but Violet and Jeff had the sidewalk to themselves. It was cold, but Violet was still warm from being inside. She pulled her collar up around her neck and dug her hands deep inside her pockets.

"Have you ever been sorry for something you've said?" Jeff suddenly asked.

"Frequently," Violet said. "I don't always think before I speak. Even when I do, I sometimes say the wrong thing."

"I never think," Jeff said as though the words were something he wanted to cast away in anger. "Or if I do, I only think of what I can say to hurt people the most."

"You're blunt, even rude at times, but I don't think you try to hurt people."

"I have. I did everything I could to make George send Rose away. After he married her, I tried to force him to choose between her and me."

Violet thought of the woman she'd met only briefly. It was hard to imagine anyone not admiring her. "I thought everybody loved Rose."

"I couldn't forget her father had been an officer in the Union Army. All these years I've held it against her, like a sword at her throat."

"How could anything that happened tonight—"

"I've been just as bad about Fern," Jeff said. "I've never let her forget her father was a Jayhawk or that she used to wear pants and still cusses."

Suddenly she understood. "You're feeling guilty."

His scowl deepened. "When you said she would die, everything was suddenly different. She's been a good wife to Madison. Certainly nobody else could dissolve his black tempers as she can. She's stayed pregnant with his sons even though she must have been afraid from the first something like this could happen. She controls those boys just as firmly as she used to control her cows. She makes sure they have everything they need to be happy, but she draws a line and keeps their toes firmly to it. If she dies, she'll take a lot of good with her. And I never told her. She still thinks I hate her."

"Did you ever hate her?"

"No." Jeff stopped, clearly disturbed by his discovery. "I used to think I did, but it wasn't Fern. It was everything else."

"Then you ought to tell her. I'm sure she'd be glad to hear it."

"She won't believe me. None of them will."

"Why not?"

"Because I never say anything nice to anybody. I've been mean and cruel my whole life."

"Surely not all the time."

"Ever since I can remember."

"You must have felt different once."

He stopped, a far-off look in his eyes. "Once, before the war, when I was sixteen, when I thought the world would always be the same, when I thought I would always be the same."

"What happened?"

"We got kicked out of Virginia. Then my father forced me to volunteer. I lost my arm, spent two years as a prisoner of war, and saw Virginia destroyed. After that I came to Texas to find both parents dead and my survival dependent on a dirty ranch and filthy cows I hated."

"But you and your family have done marvelously well."

"But I'm not like that sixteen-year-old kid any more. I'm somebody totally different. Somebody I don't like very much."

He started walking rapidly. Violet followed with lagging steps. She should have seen that before. No man lashed out at the world the way Jeff did unless he was even more angry at himself. But she realized it wasn't something she could change. Rage had been a part of him for a long time. Only he could alter it.

But she felt certain he could. All traces of that 16-year-old hadn't been erased. Some still lingered. Essie Brown had seen them. So could others. Violet had a feeling they were trying to work their way to the surface even now. Otherwise Jeff wouldn't be so upset over things he'd said and done years ago.

He stopped and turned. Violet hurried to catch up with him. The cold had penetrated her coat, and it was hard to keep her teeth from chattering. As they left the business district and reached the more open streets of the residential district, an icy wind whistled down off the mountains. In the distance, snowcapped peaks glistened in the moonlight. As Violet and Jeff turned into Champa, she pulled her coat more tightly around her and thought wistfully of the cheery warmth of Jeff's office.

"I shouldn't have made you walk," he said when she reached him. "You're cold."

"It's not far now."

He removed a glove and put his hand to her cheek. "You're freezing. As usual I never thought of anybody but myself." He took off his overcoat and put it around her shoulders.

"You'll catch your death of cold." But it was a feeble protest. The coat felt marvelously warm. She thought she might survive until she reached the school.

"The memory of all the things I've said will keep me warm." He really didn't seem to be aware of the cold. The battle going on inside him consumed all of his concentration.

"You have to tell her."

"Tell who what?"

Violet wondered where Jeff's thoughts had strayed. "Fern. What you just told me."

Jeff laughed. It was a harsh sound. "You don't know about my pride. I think I'd choke on the words."

"If you don't, you'll drown in regret. If you're going to be dead either way, some good ought to come of it."

Jeff turned to give her a penetrating stare. "Painfully honest, aren't you?"

"You can't be the only one indulging in melodrama."

His expression altered completely in a flash. "You

think that all this is melodrama, that I made it up to gain sympathy?''

Instinct caused her to loop her arm in his. She would never have done it if she had been thinking. It seemed to shock him as well. "Come on. You'll freeze without your coat, and I'll be the one feeling guilty.''

He wouldn't move; so Violet said, "I'm sorry. I shouldn't have said melodrama, but it's foolish to think you can't say what you feel. If you feel it strongly enough, you'll have to say it.''

He reluctantly fell into step alongside her. "What do you think I ought to say?''

"I have no idea. You could start with what you said to me.''

"I don't want her to think I'm saying it because I'm afraid she's going to die.''

"Then maybe you can find an opportunity to compliment her on the things she's done well—made her husband happy, given him four fine sons, run a good household—I don't know. If you really want to say something, you'll find the right words.''

Violet sensed Jeff was uncomfortable with his arm linked with hers, but he didn't attempt to remove it. Nor did she.

"Why didn't I ever see this before?" Jeff asked. "It's not as if I didn't know.''

Because he was too busy hating—Violet thought he knew that. Her saying it wouldn't help.

"It doesn't matter now. It only matters that you see it at last. As soon as you let her know, you'll both feel better.''

Jeff laughed. She thought she could detect some true mirth in the sound. "No, she'll be sure I'm up to something.''

"Then you'll feel better," Violet said. "That has to be worth something.''

They walked a little distance in silence. The huge

yards of the houses of the rich were dark and silent. Grass and trees irrigated with water stolen from the South Platte River struggled to disguise the barrenness of the prairie, which only too recently had been home to buffalo and pronghorn antelope. The needles of an ambitious young pine extending over a low wrought-iron fence brushed Violet's shoulder as she walked by. The freezing ground crunched softly under her feet. They were within sight of the school. Their walk would soon be over.

Violet was no longer aware of the cold, just that Jeff walked next to her. His arm was still linked with hers, but they were still widely separated in every other way. Even their sharing only served to make her aware of how much kept them apart, still kept him from being close to anyone, even his family.

"I don't think you have to worry that Fern won't believe you. You may say things you shouldn't, but when your family needs you, like tonight, you're always there, doing anything you can, putting all differences aside."

"That's not enough," Jeff said. "They've done that and more for me."

"There's nothing stopping you from doing more."

"Yes, there is. I'm just as much of a son of a bitch as my father."

His words were said with such anger that Violet almost stopped, but Jeff pulled her along with him as they turned into the walk from the road to the school. The familiar buildings reared up out of the night, their outlines clearly delineated against the moonlit mountains in the distance.

"I hope you're not too cold," he said, all confidences apparently at an end. "Next time insist I hire a carriage."

"I've enjoyed the walk," Violet said. "You're the one who is freezing." She started to withdraw her arm from Jeff's so she that could return his coat. He wouldn't let her until they reached the dormitory. Then he withdrew his arm, took her by the shoulders, and turned her toward him.

"I don't know why you waste your time on me. I've said worse things about you than Fern."

"I don't—"

"But I'm grateful you have. I may never get the courage to say this again; so don't interrupt me. I don't know what it is about you that seems different from any woman I've ever met. I've spent hours thinking about it, and I still can't figure it out. I've even started to dream about you."

Violet felt the warmth of pleasure surge through her. She had waited so long to hear something more than the most basic compliments from Jeff. His words were like balm to her soul.

"Has anybody ever told you how lovely you are?" Jeff asked. "You probably think your hair is your most stunning asset, but it's your eyes. They're such a deep blue they're almost violet. Is that how you got your name?"

Violet nodded, and Jeff said, "They do make a stunning contrast with your hair. But all of you is beautiful, from the trimness of your figure to the softness of your skin."

He removed his glove and took her cheek in the palm of his hand. She leaned against his hand, aware of the warmth, the strength, the roughness of his skin. She couldn't tell him, she wouldn't tell him, of the thoughts that had passed through her mind or filled her dreams for the last weeks. Nor would she tell him that his compliments seemed tame to her tortured senses, that she longed for more.

"I know I've said some pretty terrible things about your being a Yankee. But I don't feel that way anymore. You have an understanding, a feeling of caring about you that seems to make a lot of other things unimportant. I never felt this way about a woman before. I never thought I would like it so much.''

Violet nearly melted as his lips found hers in a long, sensual kiss, which was no mere brushing of the lips, nor a harsh kiss wrung out of him against his will. It was the kiss of a man who liked what he was doing and was doing it very well.

His hand had moved to the back of her neck, where it cradled her head, holding her mouth to his. His lips felt full and warm. They captured hers, covering them, moistening them. Shivers raced from one end of Violet to the other when he traced her lips with the tip of his tongue. It felt so forbidden, so wonderful. His tongue tickled the corner of her mouth, then forced her lips apart as it invaded her mouth.

"Has no one ever kissed you like this?" Jeff asked, his face so close that his breath warmed her cheeks.

"No," she said, her voice so unsteady it was a whisper.

"You should be kissed like this until every part of you sings with desire."

Apparently he wasn't aware of it, but her chorus of desire had been hitting high notes for some time. Another few minutes like that, and it was going to go completely off the scale.

Violet knew she ought to go inside, but she couldn't summon the will to move. His tongue snaked between her lips, and she found herself opening to him. His tongue brushed her teeth and teased her gums. She shivered with desire when he took her lower lip between his teeth and gently pulled it inside his mouth. When his hand slid down her back and pressed her body against his, she thought she would melt into a puddle at his feet. She barely felt able to stand on her own; the strength was slowly draining from her body.

Violet tried to concentrate on Jeff's lips as he placed

kisses on her eyelids. She tried to think of the power of his grasp as he held her close. But every other sensation was singed into nothingness by the blazing heat of his groin, where it pressed against her abdomen. Jeff's feeling for her was just as strong as hers for him.

"If you're going to keep that up for much longer, I suggest you come inside." Harvey McKee's voice coming from behind Violet caused her to start so violently that she bumped her forehead against Jeff's. Heat rose in her cheeks. She turned to find Harvey framed in the doorway by light from inside the parlor.

"I was just about to come in," Violet said, quickly handing Jeff his coat.

"I was saying good night," Jeff said.

"Don't let me stop you," Harvey said.

Violet thought Jeff sounded nearly as embarrassed as she did. He would find it impossible to let anyone know his feelings. They were such a closely guarded secret she sometimes wondered if Jeff knew himself.

"Why are you here?" Violet asked.

"I have some news for you."

"I must go," Violet said, turning to Jeff. "Tell Madison not to leave Fern alone until the doctor gets here."

"I will. Good night, and thanks for helping." Jeff turned and walked slowly away.

"It doesn't look as if you took my warning seriously," Harvey said as he followed Violet into the parlor.

"I warned myself about Jeff Randolph long before you did," Violet said, irritated. "I have no intention of letting a little kiss cause me to do anything foolish."

"That was more than a little kiss."

"Then let's say it will have little consequence," Violet said. "Now what news do you have about my mine?" She could tell he didn't want to change the subject, but she was determined. She wasn't going to discuss her feelings for Jeff with anybody, least of all Harvey McKee.

"We've had an offer to sell."

"No," Violet said. "I want the mine. I won't accept anything else."

"Close that window and come to bed, Betty Sue," a sleepy voice said. "You'll never be able to get up in time for breakfast. Miss Goodwin will be angry."

"I don't think she'll care," Betty Sue said.

"Sure, she will. She's a stickler for the rules."

But not when they apply to herself, Betty Sue thought as she watched Jeff walk down the flagstone walk. Wait until she told her mama.

Chapter Twenty

Monty Randolph was waiting the first time Violet took Aurelia and Juliette to their Aunt Fern's for the weekend. "You're officially relieved of responsibility," he said with a disarming smile. "They figure I'm good enough for baby-sitting."

"We're not babies," Aurelia said.

"I know," Monty said, making a face. "You were sweet little darlings back then."

"Miss Goodwin thinks we're sweet now."

Monty laughed. "Miss Goodwin is paid not to say what she really thinks. Rose is expecting you up at the house for tea and gossip." Monty made another face at the twins, and they giggled. "I'm not sure it's better than being saddled with these two." He scooped them up, one under each arm, and headed toward the barn accompanied by squeals of laughter.

Violet smiled. Miss Settle would be horrified, but the twins loved it. Violet started toward the house, glad to have most of the day to herself. She was relieved when she found Rose alone with Fern.

As soon as Violet had been seated and handed a cup of hot tea, Rose continued the conversation she'd been having with Fern. "Have you seen Jeff since then?"

"No," Fern said. "I think all that work has finally caused his mind to snap."

"I don't think that's the problem," Rose said, her brow creased in thought, "but something is definitely wrong. He's never done anything like this."

"Like what?" Violet asked, afraid to let them see how anxious she was. "Has he been hurt?"

"No," Fern said. "He marched in here three mornings ago—at 6:30, mind you! He woke Madison and me out of a sound sleep and proceeded to apologize for all the things that he's said about me ever since I married Madison. Then he started listing my virtues until I hardly recognized myself. Madison swore he was drunk."

"George is worried about him," Rose said to Violet. "He did much the same thing with me. If I hadn't been sitting down, I think I would have fallen. I've never been reluctant to tell Jeff what I thought, but by the time he got through, I was regretting half of what I had said."

"We were hoping you might know what set him off," Fern said to Violet. "We're all at a loss."

"No," Violet said, gazing into her teacup once more. "I have no idea."

"Jeff never apologizes," Rose said. "He'll probably turn up in a few days and have forgotten all about it."

"I don't think so," Fern said. "He was even nice to the boys. The boys! He usually can't stand them for more than five minutes."

"I think something did happen," Rose said, "something so profound it has finally broken the hold of his self-absorption with his arm and the war." She looked at Violet.

"But what could it have been?" Fern asked.

"I don't know," Rose said, "but I think he'll do

287

something totally unexpected soon.''

"Like what?'' Fern asked.

"I have no idea.'' But Rose continued to study Violet as though she expected the other woman to provide the explanation.

"How are plans progressing for the rodeo?'' Violet asked. She had to get the women talking about something else. Jeff had apologized and he seemed to mean it. As a result Rose was waiting for him to do something unexpected—like fall in love with a Yankee woman!

Jeff had kissed her as if he had never wanted to stop. Violet had thought of little else the past three days. She had moved through her duties like a ghost. Even the children knew something was bothering her. She wanted to see him so badly she almost had to bite her tongue to keep from asking about him.

But the sensible part of her brain kept reminding her that Jeff had never said anything about a future relationship. He might have been able to stand kissing her half the night, but he had been a bachelor too long to give up his freedom without a lot of foot-dragging. Violet had enjoyed the kisses as much as Jeff, but she wasn't about to force any man to the altar.

She knew what it meant to take care of a man. The promise of future independence, a future of worrying about no one but herself, was too tempting to ignore. Jeff, Harvey McKee, or any other man was going to have to do more than hand out a few kisses or invitations to dinner.

Violet pulled her galloping thoughts up short. All her speculation was fruitless. She'd better pay attention to what Rose was saying. The rodeo was coming up soon, and she wanted to know how Fern was getting along. She didn't look any better. Violet had hoped things wouldn't get worse before Dr. Ulmstead arrived.

"Monty has done a wonderful job,'' Rose was saying.

"Wait until you see what he has planned. We've already sent for William Henry and Elizabeth. They ought to be here tomorrow."

The brother and sister who never got into trouble. Violet wasn't sure that bringing them there was a good idea.

"I had a terrible time convincing Monty not to send for Hen," Fern said. "Then just as I had talked him out of it, he got a telegram. Would you believe Laurel is pregnant again!" She laughed and turned to Violet. "Maybe we should ask your doctor to build his clinic in Denver. At the rate we're going, he won't need any other patients."

"Is Hen coming?" Violet asked.

"Not until spring," Fern said.

"Good. You don't need Adam and Jordy stirring up your boys," Rose said.

"You think Monty is wild by himself," Fern said to Violet. "Get him together with Hen, and Laurel and Iris might as well not exist. Besides, Hen doesn't like Iris very much."

"Jeff changed his mind," Rose said to her sister-in-law. "Maybe Hen will, too."

"Not both in one year," Fern said, holding her heart in mock shock. "I don't think I could stand it."

Both women laughed. Then Rose said to Violet, "I'm sorry we've spent so much time gossiping about family. It can't be much fun for you."

"I enjoy hearing about your family," Violet said. "I don't have a family."

Rose reached over and gave Violet's hand a squeeze. "Neither did we. That's why it's so nice to be part of a large family now. None of us completely gets over our losses. But when we get together, it's difficult to think of anything but Randolphs."

"Most of them will be at the rodeo," Fern said. "It'll almost be like a gathering of the clan."

Violet wondered if Jeff would be there. The entire school was going, even Miss Settle.

The door opened, and George and Madison entered the room. Madison went straight to his wife, searched her face. "How are you doing?" he asked, worry in his voice.

"I'm fine," Fern said. "I feel better, having someone to talk to."

"Don't tire yourself. Dr. Ulmstead said you were to stay in bed until he got here."

"I might as well be in bed. I don't do anything but walk from one chair to the next."

As Madison continued to fuss over his wife, George greeted Violet.

"How are the girls doing?" Rose asked as George pulled a chair up next to his wife. "Is Monty ready to send them back to the school yet?"

George chuckled. "He was doing fine until Iris showed up ready to ride. At that point, he forgot about the twins. They went off with the boys and one of the grooms."

"Iris refuses to remain inside," Rose said. "She's determined to ride."

"I'm glad I'm not part of that confrontation," Fern said. She gripped her husband's hand as he settled down next to her. "I just hope the sparks don't set the hay on fire."

"I don't know how those two stand it," Rose said. "I think they actually like fighting with each other."

"Of course they do," Madison said. "Have you ever known Monty when he wasn't fighting with somebody?"

"You can't believe how quiet our house was after he moved to Wyoming," Rose said. "It took me several months to get used to it."

"But there was a great deal more work to be done," George said in Monty's defense. "Whatever you say about Monty, he can do more work than anybody I know.''

''And get into more trouble,'' Fern added.

''No, Zac holds that title,'' Rose said.

''Zac?'' Violet asked. She hadn't heard about him.

''He's the black sheep in a family of black sheep,'' Madison said. ''He's taking his floating crap game all over the West. Sometimes I think he's more like Pa than any of us.''

Before anyone could launch into a list of Zac's iniquities, the door opened and Monty and Iris entered the room.

''You can't treat me like a baby, Monty Randolph,'' Iris was saying. ''I'm barely two months pregnant. I can go riding for at least a month yet.''

''You put your bottom in a saddle, and I'll lock you in your room.''

''Don't be ridiculous. I'll climb out the window.''

Monty ground his teeth. ''You tell her, Rose.''

''If you'll remember, I drove a wagon the day I delivered the twins,'' Rose said.

''Because Fern was in trouble.''

''She did it with Elizabeth, too,'' George said. ''You'll get no help from that quarter.''

Monty turned to Fern, but Madison shook his head. ''If Fern weren't feeling so rotten, she'd be itching to race you across the next hillside. It's all I can do to keep her from putting on her guns and that hideous vest she used to wear.''

''It wasn't hideous,'' Fern said.

''There,'' Iris said. ''Now have a cup of tea and sit down.''

Monty made a face. ''I'm tempted to ask Madison for some of his brandy.''

''It won't do any good,'' Madison said. ''She'll be just as cantankerous after you've finished.''

"You two stop arguing and tell us about the rodeo," Fern said.

That invitation wrought an immediate change in Monty's mood. He launched into a detailed description of all the plans. Violet welcomed the recitation, hoping it would keep her mind off Jeff, but it didn't work. Monty reminded her too strongly of the man who was rapidly becoming an obsession with her.

Monty was full of energy. It spilled from him like water tumbling over rocks. He talked and laughed and moved constantly. He was like an inexhaustible center of activity, too vibrant to keep still.

Jeff had that same energy, that same intensity, but it was dark, smoldering, angry, tightly contained. It almost never allowed him to laugh. It drove him to work harder and harder, to distance himself from people. Monty seemed to find fun in everything he did, even fighting with his wife. Jeff never seemed to have any fun—not even his work gave him pleasure.

A smothered groan from Fern snapped Violet's train of thought. Fern's hand moved to her belly. "I think my labor's started."

"It can't be," Madison said, his face a study in worry. "You still have a month to go."

"I've done this before," Fern said, struggling to sit up. "I remember what it feels like."

"We should get her to bed," Rose said.

"I think you ought to take her to the hospital," Violet said, and all eyes turned to her. "She's going to have trouble. She's been uncomfortable for weeks. When is Dr. Ulmstead supposed to arrive?"

"Tonight. I have someone meeting him at the train."

Fern attempted to get to her feet, but she didn't have the strength.

"I'll get the carriage," Monty said and dashed from the room.

"Don't you worry," Madison said as he lifted his

wife out of the chair. "Dr. Ulmstead will be here about ten o'clock."

Violet had a terrible feeling that might be too late.

"She's bleeding," Violet told the doctor after they had made Fern as comfortable as possible.

"I know that, Miss Goodwin," the doctor said, angry at her interference. "What do you expect me to do?"

"She could die if it gets worse."

"I'm well aware of that. Women die in childbirth all the time."

"You have to stop the bleeding."

"There are some things doctors can't do, Miss Goodwin. Stopping that kind of bleeding is one of them."

Violet bit her tongue and hoped that Dr. Ulmstead would reach Denver in time. Madison sent bulletins every 30 minutes by telegraph to the stations along the track. They were handed to the doctor when the train stopped for water or fuel. The only message the doctor had sent was to keep Fern as still as possible and monitor the bleeding.

It was still just a trickle, but Violet knew something was torn. It could break loose at any time. If it did, Fern could die in minutes. So could the baby.

The tension in the waiting room was grim. All the family was there, except Jeff. He was still at his office. Everyone turned toward a young man who entered with a telegram in his hand. He handed it to Madison.

"What did the doctor say this time?" George asked.

"It's not from the doctor," Madison said. "It's from the train station at Bennett. There's another train on the track. It's headed straight toward the doctor's train."

"I thought you had arranged for the tracks to be clear," George said.

Madison crushed the telegram in his hand. "I did, but some son of a bitch has put his train on the track thinking he can take advantage of a straight shot to Kansas City. I have to find Jeff.''

"I'll go," George offered. "You can't leave Fern."

Violet jumped up. "I'll go. You both need to stay here. I can't do anything but argue with the doctor. That isn't helping anybody."

"I can't let you go. It's not your responsibility," George said.

"Let her go, George," Rose whispered to her husband. "If anything happens to Fern, you're the only one who could keep Madison from killing that doctor."

"Use my carriage," George said. "Tell the driver to take you anywhere you want."

Peering through the glass panel beside the door, Violet could see a light coming from the back of the bank. But no matter how loudly she knocked, she got no response.

"Let me, ma'am," the driver said. He pounded on the door with his fists. When that didn't bring a response, he kicked with his foot. Violet was afraid he'd break his toes.

"There's someone coming," the driver said. "And none too soon. You'd think he was deaf."

Jeff peered through the glass, his angry frown replaced by a look of surprise when he saw Violet. He unlocked the door.

"Fern has been taken to the hospital," Violet began without preamble. "She's in very serious condition. I came to tell you there's a train on the tracks blocking the doctor's train."

"I thought Madison had cleared the tracks."

"He did, but something happened. If the doctor doesn't get here soon, Fern is going to die."

"Keep your horse moving," Jeff said to the driver. "Come inside before you freeze," he said to Violet. He headed back to his office without waiting for her. He entered and went straight for the telephone hanging on the wall. He lifted the receiver and jiggled the cradle. "Give me the Kansas-Pacific Railroad Station," he said, "and be quick about it."

Jeff fidgeted while he waited. "This is Jeff Randolph, president of the First National Bank," he said when someone finally answered. "There's a train heading east on the Kansas-Pacific tracks. Whose is it, and where's the first siding where it can pull over?"

After a pause, Jeff said, "I don't care who told you what. If you don't answer my question immediately, you won't be working for anyone in this town ever again."

Following another pause, Jeff exploded and hung up the phone so violently that Violet was surprised it hadn't broken. "The bastard! Philip Rabin put that train on the tracks."

Jeff jiggled the phone cradle again. "Give me Arthur Tynon."

Violet recognized the name of the president of the Kansas-Pacific Railroad. Jeff turned to Violet. "Go tell the driver to hire a fresh horse. We may have some hard riding to do."

"Where's he going to find one quick enough—"

"In the stables down by the river. Hurry."

Violet scurried away as Jeff said into the phone, "Arthur, Jeff Randolph here. I have a problem I need your help with. Here's what I want you to do."

By the time Violet returned to the office, Jeff had completed his call and was putting papers on his desk into neat piles. He damped the fire in the stove, grabbed his coat, and herded Violet through the door. He locked his office and the front door.

Jeff helped her into the carriage, but didn't get in after her. "Where are you going?" she asked.

"To see Rabin."

"What are you going to do?"

"Stop that train."

"I'm coming with you."

"Go back to the hospital," Jeff said and turned away.

"I'll follow you," Violet said.

Without saying a word, Jeff got into the carriage with her.

Rabin was in his office. Jeff went in despite the clerk's efforts to stop him. He tossed the man aside as if he were a child. Rabin looked up from his work, shocked to see Jeff storming into his office. He glanced to where his man was picking himself up off the floor. Violet thought she saw fear in Rabin's eyes.

"Get your train off the track," Jeff said.

"I don't know what you mean," Rabin stammered.

"I know all about it. It can pull over at Magnolia and let our train pass."

Violet closed the office door against the goggling stares of the staff. She watched Rabin collect himself, turning into the shrewd, hard businessman who had become one of the wealthiest men in Denver.

"The hell I will. You can't come barging in here, shouting at me to—"

He never finished the sentence. Jeff's hand shot out and caught him by the throat. Violet stared in horror as she saw Jeff lift Philip Rabin out of his chair and from behind the desk by his neck. Rabin's face started to turn purple. He clawed frantically at Jeff's hand, but he couldn't break his hold. Violet couldn't figure out how Jeff managed it with one hand, but she did know Rabin was about to choke to death.

"Let him go, Jeff."

"Not until he orders that train off the track."

"He can't do that if he's dead," Violet said as calmly as she could manage. "And it won't help the situation if you're arrested for murder."

But Jeff seemed beyond the sound of her voice, beyond reason. She had never seen such deadly rage in any man. She knew then that Jeff would kill Philip Rabin if she didn't do something quickly.

"Let him go," she said, panic causing her voice to flutter. She pulled on his arm, but it was like iron. All her strength couldn't cause it to waver.

"Jeff," she said, "he's not worth going to jail. Think of what that would do to your family." She looked at Rabin. She was staggered to see that, despite his struggle for air, hatred radiated from his eyes. Philip Rabin hated Jeff Randolph. That was why he'd put that train on the track.

"Don't you see? This is what he wants. He doesn't care about that train. He's just trying to cause you and your family as much trouble as possible. If you don't put him down, he's going to succeed."

Jeff's fingers relaxed their hold, and Violet drew a deep breath. He still held Rabin, but the man's color gradually changed from blue to red.

The phone rang, and Jeff said to Violet, "Answer it. I told Arthur to call me here."

Very reluctantly, Violet picked up the receiver and placed it against her ear as she had seen Jeff do. "Hello," she spoke very uncertainly into the small horn that protruded from the box.

"Who the hell is this?" a voice crackled into Violet's ear. She jumped involuntarily. The sound of a human voice coming out of the small black earphone she held in her hand was unnerving.

"This is Violet Goodwin," she said. "I'm answering for Jeff Randolph."

"Damned peculiar," the voice grumbled. "I never knew Jeff to let a woman know his business."

"He can't come to the phone right now."

"Never mind. Just tell him it's a trainload of potatoes headed for Chicago. Rabin bribed one of the directors. He offered to split the profits with him, told him Jeff was trying to make the Denver & Pacific more powerful. The bastard is trying to play one railroad against the other.''

The man rang off. Feeling very much as if she'd just had a supernatural experience, Violet hung up the phone and repeated the message to Jeff. She was relieved to see him release Rabin. She wasn't so pleased that Jeff had let him drop to the floor.

"Now call your minion and tell him to get that train off the tracks," Jeff said.

Rabin glared at Jeff, hatred in his eyes. "Why should I do that?"

"Because there's a doctor on it," Violet said. "If he doesn't get here soon, Fern Randolph might die."

"I don't believe you," Philip said.

"Why would we lie to you?" Violet asked.

"From what my wife said, you'd do anything to get Jeff's ring on your finger—or Harvey McKee's." His lip curled. "From what Betty Sue says, you may have it already."

Rabin couldn't move fast enough to escape Jeff's fist. The blow sent Rabin hurtling against the wall. Violet threw herself between Jeff and Rabin.

"No!" she screamed, pushing on Jeff as hard as she could. "He's just saying that to make you angry. Don't play into his hands."

There was a furious pounding at the door. "Mr. Rabin!" a voice shouted. "You okay in there?"

"He's fine," Violet said without leaving her position between Jeff and the dazed Rabin.

For a moment, the issue hung in the balance. She knew that, if she hadn't gotten between them, Jeff would never have mastered his temper. Gradually he backed away.

Someone outside continued to rattle the doorknob, to try a key that didn't work, but when there was no further noise from the office, the would-be rescuer desisted.

"Why won't you call that train back?" Violet asked Rabin.

When Rabin glared at Jeff but didn't answer, Jeff said, "It must have to do with money. I've never known you to care about anything else. I'll buy the cargo from you. How much do you want for it?"

"I won't sell it!" Rabin said.

"Why not?" Violet asked. "Why do you care as long as you get your money?"

"It's business. You wouldn't understand."

"Try me."

"I don't discuss business with women."

"I can explain it," Jeff said.

Violet was pleased to see he had himself under control. She just hoped the cruel smile on his face didn't mean he had something even worse in mind.

"You know nothing about it," Rabin said, but Violet could tell from his expression that he was afraid Jeff did.

"Do you remember when I said the Chicago commodities market was in an uproar?" Jeff said to Violet.

"Yes, that was the first time you worked through the night."

"There's a potato shortage. Prices have tripled in less than a week. Philip is sending that train to Chicago, hoping to make about a five-hundred-percent profit."

Violet didn't need Rabin's admission to confirm Jeff's words. His expression of shocked fury was enough.

"I kept my clerks up all night, rounding up potatoes from every corner of the West," Jeff said to Rabin. "I've already shipped enough to cause the price to drop five dollars a ton. My last train went out this morning. I've shipped more than fifty thousand tons."

Violet did some quick calculations in her head. "That's a profit of at least two hundred and fifty thousand dollars."

"See," Jeff said to Rabin, "she can understand."

"So my potatoes aren't worth dirt," Rabin said. Shock and fury waged a battle for control of his features.

"They aren't worth what you paid for them," Jeff said. "If you'd asked me, I could have told you to save your money. Now are you going to call that train back? Or are you going to sell those potatoes to me?"

"At a loss?"

"I'm afraid so."

"You can't stop the train," Rabin said. Rage burned brightly in his eyes. "By the time it reaches your train, it will be past the siding. Your train will never get to Denver without backing up and going around."

"Before you show Miss Goodwin what a stubborn fool you can be, let me explain a few things you don't know."

Rabin's expression turned vicious. "What have you done?"

"Arthur wasn't pleased when he heard about your little trick. So he talked to Will. Will wasn't happy either. They're rivals, but they don't like being made to look like fools. They've dispatched a second train behind yours. They will simply transfer the doctor to the second train and speed him back to Denver. In the meantime, your potatoes will be sitting on the track. My brother and I are prepared to wait until they rot."

"Or the price drops so low you won't be able to sell them without a huge loss," Violet said.

"I told you she had a good head for business," Jeff said. "Maybe I should bring her to work at the bank. Think of what a combination we would make."

Sparks of hope shot through Violet, but she was quick to remind herself Jeff was taunting Philip Rabin. He probably had no thought of how his words might affect her.

"You're trying to ruin me, just like you did when you stole the railroad accounts!" Rabin said. "You've always wanted to ruin me."

There was the sound of rescues throwing themselves against the office door. They were trying to break it down.

"I only asked you to pull over and let the train carrying the doctor pass. My sister-in-law is seriously ill. Her husband cleared the tracks from Denver to Chicago. I won't let all his work be ruined now."

"But you want me to take a loss!" Rabin said.

Another crash sounded at the door, but it held.

"I don't care whether you take a loss or not," Jeff said. "I just want the tracks free. I offered to buy the cargo. If, knowing Fern's life hangs in the balance, you refuse to let that train pass, I will do everything in my power to ruin you."

"Bastard!" Rabin threw himself at Jeff. Jeff simply stepped aside. As Rabin charged by, Jeff delivered a blow to the side of his neck. Rabin stumbled over a chair and knocked over a table. The crash of glass was succeeded by the sound of splintering wood. Rabin's staff had finally forced the door open. They stopped in stunned amazement to see their employer lying in the floor amid the rubble, Jeff and Violet nowhere near him.

"Get out," Rabin screamed at his gaping staff.

"But—"

"Get out!" Rabin threw a splintered table leg at their heads. They withdrew, closing the broken door as best they could. "How much will you give me for the potatoes?"

When Jeff told him, he said, "But I'll lose money."

"Would you rather lose everything? Plus, I imagine your agent will be enraged when your shipment doesn't arrive. I doubt he'll want to work with you again."

"Stop crowing and give me the money."

"Send someone around to the bank tomorrow. I'll write you a check."

"How do I know you'll live up to your word?"

"The same way you knew I'd ruin you. Once I give my word, it's good."

"Get out," Rabin said.

"Come, Miss Goodwin. I don't think we're welcome any longer."

"I'll get you back for this!" Rabin shouted behind them. "If it takes me the rest of my life. I hope the bitch dies and the kid with her!" he screamed as they reached the door.

Jeff turned back, but Violet grabbed him by the arm. "Forget him," she said. "We have to get back to the hospital."

After a slight pause, Jeff turned and strode from the office. Violet followed, horrified that Philip Rabin could hate so much he was willing to sacrifice the life of a woman and her baby to get revenge.

"Would you really have tried to ruin him if he hadn't agreed to stop the train or sell his potatoes?" she asked Jeff as they walked down the hall toward the stairs.

"Nobody threatens my family. Any one of my brothers would have done the same thing."

"But how can you do that—destroy a man—without compunction?"

"He would have done the same to me if he could."

"Philip Rabin is a cruel, mean-spirited, detestable man. You're too kind."

Jeff stopped and turned to face her. "What makes you say that?"

Violet looked startled by the intensity of his question. "I've seen you with Essie. The only person who can do more is her father."

"Oh, that. You don't think—"

"Then there's me."

He had started forward again, but he paused. "What about you?"

"Even though I'm a damned Yankee, you still like me."

Jeff didn't say anything until they were inside the carriage. "To the hospital as fast as you can," he told the driver before climbing into the carriage.

He settled himself across from Violet. "Now tell me what makes you think I like you."

Chapter Twenty-one

Jeff had been tempted to walk to the hospital and send Violet back in the carriage. He wasn't sure it was wise to be alone with her. Either he would say something he shouldn't or he would fall prey to his emotions and let her discover how weak he was. He had virtually lived at the bank the last few days to keep from having to deal with his feelings. But he realized things were coming to a crisis.

She had made him do things he didn't want to do. He still hadn't recovered his equilibrium after talking to Fern and Rose. Nothing felt right. Worst of all, Violet made him question everything he had done for years, which frightened him.

You'll never be worth horseshit. You're nothing but a damned coward.

Jeff's father's words had haunted him his whole life. He'd led that charge against the Yankee guns at Gettysburg to escape them. He'd refused to die as he lay in the field, waiting for someone to find him, his life's blood soaking into the torn-up ground beneath him, in defiance of them. He'd started the bank and worked as much as 140 hours a week to prove them wrong. And he'd used the war and his arm to keep all his doubts at bay.

He had found peace at the bank in the rigid control he had over himself, in working harder than any other banker in Denver, knowing more, making more money. In the process, he'd distanced himself from his family, from humankind. When any emotion threatened to break through his harsh self-control, he drove it off with a few sharp and, if necessary, cruel words. But that hadn't worked on Violet.

"You don't want to like me, but you do," Violet said.

Silence. What did she expect him to do? Admit his weakness?

"After spending years trying to convince everybody Yankees are evil, you can't possibly admit you like one. Of course you don't really believe Yankees are devils. It's just something you say, something you use to keep people from getting close to you."

Jeff felt himself stiffen. She thought she knew him so well. Women were like that, always thinking they knew more about a man than he knew about himself.

"You don't want people to get too close because you're afraid they won't like you. You're also afraid they will. That would upset everything, wouldn't it?"

"If this is an example of Yankee logic, I'm amazed you managed to win the war, even with twice the man-power and resources."

Violet laughed softly. "If you'd said that during the quarantine, I'd have been angry. But it's too late now. You're a fraud, Jeff Randolph. You think I don't know you, but I can see right through you."

Jeff experienced a moment of panic. Part of his defense had been not letting anyone see inside him. Could Violet have broken through that barrier?

"You're just as strong and courageous as your brothers. Maybe stronger in some ways. I know you'd win at one-armed wrestling. Even Monty isn't as strong as you are."

When Jeff remained silent, Violet said, "I don't always agree with your methods, but you love your family so much, your loyalty is so strong, you'd do anything for their sake. You're the most capable man I've ever met. You do amazing things and don't even realize it."

Jeff had geared himself up for a battle, a confrontation that never developed. Instead, Violet had attacked him from a totally unexpected angle. She had found his weak side, had said things he wanted to hear, wanted to believe. Before he could whirl to face the attack, she'd fired a salvo that had brought him to his knees.

"But the biggest fraud is that you don't like people and don't want them to like you," Violet said. "You don't work at that bank for yourself. You do it for your family. You had enough money for yourself years ago. If you'd give them a chance, I think your family would tell you how much they appreciate it. But you're so afraid of being hurt that you won't let them know you care."

Jeff fought against the growing desire to have Violet say more. Like a man grabbing at branches to keep from being swept away by a floodtide, he searched for something to say. "You still haven't told me why you think I like you."

Violet smiled again. He could barely see her in the shadows, but he knew her smile. It had become part of his thinking. He knew how her eyes sparkled when she was happy, how they flashed when she was angry, how they became clouded when she was unhappy. He could remember the taste of her lips when he kissed her, the warmth of her breath, the feel of her soft body against him. He longed to reach out and touch her, to pull her against him and kiss her until the gnawing fear was banished.

But he was weak at that moment. He couldn't resist her magic. Even a slight touch might send him hurtling over the edge.

"When a woman likes a man, she can always tell if he likes her back," Violet said.

Jeff stopped breathing. Something within him burst from its long bondage. He wanted to know what Violet meant by like. He needed to know. He had never needed anyone before. He hadn't let himself. People died. Things changed. It hurt too much.

He had always felt he could turn his back on anybody if necessary, even his own family. But he knew the members of his family were as vital to him as the air he breathed. They always had been. If he drew his strength from anywhere, it was from the certain knowledge that no matter what he did they would never desert him.

And his arm didn't make any difference in how they saw him. He didn't know why he hadn't seen it before. Maybe he'd been too angry to listen when they had told him. Then why was he listening to Violet? Why was he desperately hoping she was right and he was wrong?

Obviously he hoped she had meant it when she had said she liked him. He hadn't admitted it to himself before, but he'd always been afraid no one could. After Julia Wilcox, he'd been afraid going back to Virginia wouldn't make any difference. He was afraid, but he had to take the chance. He had to know.

The carriage pulled to a stop in front of the hospital. Jeff didn't want to get out even though caution urged him to run. There were so many questions he wanted to ask. But there wasn't time. Violet was climbing out of the carriage.

"How is she?" Violet asked the minute Jeff and she reached the floor.

"The bleeding is worse," Rose said.

"Has she had the baby?"

"No."

"Have you heard from the doctor?"

"His train made it without stopping. Now it's a question of whether he can get here in time, and whether he can do anything for Fern if he does."

"Can't the doctor here do anything?" Violet asked.

"Madison won't let him. He's so angry they couldn't help her before that he won't let them come near her. He's been asking for you."

Violet felt terrible. She didn't want to give Madison false hope. "I can't do anything."

"I know," Rose said. "It just makes him feel better to have you around. You're the only one who seemed to know what was really happening. He's pinning his faith on you and Dr. Ulmstead. We all are."

"We can't work miracles. It may already be too late."

"We know that. But none of us dares think what would happen to Madison if she dies."

"Good God!" Dr. Ulmstead said as soon as he examined Fern.

Nearly unconscious, she was dead white. Violet feared each breath was going to be her last.

"You call yourself a hospital!" Ulmstead said. "You've nearly let this woman die." Doctors and nurses stared white-faced at the flushed little German.

"Don't stand there gaping like so many idiots. Get her ready for surgery. Then if you can find a god who's not too busy to listen to fools like you, pray I haven't come too late to undo what you've done. Violet, I want you to assist. Where can I wash up?"

After casting a worried look at his wife, Madison followed the doctor as he began stripping off his clothes. "What are you going to do?"

"Who the hell are you? Get this man out of here!"

Dr. Ulmstead shouted at no one in particular. "How am I supposed to work with people walking in and out like it's a candy shop?"

"I'm her husband," Madison said, "and if you don't tell me what you're going to do, I'll break every bone in your body one at a time."

Dr. Ulmstead stopped long enough to return Madison's look. "So you're the man who cleared the tracks across the whole country. I didn't know anybody outside of New York had that much power." Dr. Ulmstead stripped to the waist and began washing his arms from the elbows down.

"What are you going to do?" Madison asked again.

"I'm going to try to save your wife and the baby, but quite frankly I don't know if I can."

"Why are you wasting time here?"

"Washing. I don't want to cause an infection. Don't worry. I'll be ready before she is."

Madison seemed to deflate. "What's wrong?"

"She's bleeding to death. The baby may already be dead. I won't know until I cut her open."

Madison blanched. "I won't let you touch her with a knife."

Dr. Ulmstead stopped. "Then you'd better call for a priest, minister, rabbi, or whoever you want. She and the baby will be dead inside half an hour. She hasn't the strength to turn over much less deliver a baby. She'd bleed to death first anyway."

Madison turned to Violet, who said, "It's the only way."

"I have to have my diagnosis confirmed by a nurse?" Dr. Ulmstead growled.

Madison ignored his pique. "Save her, and you can name your price."

"I'd do my best to save her without a fee," Dr. Ulmstead said, "but I'll hold you to that promise." He held out his hands to be dried. "Now go away. The best thing

309

you can do for your wife is to leave her to me.''

Jeff took Madison by the shoulder. ''Come on. You did your part getting him here. Now it's his turn.''

Violet watched Jeff take his brother away.

''Hop to it, Violet,'' Dr. Ulmstead said. ''We have to save that woman. I mean to bleed that man's pockets good and proper.''

An hour later Dr. Ulmstead tied off the last stitch. ''That's done it,'' he said. ''Barring something unexpected, she'll live. But she won't recover soon enough to nurse that son of hers.''

Violet had to fight back tears. The relief was so great that she felt almost too weak to stand. The operation had been difficult. There had been so little time. For a while, it had been touch and go.

Dr. Ulmstead delivered the baby by cesarean section, but it had been necessary to remove Fern's womb in order to stop the bleeding. She had lost a lot of blood and would be weak for some time. She would recover, but she would never have that blond daughter she wanted.

''You'd better go tell the family,'' Violet said.

''You do it,'' Ulmstead said. ''If you hadn't bribed me into coming, they wouldn't have anything to celebrate.''

''Make sure you tell them that.''

''I will.''

''I was only kidding,'' Violet said, embarrassed. She didn't want anybody feeling grateful.

''Now go on,'' the doctor said. ''I'll be out in a minute. If I show up with blood all over me, they'll be sure she's dead.''

It took Violet only a minute to clean up. She decided to take the baby with her. He lay in her arms, tiny, quiet, and perfect. She wondered if Fern would mind that the child was also dark like his father. She wondered if she would regret that she would never have a daughter, or at least a son, who looked like her. If Violet ever had children, she'd want daughters, at least one with red hair.

No, Violet decided. Fern could be happy that all her children looked like the man she loved. And Violet realized she'd feel the same about Jeff. Nothing could be more wonderful than seeing his features reflected in young growing faces. She had to stop before she started to cry.

The family was waiting when Violet entered the room. They fell silent as they turned their strained faces toward her. Madison started toward her, more anguish in his face than she had thought one man could feel.

"Fern's going to be all right," she said, unable to postpone for even a moment the news they awaited so anxiously. "You can see her as soon as she comes out from under the anesthesia."

Madison sobbed with relief. Iris put her arms around him. He cried without shame.

"She also presented you with a beautiful son," Violet said.

Madison was too shaken to take his son, but Rose was quick to offer herself as a substitute.

"You'll need to find a nurse for him," Violet told Rose in a low voice as she crooned to the baby. "Fern will be too weak to do anything for some weeks."

"We'll take care of that," Rose said. She walked away to show the baby to its proud family.

George approached Violet. "I'm sure Madison will want to express his appreciation when he's feeling more himself, but I want to thank you on behalf of the family for what you've done. I suspect we would not have reached this happy resolution without your help."

"It's Dr. Ulmstead you have to thank. He'll be out as soon as he gets cleaned up."

George looked at her closely. "You look tired. I expect you would like to go home. I'll see there's a carriage waiting when you're ready.''

''That's not necessary. The school's only a short distance away.''

''Even if it weren't cold and dark, I wouldn't allow you to walk.''

''Ask Jeff to take her home,'' Rose said.

''No one needs to see me home,'' Violet said. I'm sure Jeff would prefer to stay with his family.''

''It won't take me long to get back,'' Jeff said.

''Why don't you spend the night at the hotel?'' Daisy said. ''You could get a good night's rest and go back to the school in the morning.''

''I've been away long enough. Besides, Miss Settle is probably ready to kill me. I didn't think to send her a note explaining why the twins and I didn't return.''

''Don't worry,'' Jeff said. ''I'll take care of that. You sure you won't go to the hotel?''

''I really can't.''

''I don't think we ought to let you go without doing something to show how thankful we are,'' Daisy said.

Rose smiled. ''Jeff will invite her to the charity ball. You can invite her to stay in the hotel then.''

Violet was exhausted. It had been a terribly long day. First getting the twins to the ranch, then the crisis over Fern, the trip to Philip Rabin's office, and assisting in the operating room. Finally, she had the added worry of what Miss Settle was going to do about her unexplained absence. Violet would have loved to have spent a few minutes alone with Jeff, but she was too exhausted to deal with invitations to balls and nights in the hotel. She managed to get away without giving anybody an answer.

''You look exhausted,'' Jeff said as he helped her into the carriage.''

''I am,'' Violet said. ''I don't think I've ever been so tired, not even when Jonas was still alive.''

She liked the sound of Jeff's voice. It was soothing

and comforting. He was intense, much too edgy—she expected he would be for the rest of his life—but there was a difference that night. There was nothing frantic about him, nothing so intense it seemed about ready to strike, to lash out. She wanted to ask him what had brought about the difference, but she was too weary. She didn't think she could listen long enough to hear his answer.

"Will you go to the ball with me?" Jeff asked.

The fatigue began to recede. She hadn't taken Rose's suggestion seriously. She didn't think Jeff had either. She couldn't tell whether he was asking her because of Rose or because he really wanted her to go with him.

She answered her own question almost immediately. Jeff never went to social events. He had told her so. He was inviting her because he didn't see how he could do anything else.

She almost said yes. She wanted to. She couldn't imagine anything more pleasant than spending an evening with Jeff, especially when he was like that. It would be easy to accept. She wouldn't have to say anything. Just nod her head. Mutter something indistinct. Even a murmur was likely to have been taken for an affirmative.

Violet wondered if Jeff knew how to dance. She'd probably have to wear boots to protect her feet. He'd be the most handsome man there. She'd be the envy of every woman in the room. With that thought, reality reared its ugly head.

"Thank you, but no," she said.

"Why?"

Violet didn't know why Jeff had to ask that question. He had to be relieved. He ought to have let it go at that.

"Surely you know the reason," Violet said.

"If I did, I wouldn't have asked." A trace of the old efficient banker surfaced.

"I don't belong at a society ball," Violet said, searching her brain for answers that wouldn't hurt his feelings.

"I wouldn't know anybody but you and your family. I don't even know what charities it's for."

"It's just a dance."

"It's a high point in the social season. The parents of my students will be there. They won't relish seeing the housemother of the Wolfe School parading about in their midst."

"I didn't think you would let anything like that stop you."

"Look, Jeff. I have to earn a living. This is the only job I have. I can't afford to offend the very people who make it possible. Besides, I've been away from my job too much lately."

"I'll talk to Miss Settle."

"No!" Violet said. Her voice was sharper than she had intended. "I've asked too much as it is. Now I'd better go before I get into trouble."

"But Madison will pay for any expense."

"You don't understand," Violet said. "Housemothers aren't supposed to ask favors. They aren't supposed to expect special arrangements. They aren't supposed to be absent from their duties. They aren't supposed to be socially acquainted with the uncles of the students. I've done all of those things. I've even gotten the school involved in a rodeo."

"The twins did that."

"They wouldn't have if I had been able to control them properly."

"That's not fair."

"Maybe, but it's the way things are. You've been rich so long you've forgotten what it's like to be subject to other people's whims. Sorry. I didn't mean to say that. Look. I can't go, so let's just leave it at that. Now I'd better go in."

"Won't you go for me?"

Violet took a firm hold on her emotions before she melted completely and did something foolish.

"Why? You don't dance. You never go to society balls. You don't like Denver society."

When Jeff said nothing, Violet said, "You're asking me because Rose invited me. Don't deny it. You won't hurt my feelings. Now I have to go."

Jeff accompanied her to the door. He wanted to go in, but Violet wouldn't let him. "Hurry back to the hospital. You ought to be with your family tonight." She stood on tiptoe and kissed him. "You're a sweet man. Thanks for asking me."

Jeff was mad. Violet could tell from his unbending attitude. Well, she was sorry she'd hurt his feelings, but he would get over it. He'd soon realize she wasn't turning him down, just the chance to mingle with Denver society.

Besides, she had to admit she was a little afraid. Jeff belonged in the top echelon of society. Violet couldn't be certain he wouldn't be ashamed to be seen at the most prestigious social event of the season with a house-mother. She wasn't even a teacher, just a hired nanny. The men were bound to snicker behind Jeff's back. She didn't even want to think of what the women would say. Violet could stand many things, but she couldn't stand for Jeff to be ashamed to be seen with her.

Once inside, Violet went immediately to a window. She watched Jeff walk down the flagstone path toward the road, his steps slow, reluctant. She knew she only had to change her mind, to call him, and he would turn back.

When Jeff paused at the road and turned back to look at the building, Violet drew back. He stood there a long time, just staring.

"If Miss Settle had seen what I just saw, you'd be out on the street in a minute."

Violet jumped, startled by Beth's words. She hadn't even heard her enter the parlor. "What do you mean?" Violet asked, though she knew perfectly well.

"Miss Settle doesn't hold with the staff mixing with

the families. She fired a teacher just before you came because she thought the woman was getting too familiar with one of the widowed fathers. If she'd seen you kiss Mr. Randolph, she'd have gone off in a dead faint.''

''We did nothing improper,'' Violet said.

''I never said you did. I'm just warning you.'' Beth's frown changed instantly into a bright grin. ''Now you tell me everything that happened. Miss Settle nearly had a fit when you and the twins didn't come back.''

Jeff felt the old familiar fears gnawing at the edges of his mind. He had never been able to accept any kind of refusal without thinking it was because something was wrong with him. His empty left sleeve lay in his lap, a silent accusation that had lost none of its power to make him feel inadequate after all those years. Even when his reason told him it was nonsense, he couldn't shake the nagging fear.

At times like that, he wished that ball had killed him. Would he never be able to escape from the perpetual feeling of being only part of a man?

Jeff tried to make himself believe that Violet had no reason for refusing other than the ones she had given him. He might not like them, but they were reasonable. Why couldn't he accept what she had said and let it go? Why did he have to keep torturing himself?

The reason was he liked her more and more each day. He was afraid she was backing away. All his life he'd been rejecting people before they could reject him. But he had to admit he had met a woman whose acceptance he wanted more than anything else on earth, and he was petrified she wouldn't give it. Her turning down his invitation was the first time she had refused him, but it was also the first time he'd tried to do anything more than kiss her.

Jeff was afraid that, when it came to a more serious relationship, she would prefer someone like Harvey

McKee, who always seemed to be turning up. Violet liked him. And why not? Rich and well liked by everybody, Harvey had both arms. There was no reason why Violet shouldn't like Harvey better than she liked Jeff. He had nothing to offer except a rotten disposition, an uncertain temper, and a missing arm.

Jeff told himself to be sensible for once. He had finally accepted that his family loved him for himself. Despite all the things he had said, they had turned to him that night without hesitation. There had never been any feeling that he was less of a man than George or Madison or Monty or Tyler.

Violet had said he was the most capable man she knew. He hoped it was so. He wanted it to be so. A man like that wouldn't constantly look for ways to blame himself. He would live life without casting blame. Jeff could do that. He would do that. He didn't want Violet to be disappointed in him.

Jeff lay still while his trainer worked the last heat from his muscles. He knew he had worked his body too hard, dangerously hard in fact, but he didn't care. He had done everything dangerously hard recently.

"I know you don't like me telling you what to do," his trainer said, "but it's what you pay me for. And I wouldn't be doing my duty if I didn't warn you that you're going to hurt yourself if you keep up like this."

"I know what's too much."

"Maybe when you're sitting at your desk, but when you get to lifting those weights, you push yourself too hard. It's as if you're trying to punish yourself, see what it takes to break you."

Maybe Jeff was. He wasn't very fond of himself just then. Maybe it was his way of punishing himself for liking Violet.

"At least take tomorrow off," his trainer said. "Your body needs some time to recover."

"We'll see," Jeff said. Work helped to keep his mind off Violet. But not even working around the clock could release the tension or dispel the sense that something was about to explode inside of him. Only brutal exercise could give him a few hours' relief.

"Louise wants to know when you're coming to see her again."

Jeff had wondered how long it would take his trainer to get around to asking that. Jeff hadn't seen Louise since the night she'd sent him away. He knew that his trainer had a soft spot for her. He was always hanging around her place. Jeff wondered how deep his interest went. He hoped his trainer didn't love Louise. She was a good woman, but Jeff doubted she'd consider settling down with one man, not even if that man wanted to marry her.

"Is she still holding my nights for me?" Jeff asked.

"I don't know what she does with her time."

No, he hadn't thought so. It was just as well. "Tell her I don't know when I'll be back."

Jeff hadn't felt any desire to return to Louise's bed. Violet occupied his mind to the exclusion of all other females.

Chapter Twenty-two

Violet stared at Miss Settle, her brain in a whirl. "But I can't go to the ball with Mr. McKee."

"I realize it would place you in a social circle completely beyond your experience," Miss Settle said, her expression stiffly formal, "but it's only for one night. It had been my intention to attend as the school's representative, but I'm not up to it."

"But why me? Why not one of the teachers or someone more familiar with Denver society?"

"I made the same suggestion," Miss Settle said. Her gaze became disapproving as she turned to Harvey. "But Mr. McKee insists he will only go with you."

"What man wouldn't want to be seen with one of the prettiest women in Denver?" Harvey said. "Besides, I've never made any secret of the fact that I enjoy your company."

Miss Settle's expression became even more forbidding. "I wasn't aware you knew Mr. McKee, yet he tells me he's seen you several times at the school."

"He's handling my uncle's estate," Violet said.

"So he told me," Miss Settle said, her displeasure not mitigated in the least. "I hope it will soon be settled satisfactorily."

"There are several problems," Harvey said. "I expect it will take a while yet."

Miss Settle didn't appear pleased by his response. "It won't do for people to think you're setting your cap for Mr. McKee. But I don't suppose attending one ball would be enough to start rumors, particularly not after I've explained to everyone you're only there as a substitute for me."

"I won't have anyone thinking I'm setting my cap for Harvey . . . Mr. McKee," Violet said, beginning to get angry.

"Well, it's something that will be assumed," Miss Settle said. "Mr. McKee's wife died about a year ago. He can't be expected to remain single for long. Any woman seen in his company is bound to become the object of speculation."

"Then I'm surprised you should ask me to attend the ball in his company," Violet said.

"I assure you that no one will think anything improper," Harvey said. "Most of the people attending know you work for the school. When I explain Miss Settle is ill, they'll understand."

"I appreciate your concern," Violet said, "but I must ask you to choose someone else."

"It's too late," Miss Settle said. "I've already told him you'll go. Besides, there isn't time to get anyone else. The ball is tomorrow night."

Violet felt almost too weak to protest. She was to be ready to go to the biggest society ball of the year in only one day? Impossible. She had nothing even remotely resembling a ball gown. But that wasn't the worst. She couldn't go with Harvey after refusing Jeff.

"Thank you for thinking of me, Mr. McKee, but it's

impossible for me to go with you. I've already told Mr. Randolph I couldn't go with him. I can't now show up with you.''

"Mr. Randolph asked you to the charity ball!" Miss Settle said, as surprised as she was displeased. "Why should he do that?"

"I don't know. I didn't ask him."

"And you refused?"

"Yes."

"Why?"

Violet thought it was none of Miss Settle's business, but she could see she would have to satisfy the head-mistress's curiosity if she was to keep her job. "I thought he did it out of a sense of duty. I would be very much out of place at a society ball. Besides, I have spent more than enough time away from my duties."

Miss Settle looked pleased with her answer. "Well, it can't be helped. Just make sure you comport yourself with discretion."

"You don't understand," Violet said, beginning to feel desperate. "If I go with Mr. McKee, Mr. Randolph will think I don't like him."

Miss Settle's expression turned glacial. "And do you?"

"That's not the point," Violet said as matter-of-factly as she could. "I can't go to the dance with someone else after refusing Mr. Randolph. He'll feel insulted."

Miss Settle's expression relaxed a little. "If that's your only worry, you can ease your mind. I'll write him myself and explain you're going in my place. He'll understand."

Violet doubted it. "I'd rather Mr. McKee choose another companion."

"Miss Goodwin, I suppose you know we're in the process of raising money to build a boy's school."

"Yes, ma'am."

"And that we're also raising money for a hospital."

"Yes, Mr. Randolph told me about that." She shouldn't have mentioned Jeff. That would only upset Miss Settle further.

"Well, Mr. McKee is the best fundraiser in town. He has an uncanny ability to encourage others to give more than they originally intended. Denver needs that school and that hospital. It is imperative you attend the ball with Mr. McKee."

If Violet hadn't heard it herself, she wouldn't have believed even Miss Settle was crass enough to make such a statement in front of Harvey. "But Mr. Randolph—"

"I personally guarantee Mr. Randolph will understand," Miss Settle said. "Besides, no one has ever seen him on a dance floor. I can't imagine why he should have asked you."

Violet could think of nothing else to say. Clearly she either went or she lost her job. She hoped Jeff would understand. She was relieved he wouldn't be there. She would go to his office as soon as she could and explain things to him. She didn't want to take a chance on his misunderstanding.

"Now I suggest you stop the foolish objections and see about getting yourself ready for this ball," Miss Settle said, dismissing Violet. "Most of the women who'll be there have been getting ready for weeks."

Clara Rabin finished reading the note. At first, she nearly shook with anger. Gradually her expression became thoughtful. Then she smiled. She looked at the note once more and then up at her husband, who was eating his breakfast.

"Philip, I have just received a note from Miss Settle. Violet Goodwin is going to the ball with Harvey McKee."

"I don't give a damn what that bitch does," Philip Rabin growled. He slammed his coffee cup down so hard that some of the liquid spilled into the saucer.

"Eleanor Settle is ill. Miss Goodwin is going in her place. I would have thought either Eleanor or Harvey could have found a more suitable escort, but that isn't the point."

"Then what is?" her husband said.

"According to Betty Sue, Jeff Randolph is sweet on Miss Goodwin."

"I told you never to mention that man's name in my presence again!" Philip said. "When I think of the money he cost me, I could kill him."

"Miss Settle also said he asked Miss Goodwin to the ball. She refused."

"I don't believe it," Philip said. "Jeff never goes to balls."

"Eleanor got it from Miss Goodwin."

"I don't care where she got it. The bitch was probably lying."

"Suppose she wasn't. Suppose Jeff could see her at the ball, dancing and enjoying herself with another man, he'd be furious. You know how morbidly self-conscious he is about that stump."

"He won't be there."

"You can get him to come," Clara said.

"How?"

"He'll do anything for that bank. After he gets there, you can needle him about women not liking him because of his arm. I'll take care of Miss Goodwin. She's a stiff-necked Puritan. I'll convince her everybody thinks she's running after Jeff. When we bring them together, she'll take one look at him and run the other way. If you say the right things, he'll think she can't stand him because he's a cripple."

Philip had stopped eating. "I'd like to see the bastard dead."

"You won't," Clara said. "But this will be almost as good. It'll eat at him for years."

"You really think it'll work?"

"It depends on your getting him to the ball. Can you?"

"Let me think about it."

"Why me?" the man asked.

"Because he'll be suspicious of anything I say," Philip said.

"Why do you want to make a deal with him? Everybody knows you hate him."

"Money's money."

"I won't do it. You're up to something. I don't want him coming after me when he finds out I've misled him."

Philip dropped all pretense of friendliness. "Do it or I yank the financing out from under your company."

The man blanched. "I can get more financing."

"Not before you lose ninety percent of what you have."

The man attempted to defy Philip, but his resistance wilted under Philip's fierce gaze. "What do you want me to say?" he asked at last.

Violet groaned. She should have guessed the ball would have been held at the Windsor Hotel. Jeff wouldn't be present to see her, but the rest of his family would.

"I don't care how many young sprigs want to dance with you. I'm your escort," Harvey McKee said, giving her hand a pat. "You can forget what Eleanor said. I'm not wasting my evening twisting arms for the hospital."

Violet couldn't help being pleased with the compliment. She liked Harvey. He was exactly the kind of man most people would have thought suitable for a woman of her advanced years. But another man already held her heart. Even if Jeff never returned her feelings, she could never love Harvey.

"Please don't neglect your duty for me," she said.

"I'm not. I'm doing it for myself," Harvey said, tucking her arm more tightly in his. "I plan to enjoy the evening."

An evening she dreaded. Violet doubted society would look any more kindly on her being with Harvey than with Jeff.

She didn't want to leave the carriage. She had worn her most elegant dress, but the addition of a broach and shawl couldn't hide the fact it was not a ball gown. She imagined the women would look on her with pity. She offered up a silent prayer that Harvey would soon settle the claim to her mine and that she would become rich enough to buy at least one decent gown before she left Denver. Not that she expected to be invited to another ball.

"It looks as if everybody is here tonight," Harvey said, noticing the line of carriages behind them.

Violet stifled an insane impulse to gather up her skirts and run back to the school as fast as she could. It was only five blocks away. Instead she took a deep breath, stepped down to the sidewalk, and allowed Harvey to escort her inside.

The hotel was already crowded. The entire lower floor had been opened up to form one huge room with spaces for people to sit, talk in small groups, or eat. There was plenty of space left for those who wished to dance. A small orchestra was already playing a slow lilting tune Violet didn't recognize.

A brief survey of the women present convinced Violet that half the wealth of the West was in the room. Violet saw headdresses with ostrich feathers that swept the air; half the women seemed to have found a way to incorporate mink, ermine, sable, or silver fox into their dresses. Gowns of silk, velvet, and satin shimmered in the light; jewels worth an emperor's ransom decorated the ears, throats, and bosoms of the cream of Denver society. The room buzzed with the sound of hundreds of voices. Violet didn't see a single person she knew.

"A good gathering," Harvey said. He kept Violet close to his side as he moved through the room, greeting guests, introducing her as he went. Violet didn't mind that few people seemed to be interested in meeting her. She hoped no one would remember her face after that evening. But the moment the orchestra stuck up a popular dance tune, that hope died a swift death.

Men converged on her from several directions. Fortunately, since shock held her mute, Harvey refused all requests. "I brought the lady, and I mean to get the first dance," he announced. "The first several as a matter of fact."

Harvey couldn't dance, and Violet wasn't much better. She explained that most people in New England disapproved of dancing. Harvey merely laughed and led her onto the floor for a second dance. After that, he turned her over to a succession of partners he selected with care.

Violet smiled to herself when she realized that they were all either too young for her or puffing octogenarians old enough to be her grandfather. She used the arrival of Rose and George as an excuse to leave the dance floor before her present partner suffered a heart attack. She was extremely grateful when Rose greeted her like an old friend.

"Thank goodness," Rose whispered. "You're the first person I recognize."

"Same here," Violet said. "I wouldn't be here, but Miss Settle fell ill and forced me to come in her place."

As Harvey and George fell into conversation, Daisy Randolph came over to add her welcome, and Violet began to feel a little better. Rose was beautifully gowned, but Daisy wore a gown of even plainer design than Violet's dress.

"Iris and Monty will be down in a little while," Daisy

told Rose. She laughed. "She's still trying to decide which gown to wear. Monty can't make up his mind which one he likes best."

"She'll look beautiful no matter what she wears," Violet said.

"No lovelier than you," Harvey said.

"Wait until you see her," Violet said.

Iris appeared a few minutes later, wearing a white silk gown embroidered with hundreds of pearls. A magnificent set of emeralds, especially chosen to match her eyes, flashed from her throat and earlobes. Her face was perfect as always, but every eye in the room was drawn to her hair. Swept up on her head and held in place by a series of emerald-studded pins, it cast every woman in the room into insignificance.

"I have never seen such hair," Rose said aloud.

"Violet's hair is just as beautiful," Harvey said.

Violet knew he couldn't mean it—no one could, not after seeing Iris—but it made her smile with pleasure. She wondered what Jeff would have said. No, she didn't. Jeff was a pragmatist. He might prefer Violet, but he would be the first to admit that Iris was a beauty without peer.

"I was feeling quite pleased with myself until now," Rose told Iris as she greeted her with a kiss. "You make me feel positively dowdy."

"She's a corker, isn't she?" Monty said, practically bursting with pride.

"I'm sure she's the best-looking woman in Colorado," Rose said. "Now get her out of my sight, or I'll be depressed for the rest of the evening. Come, George. Dance with me and tell me how beautiful I am."

George took his wife's hand. "You know I've always thought so."

"I know," Rose said smiling up at him, "but it's easier to believe when Iris isn't around."

"That's right," Iris said in mock anger. "Make me feel like the plague."

"Come dance with me," Monty said. "I'll whisper sweet nothings in your ear."

"You're more likely to bite it and cause me to squeal," Iris said, flushing with pleasure.

"Not a bad idea," Monty said, leading his wife away.

"Why don't you dance with Daisy?" Violet said to Harvey. "I still need some time to catch my breath."

"Thanks, but I'm waiting for Tyler," Daisy said, "though I may have to go fetch him from the kitchens. Would you believe he's actually tasting sauces and peering into ovens in a starched shirt and tails?"

The next hour passed rather pleasantly for Violet. Harvey proved to be an attentive escort and pleasant conversationalist—except when she tried to talk to him about her claim.

"I always keep business for the office. Tonight is for fun."

When she wasn't dancing, she spent the time with the Randolphs. Gradually her mood improved. It was impossible not to be cheerful with Iris and Monty around. Tyler finally emerged from the kitchen to make Daisy's evening complete. It didn't take long for Violet to realize all three Randolph couples were completely, hopelessly in love. Fern and Madison were no different. He had stayed home because she couldn't come.

Randolph men obviously made good husbands. It just took the right key to unlock their hearts. Violet wondered if she would ever manage to unlock Jeff's heart. Feeling a little too blue to be around all this happiness, Violet excused herself to go to the ladies' lounge.

The first person Jeff saw when he entered the hotel was Philip Rabin. If he hadn't known better, he would have sworn Philip had been waiting for him.

"You not dressed for a ball," Philip said, making no

attempt to hide his dislike for Jeff. "Maybe you think your money is enough." Philip looked pointedly at Jeff's empty sleeve. "Then again, I guess not even money is enough to make up for that empty sleeve flapping at your side."

Jeff's fist curled into a tight ball, a fact Philip didn't miss.

"You'd love to hit me, wouldn't you?" Rabin taunted. "But not even smashing my face will keep you from being a cripple for the rest of your life. You'll never get a woman to dance with you."

Jeff had never understood his father's black rages until then. He would have liked nothing better than to have killed Philip Rabin with his bare hand. It took physical effort to keep from driving his fist into the man's leering face.

"What the hell do you want?" Jeff said.

"Just to welcome you to the ball," Philip said.

"I'm not here for the ball. I came to see my brothers on business."

"Afraid to put it to the test?"

"What the hell are you talking about now?"

Vicious triumph glittered in Rabin's eyes. "Afraid to see whether the women are more attracted to your money than they are repulsed by your stump?"

Jeff's hand shot out and closed around Rabin's throat. Pushing him into a corner behind several large potted plants and out of sight of the guests, Jeff gradually increased the pressure on the man's windpipe. Rabin didn't look so confident.

"I could strangle you and leave your body here. Nobody would find you for hours."

Rabin's mouth opened and closed, but no sound came out.

"I don't know why you're doing this, but I'll be gone inside half an hour," Jeff said. "Why don't you go to the bar and have a drink."

Jeff released Rabin and walked away without a backward glance.

Violet didn't want to return to the ballroom just yet. She wanted a few more minutes to herself. She found a quiet corner behind a row of potted palms. Settled into the deep chair, she was able to truly relax for the first time all evening.

She wondered what Jeff was doing. Working, of course. He never did anything else. She wondered why he had let himself be maneuvered into inviting her to the ball. She couldn't see him spending the evening dancing and making idle conversation.

But she could easily picture herself spending the evening with him, his arm around her waist, his body close to her own, his handsome face smiling down on her. She would have forgotten that she didn't have a ball gown, that she didn't know anybody, that she felt dreadfully out of place. She would have been with Jeff. Nothing else would have mattered.

She wished she had accepted his invitation. Then she could be just as happy as Rose, Iris, and Daisy. Instead she was hiding behind a palm, trying not to let everybody know she'd rather be almost anywhere but here.

She became aware of voices. She should go back. But even as she started to rise, she recognized Clara Rabin's voice. Hoping she could escape without having to greet a woman she disliked, Violet stayed where she was.

"I don't know what she thinks she's doing here," Clara was saying. "Even she must know she doesn't belong."

Violet couldn't quite hear all of the other woman's response, but she did catch the last part. "—wearing a dress. Surely she knows the difference between a party and a ball."

"What can you expect of a housemother?" Clara Rabin said. "Besides, it's probably the best she has. I doubt she's ever owned a gown."

Violet's body stiffened. The women were talking about her!

"Then she had no business coming. I can't imagine why Harvey invited her."

"It's probably that red hair," Clara said, thinly disguised scorn in her voice. "You've seen the way the men are making fools of themselves over that Iris Randolph."

"You have to admit she's quite striking."

"Brazen is more like it, but little Miss Housemother doesn't have those kind of looks to recommend her," Clara said.

"Harvey seems quite entranced with her."

"He won't be when he learns she was throwing herself at Jeff Randolph just a short time ago."

"I don't believe it! Everybody knows he can't stand Yankees."

Clara's soft laugh was not a pleasant sound. It grated on Violet's nerves. "Apparently Miss Goodwin doesn't know that. My daughter told me all about it," Clara said in a lowered voice, which still carried with absolutely clarity.

"Told you what?"

"Jeff got himself caught at the school during the quarantine. I don't know how, but it had something to do with those horrible nieces of his. Anyway, this Goodwin woman kept throwing herself in his way the whole time. Every time he emerged from his room, she was there. She pretended she was protecting the girls, but even my thirteen-year-old daughter could see through that. She kept sending the girls to their rooms. She had dinner with him upstairs. Twice."

"Jeff Randolph! I don't believe it."

"Betty Sue doesn't lie!"

"I don't mean that," her friend said hastily. "I simply

can't imagine how she managed to corner him. I would have thought he'd climb out the window first.''

"She wouldn't let him," Clara said, delighted to be able to throw in the clincher. "She told him she'd have him arrested if he tried to leave."

"Good God!"

"Apparently she didn't give up even after the quarantine was over. My husband says she pursued him to his office, his brother's ranch, even here at the hotel. The man isn't safe from her."

"How did she meet Harvey?"

"He's handling some kind of mine claim for her. Philip says it's worthless. She's probably just using it to get her hooks into him."

"She seems to have been successful. She appears to be on terms with the Randolphs as well. Do you think she still has hopes of catching Jeff?"

"I'd be more interested in knowing how she talked Harvey into inviting her this evening," Clara said.

"I'm here in Miss Settle's place," Violet said as she emerged from behind the palm. "She was taken ill yesterday afternoon."

The two women reacted with shock. The second woman's was genuine. It took Violet only a moment to realize Clara Rabin's was feigned. She had known Violet was there all along. She must have seen her enter the lounge and followed her, intending all along for Violet to overhear every word she had to say.

For a moment, Violet was so angry she couldn't speak. Then as the two women stammered apologies, she managed to get control of her temper. Nothing would make Clara happier than to see Violet upset. She was determined to deny her that pleasure.

"As for getting my hooks into a rich husband, I haven't decided which one I want yet. You ladies know them both so much better than I do. Which one would you recommend? A woman does have to be careful, you know.''

Violet had the pleasure of seeing Clara Rabin gape. ''I understand Jeff Randolph has a lot more money, but he is a cripple. On the other hand, Harvey's older. He's not likely to live as long. I think he might appreciate a young and pretty wife more than Mr. Randolph. What do you think?''

''I think you're the most brazen fortune hunter I've ever come across,'' Clara said.

''As brazen as you?'' Violet said. ''Why I'm truly flattered.''

''You'll never catch anything in that dress,'' Clara said, struggling to make a comeback.

''I'll catch exactly what I came to catch,'' Violet said, her anger flashing from her eyes. ''Nothing. Oh, close your mouth, Clara. You look like a landed fish. You can both relax. I'm not here to make off with any of your men. But if I were, you wouldn't stop me.'' Violet turned to leave.

''I haven't given you permission to use my first name,'' Clara Rabin said. ''And don't turn your back on me. I haven't finished talking to you.'' When Violet didn't look back, Clara followed her. ''You won't marry Jeff Randolph regardless of how much you play up to his family. You can't fool me. You don't want Harvey. He doesn't have a tenth of Jeff's wealth. You only came with Harvey because you thought Jeff would be here and you could make him jealous. Everybody here knows it. They're laughing at you.''

Violet stopped and turned around. ''And how do they know it, Clara?'' Violet asked, her voice more calm than she felt.

''Because I told them,'' Clara said defiantly.

Suddenly Violet could stand no more. She no longer wanted to defy Clara Rabin or anybody else. She just wanted to get out of the lounge before she burst into tears. She had to leave the ball. She had to go home. She didn't know what she would tell Harvey, but she couldn't stay a minute longer.

She turned on her heel. Clara started to follow, but her friend reached out and grabbed her arm.

"Let her go. I think you've said enough."

"I haven't said nearly enough," Clara said.

Violet didn't know how she found her way back to Harvey. She didn't care that an angry Clara Rabin followed in her wake. Violet wanted only to reach Harvey and ask him to take her home before tears overcame her.

Harvey saw her coming, broke off his conversation, and turned to her. Violet took his arm and stood close so that she could whisper her request in his ear. Just then Jeff stepped forward from where he'd been talking to George.

Chapter Twenty-three

Violet stared at Jeff in horror. Her heart almost stopped beating. She could see the shock on his face, the immediate calcification of his smile. She knew she ought to say something, but she couldn't think of a single word that wouldn't condemn her. Realizing that Clara Rabin was right behind her ready to misinterpret anything she might say—as well as broadcast her misinterpretations to everyone in the ballroom—rendered her nearly speechless.

Clinging to Harvey, she said, "I'm not feeling well. I'd like to go home."

"Are you sick?" Rose asked.

"Maybe you ought to lie down first," Iris said. "The carriage ride might make you feel even worse."

Violet's gaze flew to Jeff. She saw no sympathy or concern in his expression. Only hurt and anger. She saw him withdraw into himself, pull back beyond her reach. Everything left was hard, impenetrable.

"Thank you, but I'd rather go home."

"Why don't you take her, Jeff?" Rose said. "You weren't going to stay anyway."

Violet couldn't stop herself from glancing up at Jeff. She hoped her face didn't show how much she hoped he would accept Rose's suggestion. She desperately wanted a few minutes alone with him.

"She came with Harvey," Jeff said. "I wouldn't think of intruding."

He sounded icily polite, but his words might as well have been dipped in poison. He had absolutely no intention of leaving the hotel with her. Violet had never seen him look so hurt, so baffled, or so icily indifferent. It made her heart ache to look at him. It made her heart sink to think she was the cause of his pain.

Obviously Miss Settle's note hadn't explained the situation clearly. The present moment wasn't a good time to attempt to justify herself, but she had to try.

"You're probably wondering what I'm doing here when—"

Blue fury flashed from his eyes. "I never wonder about Yankees," he said, cutting her off. "I know they're capable of anything."

Through the hurt and humiliation, Violet felt herself begin to get angry. He was condemning her without giving her a chance to explain. He was just assuming again, as he always did when he was hurt. "Surely you don't think I would—"

"Nor do I concern myself with their motives," he said, crushing her effort to explain her presence. "Why look for honor where you know it doesn't exist?"

Violet's temper flared up. She didn't know why he should think he was the only one with feelings or the only one who could be hurt. She was tired of his self-absorption. As much as she loved him, she wondered if he'd ever be able to think of anyone before himself.

"You wouldn't know honor if it bit you on your stump," Violet said.

"Oh, so you did notice my stump?" Jeff said, waving his sleeve at Violet.

"How could I help noticing it?" Violet said. "It seems to be the sum total of your existence. I can't imagine a more appropriate symbol of your life. A perfect creation damaged in its prime, carefully preserved in its altered form to cause misery for all."

With a sob, Violet grabbed her shawl and ran from the room.

Jeff watched Violet bolt from the room, Harvey McKee following in her wake. The pain inside him was so deep, so intense, he felt as if it was tearing him apart. He didn't want anyone to know Violet Goodwin didn't want to dance with a one-armed man. He didn't want anybody to know he loved her.

Rose turned on Jeff, her brown eyes ablaze with fury. "I thought I had seen you at your worst, but that was the most despicable thing I've ever seen a Randolph do. I've always said you were spoiled, rude, and utterly thoughtless, but I wouldn't have believed you could be wantonly cruel. You should be beaten for what you did. If we weren't in public, I'd hit you myself."

"Go ahead. One of us ought to feel better."

"Spare me your self-pity," Rose said.

"I hope she isn't really sick," Iris said, attempting to fill the awkward silence that followed. "I thought she was in good spirits."

"She certainly seemed to be enjoying the dancing," Monty said.

"Why wouldn't she, with all those men crowding around her?"

So she had enjoyed the dance, Jeff thought. There could be no other explanation. Despite everything she said about her brother, when it came right down to it, she wasn't any different from any other woman.

Jeff wondered what Violet would have said if he

hadn't surprised her. She'd probably have had some perfectly logical reason why she couldn't dance with him. But he hadn't given her time to think. She had been too shocked to hide her real feelings.

Jeff felt cold and empty inside. He hadn't allowed himself to believe it, but he had fallen in love with Violet. He had denied the attraction from the moment he had met her. He had told himself he invited her to dinner because he didn't want to waste food. He had told himself he was protecting her from Miss Settle. He had told himself any number of lies to account for his desire to be with her, to be able to look at her, to touch her, to kiss her. But that night, the minute he had stepped from behind George and come face-to-face with her, he had known he loved her. Then she had backed away from him.

"Aren't you going to make some attempt to defend yourself?" Rose said.

"What do you want me to say?" Jeff asked.

"There's nothing you can say to excuse what you did."

"Then there's no point in saying anything."

Rose directed a perplexed look at him, then said, "Come dance with me."

Jeff was certain she couldn't want to dance unless she meant to murder him in the middle of the dance floor. But Rose took him by the arm and pulled him along. He moved as if in a trance. He didn't even notice when Rose made an unexpected turn and led him to an area set aside for people who wanted a little privacy. She sat down and patted the seat next to her. He sat.

"Why must you always behave like an angry nest of hornets?" Rose asked as soon as he was seated.

Jeff didn't answer. He couldn't. He felt like the victim of a thousand hornets.

Rose watched him closely. The angry flame in her eyes had died down. "Tell me what's wrong."

Jeff started as one coming out of a spell. "What do you mean?" he asked, trying to gather his wits.

"Jeff Randolph, I've known you for nearly fifteen years. We've fought, disagreed, even disliked each other, but you've never been mean or vicious. You were both tonight. Why?"

He couldn't answer. It wouldn't have made any difference. Rose wouldn't understand the demons that drove him. She never had.

"If you don't want to tell me, just say so, but I know something's wrong, and I know it has to do with Violet."

"How do you know that?"

Rose frowned impatiently. "You take one look at Violet with another man, act like a jealous lover, and ask how I know something is wrong!" She made a noise that sounded an awful lot like derision. "Maybe you've forgotten you apologized to Fern, Iris, and myself for all the nasty things you said about us. We were almost ready to send for the doctor. We were certain you had fallen on your head."

Jeff didn't smile. He didn't feel like it. He hated having people know anything about what was going on inside him, but just then he didn't care enough to think up some plausible excuse. Nothing had changed. His life was always going to be the same. He didn't care about much of anything anymore.

He gathered himself and stood up. "I have work to do. I'll walk you back."

"Is that all you have to say? You have work to do?"

"Yes."

"That woman means something to you, Jeff. Don't try to deny it. Something happened tonight—I have no idea what—but if you're not careful, you're going to let it cost you something you want very much."

"George must know we're not on the dance floor."

"Jeff Randolph, there are times when you make me

so angry I could shake the life out of you.''

"Don't bother. It's already gone. Now let's go back before George comes looking for you. I don't know if he'd believe I'd try to run off with you, but you should never underestimate the gullibility of a Randolph.''

Rose took Jeff by the arm and forced him to look at her. "You love her, don't you?''

"She's a Yankee, Rose. A real New England bred, raised, and trained Yankee. She thinks Robert E. Lee was the biggest villain of the war. How could I love somebody like that?''

"I don't know. I imagine you fought it as hard as you could, but you do love her.''

Jeff took Rose by the elbow and they started back. "I was attracted to her. She's a lovely woman.''

"I'm not a fool, Jeff Randolph. Don't talk to me unless you intend to tell me the truth.''

But Jeff didn't mean to tell anyone the truth. Maybe if he tried hard enough, he could forget it himself.

Violet used Harvey's handkerchief to dry her eyes. "Thanks for listening to me," she said. "I feel remarkably stupid, but I feel better for having somebody to talk to.''

Harvey patted her hand. "I only wish you'd fallen in love with me instead.''

"So do I," Violet said. "You're a wonderful man. You'll make some woman a perfect husband.''

"Are you certain you can't be that woman?''

"There's no cure for stupidity," Violet said. "Once you're stupid, you're stupid for the rest of your life.''

"I take that to mean no.''

"I'm sorry. I wish I could. Truly I do. But I love that miserable, festering mass of anger and self-pity. I can't for the life of me figure out why.''

"What are you going to do?''

"Keep working, never set eyes on him again, and go

back to Massachusetts as soon as I can. I don't know. I'd leave right now if I had the money."

"I can give you—"

"You're doing more than enough for me as it is. Now we'd better get back. Miss Settle is going to want a full report on the evening. I have to think of something to tell her."

Harvey gave the driver the signal to start the carriage. They had stopped two blocks away from the school to give Violet time to calm herself.

"I'm worried about what Clara Rabin will tell Miss Settle," Violet said.

"I'll back anything you say," Harvey said.

"I wasn't discreet. I imagine half the people there saw me leave at a gallop."

"Just tell her you were about to be ill. She can't blame you for that."

The carriage turned the corner on to Champa Street, and Violet said, "After the trouble I've caused her, I imagine she's ready to believe anything of me."

"Eleanor is a little rigid, but she's not—"

Violet grabbed Harvey's arm. "That's Jeff!" she said, pointing to a man who had just gotten out of a carriage in front of the school. "I don't want to see him."

Harvey called to the driver to stop the carriage. "We can wait here until he leaves."

"You don't know Jeff. He won't leave. He'll wait all night if necessary."

"Surely not."

"You'll see."

A short time later, Jeff came out to the road, sent the carriage away, and returned to the porch to wait.

"I'll speak to him," Harvey said.

"No, it won't solve anything. I need some place to stay until tomorrow."

"You can use my house."

"It would ruin me."

"I'll spend the night elsewhere."

"It wouldn't make any difference."

"Then go to a hotel."

"It would amount to the same thing."

"I can't think of any place where your reputation won't be in jeopardy."

"I can," Violet said. "I know the perfect place."

Jeff looked at his watch. 12:21 a.m. He didn't know where Violet and Harvey could have gone. He had expected her to be in the dormitory when he had reached the school. He would wait a little while. He had to see her.

He had been a fool. He had let Philip Rabin get him mad, play on his fears, plant one pernicious thought in his head. Then when he had seen Violet with Harvey, he could think of nothing but that she didn't want him because of his arm. True to the habit of years, he had jumped to conclusions. His tongue had followed up by saying the most hurtful things he could think of.

Then as he had stormed out of the hotel, too angry to speak to anyone he passed, his hand had delved into his pocket to finger an envelope there. As he left the hotel, he remembered it was a note from Miss Settle, one he'd been too busy to read earlier. He had thrust it into his pocket and forgotten it. He read it by the soft light of a streetlight.

Afterward, he had felt like a fool, a cruel, mean-spirited fool. He desperately wanted to find Violet, to explain, to beg her forgiveness. He loved her, God forgive him. He didn't know how it had happened, but he did. He thought she loved him, too, but he didn't know if she loved him enough to forgive him for what he'd done earlier. He had to find out.

He looked at his watch again. He couldn't stand around waiting. He would look for her.

*   *   *

Jeff rang Harvey's bell again. No answer. It was the second time he had come by. It was the second time no one answered.

Jeff's eagerness had waned. He couldn't figure out where Violet could be. He didn't know why she hadn't returned to the school. He didn't know why Harvey hadn't come home. All kinds of horrible thoughts chased themselves through his mind, but Jeff did his best to ignore them, to keep his faith in Violet.

She wouldn't have stayed out all night with Harvey. He just knew she wouldn't. But if not, where were they?

"She still hasn't come home," Beth said. "I'm worried sick about her."

"She didn't send a message?"

"Not a word."

Jeff looked at his watch. 4:07 a.m. He might as well accept it. Violet wasn't coming home. She wasn't sick. He'd checked every hospital in Denver. He couldn't find her at any hotel. Clearly she didn't want to see him.

He had felt hope wane over the last hours. She didn't love him. She couldn't and disappear like that. She would have known he didn't mean what he had said. She would have known he would have wanted to see her as soon as he had cooled off. She would have known he couldn't have slept until he had. But she didn't love him—or care.

Jeff walked down the flagstone path. When he reached the road, he headed in the direction of Fourteenth Street. It was time to go home. It was time to realize it was over. Whatever hope he had was gone. And he had no one to blame but himself.

"Fern said I would find you hot and sweaty."

Jeff looked up to see George entering his training room.

George wrinkled his nose. "This place smells as bad

as a cow barn. And you said Texas stank.''

''It does,'' Jeff said, sitting up. ''That's all for today, Ed. Same time tomorrow.''

''I thought I might talk you into coming out to the ranch for the weekend,'' George said.

Jeff eyed his brother. ''They don't want me there, especially with the house full of relatives. That's usually the time everybody hopes I'll work all weekend.''

''William Henry and Elizabeth arrived from Texas.''

''They're your children, not mine.''

George settled himself in a chair, not the least bit disturbed by Jeff's answers. ''They're worried about you. After last night, you couldn't expect anything else,'' George said, his look veiled.

''Does that include you?'' Jeff asked as he dropped the towel from around his waist and shrugged into a robe. Since he had cooled down, he felt cold.

''I'm not certain worry is the best word, but it'll do. You can't go around apologizing to all and sundry after fifteen years of being a son of a bitch, show up at a charity ball and insult a woman in public, then not expect people to wonder. The general consensus is that something cataclysmic happened to you. However, since there has been no record of seismic activity in Denver during the past week, speculation is rife.''

''Good. I'd hate for the family to have nothing to talk about.''

''There's no shortage of topics, not with two women pregnant and a third coming to join them in the spring.''

''I'm surprised they even remembered me,'' Jeff said.

''You underestimate the family's interest in you.''

''I'm well aware of my value as an irritant. I give everybody a common annoyance so they won't have time to realize how little they care about each other.''

Ed picked up an armload of towels and left the room.

Some of the sunshine seemed to go out of George's expression. ''When you said what you did to Rose and the others, I hoped you'd finally come to terms with the anger that's been locked inside you all these years. I didn't know what might have happened, but I hoped it had made you happy. I couldn't have wanted it for anyone more than you."

Jeff felt the ball of angry resistance dissolve. Ever since he could remember, George had been trying to fix what couldn't be fixed. Of all the family, he came closest to understanding how Jeff felt.

"You'll be happy to know nothing cataclysmic happened," Jeff said. "The other night when we were trying to convince that doctor to come see Fern, Violet told him Fern would die."

"I was afraid of that."

"I realized that, if she died, I would never have thanked her for the good she's done for Madison. The same goes for Rose and Iris. That was all. Nothing more than a little belated fair play."

George's skepticism was blatant. "There's more to it than that, but if you don't want to tell me, I won't ask." He got to his feet. "I'd better be going. Monty is organizing this rodeo for Rose. I have to keep an eye on him to make sure it won't grow so big that I have to bring up half of Texas on the next train."

"Sit back down, George. Now that you're here, there's something I want to talk to you about." After George settled back into his chair, Jeff said, "I'm thinking about resigning from the bank. It's time I went back to Virginia."

Jeff hated having to explain anything to George or Rose. The rest of his family took what he said at face value, and that was the end of it, but not George or Rose. They would listen to every word, remember the inflection of each sound, the way he looked, the way he stood, whether he fidgeted or stood still, whether he looked them in the eye or avoided their gaze. Then they would come to a pretty fair understanding of what Jeff had tried so hard to hide from them.

"Isn't this rather sudden?" George asked.

"Not really. I'd been hoping the whole family would want to return. You told me they wouldn't, but I still hoped. Well, I finally realized nobody wants to go back except me. I'm not getting any younger. If I want to get married, I'd better go before I get so old nobody will have me."

"Why are you going back to Virginia?"

"I've always meant to go back," Jeff said.

"I know that. I just want to know what you hope to accomplish that you can't do here. You realize the family will miss you. There's no one to take your place."

"Madison could. You, too, if you wanted."

"Neither of us could do half as well as you."

"I'm going."

"Nobody will try to stop you."

Jeff could feel George looking at him, trying to see inside his head—and heart. "You still want to know why, don't you?"

"Wouldn't you if I suddenly announced I was going to sell the ranch and run off a thousand miles to a place where I no longer had any family or connections? The family needs you. It depends on you. We'll need some time to decide what to do about your leaving. I'm not the only one who'll want to know the reason."

"I'm thirty-seven, George. I can't keep putting off my life."

"What have you been doing these past fifteen years?"

"Waiting," Jeff said.

"Waiting for what?"

"For everything. For a life that could never be again. Rose says I've been a great fool most of my life. She's right. I finally learned what you tried to tell me years ago. It's over, gone, vanished. Nothing will bring it back. You see, I thought if we could all go back, somehow it would. I was stupid. I know that now. I guess I just wanted it so badly I wouldn't let myself see the truth.''

"What are you going to do when you get there?"

"I don't know. I've talked about the disabled veterans my whole life, but I've never done anything for them. Maybe it's not too late."

"When did you start thinking about that?"

"I've had the idea for some time now." He wasn't about to tell George that he'd gotten it from Violet. "I'm sure Virginia can use a banker who's interested in keeping money in the state."

"Are you going to rebuild Ashburn?"

"I don't know. I'll probably wait until I get married to decide."

"Do you have anybody in mind—for your wife, I mean? You haven't been back in ten years."

Jeff couldn't tell George he was going back without having picked out a bride, but George must have known that already. He would also know the prospects were slim. Most girls of marriageable age were too young to remember the war or understand how it affected the men who had fought in it. Their parents had told them about it, but they hadn't experienced it. It wasn't real to them. It hadn't been real for Julia Wilcox. It would be even less real for younger girls.

Jeff was scared. He wouldn't admit it to George, but he was scared right down to his toes. He'd always said that he was going back, but he'd never actually decided to do it until that moment. He knew he would only get one chance. If it didn't work, he would spend the rest of his life in Denver, Chicago, St. Louis, San Francisco, or some other city that meant nothing to him.

He had to belong. He had to feel there was a place that needed him. Part of that feeling had to come from a woman who wanted him for her husband and lover, not because he belonged to a famous family or because he was rich. It was a tall order to fill, maybe more difficult than anything he'd done in his life, but he had to try.

Violet could have done it. If he hadn't made such a fool of himself at the ball, she might have. She didn't care about his arm, the past, or his terrible bitterness. She loved him just as he was.

He had to find her and talk to her. Maybe she couldn't love him any longer—he hoped she could even though he knew he didn't deserve it—but he couldn't leave without seeing her again.

"I don't have answers to your questions," Jeff said. "I just know it's time I go back."

George regarded his brother in silence for a long time. Finally he said, "I was hoping you would change your mind. We've been gone twenty years. A lot has happened since then. Nothing will be the same as you remember it."

"I'm not the same either. Maybe we'll fit better than you think."

"Then I have just one thing to ask of you."

"What?"

"Before you go, make certain you know what you're looking for. You can't go back to Virginia just because it's there. You have to be looking for something you can't find anywhere else, something you can't live without any longer."

"Is that all?"

"No. Decide what you're going to do if you can't find it."

Violet stood rigid before Miss Settle, unable to believe her ears. She had been fired. Actually, she was being thrown out. Miss Settle expected her to be off the school property before nightfall. Her secretary, Miss Nicholson, forced to witness the interview, cowered in the corner.

"After I gave you a wonderful job—gave it to you despite no experience as a housemother, I might add, because Mr. McKee gave you such a sterling recommendation—I find it practically impossible to credit your behavior."

Violet was unable to open her mouth to protest or ask for an explanation before Miss Settle continued. "I was never easy over that business with Mr. Randolph."

"It wouldn't have happened if you hadn't ordered me not to post a quarantine sign," Violet said.

But the truth clearly wasn't going to sway Miss Settle from the course she had decided to take.

"I didn't want to believe the things Clara Rabin told me about you. I know her daughter is jealous of the Randolph twins. But I had no choice when you started shirking your duties," Miss Settle said.

"When did I do that?" Violet asked, shocked at such an accusation after she'd worked so hard.

"Time and time again I was forced to find someone to do your work while you were off chasing Mr. Randolph."

"I never chased him."

"You went to his house, his office, his sister-in-law's home. You even talked the twins' mother into arranging this rodeo so you could see more of him."

"She asked me to—"

"Then you ran off," Miss Settle said, "and spent the whole evening waiting for Mrs. Randolph's baby, as if you were a member of the family."

"Madison asked me to help. He said he'd talk to you."

"See. There you go. That's exactly what I mean, referring to your betters by their first names."

"When you're surrounded by five men and four women all named Randolph, you have to use first names."

"Then there's your shameless behavior at the ball."

Violet didn't know why she asked. It wasn't going to make any difference, but she couldn't stop herself. "What shameless behavior?"

"Don't think you're going to slip anything by me. Clara Rabin told me all about how you threw yourself at every man there. She also told me about your inexcusably rude behavior when she tried to hint, ever so gently, that you might not be making the kind of impression that would reflect favorably on the school. Then there is the matter of your not coming in until the morning after the ball."

"Would you like to know where I spent the night and why?"

"Clara Rabin gave me sufficient information to guess."

Violet took a deep breath. "I don't expect you to believe me, but Clara Rabin is a liar. She has spent the last weeks spreading rumors about me. I don't know why. She can't possibly think I can do anything to harm her."

"Mrs. Rabin is a leader of Denver society," Miss Settle announced, red anger spots flaming in her powder-white cheeks. "She doesn't like seeing people attempt to climb above their stations."

Violet was getting very angry. She was sick and tired of being blamed for everything that happened. "All of Denver society is above their stations. They were nothing but dirt farmers, shopkeepers, and grubby miners until they got rich on gold. They're lucky that people like the Randolphs even talk to them."

"Miss Goodwin! I will not have you—"

Violet lost her temper. "Save your breath. Now that I see the kind of person you are, the kind of person you admire, I wouldn't stay here if you doubled my salary. But allow me to give you a piece of advice. I wouldn't tie my star too closely to the Rabins. There are quite a few people in Denver who have a very poor opinion of them."

Miss Settle rose from her chair, swelling like a puffed toad. "How dare you presume to give me advice. Miss Nicholson, I want you to bear witness to her presumption."

"There's no need for anybody to bear witness to anything," Violet said, her temper once again under control. "I will see to it that our paths never cross again. Now I would like my full wages."

"You will get what I decide to give you. Under the circumstances—"

"Under the circumstances, you have broken the contract. If necessary, the Randolphs will bear witness to the fact that you approved my absences. The rest of your reasons are pure spite. They would not stand up in court."

"You wouldn't dare sue."

"Deny me my wages, and you'll have a suit on your desk before noon tomorrow. When I finish, this school will be a thing of the past."

"What can you say?" Miss Settle asked.

Violet couldn't help but smirk. She knew she shouldn't, but she couldn't resist. "You and Clara Rabin have made things up. So can I."

Miss Settle glared at Violet, as though trying to weigh her determination. "You wouldn't dare."

"If you believe I have any influence over Harvey McKee, believe I'll hire him to handle my case. If you believe I have any influence over Jeff Randolph, believe I'll call upon his family to back every statement I make."

Miss Settle looked aghast, but she also looked uncertain. Violet knew that the headmistress had never gotten over Harvey insisting she be the one to take Miss Settle's place.

"See that she's paid, Miss Nicholson. Immediately. I want her off the grounds within the hour."

Chapter Twenty-four

"She's not here," Beth said.

"When do you expect her back?" Jeff asked. He had stayed away for three days, but he couldn't stand it any longer. Violet might not want to see him, but he had to see her. He couldn't sleep, eat, or work. His life was falling apart, and all because of a copper-headed sorceress from New England.

"She's not coming back."

"What do you mean?" Jeff asked.

"Miss Settle fired her. She's gone."

Jeff was dazed. He hadn't anticipated anything like that. He was caught between anger at Miss Settle and worry over Violet. "When did she leave?"

"The day after the ball."

She had been gone for a whole day, and Jeff hadn't known it. He could have kicked himself. She didn't have any money or anywhere to go. She might have gone back to Massachusetts. Jolted by shock and anger, he stormed out of the building, along the path, and into the main building. Classes must have been changing. Young girls seemed to be everywhere, all hurrying in different directions.

"Where's Miss Settle's office?" he asked one.

"There," the girl said, pointing to a closed door at the back of the hall before dashing away. Jeff burst into the office without knocking. He strode past an open-mouthed secretary. He flung open the inner door to find Clara Rabin and Miss Settle in deep conversation. They broke off abruptly.

Ignoring Clara, he walked up to Miss Settle's desk, planting himself right in front of her. "Where's Violet Goodwin? And why the hell did you fire her?"

Miss Settle stared at him, her mouth open. Clara recovered more quickly, the glitter in her eyes belying the smile on her lips.

"I can't believe you're interested in the whereabouts of an ordinary housemother," she said, her smile arched and false. "Not after the way she turned her back on you at the ball."

"Get out, Clara," Jeff growled. "I came to talk to Miss Settle, not listen to your poison."

"I was here first," Clara said. "I don't intend to leave until I'm done."

"You'll walk or I'll drag you, but you'll leave now."

"Mr. Randolph!" Miss Settle said, half rising from her chair. "You can't come in here and—"

"Sit down!" Jeff slammed his open palm on the desk to punctuate his command, and Miss Settle sat. "Get out, Clara! And if I find you had anything to do with this, you'll have a lot more to worry about than an unfinished conversation."

Clara Rabin glared at him, hatred in her eyes, but Jeff saw fear as well. Just as he suspected. Clara had had a hand in everything.

"I'll be back to see you later, Eleanor," Clara said to Miss Settle in an attempt to exit with as much grace as possible. "Maybe we won't be interrupted then."

Jeff's gaze hurried Clara's departure. Then he turned his fury on Miss Settle. "Now," he said, bending forward over the headmistress's desk until their faces were only inches apart, "I want to know why Miss Goodwin was fired."

"Her work was not satisfactory."

"How?"

"On more than one occasion she failed to attend to her responsibilities," Miss Settle said.

"When?"

"S-several times."

"When?" Jeff said, the open palm slapping the desk once again.

"She didn't return with the twins."

"My brother's wife went into premature labor. As the only nurse present, Violet volunteered to do anything she could to help."

"But she didn't come back."

"She had to help with the operation. The doctor said she was the only one who knew enough."

Miss Settle's smile was brittle. "I'm sure there are many others who—"

Jeff's gaze narrowed. "Do I understand you to be setting your medical opinion against that of an expert brought in all the way from Boston?"

"No," Miss Settle stammered.

"When else?"

"There were several other times," Miss Settle said vaguely.

"I assume you don't mean the time she spent two days in the hotel after being locked up with those girls in quarantine, or the time my brother made special arrangements, or the times she accompanied my nieces to visit their aunt."

"That was quite a number of times."

"All approved by you. What else? There has to be more."

Miss Settle looked very uncomfortable. "She didn't come back until the morning after the ball."

Jeff felt something inside him squeeze until it hurt. That had been eating at him for days, but he wasn't going to let Miss Settle know it.

"Did you ask her where she had gone?" Jeff said.

"Certainly not. I don't—"

"So you condemned her without a shred of evidence."

"Clara said—"

"But you had no evidence."

"She didn't deny it," Miss Settle said.

"Would you have believed her if she had?"

Jeff had doubted Violet, and he was in love with her. How could he expect more of Miss Settle?

"There has been some talk among the parents," Miss Settle said. "Many of them are displeased with Miss Goodwin's behavior."

"In what way?"

"She's been reaching above her station."

"Who says?" Jeff asked.

"Several people."

"Name them!"

"Clara Rabin, for one," Miss Settle said, driven to the wall. "And Violet was extremely rude to me when I called her in."

"You pompous old fool! Don't you realize Clara Rabin is using you to get to me through Violet? She hates me. Betty Sue hates the twins. They've turned on Violet because they think she's helpless. You were the one who insisted she go to the ball, even though she told you she didn't want to go. She can't help it if men would rather dance with a pretty woman than a pinched-faced crone like Clara."

Miss Settle was white-faced with consternation. "Mrs. Rabin said—"

"Clara is a liar—always has been—and you're a fool to believe her. You're an even bigger fool if you think Clara will lift a finger to help you when you find yourself out of a job."

Miss Settle's complexion turned ashen. "What do you mean? You wouldn't dare—"

"If I find any harm has come to Violet, you'd better not be here when I get back. Now where is she?"

"I don't know. I don't concern myself with people who fail in their jobs. Nor do I provide references."

"You'd better hope the board feels differently about you."

Miss Settle's courage collapsed like an undercooked souffle.

"Where does she live?" Jeff asked.

"I told you I don't know."

"Who does?"

"Miss Nicholson ought to have a record—"

Jeff left without waiting to hear the rest of her sentence. Clara Rabin waited outside the door, her chin tilted defiantly when she saw Jeff.

He approached her slowly, and Clara quailed before his rage. "You'd better hope nothing has happened to Violet," he said, his voice tight and rasping. "If she has suffered even the slightest mishap, I'm liable to ignore a lifetime's habit and do violence to a woman."

"She left most of her things in the attic," Beth told Jeff. "She said she'd be back for them."

"Did she say where she was going?"

"No."

"Do you have any idea?" Jeff asked.

"No."

"Is there anybody in town she might have gone to?"

"Not that I know of. She doesn't know anybody but that lawyer."

"What lawyer?"

"The one who took her to the ball."

"I have no idea where she went," Harvey told Jeff. "I haven't seen her since the night of the ball."

"The day after," Jeff said.

The space between the two men was charged with powerful emotional energy. The looks they exchanged were openly unfriendly.

"She saw your carriage pull up before the school," Harvey said. "She didn't want to see you. I took her where she wanted to go. I didn't see her again until the next day." Harvey waited, expectant. "Aren't you going to ask where she went?"

"No," Jeff said, tightly controlling his own doubts and stampeding curiosity. He would have faith in Violet. For once in his life, he wouldn't jump to a conclusion.

Harvey looked displeased with Jeff's answer. "You realize she loves you, don't you?"

Jeff's heart leapt into his throat. "How would you know that?"

"She told me. After the brutal way you treated her, she had to talk to someone. We stopped to give her time to pull herself together. That's why you reached the school before we did. I did everything I could to cut you out, but she won't have me." Harvey gave a rueful smile. "I don't think it'll do you much good though. She swears she's never going to come within a thousand miles of you again."

Jeff wasn't pleased Violet had confided in Harvey, but he pushed his own pride aside. "I have to find her to explain."

"You'd do better to start by begging her forgiveness."

"Don't tell me what to do!"

"Somebody ought to. You can't seem to figure out even simple things by yourself."

Jeff struggled to hold his temper in check. It was pointless to get angry just because Harvey had spoken the truth. Besides, it wouldn't help him find Violet. "Do you know where she could have gone?"

"No."

"Does she know anybody else in town?" Jeff asked.

"Not that I know of. She had an uncle who died before she reached Denver, but he wasn't married. I'm handling her claim on his mine."

"What mine?"

"The Little Johnny. He left it to Violet, but it's in dispute."

So that was where she hoped to get her money. Poor girl. She had no idea what a tangle things were in. Jeff got to his feet. "Then that's where she's gone?"

"To Leadville?" Harvey said. "Don't be crazy. I've told her she can't go there. It's probably the most dangerous town in Colorado right now."

"That's why I have to leave immediately."

Leadville was a carbuncle on the virgin purity of the Rocky Mountains. Jeff entered from the south on the Denver and Rio Grande Railroad. The tracks paralleled the Arkansas River as it traveled toward its source a few miles north of Leadville. Thrown up overnight in a valley at the oxygen-sparse altitude of 10,152 feet, Leadville clung to the mineral-rich slopes of the Mosquito Range, their snow-clad peaks towering 4,000 feet over the town. Across the valley, the even more impressive Sawatch Range had flung itself up against the sky, the peaks of Mount Massive and Mount Elbert the highest in Colorado.

About five miles below Leadville, the narrow valley of the Arkansas widened into a beautiful grassy valley three miles wide and at least ten miles long. Seen against that pristine beauty, the flow of effluent from Leadville's mines was like pus from a suppurating wound.

The hillsides, stripped of their trees, lay exposed to the weather, their flanks pockmarked by what looked like huge prairie-dog mounds, piles of waste, and hastily constructed buildings. Leadville's wide streets were muddy, choked with wagons and pedestrian traffic, seemingly all male, filthy, and exhausted. The streets were lined with woodframe buildings, half of them saloons, advertising anything that could be brought over the mountains by train, wagon, or on foot for sale at prices several times higher than the same items could be had in Denver.

Jeff went straight to the Clarenden Hotel, the newest hotel in Leadville. It didn't compare to anything in Denver, but a panoramic view of the ravaged mountainsides could be obtained from its upper windows. "My name is Jeff Randolph. I want to know if you have a Miss Violet Goodwin staying here."

When the clerk stared at him as if he had lost his mind, Jeff said in a dangerously quiet voice, "I have traveled all night. I'm tired, I'm dirty, and I'm out of patience. Answer my question!"

"I can't tell you that," the clerk stammered fearfully.

Jeff grasped the boy by the collar, pulled him across the desk, and deposited him on the floor. A second frightened clerk ran off, presumably to fetch the manager. Jeff spun the guest book around so he could read the names. Violet wasn't listed there.

"If a woman were to come into town, where would she be most likely to stay?" Jeff asked the clerk as he got to his feet.

Giving Jeff a wide berth, the clerk scrambled back behind the counter. He seemed tongue-tied.

"Speak up, man," Jeff said.

"There's no women in town," the clerk said, taking care to keep out of Jeff's reach. "Leastways, not the

359

kind a woman like you'd be interested in."

"If a woman I would be interested in had come to town, where would she stay?" Jeff said, speaking to the boy slowly and distinctly.

"Nowheres. Every hotel, lodging house, and back room is full. We got people sleeping three to a bed in shifts. We can hardly get the sheets changed. There's people sleeping in the streets 'cause they can't find nowhere else."

Jeff felt a sinking feeling in the pit of his stomach. He hoped Violet had found some kind of lodging. He couldn't bear to think of her having spent the night in the streets or in a communal bed.

"Give me a list of every place in town that lets rooms."

The clerk goggled at him. "You might as well ask for a list of every building in Leadville," he said, regarding Jeff as though he were crazy. "People rent anything they got, even sheds. It ain't safe on the street. People are getting killed all the time."

"Did a beautiful woman with dark red hair come looking for a room here?"

The clerk shook his head decisively. "I ain't seen nobody like that. I woulda remembered."

The manager appeared in time to hear Jeff's question. "She came in here yesterday. But I didn't have a room to give her."

Jeff had to stifle an impulse to strangle the man. "Where did you tell her to go?"

"Everything's filled up."

"What did you tell her?" Jeff asked, deciding the man deserved to be choked.

"To go back to Denver, where she would be safe."

"Advice I'm certain she ignored."

"I can't say. She went out and never came back."

"Where should I begin looking?"

"You can go street by street asking at every house.

You never know. Somebody may have taken pity on her. She sure was a good-looking woman.''

Jeff didn't want to think of the kind of people whose pity might be aroused. If he found that anyone had harmed Violet, he would tear him limb from limb, even if he had to get somebody to help him do it.

So Jeff began the tedious and disheartening business of going from house to house, street by street. He found word of Violet many times, but she had always been turned away.

''It broke my heart to turn her out,'' one woman said, ''but I couldn't take her in, not with the rough lot I have in here. I wouldn't even trust my own husband around the likes of her.''

Jeff found men sleeping in places a dog wouldn't use. People came to Leadville to get rich quick. They figured they could put up with any kind of conditions for as long as the silver held out.

It was after dusk when Jeff walked into the Grand Hotel on Chestnut Street to find Violet sitting in the lobby, her satchel between her feet, a wary eye on the male occupants of the lobby. His feeling of relief was so great he felt too weak to speak. For a moment all he could do was look at her.

Her emerald-green dress was badly crushed, its hem heavy with mud. Her hair had come down and been repinned. Her expression was grim; her cheeks were white. Her mouth was set firmly; her eyes dared anyone to come near her. She was the most beautiful sight he'd ever seen.

He knew absolutely and without question that he wanted to marry her, that he wanted to spend the rest of his life trying to make up for the terrible things that he had said at the ball.

Most important of all, Jeff was going to protect Violet. Never again would she have no place to go. Never again would she be at the mercy of women like Clara

Rabin or Eleanor Settle. She was going to be Mrs. Thomas Jefferson Randolph, and any protection his money couldn't give her, his fist would.

"Violet," he said softly. Her name was lost in the hubbub of voices and the sound of heavy boots on the hotel's wood floors. "Violet," he called a little louder.

She looked up, startled. He saw her eyes light up, her expression lift. For a fraction of a second she seemed happy to see him. Then everything changed. She looked at him the way Miss Settle must have looked at Violet when she was about to fire her. "What are you doing here?"

Why had he come: to take her home, ask her forgiveness, take care of her, ask her to marry him? All of that and much more. But where did he begin? There was so much he wanted to say, needed to explain. So much more he had to know.

"I followed you. Surely you knew I would."

"After what you said, I thought you'd want to keep as far away from me as possible."

"I want to apologize for that. I let Philip Rabin get me worked up. When I saw you with Harvey, leaning on his arm, looking up at him as if you thought he was the only man in the world, everything went out of control. I was dying inside. At the same time I was so angry I couldn't think straight."

"You've always been good at getting angry," Violet said, her expression unrelenting. "You're not so good with your other emotions."

"I know, and I'm sorry. You were right when you said I used my anger to get my way, to control people, to keep them from getting close. You were right about so many things."

"I'm glad I did something right. Now you'd best go about your business. You're attracting attention. I've done enough of that already." She indicated several men who were quite openly eavesdropping on their conversation.

"Don't worry about that. You're coming with me."

Violet blistered Jeff with a bleak stare. "Why would I do something as stupid as to go with a man who can't stand me or anybody else born within five hundred miles of my birthplace?"

"Because I love you," Jeff said in a low voice. "I want to marry you."

Jeff couldn't figure out what was going through Violet's mind. Once more he thought he saw a flash of something warm, but it was gone almost immediately. Nothing remained but the cold, hard expression.

"I don't believe you know what love is. I'm not even sure I think you can learn, but I am certain you don't love me. As far as I can tell, you don't love anybody or anything—except possibly Virginia and your obsession with the true Southern woman."

"I'm finally able to admit I love a lot of people. I was just afraid they wouldn't love me back."

Violet looked unbelieving, like a housemother listening to a child trying to lie her way out of punishment. "And what brought about this revelation?"

She was terribly angry, angry enough to forget the tightening circle of listeners, angry enough to forget to keep her voice low. Jeff had never seen her so unforgiving.

"You," Jeff said.

"Me!" Violet's laugh was harsh and cynical. "Do you expect me to believe a Yankee female, the lowest and most despised creature in God's creation, has caused the great Jeff Randolph to have a change of heart? Once I thought Essie had found the way to something worthwhile inside of you. I don't know what she found, but she must have used it all up. There's nothing there anymore. Now go away, Jeff. I have things to do."

"You may not believe me when I say I love you, but you'd better believe me when I say you aren't going to get your mine back by just sitting here."

"What do you know about my mine?"

"I know that two men dispute its ownership. I also know no silver has been taken out of it since your uncle died."

"Doesn't that sound odd to you?" Violet said.

"Very. But you can't do anything about it by talking. Where are you staying?"

"Here."

"I thought they didn't have any rooms."

"I said here," Violet said, pointing to the chair on which she sat.

"You stayed in this lobby all night?" Jeff asked and Violet nodded. "You can't do that. You can have my room."

"You can't have a room. I must have knocked on every door in town yesterday." Suddenly she let her head roll back, her gaze going to the ceiling. "Of course you have a room. You probably keep one at the best hotel just in case you need it."

"I'm staying in Horace Tabor's private suite at the opera house," Jeff said. "He let me borrow it. I want you to use it."

"No."

"You can't stay here."

"Why not?"

"It's not safe."

"I was safe last night," Violet said.

"Look at you. You're exhausted. Your clothes are a wreck, and your hair is coming down."

"This from a man who says he loves me and wants to marry me," Violet said to the circle of curious on-lookers who'd gathered close to follow this showdown.

"I love you enough to care about your safety. I may not have acted like it in the past, but I hope you'll give me a chance to prove it now."

"Some other time. I'm too tired now."

"You can have my bed, lady," one man said. "Won't be nobody in it but me."

"She's going to take my room," Jeff said.

"No," Violet said.

"Take it," the man said.

"I'll stay here," Violet said.

"I won't have my future wife spending the night in a hotel lobby stared at by anybody who wanders in."

"I'm not going to be your wife."

"Yes, you are," Jeff said, sensing she was weakening. He didn't know why he was sure of it, but he was. "You're going with me right now. You're going to have a bath, something to eat, and a long night's sleep."

"Where are you going to sleep?" the man asked.

"Yeah, where?" another man said.

"In the lobby if I have to," Jeff said.

"You're not used to roughing it," Violet said. "I am. Since I'm here, I might as well stay."

"You're coming with me."

"No, I'm not."

Jeff gave Violet a particularly angry scowl. "Stand up and say that."

Goaded, Violet immediately got to her feet. "I'm not going with you, Jeff Randolph. Not now. Naaaahhh!" she shrieked.

Jeff had bent down and wrapped his arm around the back of her legs tipping her forward. He stood up with Violet neatly thrown over his shoulder like a sack of flour.

"I'd appreciate it if you'd bring her luggage," Jeff said to the man who'd offered Violet his room. "Since I have only one arm, she's about all I can handle."

The onlookers had tensed when Jeff had swooped down on Violet, but the man winked. "Don't mind if I do. It's always a pleasure to see a man who knows how to handle a spirited woman."

"You let me down this minute, Jeff Randolph," Violet said, trying unsuccessfully to twist out of his grip. She pounded him on the back and kicked her heels furiously. It did no good. Jeff had a secure hold on her, and he was much too strong for her struggles to break his hold.

"You can keep on squealing if you want," Jeff said, "but we'll attract less attention in the street if you're quiet."

"If you dare carry me through the streets over your shoulder, I'll never speak to you again."

"That'll leave more time for kissing," Jeff whispered. "You do remember how much I like kissing you."

"You barbarian!" Violet hissed as Jeff carried her across the lobby and out onto the boardwalk.

"You always said I was used to getting what I wanted," Jeff said. "Well, I've never wanted anything as much as I want you. You can imagine how far I'm willing to go."

"And you can be sure I'll go just as far to see I'm not what you get."

Jeff carried Violet down Chestnut Street and then turned north on Harrison. The Tabor Opera House was on the corner of Harrison and St. Louis, two-and-a-half blocks away. Jeff passed 13 saloons, seven tobacco shops, six clothing stores, and seven jewelers and pawnbrokers. He also passed signs advertising billiard halls, banks, barbers, doctors, dentists, rooms to let, and the undertaker.

Jeff saw his image reflected in several windows as he passed by, but he found it impossible to believe he was actually walking down the streets of Leadville with the woman he planned to marry over his shoulder. He felt like some primitive caveman or Viking. His family would be stunned. Nobody in Denver would believe it.

He'd never done anything so insane in his life. And he'd never felt better. It made George's spur-of-the-moment decision to marry Rose look like a well-thought-out plan. He knew Violet was going to try to kill him the minute she got her feet on the ground, but he didn't care. Never in his life had he felt more like a man. His father might not have been proud of him—he certainly wouldn't equate Jeff's present endeavor with glorious service in the cause of the South—but for once in his life Jeff didn't feel inferior to anyone.

Along the boardwalk, on the street, and from windows and doorways, men stopped to watch as Jeff passed. Some grinned. Some whistled or cheered. Everyone seemed ready to applaud him. He'd never done anything popular in his entire life. He wasn't used to approval. He was actually relieved when they reached the opera house and entered the lobby. Behind the ticket window, the clerk's mouth fell open.

"Get the key and open the apartments," Jeff said, and the man obeyed wordlessly.

"Who you got there?" one stranger asked.

"My wife, as soon as I can get her in front of a preacher," Jeff said.

"I wouldn't wait if I was you," the man said.

"She's worth it," Jeff said, following the clerk up the steps. A couple of men hanging around the ticket window tried to tag along, but the man with the luggage blocked their way.

"Let 'm be," he said. "You'll get a chance to gawk later."

The clerk scurried up the long staircase, casting glances over his shoulder as though to assure himself he wasn't hallucinating. Violet remained quiet, her body rigid. The young man unlocked the door, then stepped back.

"You can set the bags in the bedroom," Jeff said to his companion. "Thanks. I couldn't have done it without you."

"You'd have found a way," the man said with a wide, conspiratorial grin. "You randy young fellas always find a way. Come along," he said to the clerk, who stood with his mouth open. "You got tickets to sell. I got a woman to see."

Once the door was closed, Jeff allowed Violet to slide from his shoulder to the floor in the middle of an elegant sitting room decorated in green velvet. Even before her feet hit the thick imported carpet, Jeff had his arm around her and was kissing her. Then he let her go and jumped back before she could hit him with the arm she had drawn back.

"I'll send somebody up with hot water. When you get changed, we can have dinner." He vaulted over a sofa to get beyond the range of her nails. "Afterward we can talk about your mine. But first we have to talk about wedding plans."

Violet climbed across the sofa after him. Jeff scooted around the end of the sofa and darted toward the door. "I'd like to get married before Rose goes back to Texas. She loves weddings."

Jeff bolted through the door and pulled it closed behind him. Violet pounded on the door, kicked it when he didn't open it, called him names he hadn't heard since his army days, and promised to do things that would seriously threaten his general health.

Jeff just laughed. He laughed so hard he thought he might never stop. He didn't care. It felt good. He felt happier than he could remember ever feeling. Violet was going to kill him when he opened that door. She was going to swear at him and refuse to do anything he asked. He didn't care. He loved her and she loved him. He was going to marry her. The rest of it didn't matter.

Chapter Twenty-five

Violet raged in impotent fury. Delivering a last exasperated kick at the wood panels, she attacked her luggage. She succeeded only in hurting her toes, which made her madder. She caught sight of herself in the mirror: her hair coming down, her face flushed, the lace of her collar twisted and torn. Then she got madder still. She would never recover from the humiliation of being carried through the streets over Jeff's shoulder like an erring wife. She'd never be able to face anybody in that town again. She'd have to steal away on a dark moonless night. She would never get her mine, and it was all Jeff Randolph's fault.

He had acted like a marauding barbarian raiding a village for women, carrying off his spoils like a badge of accomplishment. He wouldn't have treated his Southern belle like that. What made him think she'd like it, even if she was a Yankee? She ground her teeth in frustration.

But then her life had fallen apart from the moment

she had met him. No, from the day she left Massachusetts. No, from the day that awful war started. It didn't matter when it started, Jeff had destroyed everything. She had fled Denver to get away from him, but he'd followed her to perpetrate the final indignity.

And he said he loved her and wanted to marry her! It would snow at high noon on Cape Cod in mid-August before she married Jeff Randolph.

But it was very hard to stay in a flaming rage when the object of her fury had already made his escape. It was even more difficult when he'd just solved her most pressing problem and set her down in a private suite in a town where even the dogs had to fight for a place to sleep. It was impossible when she loved the fool, even though she would have traded her silver mine for the chance to choke the life out of him.

Abandoning any hope of making Jeff suffer the agonies he deserved, Violet looked around her. She was in an elegant sitting room. The tall windows were hung with green silk drapes. Chairs and sofas were covered in green velvet. A thick carpet covered the floor. Tiffany gas lamps flooded the room with soft light. Through one door she discovered a small dining room, through the other a large bedroom. There was a spacious bathroom attached to that. The room was no ordinary hotel room.

How, in a town without a single room for rent, had Jeff managed to come up with a private suite? The same way he'd managed to find all those potatoes when no one else had been able to. He was a genius. His only blind spot was people—women and Southern belles in particular. She wondered how she had managed to crack the ring of fire, if she really had, if he really did love her.

Violet's heart started to beat faster. It had finally sunk in. Jeff said that he loved her. He wanted to marry her.

Violet stared at herself in the mirror. She looked a wreck. She'd have to do something before he came back.

She returned to the sitting room to get her suitcase when a knock came at the door.

She immediately forgot her softened mood. She remembered only the humiliation of that walk through town. She jerked the door open. "How dare you come back. I'll—"

Two nervous young men stood before her holding buckets of hot water. "Mr. Randolph said we was to bring you these."

Violet wanted a bath more than anything. She could practically feel the grit on her skull. After spending the night sitting up in the hotel lobby wide awake, stiff with fear, she was exhausted. She could already feel the soothing sensation of the hot scented water as it soaked away the grime and loosened the tension in her body.

But Jeff had sent the bath. She would have nothing to do with it. "Take it back."

"Mr. Randolph said you was to have a bath," one of the men said apologetically. "He said if you was to refuse, I was to go downstairs and get him."

Violet had a severe struggle within herself. After what had already happened, she had no doubt Jeff would force her to endure further humiliation if she refused. She had every intention of making him pay dearly for her disgrace, but she had no desire to be embarrassed further. Besides, she desperately wanted a bath.

"Very well, bring it in. I would like the key to this suite," she said as the men started to leave.

"Mr. Randolph has it."

"There must be another one."

"He has both of them. He said to tell you he'd be outside the door. Nobody'll bother you, ma'am."

Violet added another sin to Jeff's rapidly growing list. Only torture could even his account. The two young men soon returned with more buckets of steaming water. Violet was tempted to run out the door and look for the rear exits. But she was certain Jeff had them blocked.

Besides, she had nowhere to go.

She might be as mad as a hornet, but for the first time since coming to Leadville, she wasn't scared senseless. She would never forget the ride across the mountains, the day spent in a fruitless search for even the most humble lodgings, the hungry stares of the thousands of filthy, exhausted men who thronged the town, or the nerve-racking night she'd spent in the Grand Hotel lobby.

She would have her bath. Then she would decide what to do about Jefferson Randolph.

Violet relaxed in the soothing hot water. As the heat eased the tension and she began to feel the weight of her exhaustion, she became a little less determined to murder Jeff. She still intended to devise some form of torture. Not only would he learn it was unacceptable to carry a lady through the streets like a rolled up carpet, even a female from Massachusetts, but he would also learn she could not be humiliated one moment and made love to the next. She contemplated one form of torture after another. But instead of enjoying the thought of his lifeblood draining into the carpet or the sound of his bones breaking, she found herself wanting to stare into his eyes, touch his body, or kiss his lips to see if they were as soft as she remembered.

Clearly, a hot bath was not the place to contemplate revenge. She would have to wait until she was back on her feet or until she was back on the street trying to stare down the men who had followed her with leering gazes. Jeff Randolph had committed enough sins to deserve an unmerciful punishment. She just had to make herself remember them.

By the time Violet had washed her hair, covered her body with scented powder, and changed into a clean dress, she was furious with herself. She felt thankful Jeff had found her. She kept telling herself she still meant to slit his throat, but all she could feel was gratitude that she didn't have to spend another night in the Grand Hotel lobby.

She had never expected Jeff to feel guilty over the way he had treated her. She certainly hadn't expected him to follow her to Leadville.

She wondered what the real reason behind his being in Leadville could be. She'd have been less surprised if Harvey had followed her. But Harvey hadn't stood kissing her within sight of the students and faculty of the Wolfe School. Harvey hadn't pulled her away from her duties time after time. Harvey hadn't mortified her before half of Denver society. Harvey hadn't followed her, forcing her to spend the night away from the dormitory. Harvey hadn't caused her to lose her job.

It couldn't be anything but guilt, so much guilt that Jeff had felt compelled to say he loved her and wanted to marry her. It was a nice thing to say, but it was no substitute for a job. She doubted it would make her feel better about being without money, prospects, or any knowledge of how to acquire either.

A knock on the outer door interrupted Violet's thoughts. Jeff! She found she wasn't nearly as angry as she wanted to be. She had intended to tell him she never wanted to see or hear from him again, but that intention evaporated when she opened the door and a young man handed her a bouquet of flowers.

She didn't know what she wanted to do. She'd have to wait to see what Jeff had to say for himself. She was honest enough to admit that she was glad he was in Leadville. She could be furious all she wanted at his treatment of her, but she'd rather feel safe.

After another knock, Violet opened the door, her mouth open to tell Jeff she wasn't going to speak to him. But she came face-to-face with the two men again. They were back with a white tablecloth and china. No sooner

373

had they set the table than another man brought in a dinner of hot vegetables and beef.

Violet realized she was starved. She hadn't eaten all day. But the table was set for two. "Where is Mr. Randolph?"

"Downstairs."

"Is he coming up?"

"He said he would if you asked for him."

Violet was tempted to close the door and eat every last bite herself, but she was an honest and fair woman. She knew she wouldn't enjoy the food unless Jeff shared it with her. She might be angry and want to do terrible things to him, but the meal would have no flavor without him. She also knew he could have stayed in his bank, quietly counting his money, and let her disappear from the face of the earth. Nobody would have known or cared.

"Tell him to come up in five minutes," she said, then returned to the bedroom and her mirror.

Violet hadn't done half the things she wanted when a knock came on the door. She felt her pulse quicken. There she was, wanting to be angry at him, and she felt like a girl opening the door for her first gentleman caller. She took one last glance in the mirror. She was a silly, foolish female who deserved to be carted through the streets if she couldn't manage at least one frown.

The moment Violet set eyes on Jeff, all her intentions faded and her frown turned into a smile of welcome. She tried to call it back and she tried to say something cutting, but she couldn't. Jeff had always had the power to reduce her brain to jelly. That night was no exception.

He looked so handsome she could hardly get out the words. But she succeeded in saying, "Come in."

"You sure you're not planning to invite me in and then dump the beef over my head?"

Violet smiled again. It had to be a foolish smile. She

felt foolish. "I considered it, but I'm too hungry."

Jeff stepped inside, still looking doubtful of his welcome, ready to make an emergency escape if necessary. "No poison, no hidden guns?"

Violet smiled again, that time with satisfaction. He did feel guilty. Very guilty. Wonderful.

"No, I'm still mulling over my revenge. But I'll tell you right now I don't intend to give you any more warning than you gave me."

Jeff flashed a broad smile that caused Violet's heart to flutter uncertainly. But not half as fast as when he pulled her close and kissed her hard. She felt dizzy. Her heartbeat still hadn't evened out when he pulled out her chair, and she sat down.

"Would you have come with me if I'd given you a choice?" he asked as he took his own seat.

"Probably not. I wouldn't have believed you would carry me through the streets. I still find it hard to believe."

Jeff smiled again, and the effect on her was just as disconcerting. Maybe it was a good thing he didn't smile too often. "We Randolphs are men of our word."

"I'll remember that. Now would you please explain about this apartment?" She needed to talk about something unconnected with either of them. She needed time to calm her pulse and marshal her thoughts. "How are you always able to conjure up luxury accommodations out of the air?"

"We're in Horace Tabor's private apartment in his opera house. He moved to Denver two years ago; so nobody uses it now. He's always glad to let me use it."

Violet had heard of the eccentric millionaire. She should have known he and Jeff would get along famously.

"You'd better eat your dinner," she said, determined to restrict the conversation to everyday topics. "I don't imagine it's easy to find a meal like this in Leadville, even for a Randolph. It's a little too far for Tyler to send it over from the hotel.''

''I'm not here for the food.''

''Then what are you here for?'' She realized she had slipped the minute the words were out of her mouth.

''I told you. I love you. I want to marry you.''

Violet found it increasingly difficult to maintain her skepticism—or her desire to talk about the vegetables—in the face of Jeff's repeated declarations. She wanted so much for them to be true that it was almost impossible to keep disbelieving him. Still, she wouldn't give in, at least not yet.

''Just when did you reach this momentous decision? As I recall, the last time we spoke—''

''I didn't mean it. I was angry. I thought you had refused me because of my arm. I couldn't—''

''What?'' Violet said.

''I thought you had refused to go to the dance with me because of my arm.''

''I think work has addled your brain,'' Violet said. ''After I let you kiss me in the hallway of the Windsor Hotel and on the steps of the school, you think I'd start worrying about your arm now?''

Jeff had the good grace to look chagrined. ''When you've gone as many years as I have being absolutely certain every slight, every rude comment, every questionable glance is the result of being crippled, you can't think of anything else. When you've spent most of your life feeling that you're only part of a man, it's hard to think of yourself any other way.''

''But I told you about Jonas,'' Violet said.

''Reason has nothing to do with it. After twenty years of thinking one way, it's not easy to change. I'm counting on you to help me.''

He was trying to gain her sympathy, and he was succeeding. She almost wanted to apologize for having doubted him. If he could manipulate people as quickly and as well as he had manipulated her, no wonder he owned the biggest bank in the West. If she'd had any money, she'd have put every cent in his bank just to make him feel better.

Violet tried to remind herself that Jeff had been kind and flattering before, only to revert to his old self in moments of stress. She firmly believed she didn't know a man's true character until he was under extreme adversity. She had seen Jeff at his worst, and she didn't like what she had seen.

"That's something you have to do for yourself," she said. "Nobody can do it for you."

Jeff stopped eating and looked at her. He seemed to be searching her face for clues to her thoughts. "Does that mean you won't help me?"

Of course it didn't. She couldn't look into those eyes and see the pain there and not want to do everything she could to drive it away.

"It means, until you think well of yourself, you can't believe anyone else does. You know what I think—I've told you—yet you thought I would go to a dance with Harvey because I didn't want to be seen with a one-armed man."

Jeff chewed his food in silence. She couldn't imagine how he could think any woman would worry about his arm. He was so handsome he took her breath away. He was so tall and strong it made her proud to know him. It made her squirm in her seat just to be near him. She couldn't imagine other women wouldn't feel the same way.

Violet moved and their knees brushed. It was a slight thing, but it caused alarms to go off all through her body. Immediately she thought of the morning she had seen him lifting weights while wearing those skimpy pants. She lost interest in her food. She felt heat travel through her like an incoming tide. But she was determined neither her body nor her emotions were going to rule her head. For once, she was going to approach the problem of Jeff Randolph with cold, hard reason.

"What are you going to do here in Leadville?" she asked, hoping a change in subject would ease the tension she felt.

"Convince you to go back to Denver and marry me."

She had to give him one thing. He was persistent. "Besides that. Are you going to do anything with those mines Madison was looking into?"

"There's only one left. It's suddenly started producing, and the owners want a lot more for it."

"Are you going to buy it?"

"I don't know. Madison doesn't trust the men. He says there's something wrong. Madison has an instinct for these things. He hasn't been wrong yet."

Violet wanted to ask Jeff to help with her mine. It was on the tip of her tongue, but she couldn't make herself do it. That was one thing she wanted to do for herself.

"It's next to your mine," Jeff said.

"What is?"

"The Silver Wave. The mine I'm considering buying. I thought I might look into yours as well."

"I can do that myself."

"You can look, too, but we're liable to find different things."

"How do you mean?"

"People say different things to men and women."

"Are you implying they won't tell me the truth?"

"We'll see."

Violet pushed aside the rest of her meal. She had a terrible feeling the mine was floating farther and farther out of her grasp. "Would you like some coffee?"

"Yes."

She poured a cup and handed it to Jeff, but her mind was busy wondering what he really meant to do.

"I want you to promise me you won't do anything

without telling me first," Jeff said.

His comment riveted Violet's attention. "Why should I do that?"

"There are fortunes to be won out there. This town is full of men willing to do anything they must to win them."

"And what makes you think you're so safe?"

"I'm not. I'm probably in more danger than you."

Violet tensed. She hadn't thought of danger to Jeff. He had always seemed so indestructible. "Why? From whom?"

"From the men who're trying to cheat me. But right now, I'm only in danger of missing the beginning of the show."

"What show?"

"We're going to the opera. We're the personal guests of Horace Tabor."

"I don't have anything to wear," Violet said. She didn't imagine the ladies of Leadville would be as extravagantly dressed as the ladies of Denver, but she expected that they would be able to tell the difference between a dress and a gown. And Violet was tired of being thrust into society looking like a poor cousin. "This dress is all I have."

"You look beautiful as always," Jeff said. "Besides, we have a private box."

Violet had become aware of movement in the building, but at that moment she could hear the sound of footsteps and conversation outside the apartment. People were already arriving at the theater. They were going to see her emerge from the apartment with Jeff. They were going to see them in the box together. Some would remember seeing Jeff carry her down the street. None would know the basis of their relationship. They would all assume she was his wife—or something else.

There was no help for it. She must decide before she stepped out of that door what she was willing to endure for the uncertain promise offered by that man.

She loved him. There was no doubt about that. She wanted to be his wife. She had tried her best to deny it, to change it, but she might as well admit it. She had been wanting to marry him for weeks. It messed up all her plans, made a shambles of her stated beliefs, knocked asunder everything she'd said about men, marriage, and the servitude expected of wives. But when everything was said and done, she wanted to marry Jeff.

She was a foolish woman to marry an emotional cripple who was convinced he was a physical cripple, a man who worked so hard he was in danger of becoming a mental cripple. But she wanted to be with him. She could help him. She would help him. But even if she couldn't, she wanted to be with him as long as he would let her. It didn't make her sound very proud, but somehow pride didn't matter. She had met many men, several of whom had been very fond of her. Two had even asked her to marry them. But she'd never felt anything more than a strong liking for any of them. Then she had met Jeff and fallen hopelessly, stupidly, in love. She was 29 years old. She wasn't likely to fall in love like that again. If he was her one chance, she meant to take him. She would worry about the consequences later.

Violet pushed her coffee away. "We'd better be going. It's rude to enter after the curtain has gone up."

The show was very far from opera as Violet knew it. It consisted of a sentimental story with a villain, a heroine in distress, and a hero who rescued her. Somehow in the course of a plot she barely followed, large numbers of scantily clad women kept finding reasons to rush out on the stage. Presumably they were friends of the heroine, but they never gave her any advice or offered any help. They seemed to confine themselves to running about in a fashion guaranteed to raise their skirts as much as possible. Their attention was entirely centered

on the men in the audience. Their songs and dances—
if their shrieks, squeals, and jumping about could be
described as either—were merely an excuse for more
limb-exposing activity.

The audience, made up almost entirely of men, whistled and hooted its approval. The few women in the theater occupied seats on the lower level and seemed to be
in no position to look down their noses at Violet. In fact,
Violet wasn't sure they were aware of her presence.

In a way, it was good the show didn't require too
much of Violet's concentration. She could hardly take
her mind off the fact that Jeff sat throughout the entire
first half with her hand in his. He didn't merely hold her
hand. Occasionally, he would turn to her to comment on
something on the stage, and he would give her hand a
squeeze. Twice he released her hand only to spend several minutes running his fingers up and down the back
of her hand. Even through gloves, the feeling was elec-
tric, much more interesting than anything taking place
on the stage.

Once he hooked her arm in his and for the next several minutes gently brushed his fingers along her fore-
arm. Violet lost the thread of the plot at that point.

They retreated to the suite for coffee during the in-
termission. When they took their seats for the second
act, Jeff put his arm around her shoulder. Even sitting
perfectly still, she found it difficult to concentrate. When
his fingers began to caress her shoulder and the side of
her neck, she found it impossible. He leaned over to
whisper something in her ear and Violet jumped.

"What's wrong?" Jeff asked.

"Nothing," she said a trifle breathlessly. "You startled me."

"A woman like you should be used to having things
whispered in her ear."

"I am," Violet said, "but by little girls."

"I'll see what I can do about changing that."

Violet couldn't understand the change in Jeff—not just his interest in her, but the change in his attitude in general. It was almost as though he had never lost his arm, as though he'd never had any doubts about himself. There was a kind of confidence she hadn't seen before. More important, there was an element of recklessness, or joie de vivre, she had never seen in him. He was practically a different person.

She wondered if he would be the same way when he got back to Denver. She could help make him believe in himself and believe that people could look at him without seeing his missing arm. She knew nothing about the hurts buried deep in his past, but she felt certain that, if he could just get past his fear of being a cripple, he could deal with whatever lay in his past. As she allowed him to pull her a little closer, she vowed she would always be at his side if he would only let her.

When the curtain fell on the last ensemble number, Jeff escorted Violet back to the suite before the customers had a chance to become interested in who was occupying the Tabor box. The remains of supper had been cleared away, the table removed, and the bath emptied. A pot of coffee sat on a table with two cups.

Violet became keenly aware that she and Jeff were alone in the suite. She was also aware there was only one bedroom, one bed, and no place else in town for Jeff to sleep. He had said nothing, but something would have to be decided soon. He would probably postpone any decision until the people finished leaving the theater, or at least until they cleared the landing outside the suite. But then he would go—or stay.

Violet suddenly realized she didn't know which she expected him to do, which she thought he would do, which she wanted him to do. She had to make up her mind in the next few minutes.

"Would you like a cup of coffee?" she asked.

"Yes," Jeff said.

Violet poured a cup and handed it to him. He liked it black.

"Did you enjoy the show?" he asked. He looked slightly ill at ease.

"It wasn't at all what I expected, but I found it amusing."

"Not what you find in Boston?"

"No, not that I've been often. I never had the time."

The sound of footsteps became less frequent, the raised voices on the boardwalk fewer. The moment of decision was approaching. She had to decide what she wanted Jeff to do.

No, she knew what she wanted him to do. She wanted him to stay with her. She wanted him to make love to her. She wanted him to know before she even began to listen to his offer of marriage that her love had nothing to do with his arm. She wanted him to believe that he was more of a man to her than any man with two arms.

Having made her decision, Violet felt all the tension flow from her body. She put down her cup of coffee. "Do you have another room?"

"No."

"Where had you planned to stay?"

"There are lots of places a man can stay," Jeff said.

"Do you have one in mind?"

"Not yet but—"

"I want you to stay with me."

Chapter Twenty-six

Jeff's hand paused with the cup halfway to his mouth. Slowly, he lowered it and set it back in its saucer. From the minute he had decided he had to find Violet, from the time he had decided to follow her to Leadville, he had known that moment would come. He had wanted it to come. He'd done everything he could to make sure it would come. Yet with it there, he felt the familiar hesitation.

"I can stay in the hotel lobby. It's not necessary for me to stay here," he said.

"I want you to stay." When Jeff glanced toward the bedroom, Violet said, "I'm not a girl anymore. I know what I'm asking. I also know there's only one bed. I want you to share it with me. I want you to make love to me. I want to make love to you."

Finally, Jeff would find out once and for all if a woman could love him despite his arm. Violet had seen him without his shirt. She hadn't cringed like Julia Wil-

cox. She had cared for her brother. She was familiar with
mangled bodies.

But Jeff didn't want her not to cringe merely because
she knew what to expect. He wanted her to love him as
if there was nothing wrong. He knew that was an unreasonable hope, but he wanted it anyway. Too many
other problems had their roots in his empty left sleeve.
If he could only lay that one fear to rest, maybe he could
deal with the others.

His father had called him a coward, had called him
half a man. His arm made him feel like half a man. He
couldn't forget the loss of the war, the loss of his home,
because he felt as if he'd lost himself, lost who he was.

Suddenly, he had a chance to rid himself of these
demons, and he was scared. If he didn't get it right, he
doubted he would ever have the courage to try again.
Looking for a wife in Virginia wasn't the answer. He
didn't love, could never love, anybody but that Yankee
woman. If she couldn't love him the way he needed to
be loved, nothing else mattered.

"Are you sure?" Jeff asked. "After tonight there'll
be no going back."

"I hope not. I don't want you to worry ever again
that someone important to you cares more about your
arm than about you. I want you to feel you have the
right to be loved just like everybody else."

"Do you love me?"

"I have for a long time," Violet said.

"Rose said you did."

"What else did Rose say?"

"She said I loved you," Jeff said.

"And do you?"

"Yes."

"Even though I'm a Yankee?"

Jeff had to smile. He wasn't the only one with doubts.
He took Violet's cup and set it down. He exchanged his

seat for a place next to her. He took her hand in his. "I think I love you more because you are a Yankee."

Violet closed her eyes and shook her head, as if she wasn't sure she had heard him correctly. "You're going to have to explain that. I thought my being a Yankee was the problem."

"It was in the beginning. I was horrified that I liked you. But I loved you so much I couldn't stop myself. Even confessing to my family wasn't as bad as losing you. Will you make me a promise?"

"What?"

"Say you'll marry me if I stay tonight."

"Only if you still feel the same way a week from now."

"Why a week?"

"Getting married is very different from falling in love. It's not always a good idea for one to follow the other. I want you to be sure I love you despite your arm. At the same time, I have a problem with your arm, too. I don't want you to marry me because you think I'm the only woman who doesn't care about it. I want you to marry me because you can't stand the idea of not marrying me, because you want me to have your children, because you want me by your side for the rest of your life.

"Up until now, everything in your life has been tied up with your arm. But loving me, marrying me, and wanting to spend the rest of your life with me have nothing to do with it. I want that out of the way, finished, forgotten before you ask me again."

Jeff didn't know what to say. He'd spent years wondering if any woman could forget his arm, and Violet was saying she wouldn't marry him if he couldn't forget it. He didn't know if he could. After so many years, he felt that the person he had become was inextricably bound up with his arm. He'd kept the burden strapped to his back for so long he'd forgotten how it felt to be without it.

But he felt excited by the possibility of freeing himself from the curse he'd nearly let destroy his life. He would try—he had to try—but he needed Violet's help. He couldn't do it alone.

It was his one chance. He didn't mean to lose it. But it wasn't just an opportunity to free himself from a demon that had blighted his life and riddled his hopes for nearly two decades. It was his chance to marry the woman he loved, the only woman he'd ever loved. He didn't have to decide which was more important. It was impossible to have one without the other.

"I'll ask you now, tomorrow, the next day, and every day after that until you say yes," Jeff said.

"Are you sure you can face the world, not to mention your family, after what you've said about Yankees?"

"Losing you would be much worse."

"You keep talking like this, and I might not make you wait a week."

"Come here," Jeff said.

When Violet came and put her arms around him, Jeff pulled her close. He marveled at how different it was from being with Louise. He could spend hours looking at Violet, never touching her, and not feel cheated. He had already spent a lot of time kissing her, and he didn't feel he had even begun to experience a tenth of the pleasure he would find in her lips.

He liked the feel of her body as it leaned against his own, the feel of her arms around him. He'd never been close to anyone that way. He'd always kept his distance, physically, mentally, and emotionally. At that moment, he wanted to be as close to Violet as possible. It was something he'd wanted for years, longer even than he'd wanted to get his arm back. There had been times when it seemed getting his arm back would have been easier.

That was all changed. He missed his arm in a new

way. It was awkward to have only one arm to hold Violet, not that she wasn't already as close as physically possible. There was a kind of extra special joy in being able to hold someone he loved, to pull her so tightly against him he thought he'd crush her.

Jeff had seen his brothers do it. He'd sometimes wondered how Iris survived Monty's bear hugs. He would have to look for some other way to make their togetherness special. He'd had enough of being angry because he couldn't do things other people could. He didn't want to be jealous of anybody ever again. He had Violet. That was more than anybody else had.

"Making love to a one-armed man isn't going to be easy," Jeff said. His gaze never wavered. "Most women expect the man to do everything. You're going to have to help."

Violet pulled his face down until she could kiss his lips. "I always understood it took two to make love."

Violet knew she was taking a gamble. She wasn't gambling that Jeff could love her. She felt certain he did. After everything he'd said about Yankees, he wouldn't have followed her if he didn't. She was gambling he could fall in love like any other man. She didn't mind his stump. She didn't even think about it most of the time. It was part of him, like his smile and his muscles.

But she was selfish enough not to want to marry Jeff's fears. She wanted him to get past them, more for himself than for her. He would never be able to completely forget his arm. It would limit some things he did and slow others. At times he would need help. That she could accept, but she didn't know if Jeff could. If he could, he would be a different person. He would be the man Essie adored, the one Violet knew was hidden inside.

Jeff's kisses scattered Violet's thoughts. She always did like kissing him. She wondered why she hadn't found as much pleasure with Nathan. He had been attractive, fervent, intent on making Violet his wife. Nathan's kisses weren't very different from Jeff's, but the effect on her wasn't even remotely the same.

Nathan's kisses left her unmoved. Jeff's kisses left her shaken and wanting more. Nathan's touch was friendly and comforting. Jeff's touch awakened desire in her. Nathan's lovemaking left her wondering when the magic was supposed to start. Jeff's literally transformed her.

Violet leaned her head to one side to allow Jeff to nuzzle the side of her neck, to nibble her earlobe. Shivers raced up and down her spine when she felt his warm breath inside her ear. She'd never realized it could be so sensitive. She nearly melted when she felt his tongue trace the outer shell of her ear. She tightened her arms around him.

She knew Jeff was a big man, heavily muscled, but she never realized just how big, how well muscled. Her arms couldn't reach around his chest. She could barely concentrate with him practicing his wizardry on her neck and ear, but she gradually became aware of her breasts growing more and more sensitive where they pressed against the hardness of his chest.

Jeff didn't cease to make love to her, but one by one he pulled the pins out of her hair and dropped them on the floor. With each one, she felt more relaxed, more uninhibited, more aware of her own desire to explore Jeff's body. She unbuttoned his shirt and slipped her hand inside.

Touching his chest was like running her hands over soft steel—beautifully sculpted and contoured steel. Violet had touched her father and brother many times without thinking. At that moment she felt so acutely aware that she could have mapped each square inch she touched. Her roving fingers encountered Jeff's nipple. She felt his body tense. Tentatively her fingers explored its softness. She was amazed to feel it grow firm under her touch. She was equally astonished at the immediate and spectacular response in her own nipples.

Jeff deposited the last pin on the floor. He gently massaged the base of her neck, making it difficult for her to concentrate on her explorations. No man had seen her hair down since she was a child. No man had ever massaged the back of her neck and base of her skull until she felt nearly limp and yet tingly and excited all at the same time.

Violet liked Jeff's touch on her skin. His hands were soft but strong. She liked his kisses even more. His lips were warm and soft. The pressure was gentle and questing as he tasted her mouth. She responded by taking his lip between her teeth until it drew a groan of pleasure from him.

Violet felt his hand slide down her back. He began to undo the buttons of her dress. She put her arms around his neck. For each button he undid, she placed a kiss on his neck, his ear, his mouth. Jeff splayed his fingers across the bare skin of her shoulders. Gently he pushed the dress off her shoulders and down her arms. His lips left trails of kisses across her ultrasensitive skin.

She loosened his tie and opened his shirt. She had dreamed of caressing his whole torso ever since that first morning she had seen him exercising. It was no longer enough to be able to touch him. She wanted to see, taste, smell, absorb him into her being until the lust that had plagued her body was finally appeased. She slipped his coat off and let it drop to the floor. Then she pushed his shirt over his shoulders.

At last, his glorious body and his magnificent chest were hers to touch and caress and fondle. In a feverish burst of activity, she covered his chest with kisses. Then, feeling as though she had at last taken the edge off an old, aching longing, she slipped her arms around him and leaned her head against him.

He smelled of spices and mint. Her father and brother

hadn't scented their bodies, but she liked it. She breathed deeply, enjoying the faint scent of the male animal that mingled with the cologne. With her ear pressed to his chest, she could hear his heart beat, feel the blood as it coursed through his veins. His muscles quivered and tensed under his skin. She felt as though she held lightning in a bottle.

Violet could hardly believe she was holding Jeff Randolph. Naked to the waist, the object of her dreams was in her arms, hers to do with as she wished. And all she wanted to do was hold him, to glory in the possession of him—not that she could ever possess him. Even in a still moment such as that, there was an energy about him that defied possession by any mortal. Coiled, cocked, and loaded, it needed only a spark to set it off. Violet wondered if Jeff would be the same if it exploded. She had already been changed.

"I want to see your face." Jeff took her chin in his hand. He brushed the hair back from her face with his stump. "Have I told you you're beautiful?" When Violet shook her head, he said, "Bankers are supposed to be thorough, never overlooking the slightest detail."

"You can start making up for past oversights now." She smiled up at him. She knew it was a foolish smile, the smile of a woman who had everything it took to make her happy and didn't care who knew it. "I think I can spare a few moments to listen. But you have to hurry. There are other important things on the agenda."

"You are beautiful. I thought so from the first, but I wouldn't let myself admit it. I told myself your hair was too dark, your clothes too extravagant, your eyes too blue. I told myself anything except that I liked the way you looked and could have spent hours just watching you."

An involuntary chuckle escaped Violet. "You make me sound like some sort of bird and you like an ornithologist."

Jeff kissed her lightly on the lips. "You were the rarest of birds, a Yankee sparrow able to dissolve the layers of anger and hatred I'd covered myself with all these years."

"I'd rather be a robin or a bluebird. At least make me a cardinal."

"Cardinals don't have lips I long to kiss."

"I should think it would be uncomfortable to kiss a beak, especially if it had a worm in it," Violet said.

Jeff grabbed her tighter and swung her over backward. "Don't make fun of me, woman," he said in mock fury. "I will have my way with you."

"I was wondering when you would get around to that."

"Damn!" Jeff said as he held her suspended only a few feet above the floor. "I wish I still had two hands."

"What would you do?" Violet asked, completely unconcerned that she was suspended only a few inches from the floor. She knew Jeff was too strong to drop her.

"I'd open your chemise while I still had you helpless."

Violet pushed down the top of her gown and undid the laces of her chemise. "Like this?"

The laughter had gone out of Jeff's eyes, replaced by something much warmer. "I'd open it so I could see your breasts."

Violet pulled the sides of her chemise as far back as she could. "Is this far enough?"

Jeff's answer was to lower his head until he could kiss the soft mounds of her breasts. Violet thought she would swoon. It was all she could do to slide her arms around Jeff's neck. She felt completely disoriented, out of control, at his mercy.

Jeff whispered softly in her ear, "I wish I could carry you to the bedroom, but I'm afraid you'll have to walk."

The blood came rushing to Violet's head when he sat

her up. It made her dizzy. Jeff pulled her to her feet. She leaned on him as they walked together to the bedroom. There might be several things Jeff couldn't do, but taking Violet's dress off wasn't one of them. The chemise was just as easy.

"Now your stockings," Jeff whispered.

Violet peeled her stockings down her legs one at a time. All the while she kept her gaze on Jeff. She was proud of her legs. They were slim and well formed. She enjoyed the look of appreciation that appeared in Jeff's eyes. He reached out to remove her shift.

"Not before you let me undress you," she teased.

Violet had undressed both her father and brother, but taking off Jeff's clothes was a whole new experience. Jeff's body was young and strong and firm and very much aroused. Knowing that caused her fingers to fumble at their familiar tasks. His shirt wasn't the problem. It was his pants. She kept remembering the tight pants he'd worn that morning she had found him exercising. The pants he wore that night weren't similar in the least, but they were no more able to disguise his aroused condition. The two stood facing each other, Violet in her shift, Jeff in his shorts.

"I never told you that you're beautiful," she whispered. "I thought so the first time I saw you. I didn't know how beautiful until that morning I saw you exercising."

Jeff slipped her shift off one shoulder. "You were horrified. You couldn't wait to escape."

"I was terrified of what seeing your body was doing to me." She pulled at the drawstring on his shorts.

"What's it doing now?" he asked as he slipped the shift off her other shoulder. The garment slid from her body and pooled at her feet.

"The same thing," Violet said. She pulled the knot loose. A slight tug and Jeff's pants lay on the floor as well.

393

"What's that?" Jeff asked. One fingertip traced a line along Violet's jaw, across her lips, down her chin and neck, across her shoulder and down to the tingling nipple.

"My entire body feels as if it's on fire. I feel as if I'm about to burn up."

"I wouldn't like that."

Jeff's fingertip circled and recircled Violet's nipple until she felt reduced to a single point of aching sensitivity.

"The strangest feeling is in my belly," Violet said. "A weakness seems to be flowing from it to every part of my body. My muscles tremble. I can hardly stand up."

"Then let's lie down."

They lay beside one another, but Violet didn't feel any change in the weakness consuming her. Only Jeff's attentions to her breasts enabled her to think of anything beyond his erection nudging her thigh.

She lost track of everything else when he touched her other breast with his hot tongue. She felt assaulted; her body felt ignited. With finger and tongue, he teased and tortured her nipple until she heard herself groan with pleasure. She couldn't lie still. She ran her hand over his shoulders, his back, his neck, pressing into his flesh harder and harder as the exquisite agony in her breasts increased.

Violet was disappointed when Jeff's lips deserted her breasts, but the tension spiraled another notch when he started planting kisses across her stomach and down to her navel. He teased it with his tongue before angling over to one hip. Violet felt her body tense involuntarily. She tried to relax, but it was impossible. She knew what was coming next. But it didn't.

Jeff took her hand and settled a nest of kisses in her palm. Then trailing his way up her arm, her returned his attention to her breast. Only that time he took her nipple between his teeth and pulled gently. Violet gasped. Pleasure exploded through her. It was a moment before she realized he had moved his hand to the inside of her thigh. Before her body had time to clamp down in panic, he had invaded her.

Violet nearly rose off the bed. She had known what to expect, but she'd had no idea of the effect it would have on her. Jeff seemed to have found a spot that was excruciatingly sensitive. Soon she was trembling. She forgot the feel of his lips on her breast. She forgot his kisses. She could think only of what his hand was doing to her.

Pulsating waves began to wash over her, taking her with them. The waves grew higher and stronger, deeper and longer. She moaned and writhed as Jeff continued to touch her. Then there was a convulsive push, and suddenly the pressure was released, and it all drained away. Violet floated down like a feather on a soft ocean breeze.

It was several moments before her breathing returned to normal. She looked at Jeff. He was smiling. "What did you do?" she asked when she could speak.

"I'll tell you someday. Now we come to the part where you have to help."

After what she had just experienced, Violet wondered how there could be anything more. "What do you want me to do?"

"First I want you to touch me," Jeff said. "Be careful," he said when she was quick to sit up. "You need to be very gentle."

"Why?"

"I'll explain that someday, too."

"You're leaving out an awful lot."

Jeff smiled ruefully. "It's about all I can handle in one day."

She touched him. He was hard and warm and soft.

"Very carefully put your hand around me," he said.

Violet reluctantly followed his orders. It seemed strange.

"Now I want you to sit astride me, Violet. We can make love the conventional way, but this is much better for me."

Violet didn't need to know anymore. She straddled Jeff, but she felt uncertain.

"Now sit down slowly," he said.

Despite the tension, Violet lowered her body until she felt the pressure of Jeff against her. She hesitated before lowering herself still further.

"This may hurt a little, but it won't last long," Jeff said.

Before Violet had time to ask what he meant, Jeff thrust into her. A sharp pain shot through her body. Before she could flinch, Jeff pulled her down until he had entered her all the way.

"Now kiss me," he said.

As Violet leaned forward, Jeff began to move within her. Before long, she realized she was feeling the same sensations she had felt moments ago, only they were more intense. Instinctively she began to move with Jeff, rising when he drew away, then lowering her body to meet his.

Gradually she forgot his kisses, his hands on her body, everything except the feeling that was spreading through her loins, causing the muscles to bunch and her breath to come in gasps. She was vaguely aware Jeff had increased his tempo to match hers, but she was hardly aware of anything except the urgency that drove to meet the need buried deep inside her. Angling her body, she drove Jeff deep inside her. Still it remained just out of reach.

She became swallowed up by her own need. Increasing her tempo, Violet felt herself approach the outer ring of her need. Each thrust seemed to bring her closer to the core. Straining every muscle, Violet drove Jeff deeper and deeper until she felt the waves begin to grow, each higher and wilder than the last. Almost frantic, she forced her body to go faster, to ride higher, to experience more intensely until she reached the core at last and release flooded her body.

She was vaguely aware of Jeff as he tensed and drove into her with a few hard thrusts. Violet collapsed on top of Jeff as she felt the heat of his seed released within her.

Violet lay snuggled against Jeff's side, his arm around her. She was quiet. She didn't feel like talking. It was going to take her a while to adjust to what had just happened. It was more than her first experience at making love. It was even more than making love to the man she loved. It was more than the loss of her virginity. She felt recreated.

That sounded a little foolish, but that was how she felt. And it had little to do with the physical experience. Something had happened between her and Jeff that changed everything between them forever. A part of him belonged to her, a part of her to him. No matter what happened in the next few days or the next several years, they could never take it back again.

She wasn't the same woman who'd invited him to make love to her. She didn't know who she was or how she had been changed, but she began to understand the special relationship that existed between Jeff's brothers and their wives. She felt as though their souls had merged. No matter where she went, no matter what happened to her, she could never be fully separated from him.

"Are you sorry?" Jeff asked.

"Yes," she said, then felt him tense. "Sorry it took me so many years to find you."

He pulled her closer and kissed the top of her head, and she asked, "How about you?"

"I'm not sorry in the least. If I hadn't been such a son of a bitch all these years, I'd probably have married someone else. Then I'd have been mad as hell when I finally found you."

Violet liked that, but she couldn't help pushing him to expand on the subject a little more. "You'd have found some beautiful Southern belle who was everything you wanted. You wouldn't even have noticed a Yankee."

"I'd have noticed you," Jeff said. "I did from the first."

"Me, too," Violet said. "One look at your body, and I was consumed by lust."

Jeff twisted until he could see her face. "You?"

"Yes. Mortifying, isn't it?"

"Your husband-to-be is delighted. Lust can be a wonderful thing."

"We agreed to wait awhile before we spoke of marriage," Violet said, pulling away and sitting up. "You promised, and Randolphs don't go back on their word. You told me that."

Jeff pulled Violet back down. "Maybe not, but Randolphs don't always like it."

Violet giggled. "That's okay. I'd be upset if you did."

"Are you going to torture me, woman?"

"I'm not sure," Violet said, with another giggle. "I'll have to think about it."

"While you're thinking, I'll just. . . ."

Violet didn't do any more thinking for a while.

Chapter Twenty-seven

Jeff sat at a table in the Hattenback Saloon on the corner of State and Harrison. Miners came in at all hours of the night, some to eat, others to drink. All were waiting for their time in the few beds for hire in Leadville, most of which were rented out in eight-hour shifts. While they waited, they ate, talked, drank, and gambled. Most were too tired or too drunk to know or care what they said.

No one would have recognized Jefferson Randolph, president of the First National Bank of Denver. All they saw was a man just as dirty as everybody else, leaning on what was left of his arm after a mine accident.

Finally the man Jeff had been waiting for, Pete Colfax, entered the saloon. Jeff kicked the chair out from under a man snoring with his head on the table. "Go find another table," Jeff said, his voice rough and threatening. "You snore too damned loud."

The man picked himself up and shuffled off to find someplace else to sleep until it was time to go back to work. Jeff waited as Pete searched the room for a chair.

The chair next to Jeff was the only empty one in the saloon. Pete came over and sat down without introducing himself. Jeff let him down a whiskey.

"Been a hard shift?" he asked.

"They're all of them hard," Pete said, pouring himself another whiskey. He glanced at Jeff's empty sleeve. "You ought to know if anybody does." He swallowed his whiskey, then looked at Jeff again. "Don't remember seeing you about."

"Went away after this happened. Can't do much with one arm." When Pete didn't comment, Jeff said, "Then I heard the Silver Wave was producing again. I figured they owed me; so I come back. I mean to collect."

Pete spat out a foul epithet. "You won't get nothing out of that pair."

"Why not? I heard they made a big strike." When Pete said nothing, Jeff repeated in a harsh voice, "They owe me."

"If you mean to get anything, you'd better get it soon," the miner said in a lowered voice.

"Why?" Jeff asked, but Pete wouldn't answer. "I wouldn't have come back, but I got a wife and kids to think about." Jeff tried to shift from sounding angry and threatening to defeated and hopeless. He wished he had Zac's talents. The boy would have had the miner in the palm of his hand in minutes. "The wife's swelling up with another kid. There's no way to get food during winter except by working in the mines."

Pete downed two drinks, one right after the other. Jeff could tell the other man wanted to say something, but caution made him hold his tongue.

"You got to think Harlan and Chapman would act kindly since I was injured in their mine."

"They're more likely to throw you out," Pete said.

"Why?" Jeff asked, his voice full of disbelief.

"Those bastards would steal from their mother if they got the chance!" Pete said. Realizing he'd spoken too loud, Pete looked nervous, as if he was ready to jump up and leave before he said any more.

Jeff pretended to take a deep draw on his beer. He'd pour some more of it on the floor as soon as the miner wasn't looking.

"Maybe I ought to see if I can find work at the Little Johnny," Jeff said, trying to sound half drunk. "Eli Goodwin is a good man."

"Eli's dead and the mine gave out." Pete downed another whiskey. Jeff could tell he was becoming less cautious. "You take my advice and clear out, or your wife's liable not to have a father for her baby."

"That seems strange," Jeff said. "One mine turning rich just as the other turned poor, one pair getting rich just as the other one died."

"It ain't as strange as you would think," Pete whispered. "There's ways."

"What ways?" Jeff asked.

Pete lowered his voice. "I ain't sure. I used to work for Harlan and Chapman. The Silver Wave was cleaned out. They was trying to sell it, but nobody wanted it. The Little Johnny right next to it was played out, too. Folks said Eli Goodwin was crazy to buy it. But about a month later, Eli starts telling everybody he's made a big strike.

"All of a sudden Harlan and Chapman up and fired me and everybody else who worked for them. They said that their money was gone, that they couldn't keep working a played-out mine. It wasn't a week later that I heard that Eli Goodwin met with an accident. Harlan and Chapman found the cave-in. They said they didn't find no silver. They figured Eli was planning to salt the mine and try to sell it. Meanwhile, somebody files a claim against the Little Johnny. They ain't in town. Eli's kin ain't in town. So the mine stays closed. Unless somebody buys it, it's likely to stay closed a long time.

"That's when the Silver Wave starts producing

again." Pete lowered his head until his mouth was close to Jeff's ear. "Peculiar thing. Nobody works the Silver Wave but Harlan and Chapman. They could bring up a lot more if they was to hire the old crew back, but they don't want us."

"Did they sink a new shaft?"

"They said they found a new deposit in one of the old tunnels."

"Hasn't anybody wondered why their success should coincide with the Little Johnny's failure?" Jeff asked.

Pete indicated Jeff was to lower his voice. "That kind of question could get you killed. A lot of funny things go on in those mines."

"But you've wondered, haven't you?"

Pete nodded. "But I don't suppose you could tell nothing without going into the Little Johnny."

"Or the Silver Wave," Jeff said.

"Can't. Harlan and Chapman never leave it. They even sleep there."

"You think they're pulling silver out of the Little Johnny and using it to salt the Silver Wave?"

"That's what I thought at first. But I watched one whole night. Nobody went near the Little Johnny, yet the silver came up just like usual next day."

Jeff had never been in a mine, but it seemed to him that the only explanation for the sudden reversal of fortunes in the two mines was that their tunnels met. Harlan and Chapman were taking ore from the Little Johnny out through the Silver Wave tunnels.

"Can you get me down into the Little Johnny?"

"What you want to do that for?" Pete asked.

"I need money. I can't work with this arm. If I can find out what they're doing, maybe they'll pay me to keep what I know to myself."

"I wouldn't mess around with those two. Besides, the mine's not safe. Part of it caved in on Eli. It was so bad they didn't even bring his body up."

"Was anybody else hurt?" Jeff asked.

"He was working alone. Harlan and Chapman claimed they were passing by the shaft when they heard an explosion. They went down and found the cave-in. Everybody thought they was heroes to even go in there."

Jeff knew he had to get into that mine. Whatever was being done, or had been done, the secrets were all underground.

"Will you help me?" Jeff asked.

"You gotta be crazy," Pete said.

"I have to know."

"Why the hell are you so damned curious? You can get killed."

"I might as well be dead without an arm," Jeff said. "It's a chance I got to take."

The miner thought for a while. "I hate those sons of bitches. They're getting away with something. I'll help you, but I ain't going down with you. I'll let you down in the bucket. You're on your own after that."

"You got some equipment I can borrow?" Jeff said.

"There's plenty at the mine. Nobody'll miss it."

Violet rolled over. Only half awake, she reached out for Jeff. It took her a moment to realize she was alone in the bed. She sat up, wide awake. Why had Jeff left without saying anything to her? And where had he gone?

A sign was nailed to the shaft.

MINE UNSAFE
DO NOT ENTER

"They put that sign up right after Eli died," Pete said. "They said they'd leave it there until the claim was settled."

Jeff didn't like the feeling in the pit of his stomach. He hadn't liked facing enemy fire during the war, but at least it was daylight. He could see then. Going down into a tunnel nearly a hundred feet deep was quite different.

You're a coward! I'm ashamed to be your father!

For the first time in Jeff's life, the memory of his father's words didn't make him sick to his stomach. He was fearful. He was facing the unknown. He'd never been underground. Someone might already have committed murder. A fortune was at stake. He would be a fool not to be afraid.

But Jeff wasn't going to back out. The answer was in the mine. If the only way to find it was to go down that shaft, he'd go. But he didn't have to like it.

''I'll lower you all the way to the bottom,'' Pete said. ''It'll be easier to find the other tunnels coming up than going down.''

''How will I signal you when I'm ready to go to another level or when it's time to stop?''

''There's marks on the cable for the different tunnels,'' Pete said. ''You use the bells if you want to go up or down. One is up; two is down. Be careful when you climb into the bucket. More than one man's turned it over and pitched headlong to the bottom.''

Jeff took care not to upset the bucket when he climbed in. He was armed with a pocketful of candles, a box of matches, and a pick.

''This whim ain't going to be quiet,'' Pete said. ''If I stop all of a sudden, it's because somebody's getting curious.''

The whim squeaked and groaned. Jeff hoped the rope would hold. He decided going down in the mine wasn't an experience he wanted to repeat anytime soon. He held his lit candle up as the big metal bucket descended too swiftly for his comfort. Walls of rough stone flashed by. In places they had been reinforced with timbers to keep them from caving in. Jeff would have felt better if the owners had used three or four times as much reinforcing.

Jeff passed three tunnels on the way down, each about 30 feet apart. At one he thought he caught the fetid odor of urine and dung, but he told himself that was impossible. An animal would have to be living in the tunnel to create such a strong smell.

The bucket slowed and Jeff braced himself for the landing. Even then it was so jarring he fell against the side of the bucket, barely escaping injury. Relieved to be at the bottom at last, Jeff climbed out of the bucket and briefly inspected the tunnels that ran off in opposite directions. He had already worked out a way of numbering them to keep from getting lost. Scratching a number in the floor of the first tunnel, he entered.

Jeff stared at the dark stain on the ground. He was certain it was blood. He walked slowly along the tunnel, bending over as the ceiling dropped lower. It wasn't braced, and he didn't feel comfortable. Before long he began to smell something unpleasant. At the end of the tunnel he found a pile of rocks. That was no cave-in. The rocks had been stacked.

Jeff held his breath in an attempt to keep his stomach from rebelling. He had to remove some of the rocks. He had to know if his suspicions were correct.

A half hour later Jeff had uncovered the body of a man. The cold dampness of the cave had slowed the process of decay, but Jeff retched twice. There was no question of moving the body; so he had to find some identification. Despite gagging constantly, Jeff searched the clothing. He found a wallet.

It was Eli Goodwin, and he had been killed by having his head bashed in, probably where Jeff saw the first blood. Jeff thought he heard the faint protesting squeal of the whim, but he was too nauseated to think of anything but finishing his search and getting out of the mine. He nerved himself to search the rest of Eli's clothing, but there was nothing else.

Jeff retched again. Hoping his stomach would hold out until he got beyond the smell, he retreated down the tunnel. He would have to see that Violet's uncle received a decent burial, but right then he couldn't wait to get as far away from the body as possible.

"I told you I heard that whim," one man said to the other. "I would recognize the sound of it in my sleep."

"Who'd be going into that mine? Everybody thinks it's about to cave in."

"I don't know, but we better make sure they don't come up again."

The two men approached silently, using the numerous buildings, sheds, and pieces of equipment to cover their approach.

"That's Colfax hanging over the shaft," one said. "What the hell is he doing here?"

"I don't know, but he always was trouble." The man picked up a small log. "He won't be much longer."

"Ed, don't—"

"Shh!" It was the work of no more than a minute to sneak up behind Colfax and hit him over the head with the log. Ed had to pull him back to keep him from falling into the shaft.

"Bring up the bucket," Ed said. The whim began to creak and groan. Minutes later the bucket rose to the surface. "Give me a hand," Ed said.

The two men lifted Colfax's inert body and dumped it down the shaft. A muffled thump told them when it hit bottom.

"Won't nobody miss Colfax," Ed said. "If they do, they won't care."

"What about whoever's down there?"

"If anybody does miss him, they won't know where to look."

When Jeff reached the shaft, he found he had been right. The bucket was gone. Who had removed it and why? He stared at the empty shaft while the implications sank in. He was in the bottom of the mine with no way to get out.

Something hit Jeff on the shoulder and knocked him to the ground. He dropped his candle. It went out. He lay on the cold, damp rock, dazed, waiting for his head to stop spinning. He felt his limbs. They weren't broken. He could tell from the warm, wet feeling in his shirt that his stump was bleeding. He hoped it wasn't serious. He could bleed to death.

Jeff pulled several candles from his pocket until he found one that wasn't broken. Holding it between his knees, he struck a match on the shaft floor and lighted the candle. He held it over his head. Pete Colfax's body lay inches away, his head smashed almost beyond recognition. Jeff retched again.

When he recovered his strength, he withdrew a short distance down the tunnel. Using candle wax to anchor them, he lit three candles and placed them in a semicircle. Then he leaned back against the tunnel wall. It was rough and cold, but he pushed the discomfort out of his mind. He had to think.

No one knew he was down there. No one was coming to rescue him. Only Violet would know that he was gone, and he hadn't told her where. He hoped she wouldn't think he had deserted her after one night of love. He hoped she would know he meant to come back. He hoped she would mount a search to find him.

Violet was worried when Jeff wasn't back when she woke. As the morning wore on, she became nearly frantic. Never once did she believe he had deserted her. If Jeff had decided he'd made a mistake, he'd have told her. He wasn't the most sensitive man in the world, but he wasn't a coward.

But Violet didn't believe he had left her. She remembered the way she'd felt last night. She knew Jeff had felt it, too. He would never leave her after that. Besides, he hadn't taken any of his clothes. Even his money was still in his pockets. Something had happened to him that prevented him from coming back or sending a message.

Once she reached that conclusion, Violet became prey to all sorts of fears. Who would have wanted to stop Jeff from coming back? Why? How? She didn't want to answer that last question. She couldn't help thinking of her uncle.

But Violet was certain Jeff was alive. She would have felt it if he were dead. It was up to her to figure out what had happened to him. After a good hour spent studying and discarding possibilities, she decided his disappearance must have to do with the mines, either the one he was going to buy or hers.

But that didn't help much. What could he have been doing in the middle of the night? By process of elimination, she decided he must have gone to the mines. It was unlikely he'd be calling on a lawyer in the middle of the night. And if he had, he wouldn't have stayed long. He was an important man. Everybody in Leadville would probably recognize Jeff's name and fall over himself trying to please Jeff.

But she had to get information, and she had to start somewhere. She knew where all the lawyers had their offices. She'd walked every street the day before.

The fourth lawyer she visited had his offices above the Bank of Leadville. He not only dealt with the Randolph family; he had also dealt with Eli Goodwin. He knew the location of both mines.

"They're next to each other on Freyer Hill. Why do you want to know?"

Violet didn't like the man's attitude. He acted as if

she was wasting his time asking questions about things that were none of her business. She could easily have changed his mind, but she didn't want to tell him any more than necessary. She didn't know whom she could trust.

"I'm interested in the Little Johnny," she said. "Mr. Randolph was going to show me around, but he hasn't turned up this morning. Could you take me there?"

"I'm afraid I don't have time." Which, if his expression could be trusted, translated as, "I can't be bothered."

"Maybe one of your clerks could help me," Violet said.

"It's not safe for a woman to go into those hills. Not a good idea either with all those men about."

"Well, I'm going," Violet said, getting to her feet. "When I do see Mr. Randolph, I mean to tell him how uncooperative you've been."

The lawyer's entire attitude changed immediately from barely concealed impatience to smiling helpfulness. Violet was right. Whoever was responsible for Jeff's disappearance was not a member of the legal community. The only possibility left was that somebody didn't want him to find out about the mines. That meant either something awful had happened to Uncle Eli, the claim was false, or both.

Violet found herself getting scared. If the situation was as serious as she suspected, she could be in great danger. If somebody had already killed Uncle Eli and Jeff, the murderer wouldn't balk at trying to kill her as well.

Violet went straight to the telegraph office and sent two telegrams, one each to George and Madison. But not for a moment did she consider waiting for them to reach Leadville. Jeff was in danger, and every minute counted.

* * *

"You sure you want to go to the mine?" the clerk asked. He was an older man, rough looking, not at all the kind of person Violet expected to be serving as a clerk in a respectable law office.

"I can't see anything from here," Violet said.

Violet could see quite a lot. The mine had been staked out on a hill at the foot of the Mosquito Range. Nearly all the spruce, aspen, and pine trees for miles had been cut down. Their stumps remained as reminders of the way nature had intended the slopes to look. Each mine was composed of several buildings. Slag heaps of refuse from the mines could be found on all sides. The rock varied from yellow through gray to almost white. The mines were so close that a bulwark had to be built around some slag piles to keep them from falling on the mines farther down the hill.

Violet got down from the buggy and picked her way across the hillside to the Little Johnny mine.

"It's closed," the clerk said. "It has been since the cave-in that killed Eli."

"Who found him?"

"Harlan and Chapman. They own the Silver Wave right over there. It started producing again just after the Little Johnny closed. They're trying to sell it."

"The mines don't seem to be far enough apart to keep their tunnels from running into each other," Violet said.

"All the mines are close together up here. That's why there are so many cross claims."

But Violet could tell the same idea had occurred to both of them. "What if—"

She didn't get to finish her sentence. A tall, grubby man with an unfriendly face approached them. "It's dangerous for a lady to be up here," he said. His expression looked welcoming, but Violet decided his eyes told a different story.

"I've never seen a mine," Violet said. "I just had to see one before I left Leadville."

"Well you can't see that one. It's closed."

"I already told her," the clerk said.

Violet noticed a change in the clerk's attitude. He didn't like the man either.

"Who are you?" Violet asked bluntly.

"I'm David Chapman. I'm part owner of the Silver Wave."

"Can I see your mine?" Violet asked. She decided she didn't trust the man. She'd do better if she acted a bit silly. "I'm just dying to see one. They talk about it all the time in Denver. Just think. I'd be able to tell my friends I had been down in a mine. I'd be the envy of everybody I know."

"Sorry, ma'am, but you can't go down. The men go down in those buckets." He pointed to the bucket in the Little Johnny shaft. "They're dangerous. Quite a few men have been killed falling out of them."

Chills of cold fear ran up and down Violet's spine. She felt certain Jeff had ridden in one of those buckets. Maybe that very one. She prayed he wasn't one of the men who had died.

She walked over to the edge of the shaft and looked down.

"Oh, it's dark inside. How do you see?"

"We use candles," Chapman said. "Some mine owners prefer to use oil lamps, but they can cause fires."

"You sure I can't ride down in the bucket?" Violet asked. "It looks like so much fun."

"No, ma'am. It's too dangerous."

"Yoo-hoo!" Violet called into the dark hole. She showed foolish excitement when a faint echo answered back. "Can I have a piece of silver? I just have to have something to show my friends."

"It doesn't come in pieces, ma'am. It's in rocks."

Violet made her most disappointed face. "I think it's terrible I have to go home with nothing. Who's going to believe I've actually seen a mine?"

"Come with me, ma'am," Chapman said.

Violet and the clerk followed Chapman to the shaft of the Silver Wave. A few minutes later the bucket came to the surface loaded with ore. Chapman took two pieces from the bucket and handed them to Violet.

"But they're nothing but black rocks," she said, dismayed.

"That's what silver ore looks like," Chapman said. "We have to smelt it down to get the silver out of it. Show that to your friends. At least they won't think the silver's lying around on the ground for us to pick up."

"Thank you," Violet said, trying to sound as dismayed as possible when she was actually thrilled. If, as she suspected, the silver had come from her uncle's mine, she held in her hand the proof that Chapman was stealing. The ore from different veins was as identifiable as a fingerprint.

"Now I suggest you go back to your hotel. It's not safe up here. There are tunnels under all of these hills."

Violet kept up her foolish act, chattering away like the half-wit she hoped Chapman would believe she was. The moment she was out of sight, she turned to the clerk. "You have to bring me back here tonight," she said.

"What for?"

"We have to find some silver from my uncle's mine. I'm going to prove these came from the same place."

Jeff started awake from a state of semiconsciousness. He thought a shadow had crossed the opening to the shaft, as though someone had leaned over to look inside. He thought he had heard Violet's voice. He scrambled to his feet and called out, but the cold air at the bottom of the tunnel had made him hoarse. He doubted the sound of his voice could reach the surface even if someone was listening for it. He tried again and waited, but he heard nothing, saw nothing.

He must have been hallucinating. The cold, the dark, and the utter silence had had a deadening effect on his senses. After so many hours, he seemed to be approaching a state of suspended animation. He tried to fight it, but he felt himself gradually losing the battle.

Don't be a fool. Let it come. That way you won't know when you die.

But Jeff didn't mean to die. He didn't know how, but he meant to live a good many years yet. He hadn't found Violet only to lose her.

Later that night, with the ore samples locked away in the lawyer's safe, Violet and the clerk returned to the Little Johnny Mine. A second man accompanied them.

"I insist on going down in the bucket with you," Violet said. "I don't care how dangerous it is. I have to convince myself Jeff was never in that mine."

"Why would he have come here?" the clerk asked.

"I don't know, but something kept him from returning. I have a feeling it had something to do with these mines."

"You be careful with that pick, miss," the clerk said. "You can hurt yourself going down the shaft."

"Just help me into the bucket." Violet had to keep her courage up for the benefit of the men who were helping her. To herself, she admitted she was petrified. The thought of being in a bucket suspended over a shaft more than a hundred feet deep scared her almost senseless.

"Let me get in first," the clerk said. "Then Tom and I will both help you."

Violet got into the bucket without any trouble, but the swaying motion immediately unsettled her stomach so badly that she feared she would throw up. When Tom began to man the whim and the bucket began to sink, she was certain she would faint, throw up, or both.

"Hold on, ma'am," the clerk said. "It sounds as bad

as can be, but you'll be at the bottom before you know it.''

Violet knew there was no way she could reach the bottom soon enough. Once she did that, she would have to ride the terrifying contraption to the surface again. She kept reminding herself that she was looking for Jeff. She could endure anything as long as she found him. She wanted to get her mine back as well, but Jeff was what really mattered. The trip into the bowels of the earth was making that agonizingly clear.

Jeff gradually emerged from his stupor. The bucket was coming down the shaft. Someone was coming. Euphoria was immediately tempered by caution. The only people who knew he was there were the people who had killed Pete Colfax. They might be coming to get him.

Willing his body to shed its lethargy, Jeff moved deeper into the tunnel. He had every intention of knowing who had come down before he revealed himself.

"Are they in the bucket, Tom?" David Chapman asked.

"Sure are, Mr. Chapman. They ought to be about halfway down by now. You want me to drop them?"

"No. Once they reach bottom, untie the rope and throw it in after them. Everybody will think it rotted through. Nobody will bother to install a new one for a worthless mine.''

Tom played with the whim, letting the bucket descend too fast, then bringing it to a jerky halt.

"What are you doing?" Chapman asked.

"Giving them a little fun," Tom said, grinning. "They ain't going to have nothing to do when they reach the bottom.''

The two men watched in silence. Then Chapman said, "It was smart of you to tell me what that silly female intended to do.''

"I thought you'd want to know. What do you want me to do when I'm done here?"

"Come to the Silver Wave."

"You got my money?"

"Sure. I got everything."

Jeff couldn't believe his ears. It was Violet's voice that he heard floating down the shaft. He struggled to drive away the drugged feeling that still clung to his senses. Somehow she had found him. He was safe.

Pete! His body was still lying at the bottom of the shaft. Jeff didn't want Violet to see the dead man. Forcing his sluggish muscles to act, Jeff dragged Pete's body several yards down the opposite tunnel. Later he would have to see about a proper burial for him.

Back in the first tunnel, he fumbled for his candle. He could hardly wait to gaze on Violet's face. He could hear her talking to someone. The bucket hit the ground. A man was telling her how to get out without falling. Jeff heard Violet's feet scrape the tunnel's rough stone floor. He struck a match. He heard a gasp. He resolutely forced himself to concentrate on lighting his candle, then another and another until he had three points of light on the tunnel floor.

"Jeff!" Violet said.

Her voice was the sweetest sound he'd ever heard in his life. He stumbled forward and fell into her arms. He kissed her mouth and cheeks and eyes. He could never get enough of her.

"How did you know I was here?" he finally managed to ask.

"When you didn't come back, I knew it had to have something to do with the mines. When I met David Chapman, I knew he'd done something terrible."

"It doesn't matter. We're safe now. As soon as we reach the surface, I'll see Chapman goes to prison for the rest of his life."

A strange sound assaulted their ears. It was a swishing sound, like something moving through the air so fast it created a noise as it went. The rope. Someone had thrown the rope in after them. They were trapped in the tunnel. They were all going to die.

Chapter Twenty-eight

Jeff peered over the edge of the bucket. Most of the rope was coiled inside. The end was caught on something above.

"The rope broke!" Violet said.

"It's more likely your friend threw it in after you," Jeff said.

"But that means—"

"That means somebody wants us to die down here," Jeff said.

"But I've known Tom Blake ever since he came to Leadville," the clerk said. "He wouldn't do this to me."

"He probably found he could get a lot of money for betraying you to Harlan and Chapman," Jeff said.

"You think they did this?" Violet asked.

"If they're stealing from your uncle's mine, they'd have no other choice." Jeff tested the rope. He pulled hard on it. It wouldn't budge. "It's caught on something," he said. "I wonder what."

"Probably one of the timbers used for bracing," the clerk said.

Jeff pulled on the rope again. "It seems to be caught tight. Maybe you can climb it."

"Why?" the clerk asked. "There's nothing up there but more tunnels."

"There's no way out at this level," Jeff said. "I've been to the end of both tunnels."

"There's no way out of any of them," the clerk said.

"There's always a chance," Jeff said. "The rope's caught fast. We have to see if it will take us to the next tunnel. I'd go, but I only have one arm." It would be easiest for someone light, but Violet would never have the strength.

The clerk pulled on the rope. He seemed satisfied that it would hold. "I don't know if I can get that far. I ain't worked in a mine for a long time. My arms ain't what they used to be."

"It's our only chance," Jeff said. "If we die, you'll die with us."

"My boss will come after us."

"He doesn't know we're down here," Violet said. "He won't know you're missing until tomorrow. He'll probably wait a day or two before he starts looking for you. Then it'll take him several more days to sort through all the possibilities."

"And how do we know Chapman might not rig up another bucket on the surface so that it looks as if nobody came down here?" Jeff said.

"Okay, I'll give it a try."

"Hold the rope between your legs and pull up with both arms," Jeff said.

"I know how to do it," the clerk said, his temper edgy. "I just don't know if I can."

Jeff didn't say anything more, even when the clerk started to use his feet to push against the wall. Jeff waited, his arm around Violet, a silent prayer in his heart.

"Can you see where the rope's caught?" he said, after the clerk had climbed about ten feet.

"No." The man gasped. "It's all I can do to hold on."

"Wrap your legs around the rope," Jeff said, but the clerk continued to climb hand over hand with his feet braced against the wall.

"Will he make it?" Violet asked in a hushed whisper.

"If he can just—"

The rope slipped! The clerk lost his grip and fell to the bottom of the tunnel. Fortunately he missed hitting the bucket, which would have killed him. He merely broke his leg.

Violet rushed to his side. "We can set his leg," she said as the clerk groaned in pain, "but he needs a doctor."

Jeff looked from the man to the rope and back again. The rope was their only hope of escape. He pulled on it. It seemed to be caught again. Would it hold? Did he have the strength to pull himself up with only one hand? Could he figure out how to do it.

"Could you see where it was caught?" he asked the clerk.

"No, it'll probably slip again if you put much weight on it."

Jeff made up his mind. "I'm going to move you. If I fall, I don't want to fall on you."

"You can't go up there," Violet said.

"I have no choice."

"But you could fall. Besides, there's no way out."

"If they've been stealing silver from the Little Johnny, there has to be a tunnel that connects the two mines. It's not down here."

Violet gave him a brusque hug. "I didn't put up with

419

your rude-Yankee comments to lose you now. Be careful.''

Jeff gave her a short, fierce kiss then turned away. He had to get everything out of his mind except the task ahead. He studied the rope. Made of coarse hemp, it was about an inch thick. Jeff had to pull himself up with his right arm. Just as important, he had to find a way to keep the rope from slipping while he released his grip and secured one higher on the rope.

Jeff pulled the rope across his body and under his stump. He clamped down. That was good, but not good enough. He wrapped the rope around his body and caught it between his legs. That was much better. He secured a grip, pulled himself up about a foot, then clamped down on the rope with his arm and legs. It didn't slip.

He worked to get some kind of grip on the rope with his shoes. It wouldn't be much, but he needed to be able to push with his legs while he pulled with his arm. He was strong, but he doubted he could pull himself the 30 or so feet to the next level with just his arm. Jeff released the rope and secured a fresh hold. Using his arm and what push he could get from his feet, he raised his body six inches.

The strain of hoisting nearly 200 pounds was enormous. He felt as if his arm was about to come out of its socket. Lifting weights had never been that difficult.

Jeff concentrated on six inches at a time. After pulling himself up ten feet, he had to stop and catch his breath, to allow the muscles in his arm to rest. He was beginning to feel the strain.

He thought of Violet down below. Her life depended on him. He couldn't stop. With painstaking, deliberate effort, Jeff inched up the rope until he was about 20 feet above the bottom of the tunnel. His muscles screamed in pain; he had a painful rope burn under his left arm; his legs and feet ached from the awkward angle of the pressure he put on them, but he kept climbing. He could see an opening above. There was a tunnel up there. He could reach it if he just kept climbing.

Five feet away, he could smell the fetid aroma of dung and urine. His lungs gasped for breath; his stomach threatened to rebel. He told himself to hang on. He had to make it. When he was two feet away from the tunnel, the rope slipped.

Jeff hung on desperately though he expected to fall and die. When the rope caught again, it felt as if he was being torn apart. The rough hemp tore into the red swollen flesh of his hand, sending searing pain screaming along the nerve endings until it exploded in his brain. Gasping from sheer agony, Jeff bit his lip and struggled just to hold on. If he fell, if he slipped to the bottom, he would never make it to the top again.

He didn't fall. The rope stayed caught under his stump and wrapped around his body. If he'd been holding the rope in his hands like a normal climber, he'd have lost his grip and fallen to his death. Ironically, being one-armed had saved his life.

But he had no time to dwell on irony. After a few moments when he thought he might pass out, Jeff was able to push back the pain. Not giving himself time to feel the agony, he reached for a new grip and pulled himself up the next torturous six inches. Every part of his body screamed with pain. His brain kept sending messages through his nerve endings to his hand to let go, to back away.

Jeff fought his own body. He thought of Violet and forced himself to hold on. Each time he had to release his hold and take a new grip, he thought of Violet. He thought of the hours he wanted to spend just looking at her, brushing that gloriously thick hair, looking into her eyes, making love to her. He thought of what would happen to her if he didn't climb the rope, if he didn't find a way out, and he somehow found the strength to keep going.

When he finally pulled even with the tunnel, the sickening odor of dung and urine nearly defeated him. He fought to control his body's convulsions. Using every last reserve of energy and determination, he managed to pull himself into the tunnel and collapse on the cold, wet floor.

Look at me now, Pa, you goddamned hateful son of a bitch. I did it. You can't call me a worthless coward ever again. I climbed all the way up that rope. And I did it with just one arm.

Jeff lay on the floor, unmoving. He didn't think he could ever move again. Yet he must. His mouth was dry. His body begged for water. That was his greatest danger. He had been without water a day longer than Violet and the clerk. He would die first.

Jeff forced himself to move. Even though his hand was so painfully swollen he could hardly move his fingers, he managed to get a candle out of his pocket. He searched until he found some gravel. Using his foot, he mounded it against the candle. He could barely hold the match in his fingers. He dropped it twice before he was able to strike it. The tiny flame lighted the tunnel for only a short distance. Jeff pulled out a second candle and lit it.

Something snorted. Jeff looked around him, his heart thumping painfully in his chest. Something was in the tunnel with him. His first thought was that Chapman and Harlan had somehow found him. But they couldn't have gotten down there without using the broken bucket.

Taking a candle and holding it above his head, Jeff stared into the darkness. Getting to his feet, he walked slowly forward. Around a bend, he found himself looking at the rear end of a mule harnessed to an ore car. He had found the source of the dung and urine.

Two thoughts hit Jeff simultaneously. If there was a

mule there, someone had been bringing him water since the Little Johnny Mine was closed. He had found a way out.

Jeff was becoming used to the odor. He didn't feel like gagging all the time. Holding the light high so he could see, he stumbled past the mule to the bucket of water. Falling to his knees, he leaned his candle against the wall and scooped up a handful of water. It was fresh. He held it in his mouth, moistening the dry tissues and his tongue. Finally he swallowed. Then he drank a second and third handful. Then he stopped. He knew better than to drink too much too soon.

He stood up and looked at the mule. The animal responded to his presence, but it had been in the mine so long that it was almost blind. But that didn't matter. The mule could still help Jeff bring Violet and the clerk up to this level.

Jeff went back to the shaft. He waved his candle into the shaft. "I've found a way out!"

"How can we get up?" Violet asked.

"There's a mule up here. Get the clerk to tie a loop in the rope. We'll pull you up."

"The clerk has to go first," Violet said.

Jeff didn't like that, but he figured Violet wasn't going to change her mind. It wasn't easy getting the man over the ledge with his broken leg, but he held up remarkably well. In an even shorter time, Jeff was helping Violet into the tunnel. He wrapped his arm around her in relief.

"I thought we were going to die," she said.

"Not us," Jeff said, feeling too good to acknowledge any doubt that they would get out. "I can't be the first Randolph to die. Besides, I have too much to do."

"Like what?"

"Marry you."

Violet laughed. It was strained, not nearly full throated, but it was a laugh. "It hasn't been a week yet."

"It feels like it."

"What about that man down there?"

Jeff felt the smile freeze on his face. Had she found her uncle?

"He looks like a miner. I found him a little way down the tunnel. What happened to him?"

"Chapman threw him down the shaft for helping me," Jeff said. We'll send someone back for him once we get out." He paused. "There's another body down here."

"My uncle?"

"Yes."

"Are you sure?"

"I found his wallet. Chapman and Harlan killed him and buried him under some rocks. There was never any cave-in. This mine is not dangerous. Let me show you what I found." Jeff took her to a point beyond the water. A series of tunnels opened off in all directions. "This is where they get the ore that comes out of the Silver Wave." He picked up a piece broken off the wall. "It looks very rich."

"How do we know which way to go?" Violet asked. "There's a maze of tunnels down here."

"I'm depending on the mule to know the way they get the ore to the shaft of the Silver Wave."

"But how are you going to get us up?" the clerk asked. "Chapman and Harlan aren't going to let us get out if they can help it."

"I know that," Jeff said, "but they won't be coming down here for some hours yet. By then I'll have a plan."

"While you're thinking, you can help me make a splint and set his leg," Violet said.

Most mines worked around the clock to take out as much ore as possible in the shortest amount of time. As long as the men were underground, it didn't make any difference if it was night or day. Harlan and Chapman worked only one shift because they couldn't trust anybody else with their secret. That was the bit of luck that Jeff counted on to enable them to escape.

The wait seemed interminable, but finally Jeff heard sounds of someone approaching through the tunnel. Soon he could hear voices. Chapman and Harlan.

"I don't like all this killing," Harlan said. "Somebody's bound to find out. What good is all this money going to do us if we hang?"

"No one's going to find out," Chapman said. "No one even knows they're missing. Even if they did, they wouldn't know where to look."

"But the cripple is a Randolph," Harlan said. "Even if he's dead, his family won't give up until they find out what happened to him. They'll keep after us until they find him."

"If they ever do figure out we had anything to do with it—which I don't think they ever will—we'll have sold the mine and be in Europe with enough money to live like kings for the rest of our lives."

"I still wish we'd taken the offer we got six months ago."

"That was peanuts. Everybody knew the mine was played out."

"You should have listened to your partner, Chapman," Jeff said, stepping out of a dark recess. "He has more sense than you do."

Chapman whirled, but before he could lift a hand, Jeff hit him a blow that sent him staggering back against the tunnel wall. But Chapman was a strong man. He came charging back at Jeff, his powerful forearms ready to drive massive fists into Jeff's face. Jeff feinted, then hit Chapman in the windpipe. While the big man gasped for breath, Jeff pounded him in the body until he staggered to his knees. One last blow to the jaw knocked him out.

Jeff looked up, ready to ward off an attack from Harlan. No attack came. Using Violet's splint, the clerk had come up behind Harlan and put a bar across his windpipe. A slight increase in pressure would choke him to death.

"I think we ought to throw them down the shaft," the clerk said after they had tied Chapman up and dumped him inside the ore car.

"How are we going to get to the surface?" Violet asked.

"I bet that back-stabbing Tom Blake is at the whim," the clerk said.

"Harlan is going to help us," Jeff said. "He's going to convince Blake to help me out of the bucket."

"He won't if he knows it's you," the clerk said.

"Then we have to make sure he doesn't."

"What are you going to do?"

"I'm going to leave you here with Chapman."

"Good. If you're not back inside an hour, I'll dump him down the shaft."

"Be my guest," Jeff said. He turned to Harlan. "You said you didn't like all this killing. Here's your chance to prove it. Do what I ask, and I'll see you don't hang."

"Can you do that?"

"He's a Randolph," the clerk said. "They can do anything."

Jeff took Violet down one of the side tunnels. "I don't trust Harlan. He might not have wanted to murder anyone, but he didn't dislike it enough to stop Chapman. I'm going to put a long pole in the bucket. The minute we reach the surface, I want you to place it across the opening."

"I've never done anything like that."

"Just make sure it's through the bucket handle and rests on each side of the shaft. That way, if Blake decides to sacrifice Harlan in order to kill us, the bucket won't fall down the shaft."

"What are you going to do?"

"Get out of the bucket and stop Blake before he can do anything else. You understand?" When Violet nodded, Jeff said, "Keep down until the last minute. I don't want him to see anybody but Harlan. The minute you get that pole across the shaft, get out of the bucket. I'll help if I can, but I have to get to Blake first. Now let's go."

When they reached the ore bucket, Jeff kept Harlan away from the bell used to signal the lift operator. He put a long pole in the bucket. Then he helped Violet in, followed by Harlan. Taking the bell, he climbed into the bucket. He rang the bell once, loud and clear, then threw it down the tunnel as far as he could. It landed somewhere distant with a dull thud.

"That's so you can't send him a different signal," Jeff said.

The ride to the surface was slow. The whim must have been hand driven. "Get down," Jeff said to Violet when they were within 20 feet of the surface. "Remember what I told you."

Jeff pushed Harlan forward and crouched down behind him. He was taller than Harlan, but he hoped for the moment's advantage he needed. "Stand real still, Harlan," he said. "When the bucket stops, tell the operator that you got hurt, that you need help getting out of the bucket."

Harlan nodded, but the closer they had come to the surface, the less Jeff trusted him. The man was going to try to betray them. Just as the bucket approached the surface, Jeff reached up and took a grip on Harlan's throat. Harlan's hands flew to his neck, but Jeff's hold was too strong. His fingers pressed down on the windpipe. Harlan struggled desperately. Jeff released him just as the bucket broke the surface.

Harlan tried to call out, but no sound came from his abused vocal cords. As Jeff vaulted out of the bucket, he saw Violet slipping the pole across the shaft. The ore bucket was secured. He just had to reach Blake.

Blake took one look at Jeff and started running down

the hill. "Stop him!" Jeff said to some men working a nearby mine. "He just tried to kill a woman."

"He's a liar!" Blake said, dodging the men.

"I'm Jefferson Randolph! Stop that man!"

The miners didn't need to know more. They ran down Tom Blake.

"Hold him." Jeff hurried back for Violet.

When he reached her, Violet was out of the bucket. Harlan was also out, but he was holding his head, blood running down his face.

"What happened?" Jeff asked.

"He tried to assault me," Violet said. "So I hit him with one of the pieces of ore he tried to steal from my uncle."

"But where—"

"In my purse," Violet said. "I always carry everything I need in my purse."

Chapter Twenty-nine

"It'll be easy to prove Harlan and Chapman have been stealing from the Little Johnny," Jeff told George. They were relaxing in the Tabor suite. George had arrived on the train early that afternoon.

"There're no other workings in either mine. Nobody saw them kill Eli Goodwin, but Harlan confessed that Chapman killed the miner who helped me. Violet will get the mine and the money for all the silver Chapman and Harlan sold since the day her uncle died. That ought to come to around a half-million dollars."

"I don't suppose you're planning to go back to the Wolfe School," George said.

"I'm through being a housemother," Violet said.

"I was thinking of headmistress," George said. "Miss Settle has resigned. The board is looking for someone to fill her position."

"Violet wants to go back to Massachusetts and set up a charity for women who cared for men disabled in the war," Jeff said.

George gave Violet a glance that said he wanted an explanation.

"I'm not sure what I'm going to do," Violet said. "Things have been changing so quickly."

"I'm trying to talk her into staying in Denver," Jeff said. "I don't suppose Clara Rabin will like it, but it's about time Denver society had a new Mrs. Randolph to talk about."

George directed a speculative glance at the pair.

"Yes, I've asked her to marry me, but she hasn't said yes." Jeff got to his feet. "See if you can talk her into it while I go see the judge. I want to make certain everything's straight about Violet's mine and her money before we leave. I'll be glad to see the last of Leadville."

Jeff's departure created an awkward silence. Violet poured George another glass of milk.

"You sure you aren't hurt?" George asked Violet for the third time.

"I'm just fine. It's Jeff you ought to be worried about. I don't know how he had the strength to climb that rope with a cut in his shoulder."

"Jeff is a lot tougher than people think."

"Tougher than he thinks," Violet said.

"Yes, he has underestimated himself more than anybody else. But I hope getting all of you out of that mine will give him more self-confidence."

"He was like a different person even before he got caught in the mine," Violet said. She blushed at the memory of being carried through the streets over Jeff's shoulder. "I don't know whether it's being away from the bank or realizing he's not handicapped, but I've never seen him so cheerful. I hesitate to say it, but he's almost sweet tempered."

George laughed. "Don't ever say it to anyone. It'll embarrass Jeff, and nobody else will believe you."

Violet didn't return George's laugh. "But you do."

George sobered. "I'm closer to Jeff than the others. I

remember what he was like before the war. He won't ever be that boy again, nor will he be the embittered man he's been for the last twenty years. You're responsible for that. Are you going to marry him?''

''I told him to ask me in a few days,'' Violet said.

''Why?''

''I don't want his marrying me to have anything to do with his arm. I want to give him time to be sure of that for himself.''

''But you do love him? You want to marry him?''

''More than anything.''

George took a swallow from his milk. ''Have you talked about living in Denver?''

''We haven't talked about living anywhere, but I know Jeff could never live in Massachusetts. He hasn't changed that much.''

George's smile was wry. ''If you want Jeff to be truly happy, you'll have to go to Virginia.''

''That's the last place I want to go.''

''The part of Jeff that's missing is there. He'll never find it anywhere else.''

''I don't understand.''

''Jeff's bitterness over his arm is only part of what was wrong with him. He could have stood the losses of the war if there had been anything to go back to. But the South he loved was destroyed. Not the plantations, but the idealism, the chivalry. It wasn't a perfect world. Some of us can live without it, but others would rather die than try. My mother was one of them. She willed herself to die. My father, scoundrel that he was, rode at the head of a charge he knew he couldn't survive. Something died during those four years that can never be replaced.

''Jeff has made a life for himself here. He's a valuable member of the community, but he'll never be whole unless he returns to Virginia, unless he works to restore as much of that lost world as he can. He won't succeed. A

time such as that can't last now any more than it could
in ancient Greece or medieval France. But he'll have to
try.''

"But he's so successful as a banker.''

"That's part of the irony. He's a brilliant banker, but
he's been dying inside. He'll be happier as a struggling
farmer.''

"I don't understand.''

"I don't either. I just know the only way he can cancel out the loss of his arm is to try to restore the best of
what he lost. You can help him.''

"Me?''

"You'll understand him when others don't. Don't
misunderstand me. Jeff will never be completely happy.
Only turning back the clock could do that.''

"You don't think I will be completely happy either.''

"You'll never forget the loss of your family. But you
can make your peace if you get to know the people
you've hated for so long. People are people, no matter
what side they may be on. Once you learn that, you may
be able to forgive them—and yourself.''

"Myself.''

"Yes. You never forgave yourself for not being able
to save your brother.''

Violet looked uneasy. "Jeff always said you and Rose
could look inside people's heads. Now I know what he
means.''

"Did he ever ask you where you stayed the night after
the charity ball?'' George said.

"No.''

"Are you going to tell him you stayed with Fern?''

"Probably, but not just yet. He trusts me enough not
to want to know. I like that feeling.''

"I don't feel comfortable staying in this hotel,'' Violet said.

"There's no place else,'' Jeff said. "You can't stay

432

with Fern and Madison. Until that damned rodeo is over, they won't have room to sneeze. You can't stay at my house. You might know Hen and Laurel would insist on coming for the wedding.''

''About the wedding—''

''I know it's bigger than you wanted, but we've already had to turn down half the people who want to come. Besides, you'll be seeing them every day from now on. It's a good way to be introduced to them.''

''That's something else we need to talk about.'' Violet turned so that she could watch him more closely. She didn't want to miss a single nuance of his facial expression, to overlook a shading of his eyes. ''I don't want to live in Denver. I think we ought to move to Virginia.''

Jeff's expression froze.

''Who's been talking to you?''

''I—''

''You don't want to live in Virginia. You don't like the South. It was George. I knew I shouldn't have left you alone with him.''

''It wasn't George,'' Violet said. ''At least it wasn't George who made me decide.''

''Then who did?''

''You.''

''I never said a word. I planned to stay in Denver,'' Jeff said.

''Maybe you've forgotten, but you've been talking to me about Virginia from the day we met. You've always wanted to go back. George told me what you said to him after the charity ball.''

''A lot of things have changed since then. I didn't think you would have me.''

''You still have a lot of questions you need answered. You can't do that here.''

''What about you?'' Jeff asked.

''George said I'd never get over my anger until I got

to know Southerners as people instead of as a war machine that deprived me of my family.''

"George had no business telling you any of this."

"But he's right. You of all people ought to understand that."

"And if it doesn't work?" Jeff said.

"Then we can come back to Denver—or any other place you want to live. I don't care as long as I'm with you. I just think we ought to start in Virginia."

"Are you sure? I mean really sure?"

"Yes. I'll always wish I'd met you when I was nineteen. I feel I've missed ten years of my life. But I won't have the rest of it compromised by the past. I want to face it and get rid of all the hurt. I love you, Jeff Randolph. You're the most wonderful, the most complete man I've ever met. But I mean to have all of you. I won't have any ghosts coming between us."

Jeff held Violet close. "No matter where we go, there'll always be ghosts."

"Okay," Violet said, "you can have a little one. But the rest are going to have to haunt somebody else, or I'll sic a New England witch on them."

Epilogue

Christmas 1881

Rose and Violet sat in the carriage, watching Jeff and George inspect the framework of a huge house under construction.

"I tried to tell him we didn't need so much space," Violet said to Rose. "I can't possibly have enough children to fill such a house."

"You've made a good beginning," Rose said. She looked down at the blond baby Violet held in her arms. "Not even Fern managed to produce a child within the first year and get pregnant with another."

Violet blushed. "I suppose both of us feel we have to make up for lost time."

"Are you going with him when he campaigns?"

"I don't know. I've already told him I can't leave the home."

"George told me something about it."

"It's a combination of what Jeff and I wanted," Violet said. "We bring both Union and Confederate disabled soldiers here for a month. We give them the best medical attention we can find, pay for limbs, provide any special equipment they might need, and get them as healthy as we can. It gives them some needed care and gives their families a month of rest. When they return, they're all better able to cope with each other."

"But it's not enough for Jeff?"

"No. First it was a bank. Then he wanted to buy every ruined farm in three counties and return them to working order. Now he wants to run for the state legislature."

"You realize he's going to want to be governor someday."

Violet didn't look happy about that. "I've tried to tell him that there are thousands of men in Virginia, that he doesn't have to do everything himself, but he doesn't listen. I want a husband, not a miracle worker."

"Randolph men make some of the most difficult husbands in the world, but eventually they get the hang of it. Jeff's getting started later than the others. It may take him a little longer to settle into the job."

Summer 1882

"Are you sure you're comfortable?" Jeff asked.

"I'm fine," Violet said. "I want to enjoy the breeze as long as I can. It'll soon be too hot out in the afternoon."

"We could move to Massachusetts for the summer. It's bound to be much cooler on the Cape."

"Don't be absurd," Violet said with a spurt of laughter. "You'd never survive having a child born a Yankee."

Jeff patted her rounding stomach and smiled contentedly. "I don't know. I like having a Yankee wife. I don't think Tom would mind a Yankee sister."

Violet looked to where her son was crawling through

the grass in search of bugs, twigs, pieces of dirt, and anything else disgusting he could find to put in his mouth. Oddly enough, she felt Virginia was more her home than Massachusetts. Her new life and her new family were bound up with Virginia. She couldn't imagine living anywhere else.

She wanted to go back someday, at least for a visit, but not yet, not until she had the baby. Until she had several more babies. Most of them girls. Jeff deserved at least one Southern belle daughter, but one with enough New England common sense to keep her from being an embarrassment. Violet decided the experiment would need a pool of several daughters to work from. She doubted she would get it right the first time.

"I'm just fine," Violet said. "Besides, I don't think the doctor would let me travel that far."

"What did he say?" Jeff asked.

"He said I ought to deliver a fine, healthy baby in July. And if my husband started to bother me too much, I could move into the clinic with the men."

Jeff settled into the swing next to his wife. It hung from the limb of a huge oak tree behind the big white brick house. "I want a girl this time. One with red hair and blue eyes. One just as stubborn and hardheaded as her mother."

"I'd think one of me was enough."

"And after that, I think I'd like to stay home."

Violet sat up and turned to stare at her husband.

"I wouldn't mind running for the legislature," Jeff said, "but I don't like the idea of being away from my family. I want to be here when you jump up to see what Tom has managed to find to put in his mouth. I like seeing you move around the house, fat and sleek with our unborn child. I like having the time to soak up all the fun of being a father and a lover."

"You sure you won't miss it?" Violet said.

"The bank is enough."

"But you wanted to do so many things."

Jeff drew her to him. The kiss was long, languorous, and as sweet as the smell of the honeysuckle that climbed the wall separating the yard from the garden.

"I'm doing them," he said.

"What about Virginia?"

"Maybe someday, if you turn into a Southern belle, I'll turn to politics, just to have someone to talk to who has an opinion of her own."

Violet put her arms around her husband and settled as close to him as she could. "Virginia just lost the best governor it could ever have had," she said. "I intend to remain a damned Yankee until the very end."

Author's Note

Leadville, Colorado, was the site of one of the richest mineral deposits on earth. In its first 60 years, it produced 2 million dollars in mineral wealth, more than any single mining district in the country. Gold was discovered in the highest valley of the Arkansas River in 1860. But it was silver, first mined in 1876, that put the town on the map. For the next 15 years, Leadville was the silver capital of the world. After the silver and gold ran out, enormous deposits of lead, zinc, and copper were discovered, and finally molybdenum, an important alloy for steel used by the automobile industry. For most of the twentieth century, Leadville was the only important source of that metal in the world.

The often-told tale of Horace Tabor reflects the history of Leadville. A store owner since the earliest days of placer mining, Tabor took a half interest in a mine in exchange for grubstaking two old miners. They struck silver. From then on, Tabor could do no wrong. He used that money to buy more mines, each richer than the last.

He bought useless mines, drilled deeper, and found enormous deposits. For a time his income was over a million dollars a year. He divorced his wife to marry a pretty widow, dabbled in politics, and gave Leadville and Denver two of their most extravagant buildings—the Tabor Grand Hotel and the Tabor Opera House. Tabor lost his fortune in the crash of 1893 and died broke six years later.

Leadville didn't sink quite so low, but the mineral wealth finally gave out. From a town of nearly 30,000 in 1880, it has shrunk to a sleepy town of a few thousand, living primarily on the memory of its past. The decaying buildings, slag piles, collapsing mine shafts, and eroded hillsides are still there. But so are the snow-covered peaks and crisp mountain air—and the Tabor Opera House with its private suite.

WYOMING Wildfire

Leigh Greenwood

With the inheritance of half her uncle's Wyoming spread, Sybil Cameron feels she's gained her independence at last. Then she meeets her partner, Burch Randall–a man who believes a woman has no business running a ranch. She vows to keep her cool no matter what. Yet as Burch's muscular arms close around her, a deliciously hot feeling courses through her body.

To Burch, Sybil is a wild filly: spirited, headstrong, and in need of a man's brand. But he soon learns this is one woman not to be tamed. In fact, he finds he glories in her passionate abandon, revels in her raw courage, and wants only to take her and set the prairie ablaze in a Wyoming wildfire.

Dorchester Publishing Co., Inc.
P.O. Box 6640   __52459-7
Wayne, PA 19087-8640   **$5.99 US/$6.99 CAN**
Please add $2.50 for shipping and handling for the first book and $.75 for each book thereafter. NY and PA residents, please add appropriate sales tax. No cash, stamps, or C.O.D.s. Prices and availability subject to change.

Canadian orders require $2.00 extra postage and must be paid in U.S. dollars through a U.S. banking facility.

Name _____
Address_____
City_____ State_____ Zip_____
E-mail _____
I have enclosed $_____ in payment for the checked book(s).
Payment <u>must</u> accompany all orders. ❑ Please send a free catalog.

CHECK OUT OUR WEBSITE! www.dorchesterpub.com

Refusing to bet her future happiness on an arranged marriage, Lily Sterling flees her Virginia home to the streets of San Francisco. In the best saloon in California, she meets handsome proprietor Zac Randolph, and when the scoundrel refuses Lily's kindness, she takes the biggest gamble of her life.

___4441-2 $5.99 US/$6.99 CAN

Dorchester Publishing Co., Inc.
P.O. Box 6640
Wayne, PA 19087-8640

Please add $1.75 for shipping and handling for the first book and $.50 for each book thereafter. NY, NYC, and PA residents, please add appropriate sales tax. No cash, stamps, or C.O.D.s. All orders shipped within 6 weeks via postal service book rate. Canadian orders require $2.00 extra postage and must be paid in U.S. dollars through a U.S. banking facility.

Name_____
Address_____
City_____State_____Zip_____
I have enclosed $_____ in payment for the checked book(s).
Payment <u>must</u> accompany all orders. ❑ Please send a free catalog.
          CHECK OUT OUR WEBSITE! www.dorchesterpub.com

SEVEN BRIDES
LEIGH GREENWOOD

FERN

**"I loved *Rose*, but I absolutely loved *Fern*!
She's fabulous! An incredible job!"**
—*Romantic Times*

A man of taste and culture, James Madison Randolph enjoys the refined pleasures of life in Boston. It's been years since the suave lawyer abandoned the Randolphs' ramshackle ranch—and the dark secrets that haunted him there. But he is forced to return to the hated frontier when his brother is falsely accused of murder. What he doesn't expect is a sharp-tongued vixen who wants to gun down his entire family. As tough as any cowhand in Kansas, Fern Sproull will see her cousin's killer hang for his crime, and no smooth-talking city slicker will stop her from seeing justice done. But one look at James awakens a tender longing to taste heaven in his kiss. While the townsfolk of Abilene prepare for the trial of the century, Madison and Fern ready themselves for a knock-down, drag-out battle of the sexes that might just have two winners.

___4409-9 $5.99 US/$6.99 CAN

SEVEN BRIDES
LEIGH GREENWOOD

Iris

Rough and ready as any of the Randolph boys, Monty bristles under his eldest brother's tight rein. All he wants is to light out from Texas for a new beginning. And Iris Richmond has to get her livestock to Wyoming's open ranges before rustlers wipe her out. Monty is heading that way, but the bullheaded wrangler flat out refuses to help her. Never one to take no for an answer, Iris saddles up to coax, rope, and tame the ornery cowboy she's always desired.

___4175-8 $5.99 US/$6.99 CAN

Dorchester Publishing Co., Inc.
P.O. Box 6640
Wayne, PA 19087-8640

LEIGH GREENWOOD
The Cowboys

WINNER OF THE
ROMANTIC TIMES CAREER
ACHIEVEMENT AWARD FOR 1996

The freedom of the range, the bawling of the longhorns, the lonesome night watch beneath a vast, starry sky—they get into a man's blood until he knows there is nothing better than the life of a cowboy...except the love of a good woman.

Devastated by a ruthless betrayal, disillusioned by the War Between the States, Ward Dillon swears that he will escape his bitter past and start anew. So the San Antonio doctor trades his medical practice for the rugged life of the open trail. Yet what hope, what harmony, what hint of happiness can be his without Marina, the woman he left behind? And when she tracks Ward down, how can he resist the burning brand of passion that had once brought them searing ecstasy and promises the only peace possible for his embattled heart?

___4299-1 $5.99 US/$6.99 CAN

LEIGH GREENWOOD'S
SEVEN BRIDES
Laurel

Although Hen Randolph is the perfect choice for a sheriff in the Arizona Territory, he is no one's idea of a model husband. After the trail-weary cowboy breaks free from his six rough-and-ready brothers, he isn't about to start a family of his own. Then a beauty with a tarnished reputation catches his eye and the thought of taking a wife arouses him as never before.

But Laurel Blackthorne has been hurt too often to trust any man—least of all one she considers a ruthless, coldhearted gunslinger. Not until Hen proves that drawing quickly and shooting true aren't his only assets will she give him her heart and take her place as the newest bride to tame a Randolph's heart.

_3744-0 $5.99 US/$6.99 CAN